Works by

## Non-fiction

Seeing Beyond the Wrinkles: Stories of Ageless Courage,
Humor, and Faith

Study Guide (Seeing Beyond the Wrinkles)

The Enduring Human Spirit: Thought-provoking Stories of
Caring for our Elders


## MAC Detective Agency Mysteries

This Angel Has No Wings

This Angel Doesn't Like Chocolate

# This Angel Doesn't Like Chocolate

## Charles Tindell

P.O. Box 3358
Frederick, Maryland 21705-3358

This novel is a work of fiction. Names, characters, places and incidents either are the product of the author's imagination or are used fictitiously. Any resemblance to actual persons, living or dead, events, or locales is entirely coincidental.

First Edition-November 2005
ISBN 1-59133-120-X

Book Design: S. A. Reilly
Cover Illustration © S. A. Reilly
Manufactured/Printed in the United States of America
2005

Dedicated to:

Bill Fossum, who has been like a brother to me.

# ACKNOWLEDGMENTS

As I continue to travel my journey in putting my stories on paper, I realize more than ever that the journey is never made alone. I could not have continued on the pathway without the support and encouragement of those I have been privileged to meet along the pathway.

Acknowledgement must be made to those whose reading and critiquing of my manuscript proved invaluable. The following individuals' support and encouragement greatly helped me in my journey: Jonay Gilbertson, Jolene Grayum, Rosie Grossman, Claire Johnson, Judy Kocher, Susan Lestina, David Osborne, and Verna VanSickle. Thanks to Lisa Thorpe for taking my photograph for the book.

Special thanks are to be given to Jean K. Mattson whose editing has proven to be a lifesaver. I also want to thank Linda Wagner for her contribution to the final editing.

In addition to the individuals mentioned above, I also want to acknowledge the staff, residents, and volunteers of the Minnesota Masonic Homes/Bloomington for their ongoing support and encouragement in this process.

A word of appreciation is also expressed to the members of the South Side Writer's Group that meets weekly at the library in Eagan, MN. The feedback I have received from my peers in this group has been greatly appreciated – it is feedback I truly value since so many in the group have demonstrated their mastery of the craft of writing.

I wish to express my gratitude to my publisher, Stephanie Reilly, and to my editor-in-chief, Shawn Reilly; their patience and encouragement goes beyond the call of duty. Both have gently steered me in my journey.

Finally, I wish to thank my wife, Carol, for putting up with the long hours I have spent in front of the computer screen. I also want to thank my sons, Scott, Andrew, and Robert for their understanding of a father who is not always typical.

# Chapter 1

IT WAS THE story's bizarre headline that first caught Howie Cummin's attention that Saturday morning in late June of 1967.

Sitting at his desk, sipping a cup of coffee, he had been leisurely paging through the morning newspaper. He still had a few minutes to read the funnies before his two partners, Mick Brunner and Adam Trexler, showed up. Last night he had called and asked them to drop by the office so they could discuss any cases their detective agency was handling. It would be a short meeting, however, since they presently were between cases. That they had no clients would suit Mick fine, since he and his fiancée, Mary, were looking forward to Monday, their first official day of the summer break from teaching. Mick, a social studies teacher at a junior high, loved kids but needed to get away from them for a while. It would be a chance for him to recharge his batteries.

Adam also needed to recharge his batteries, but for a different reason. He had just finished his first year of seminary and was glad to have the summer off to wrestle through some personal faith issues. "I have to decide whether or not to go back to seminary in the fall," he confided to Howie and Mick. The unexpected ending to their first case last year didn't help matters and only served to further confuse him about the line between good and evil. "I'm not sure I can stand in the pulpit and preach on things that I have doubts about," he confessed. "And I have questions for which there seem to be no clear-cut answers, at least none that satisfy me."

The only way Howie wanted to recharge his batteries was to have a case to work on. He lived and breathed detective work. His friend, Jim Davidson, an eighteen-year veteran police detective working out of the Fifth Precinct on the North Side, told him that he had what it took to be a good detective, but suggested that he should relax and give himself some time to get established. "Loosen up a little," he had said. "You're not going to catch all the bad guys in your first year."

Although having a cup of coffee and reading the newspaper was relaxing, Howie would rather have been reviewing notes on a case. He never got to the comics, though, because of the story near the bottom right-hand corner of page six. "What the..." He set his cup down and picked up the newspaper. He had to read the headline twice to make sure he had read it right.

### Man Drowns in Chocolate

*LaMar Jones, twenty-seven years old, drowned in a vat of simmering chocolate late Thursday night at the Chocolate Angel Candy Factory in North Minneapolis. The body was found early Friday morning by an employee who had come to check on the chocolate. Scalded beyond recognition, Jones was identified by Charles Gilbertson, founder and owner of the factory. Identification could only be made on the basis of Jones' clothes and high school class ring. Police ruled the death accidental, speculating that Jones slipped and was knocked out as he fell head first into the vat. The coroner stated there was no evidence of drugs or alcohol involved. Jones had worked at the factory for the past three years as the evening janitor and was considered a valued employee.*

"Holy cow!" Howie let out a slow whistle. "What a way to go." He was rereading the story when the office door opened and Mick walked in.

"Hi, buddy," Mick said in his usual cheerful tone. Of the three of them he was the easiest going and counterbalanced Adam's at times brooding personality. "What's so interesting?"

Howie held up the newspaper and pointed toward the bottom. "This story."

"Oh, yeah? What's it about?"

"Some guy who drowned in a vat of chocolate."

Mick grimaced. "I heard about that." He walked over to the wall opposite the office door and stood before Howie's framed movie poster of *The Maltese Falcon* starring Humphrey Bogart. The poster had intentionally been hung at that spot so that it would be the first thing people saw when they came in. "Some of the other teachers at school were talking about it yesterday," he said as he eyed the poster and then straightened it to the approving nod of Howie who considered Bogart to be his role model. "I just can't imagine that happening to anyone. It had to be a terrible way to go. Poor guy."

"You can say that again." Howie took a sip of coffee and deadpanned, "Makes me not want to eat chocolate for awhile."

Mick rolled his eyes at his boss' comment and then walked over and eased into one of two leather chairs in front of Howie's desk. He always chose the one on the left because he claimed its padding conformed to his body. At six two and nearly two hundred and thirty-five pounds of solid muscle, he still retained the athletic build of his high school football years. He had Howie by a good six inches and sixty pounds. "You remember Ted Singleton, don't you?" he asked, stretching out his legs and clasping his hands behind his head, his fingers disappearing into black, curly hair that was impossible to keep combed. A broad, sloping forehead along with dark, bushy eyebrows and a nose that had been broken twice playing football gave him a menacing presence. "He's the guy that teaches English at my school."

"Yeah, I remember him." Howie disliked the man from the first time he had met him. Mick had brought Singleton over to show him the office. Singleton had found it amusing that the office had once been the living room of Howie's apartment. "So what about him?"

"He's the one who told me about it, but I didn't see the story in the newspaper. Let me read it." Mick took the paper from Howie.

While Mick read, Howie glanced around the office. Singleton had been even more amused by the furnishings. A used mahogany desk, two worn dark brown leather chairs, a secondhand couch, a dented four drawer file cabinet, and a floor-standing brass lamp with only two of the three light sockets working had gotten raised eyebrows from Singleton. Mick's friend had saved his biggest chuckle for the dentist chair sitting behind Howie's desk. The chair had been a gift from Doctor Anderson, the previous occupant who used the space for his dental office. Howie modified the chair, explaining that it would make a great conversation piece. It sure did. Singleton couldn't stop making snide remarks about it, and as if that wasn't enough, he then had the nerve to suggest that the name of their operation, *MAC Detective Agency*, be changed.

"*ABC Detective Agency* might be better," Singleton said with a smirk.

"I don't think so," Howie replied through a forced smile. "We'll stick with MAC."

"And what does that stand for?"

"It's an acronym. The M is for Mick Brunner, the A for Adam Trexler, and the C..." Howie allowed a hint of sarcasm to creep into his tone. "You look like you're smart enough to know what that stands for...or do I need to spell it out for you?"

Just before he left that day, Singleton remarked, "I still think ABC is more descriptive. It has all your initials and..." He took a quick look around the office again. "It better reflects the nature of your operation...or do I have to spell *that* out for you?"

"Howie?"

His partner's voice brought him back to the present moment. "What? Sorry, Mick. I was thinking about something." He took a deep breath, still ticked at the snide remarks that Singleton had made that day. "What did you say?"

"This story in the newspaper..."

"Yeah? What about it?"

"Can you imagine being scalded beyond recognition? That's got to be awful." Mick handed the paper back to Howie.

Howie folded the paper and put it aside. "What gets me is why they were cooking that chocolate all night, anyway."

"I don't know. I—" The downstairs door to the street entrance slammed shut. "That must be Adam," Mick said as he and Howie listened to the sounds of someone trotting up the wooden stairs. "Maybe he knows the answer."

Within moments the office door opened and Adam appeared. At six feet, a slim athletic body, and brooding bedroom eyes, Howie told him that if he didn't become a preacher he could always try male modeling. "Sorry, I know I'm a few minutes late," Adam said, brushing a shock of dark-brown hair from his forehead.

"That's okay, we haven't started," Howie said. "We've been waiting for you."

"Come and sit down." Mick motioned to the chair next to him. "We've got a question that we figure you can answer."

Adam lowered himself into the chair. His sleepy eyes and tired-sounding voice indicated that he had probably spent another night brooding about what direction his life should take. "You can ask the question but there's no guarantee I'll have the answer."

Howie picked up the newspaper and held it in front of him. "Did you happen to read the story in today's paper about the guy who drowned in a vat of chocolate?"

"Yeah, and I don't understand why things like that happen. The man was so young. It doesn't seem fair."

"I agree," Mick said. "But, by any chance, do you know why they kept a vat of chocolate simmering all night?"

Adam nodded. "I was told that it's part of the processing they do for the chocolate angels they make."

Mick slapped the desk. "See, what did I tell you?" He gave Adam a pat on the shoulder. "My man here knows all the answers."

Adam waved off Mick's remark. "I wish I did, but I don't. I just happen to know about this because—"

"No, let me," Howie said, smiling knowingly at Mick. "Because his mother found out and told him. Am I right?" he asked Adam.

"Yeah," Adam said with a look of surprise.

"How did you figure that out?" Mick asked.

"Simple." Howie leaned forward, clasping his hands on the desk. "Working down at Andy's, his mother hears whatever is going on from the customers. They confide in her just like people do with a bartender. Trust me. Waitresses and bartenders are alike in that way," he added, wanting to use every opportunity to teach his partners to think like detectives. "That hamburger joint has got to be a gold mine for information. And if anybody can get it, his mom can."

"You've got that right," Adam said. His mother, Virginia (or Virg, as she was known to all the customers), had worked at the sandwich shop nearly twenty years. There was hardly anything that went on around the North Side that she didn't hear about.

Mick stood up and bowed before Howie. "We defer to you, boss," he said with a flourish and then sat down. "That only goes to show why you're the full-time detective and we're only part-timers." He tapped Adam on the shoulder. "Maybe we should convince our boss here to open up an office down where your mom works."

Howie leaned back in his chair and smiled. Even though his friends only worked part-time, he was glad they were with him. They had been in the operation together for less than a year, but their friendship stretched back nearly thirteen years to 1954, the year they worked on a project together in woodshop in junior high. After he got his private investigator's certificate from a correspondence school, Howie had persuaded them to come in with him. "It'll be an opportunity for you guys to get some excitement into your otherwise boring and pathetically dull lives," he had argued. Even though Adam had plans of becoming a minister and Mick had a full-time teaching position, they agreed.

"Speaking of opening up another office..." Adam looked at Howie. "Do we have any cases to discuss?"

"I'm afraid not." Since opening last fall, cases had been sporadic. Howie, though, had warned his partners that it would take time to become established. And however long it took, he was determined to not only make it in the business but also prove to any skeptics that he had the smarts to be a top-notch detective.

"So this is going to be a short meeting?" Adam asked

"I wouldn't count on that," Mick said, a smug grin on his face.

Both Adam and Howie shot their partner a questioning look, but Howie took the lead. "Okay, what are you saying and why do you have that silly grin on your face?"

"I've got a client for us."

"You do? Great." Howie got out his notepad. He could feel the adrenalin flowing once again, and hoped the new case would help with their agency's cash flow. A wealthy client would be nice, but he would settle for anyone who just paid them on time.

"Who is it?"

"His name is Jerome Huntington."

Howie jotted the name in his notepad. "Okay, so who is this guy?" he asked, looking up. "A teacher friend of yours?"

"He can't be a teacher," Adam offered.

"Why not?"

"Because with that kind of name, he sounds rich."

Mick chuckled. "He's not a teacher and he's not rich." He glanced at Adam. "You're right, though, about teachers not being rich."

"Let's not get into that now," Howie said, not wanting to get sidetracked. "So, who is he?" he asked, disappointed that their potential client wasn't rolling in dough.

"One of my students."

Howie stared at Mick for a moment, pushed aside his notepad, and tossed his pencil on the desk. Leaning back in his chair, he closed his eyes for a moment. He considered anybody under the age of fifteen a rug rat. Being the only child of older parents, he grew up in quiet surroundings. Mick, on the other hand, came from a large extended family and had lots of noisy little nieces and nephews running around while he was growing up.

"Jerome is concerned about his grandmother," Mick said. "He wants to hire us on her behalf."

"For what?"

"To investigate the disappearance of her diamond ring."

"If it was stolen, tell old granny to go to the cops."

"That's the problem; she already did. The police did a preliminary investigation and came up with nothing. Jerome said that they didn't believe Nana."

Adam leaned toward Mick. "Who's Nana?"

"That's Jerome's grandmother."

"And where did she get a name like that?" Howie asked.

"That's what he called her when he was small, and the name stuck. Her real name is...just a minute, I've got it here." Mick pulled a slip of paper from his shirt pocket. "Her name is Anabel Peterson."

"Is she from the North Side?" Adam asked.

"Ah, yeah..."

Howie raised an eyebrow. "Why did you hesitate just now?" he asked Mick. "What aren't you telling us?"

"Nothing, except..."

"Except what? Come on. Out with it."

Mick offered Howie a sheepish smile. "Nothing, except that his grandmother is a resident at a nursing home."

"What!" Howie massaged his temples for a moment, wondering what he was getting into having a rug rat and a senile, old lady for clients. When he was a little kid, his father would bring him to visit his grandmother in a nursing home. Many of the people in that nursing home didn't know where they were. His own grandmother didn't recognize him. All she had talked about was the bad food and how the other residents were stealing her blind. The sights. The sounds. The smells. It wasn't a pleasant memory, and he didn't like the idea of reliving it. "You're just going to have to tell the kid 'no.' We can't—"

"I already told him we'd take it."

"You what?" Howie buried his face in his hands. That was just like Mick. His partner was devoted to kids. One of the most popular teachers at Franklin Junior High, students were always coming to him seeking advice.

"Don't worry," Mick said. "Jerome's a good kid, and he's really concerned that his grandmother is going to have a heart attack over all of this." He handed the slip of paper with her name on it to Howie. "You wouldn't want that on your conscience, would you?" When Howie didn't reply, he continued. "You wouldn't be able to sleep nights. Why, you would lose your appetite. And if I know you, you'd probably—"

"Okay, say no more," Howie said as he put up his hands in mock surrender. "We'll take it on." He copied Nana's name in his notepad and then looked up. A possible way out of this case had popped into his head. "You know, this kid and his grandmother probably aren't going to be able to pay us much."

"I realize that, but it'll help us sharpen our detective skills."

"Mick's right," Adam added. "Besides, we don't have any other clients right now anyway, do we?"

Howie shook his head. The lack of cases reminded him that he was scheduled to work that evening at the soda fountain downstairs at Kass' Drug Store. After Doctor Anderson had retired, Kass had told Howie that he would turn the former dental office into an apartment for him. He also had reduced the rent with the agreement that Howie would work a certain number of hours at the drugstore every month. It had been a generous offer and came at a critical time in Howie's life; his father had died a month earlier and he couldn't afford to stay in the duplex where he and his father had lived. "Okay, tell the kid we'll take the case."

Mick cleared his throat. "Ah...it's not as simple as that."

"What do you mean?"

"Jerome wants to interview you first before he decides to hire us."

"He wants to what?" Howie stood up, put his hands on the desk, and leaned toward Mick. "You mean to tell me that I have to put up with some snot-nosed kid asking me questions about my work. Nothing doing. I'd rather—"

"Take it easy, now," Mick said. "It's not going to hurt you to do it."

"You'd do it for other clients, wouldn't you?" Adam pointed out.

Howie plopped back down in his chair, mumbling.

Mick cupped his ear with his hand and leaned forward, his eyes twinkling with amusement. "What did you say?"

"I said being interviewed by other clients is different." Howie opened his notepad. "How old is this kid, anyway?"

"He's twelve."

"Twelve?" Adam said, his eyebrows rising slightly. "Isn't that a little young for being in eighth grade?"

"It is, but Jerome's a pretty smart kid." Mick spoke with a teacher's pride for one of his students. "His I.Q. is nearly 170. He's skipped a couple of grades already. At the rate he's going, he'll probably finish high school before he's fifteen."

"Oh, great." Howie shoved his notepad into his shirt pocket. "Just at the age where they think they know it all." He took a deep breath and let it out in an audible sigh. "All right, I'll submit to the interview, but you owe me."

Mick nodded.

"You owe me big time."

Mick nodded again.

"Tell him to come in and see me next week."

"When?"

"Wednesday afternoon," Howie said, not wanting to start the week with the kid. "Tell him to be here at three. And tell him not to be late."

After Mick and Adam left, Howie picked up the newspaper and turned to the funnies. He wasn't looking forward to meeting with Jerome Huntington. And he certainly didn't relish the thought of trying to communicate with some little old lady at a nursing home who probably didn't even remember her own name.

# Chapter 2

SEVERAL DAYS HAD passed since Howie's Saturday morning meeting with his partners. He now sat at his desk drumming his fingers waiting for Mick's student to show up. Mick had warned him that Jerome Huntington could come across a little snobbish. "Don't be too tough on him, though; he's really a good kid at heart."

At six minutes past three the door to Howie's office opened and a kid with neatly combed, short-cropped, light-brown hair and wearing black-rim glasses entered. His light-tan slacks and blue-plaid shirt looked as though they had just been ironed. The shine on his brown loafers would have put Howie's scuffed shoes to shame. A red spiral notebook was tucked under his right arm, being clutched as though it were a briefcase filled with top-secret documents.

Howie opened his mouth to say hello but then watched as his visitor walked over to the poster of Bogart, twitched his nose at it a couple of times as if dismissing it, and then glanced around the room until finally directing his gaze toward him.

"Hello, my name is Jerome Huntington," he announced in a tone exuding confidence while at the same time sounding patronizing. "I'm here to see Mr. Cummins."

"Who do you think I am, kid, the janitor?"

Jerome pushed his glasses further up upon his nose. "You're Mr. Cummins?" His thin, brown eyebrows rose as wrinkles formed on his forehead. He glanced at the door behind Howie as though expecting a *real* detective to come through it at any moment. "Aren't you sort of young to be a detective?" he asked, again glancing at the door.

"I drink a lot of milk," Howie said through clinched teeth. He pointed to the clock on the wall. "You're late!"

Jerome glanced at the clock and offered a self-righteous smile. "I believe your clock is fast. If you call for the time on the telephone, you'll find that I'm right." He waited for a reply. "Would you like the number?" he asked. "I have it memorized."

"No, that's okay." Howie reminded himself that this was a favor for Mick. "I'll call the number later."

"Are you sure?"

"Yeah...I'm sure." Howie's neck muscles tightened. The little twerp hadn't been there two minutes and he was already getting on Howie's nerves. "Why don't you have a seat so we can get started and get this over with." He stole a glance at his wristwatch and silently cursed as he made a mental note to reset his wall clock.

After Jerome made himself comfortable in the chair, he opened his notebook and took a gold pen from his shirt pocket. "Mr. Brunner told me that you'd be willing to answer some questions before my grandmother and I decide to hire you."

"Well, that's awfully nice of Mick—ah, Mr. Brunner." Howie leaned back, interlaced his fingers, and put his hands behind his head. "Go ahead and ask your questions."

"How long have you worked in the detective business?"

"What's the matter, don't you trust my experience?" Howie snapped and then added in a calmer voice, "We've been in business for about a year."

"Do you think you're good at being a detective?"

"I wouldn't be in this line of work if I didn't think I could do a good job." Howie looked on as Jerome wrote in his notebook. When the kid noticed his interest, the little know-it-all used his other hand to shield what he was writing.

"I know that Mr. Brunner works part-time for you." Jerome turned the page in his notebook. "Do you have anyone else employed who does?"

"Yeah, his name is Adam Trexler. That's T-r-e--"

"There's no need to spell it." Jerome smiled. "I'm quite proficient at spelling."

"Is that so?"

"Yes, I do it by sounding out the syllables."

Howie took note of Jerome's perfect posture, wondering if the kid would ever be caught slouching with a leg draped over the arm of the chair. "That's pretty good," he announced after the kid spelled the name of his partner out loud.

"Thank you." A look of smug satisfaction settled on Jerome's face. "I've won the spelling contest at school for the past two years." He lifted his chin slightly and smiled. "My teachers tell me I'm precocious."

"You know..." Howie snapped his fingers and pointed at Jerome. "I was just about to tell you that myself, kid."

For the next twenty minutes, Jerome went over his list of questions. "Why did you pick this location for your detective agency?"

"The owner of this building offered me the space," Howie explained. "Broadway is a good location. A lot of things happen around here that require my services."

"And who is the owner of the building?"

"What do you want to know that for?"

"I pride myself on being thorough."

Howie took a deep breath and let it out slowly. "His name is Hershel Kass, but everybody calls him Kass. He owns the drugstore downstairs. He's a short guy, heavy-set; looks like Santa Claus without the beard."

"Did you always want to be a detective?"

"Yeah, ever since high school."

While Jerome reviewed his notes, Howie thought back to that evening when he and his father were watching some detective show on television. This was several years after he graduated from high school. While Mick and Adam went on to college, he had worked two jobs helping to pay the bills and caring for a father who couldn't work full time because of health problems.

"Wasn't it your dream to become a detective some day?" his father had asked him during the commercial break.

"It still is."

"I'm glad to hear that." His father had got up from the couch and turned off the television. When he sat back down, he turned to Howie. "I know that you've been working hard to take care of me, but don't ever give up on your dream." His eyes pleaded with his son. "Promise me you won't."

His father had also reminded him that night that his mother had always said to be sure to make a positive impact in the world. Howie's mother, a fine Christian woman, died when he was in grade school. He still resented God for taking her away. When his father had died nearly three years ago, the experience had alienated him even further from any belief in a supreme spiritual being. Religion was a subject that he made clear to his partners, especially Adam, not to bring up.

Howie, however, appreciated the support Kass had shown him once he had decided to go after his dream of becoming a detective. After he got his private investigator's certificate, Kass remodeled the living room into office space for the detective agency. "Someday you'll be famous, and then you'll tell everybody that you got your start above Kass' Drugstore on Broadway." When Howie had talked Mick and Adam into joining him, Kass had thrown them a party, putting up a congratulatory banner behind the soda fountain.

"Do you live here?" Jerome asked, continuing with his interview.

"Yeah, my living quarters are beyond the door behind me." For a moment when Jerome looked at the door, Howie thought the kid was going to ask for a tour to check on his housekeeping abilities.

"And do you carry a gun?"

Howie stared at Jerome for a moment. "No, I never have and I don't plan to."

"Why is that?"

"Because of something that happened a long time ago." Bradley, his grade school best friend, had been accidentally shot in the chest by an older brother who had found their father's gun hidden behind some boxes in a closet. For a long time afterwards, Howie had nightmares about his friend lying in the casket.

"And what did happen?" Jerome asked.

Howie shook his head. "That's something that you don't need to know," he said, having always been tight-lipped with his personal life and history except with his two partners and Kass.

Jerome nodded; he was apparently smart enough to know that he shouldn't pursue the subject any further. He scribbled a few more notes and then closed his notebook. "I'd prefer someone with more experience, but since you're less than fifteen minutes from where my grandmother lives, I think we'll go with you."

"Thanks, that's mighty big of you." Howie dug out his notepad from his shirt pocket. "Now can we get down to business?" he asked, anxious to get some basic details and then send the kid on his way. "Can you tell me specifically what you want to hire us for?"

"Didn't Mr. Brunner tell you?"

"Sure, but I want to hear it from you to make sure we're talking about the same thing."

"Okay, I can understand that." Jerome leaned forward. "My grandmother's diamond ring is missing. She believes it was stolen." He adjusted his glasses. "In case you don't have her name, it's—"

"Anabel Peterson, right?"

Jerome nodded.

"Okay, now concerning this ring, are you sure she didn't just misplace it?" On several occasions Howie's grandmother had misplaced her teeth. He also had an uncle who always forgot where he parked his car whenever he went shopping in downtown Minneapolis. "Maybe she just forgot where she put it."

"Oh, no," Jerome said. "She's pretty sharp and I believe her."

"And from my understanding, the cops were involved?"

"Yes, but when they came up with nothing, she told me to hire a detective." Jerome glanced around the office. "I came to you because Nana, that's my grandmother, can't afford a lot and I figured that since you're just starting out, you'd be cheaper."

Howie smiled outwardly but inwardly cursed Mick. "We won't charge you our normal rate," he said. "Since you're a student of Mr. Brunner's, we'll give you and your grandmother a special student rate."

"And what's that?"

"Just hang on, kid. I'm figuring it out now." Howie turned to a blank page in his notepad and studied it for a moment. "Let's say twenty-five percent of the value of the ring plus expenses. I'm sure—"

"Twenty percent, plus expenses, and a time limit of two weeks." Jerome flipped a couple of pages in his notebook. "The ring is valued at nine hundred and thirty-five dollars. That means you and your partners would make one hundred and eighty-seven dollars."

"Looks like you've done your homework."

"Thank you. I usually do." Jerome closed his notebook. "One more thing."

"And what's that?"

"If you don't recover it, we only pay your expenses."

"That sounds reasonable."

Jerome smiled as if he had just negotiated a multi-million dollar business deal. "Since my grandmother put me in charge of keeping a record of the finances, I'd like a copy of your expense receipts."

"My what!"

"Your expense receipts. I—"

"I heard you." Howie rubbed his temple, reminding himself to take a couple of aspirins once the kid left. "Okay, I'll make sure you get copies of the receipts. Triplicates if you want." He leaned back and crossed his arms in front of his chest. "Now, is there anything else?"

"Yes, where do I sign?"

"Sign? Sign what?"

"The contract."

"On this case, we don't need a contract." Howie stood up and walked around to the front of the desk. "Let's shake hands, man-to-man. That's all the contract we need. I trust you, Jerome. I hope you trust me."

Jerome stared at Howie's outstretched hand for a moment and then stood up and shook it with a firmness that surprised Howie. "Here's my grandmother's telephone number in her room and the name, address, and telephone number of the nursing home." He handed Howie a slip of paper.

"*The Golden Years Retirement Home.*" Howie scratched his chin for a moment. "I think I've driven past it a couple of times."

"I'm sure you have. It's not that far away from here."

"Yeah, if I remember, it's just off Broadway. It's a white-stucco building in the middle of the block, isn't it?"

Jerome nodded. "My grandmother is expecting to see you today. I told her you'd meet with her as soon as we were done."

# Chapter 3

AT TWENTY MINUTES past four, Howie pulled up and parked across the street from the Golden Years retirement home. A block off Broadway and Queen, hemmed in on both sides by storefront businesses housed in brick two-story buildings, the three-story retirement home sat some thirty feet back from the street. Dandelions dotted what little lawn the place had, their bright-ocher color providing a sharp contrast to its stucco exterior yellowing with age.

Howie turned off the ignition and sat for a moment. The sign on the lawn had been painted in black, bold letters with the exception of the word "Golden" that had been done in burnished-gold stylized letters. He got out of the car and headed across the street. Two elderly ladies, sitting on a bench to the right of the entrance, watched him as he approached. To the left of the entrance, a man and a woman sitting in wheelchairs also kept an eye on him. A group of people, mainly women, in wheelchairs observed him from inside through floor-to-ceiling glass panels that ran along either side of the entrance. One elderly lady in the group had her nose pressed to the glass. He nodded and offered a smile to those residents sitting by the outside entrance.

"How come you ain't in school, sonny?" squeaked a frail-looking man hunched over in a wheelchair. A dusty-brown, wool lap robe covered his legs. His pea-green bulky cardigan sweater, large enough to fit a person twice his size, overwhelmed the red-checkered flannel shirt he wore. The old guy pointed a bony finger at Howie, his fingernail as yellowed as the stucco exterior of the building. "You're not skipping school, are you?"

At first, Howie thought the man was joking, but the way the old codger knitted his white, bushy eyebrows together and had his jaw thrust out suggested that he better play it straight. "No, sir, I've been out of high school for eight years."

The old guy leaned forward. He screwed his eyes so tight that Howie wondered how he could see anything. "You look mighty young for that. Got any I.D?"

"Oh pipe down, Elmer, you old coot," cried the lady sitting in the other wheelchair. "Leave the young man alone." She turned to Howie and offered him a sympathetic smile. "Don't mind him. He used to be a truant officer."

"Darn tooting I was! And a good one at that!" The one-time truant officer's jaw moved up and down as though he could be chewing a plug of tobacco. "Didn't have any young'uns skipping school when I was on duty. No, sir-reee."

Howie smiled politely and excused himself, explaining that he had someone waiting to see him. As he opened the entrance door, he noticed a cornerstone engraved with the date July 29, 1917. He glanced back at Elmer, wondering if the old coot had lived here since the place opened up nearly fifty years ago. The cantankerous geezer looked like he had traveled more than his share of miles in life, but probably not quite that many yet.

Upon entering the lobby, the detective drew the attentive looks of many of those who had watched him come up the sidewalk. Several of the ladies waved at him and he waved back. As he walked up to the reception desk he heard snatches of the conversation behind him.

"Doesn't he have such an angelic-looking face?" squealed a woman.

"And did you notice his dimples when he smiled?" another lady said. "And that reddish-blond hair?"

"How about those baby blues," cooed another female resident. "My, he sure does remind me of my grandson."

"He does?"

"Yes, except my grandson is much taller...and cuter."

Howie stood at the receptionist's desk for a moment, waiting for the silver-haired lady to finish writing a message she was receiving over the telephone. "Hello, can you tell me where I might find Mrs. Peterson?" he asked after she hung up.

"Which one?" The woman's pleasant voice complimented the twinkle in her eyes. "We have a number of residents here by that last name. And is it spelled, s-o-n, or s-e-n?" She smiled. "It makes a difference, you know."

"It's s-o-n. Her first name is Anabel."

"Oh, yes, Nana. She's in room 114." The receptionist pointed to Howie's right. "Go down to where the elevators are and take the hallway to your left. Her room is three doors past the nurses' station."

"Thank you." Howie turned to go.

"Sir, just a minute."

"Yes?"

"I don't think she's in her room."

"She isn't?"

"That woman hardly ever stays in her room unless she's sick or sleeping." The receptionist glanced at the clock above the fish tank. "Knowing her, right now she's probably out..." She tapped her chin with the end of her pencil several times. "Perhaps, you should stop at the nurses' station," she suggested. "I'm quite sure that one of the staff will know what Nana's up to at this time of day."

"Thank you, I will."

Once Howie walked past the elevators and started down the hallway, he could see a nurse up ahead speaking to someone in a wheelchair. Only the top part of the person's head could be seen above the back of the wheelchair. It was obvious from the nurse's facial expression that she wasn't very pleased with the person. As Howie got closer he could hear the nurse speaking in a quiet but stern tone of voice.

"How many times have I told you that you shouldn't be doing that?" The nurse's tone changed, reflecting now a note of exasperation. "I just can't believe you were racing down the hallway with another resident again." She put her hands on her hip. "Who were you racing this time?"

"Not going to tell!" The resident's high-pitched voice crackled with feistiness. "I'm not any stool pigeon!"

"Well, I'll find out who it was." The nurse sighed. "What in the world were you thinking of? You could've tipped over. And you almost knocked poor Agnes down."

"I told her to move aside!" the woman snapped. "She ought to know better than to get in my way. That old biddy cost me the race."

Howie walked up and stood quietly to one side, waiting. Whoever it was in the wheelchair wasn't backing down from the nurse.

"Next time she gets in my way again, I'm running her down! That'll teach her a lesson she won't forget! I'm—"

"Calm down," the nurse cautioned. "Remember your blood pressure. And besides, that isn't a very nice way to talk." The nurse paused and took a deep breath before continuing. "Why can't you use your energy in other ways?"

"Like what?"

"You could participate in some of the planned activities that we have around here."

"Humph! You mean like bingo and popcorn parties?"

"Exactly. I'm sure that—"

"They're boring."

"No, they're not."

"They're for old people."

The nurse shook her head in frustration. "But you're older than most of them."

"I don't care. Their idea of excitement is having real butter on their popcorn and getting to yell out 'Bingo.' That's not for me. I'm looking for some real action."

The nurse looked over and saw Howie. "Hello, may I help you?" she asked, sounding relieved for the distraction.

"Sorry for interrupting." When Howie moved closer, the lady in the wheelchair with hawk-like eyes gave him the once over. "The receptionist said you might be able to help me," he said to the nurse. "I'm looking for Mrs. Anabel Peterson."

"That's me!" yelled the woman in the wheelchair as she wheeled around to face him head on. Dressed in red slacks, white tennis shoes, and a deep-purple sweatshirt with the words *Old Age is Not for Sissies* emblazoned in red across the front of it, the lady looked like she was ready to race in the

Indianapolis 500. "What do you want?" she asked, casting him a stern look. "You're not one of those salesmen trying to sell me a fancy casket, are you?"

"No, ma'am."

"Because if you are, you can march right back out the door and go back to wherever you came from."

"My name is Howie Cummins." He offered his best smile, a winsome one that generally won people over, especially women. "Your grandson asked me to see you. He said that you had something to talk over with me."

"Is that so?" When she leaned forward, braided pigtails could be seen dangling just below her shoulders. "Well, I've got to make sure you're on the up-and-up. What's my grandson's first name?"

"What?"

"What's my grandson's name?" she yelled. "What's the matter? Have you got wax in your ears?"

"No, ma'am."

"So what's his name?"

"It's Jerome."

"What color hair does he have?"

Howie looked at the nurse, but she just shrugged. He turned his attention back to his gray-haired interrogator. "His hair is brown and it's cut short. He also wears glasses, and is twelve years old."

Anabel was silent for a few moments while giving him the once-over again. "Okay, I guess you're on the uppity-up." She glanced around. "We need to talk, but not here. Follow me!"

Before Howie could respond, Anabel whipped her wheelchair around and headed lickety-split down the hallway.

"Good luck," the nurse said, and then whispered, "You'll need it."

"Thanks." Howie exchanged smiles with her before starting after Anabel. He caught up to her just as she turned the corner at the end of the hallway. "Where are we going?"

"You'll know when we get there."

Howie nodded greetings at several residents coming toward them from the opposite direction: two women in wheelchairs and a man using a walker. It could have been his imagination, but the two women wheeled their chairs as close to the wall as they could as soon as they spotted Anabel.

The elderly gentleman with the walker grabbed the wall railing with one hand and shook his fist at Anabel as she went by. "I wouldn't be going anyplace with that woman!" he warned Howie. "She's a menace. A menace, I tell you!"

"Don't pay any attention to him!" Nana yelled over her shoulder. "The old fool still thinks Coolidge is President."

After several more minutes of following Nana, Howie wondered if she knew where she was going. He was just about to say something when she abruptly stopped in front of a closed door.

"We'll go in here!" she said, leading him into a small sitting area with a couple of chairs, an end table, and a lamp. "Shut the door!"

Howie closed the door, and took a chair. "Your grandson said that—"

"Shhh." Anabel put her finger to her lips, wheeled up to the door, brushed back her pigtails, and leaned her ear against the door. "I've got to make sure we're alone. Can't trust people around here. Do you know what I mean?"

"Mrs. Peterson, I—"

"Call me, Nana. Everybody else does."

"Okay, I will." Howie cleared his throat. "Nana, your grandson is concerned about you."

"Smart little fellow, isn't he?" When she stuck out her bony chin, three long wiry-black whiskers could be seen growing out of a mole. "Some in the family say he takes after me. Both of us are peas from the same pod. I was precocious when I was that age." Anabel stuck out what little chest she had. "And my precious Jerome is taking after me."

"That's nice." Howie cleared his throat again. "Now, what exactly is it that you wanted to see me about?"

"Somebody stole my rock!"

"Your what?"

"My rock!" She gave him a puzzled look. "What kind of detective are you? A rock is crook talk for a diamond."

"Of course. I forgot." Howie took a deep breath. The aspirins he had taken earlier hadn't taken effect yet. "Can you describe it for me?"

"What's there to describe? A diamond's a diamond!"

"Okay, we'll forget about that for now." Howie paused. "Are you sure it was stolen?" he asked, recalling the time he and his father once found his grandmother's teeth half-buried in the dirt of a flowerpot that sat on the windowsill in her room. "Is it possible that you maybe…just misplaced it?"

"I didn't misplace it!" Nana snapped.

"Sorry, I didn't mean—"

"I may be old but I'm not senile! Somebody took it, I tell you!" She cocked her head. "There's something fishy going on around here." Just then, the door opened and a man in a wheelchair peeked in. "Get out of here, Lyle!" she shouted.

"Why? What's going on?"

"I'm having a bowel movement and I want to be alone."

Lyle's eyes doubled in size. He glanced at Howie and then quickly shut the door.

"Gets him every time," Nana said, cackling. "Now, what were we talking about?"

"You were saying that something fishy is going on around here."

"I was?" Nana reached back, grabbed hold of one of her pigtails, wrapped it around her finger, and then let it go. "Now, I remember. There's been a number of diamond rings stolen around here."

"Did you report it to the nurses?"

"Of course I did, but they don't believe me. They think I'm a loony old lady." Nana leaned forward and stared at him for several moments. "You don't think that, do you?"

Howie forced a smile. "Oh, no...I...ah...would never think that."

"Good!" She settled back in her chair. "Because I have a friend whose diamond ring was taken on Wednesday."

"You mean Wednesday of last week?"

"Last week?" Nana scrunched up her nose. "I'm talking about yesterday."

"Yesterday was Tuesday." Howie kept his tone friendly and conversational, not wanting to give any indication that he thought she was losing it. "Today's Wednesday."

"Is that so?" Nana tugged on her pigtail. "Well, one day turns into another around here. If you'd been here as long as I have, you'd get your days mixed up too." She scratched the mole on her chin. "It must've been last week some time. Let me think now." A long minute went by before she spoke up. "It was the same day they served raisin toast for breakfast. And they do that every Wednesday. Or is it Monday?"

"I'll tell you what I'll do," Howie said, anxious to inform Mick not to take on any more cases from his students. "I'll conduct some interviews, ask some questions, and check with whoever's in charge of security around here." He pulled out his notepad. "Now, if you just give me the names of the others who are missing diamonds."

"There's Gertrude up on second floor. I don't remember her room number, but it's the one across from the drinking fountain." Nana shifted in her wheelchair. "Come to think about it, that drinking fountain doesn't work. I wonder if Gertrude knows about that." She shook her finger at Howie. "Be careful, though."

"Of the drinking fountain?"

"No, of Gertrude's roommate."

Howie rubbed his eyes. He needed some fresh air. "And why's that?"

"Because she's a snoopy little thing. She goes through Gertrude's dresser drawers when she's not there. She likes to smell her socks."

"Okay, anybody else?"

"There's Beatrice up on third. She's in room...no, wait a minute, scratch her off."

"Why's that? Did she find her diamond?"

Nana shook her head. "She croaked last week."

"I'm sorry to hear that."

"Don't be. She had two helpings of strawberry ice cream for lunch that day. That was her favorite. After lunch, she laid down for a nap and never woke up." Nana smiled, revealing nearly a perfect set of teeth. "That's the way I want to go. Nice and peaceful. I don't want any tubes in me. Not like that poor woman up on third. I—"

"Besides Gertrude, anybody else?" Howie felt bad about interrupting but he suspected that Nana could go on for quite some time.

"Clara in room 147. She's a little hard of hearing, so you'll have to speak up." Nana shifted in her wheelchair again. "That's all I can think of for now. Next time you come, I'll have some other names for you."

"Okay, this is enough for me to start on." Howie stood up. "May I take you back to your room?"

Nana shook her head and flashed a sly grin. "I'm going to wait here for Lyle. He should be back in a little while."

Before Howie excused himself, he assured her that next week he would have a chance to visit with the people she had mentioned. He said a quick good-bye and headed down the hallway toward the entrance.

"Did you find her?" the receptionist asked him as he walked by.

"I sure did," he replied as he opened the entrance door to leave. The two ladies who earlier had been sitting on the bench were gone. The one-time truant officer and his lady friend, however, were still there. As Howie walked by, he heard the old guy speak up.

"I still say we should've asked for that young'un's I.D."

"Oh, Elmer, hush your mouth."

Howie was still chuckling about Elmer's remark when he got to his car. On the drive back to the office, he would stop at the drugstore to see Kass. Throughout the years, Kass had been a good friend to him as well as to Adam and Mick. The three of them had known Kass since they had been in grade school. Many times, they had come to him for advice. This time Howie would be asking for some advice on older people. He parked the car on the side street across from his office and headed for the drugstore. The cowbell above the door clanged as he walked in. Kass was at the front register with a customer.

"Good afternoon, Howie, my boy." Kass flashed him a broad smile. "Go sit down. I'll be right with you."

Howie had no sooner sat down on one of the six stools, thankful that the others were empty, when Kass walked over.

"So how's the detective business going?"

Howie shrugged. "Not too bad. We've just been hired, but I'm not so sure it's a real case."

"And why do you say that?" Kass asked as he took a towel and began wiping the counter in front of Howie.

Without giving names, Howie shared that he had just come from the nursing home and had met with a woman who claimed that someone had stolen her diamond ring. "Kass, I'm not convinced it was stolen. She probably just misplaced it. What do you think?"

Kass scratched the top of his bald head. With a fringe of light-brown hair, he always said he could pass as a Jewish monk. "I don't know what to tell you, but I did have an uncle who was in a nursing home." He set a glass of ice water in front of Howie. "Every time we went to see him, he swore up and down that somebody had stolen money from him."

Howie took a sip of water. "So what did you do?"

"We searched his room and found the money hidden underneath some sweaters in his dresser drawer."

"Yeah, I kind of think that this case is going to turn out the same way." Howie took another sip of water. "Old people seem to have short memories."

Without warning, Kass slapped himself on the forehead with the palm of his hand. "Speak about having short memories." He offered a contrite smile. "I forgot to tell you that Mick stopped in about twenty minutes ago and told me that if you came in, to tell you to go upstairs right away because there's a woman waiting in your office."

"Really?"

"Yes, and he said she's quite attractive." Kass' eyes twinkled. "A special lady friend of yours, perhaps?"

"I'm afraid not."

"Maybe another client, then?"

"Let's hope so." Howie hopped off the stool. "See you later." Within moments, he was out the door and heading toward the street entrance of his apartment. He took the stairs two at a time, pausing for a moment on the top landing to catch his breath before opening his office door. The woman was standing in front of his Bogart poster, apparently admiring it. When she turned to see who had come in, he understood why Mick had called her attractive. With shoulder-length auburn hair and greenish-blue eyes, she was *very* attractive. She couldn't have been much more than in her mid-to-late twenties.

"Hello, my name's Howie Cummins. Sorry I wasn't here when you got here." He closed the door behind him. "I understand you wanted to see me."

"Yes, I do. My name is Stephanie. Stephanie Turner. Your partner, Mr. Brunner, said I could wait for you here."

"I'm glad you did."

"Mr. Brunner was very apologetic about having to leave, but he thought you would be back shortly."

"I hope you didn't have to wait long." Howie motioned to the leather chairs in front of his desk. "Please have a seat." He tried to see if she was wearing a ring. "Is it Miss or Mrs.?"

"It was Mrs. up until two years ago. That's when my husband and I were divorced." She moved gracefully toward the chair and sat down, smoothing her plaid skirt over her knee. "Please call me Stephanie. Mrs. Turner always made me feel so old."

"Okay, Stephanie. What can I do for you?"

Her smile quickly disappeared. "I want to hire you and your partners to investigate the death of my brother." Her voice broke and she had to compose herself before continuing. "I have reason to believe that he died under some very suspicious circumstances."

"If that's the case, don't you think this is a matter for the police?"

"They've already investigated it and have ruled his death as accidental." She leaned forward. "But I don't believe it was."

"Are you saying that your brother could've been murdered?"

Stephanie gasped. "I'm...I'm sorry but I've always thought of it as being non-accidental. I guess I've never used the term...*murdered*." She shuddered and then took a deep breath. "That sounds so horrible." She took another deep breath. "Yes, I believe he was... murdered."

Howie's adrenalin kicked in. This would be their first murder case and a chance to really establish a reputation on the North Side. He had promised himself that he would follow his mother's advice to make a positive impact upon the world. Being the best detective he could be would be his way of doing that as well as honoring the memory of his parents. And what could make a more positive impact upon the world than bringing a killer to justice? It would also be great to solve a case that the cops had written off. "I can promise you that we'll do everything we can to look into all the facts. If your brother was murdered, we'll find his killer." He took out his notepad. "Now, what was your brother's name?"

"LaMar Jones."

# Chapter 4

"LAMAR JONES?" HOWIE opened his notepad and printed the name, pondering it for several moments before turning his attention back to Stephanie. "Your brother's name sure sounds familiar, but I can't place it. Do you know if the two of us ever met?"

"I don't think so."

Howie tapped his pencil on the notepad a couple of times. He prided himself on having a good memory for names. "I know I've heard your brother's name before, but I just can't recall where."

"Perhaps you saw the article in the paper last week about his death." Stephanie's eyes narrowed and her face darkened as though a storm cloud suddenly cast its shadow upon it. "I went to the newspaper office and tracked down the reporter who had the audacity to write the story." Her nostrils flared and her breaths grew short and rapid. "I was so angry with that man!" she cried in a voice teeming with emotion. "There was absolutely no excuse for the headline he gave it. No excuse at all!"

"I'm not sure if I recall reading it." Howie laid his pencil down, leaned forward and clasped his hands on the desk. His client's attractiveness only increased with the fury she displayed. "Was it on the front page?"

"No, it was toward the back of the paper. Page seven."

"What did the headline read?"

Stephanie shifted in her chair. Several moments passed before she replied. "*Man Drowns in Chocolate!*" she said, spitting the words out as though distasteful even to speak. She looked at him as if expecting a reaction. "Isn't that terrible?" Her tone oozed with the raw rage of someone who felt they had been trampled upon by a grave injustice. She leaned forward and gripped the arms of her chair, her knuckles turning white. Her light-brown eyes grew dark. "It trivializes my brother's death!" she cried.

Howie cleared his throat, not sure how he should respond to her outburst. "You're right, it does," he finally said, recalling the off-handed remark he had made to Mick about the story. "I do remember reading it now."

"So you understand why I gave that reporter a piece of my mind? I was so angry that I screamed and pounded on his desk." Stephanie took a couple of deep breaths before collapsing back into her chair.

"Are you okay?"

She nodded and took another deep breath. Her next words were spoken in a tone slightly above a whisper. "I was at a restaurant yesterday and overheard people in the booth behind me making a joke about..." She buried her face in her hands. When she looked up, her eyes glistened with tears. "People don't understand...they just don't understand. How can people joke about something so horrible?"

Howie shrugged.

"The way my brother died. It...it had to have been awful."

"I'm sure it must've been." He handed her a box of tissues. Tears always made him uncomfortable. In these situations, he always felt like he should be doing or saying something to make the woman feel better. Perhaps that was one reason his social life was close to nil. Adam was more adept at handling something like this. His partner's bedside manner would serve him well when he became a preacher. His own bedside manner served him well, but in a different way that Adam probably wouldn't approve of. "Would you like a cup of coffee or something to eat?"

Stephanie dabbed at the corner of her eyes with a tissue and then gently blew her nose. "No thank you." She took a couple of tissues before handing the box back. "I just want to get at the truth."

"I know you do and I promise we will." Howie picked up his pencil. "Why don't you let me get some preliminary facts about the case, okay?"

Stephanie nodded.

"Good." He flipped to a new page in his notepad. "If I recall from that newspaper story, your brother worked at a candy factory here on the North Side. Am I right?"

"Yes, the Chocolate Angel Candy Factory."

Howie wrote down the name of the place as well as making a note to check to see if he still had Saturday's newspaper. If he still had the paper, he would clip out the story for his files. Maybe he would contact the reporter to see if the fellow had any additional information. Jim Davidson, his police detective friend, had advised him when he and his partners first opened the detective agency to always check out all leads, especially the ones that might be considered insignificant.

"I suppose I could do that, but wouldn't that take a lot of time?" Howie had asked.

"Sure, but if you want to be a good detective, that's what you do," Davidson had replied. "You never know when and where an important clue may turn up. Some of the best leads I've had came from sources that nobody else thought important enough to follow up on. Just take my word for it; follow all your leads."

"Thanks, I'll keep that in mind."

"You do that. And remember that if I can ever be of some help, just give me a call," Davidson had said, adding, "And call me JD, all my friends do."

JD had proven to be a good resource, but this was a case Howie wanted the agency to handle on its own. If this was a murder case, and they solved it, the word would quickly spread around the North Side, and would bring in more business. And more business would mean a better cash flow. And a better cash flow would mean that he could devote full time to detective work. "And where is this candy factory located?" he asked.

"On Eighteenth and Third." Stephanie's voice sounded calmer.

"Really? That's not too far from here." Although Howie had lived on the North Side all his life and had driven past that corner many times, he didn't recall any candy factory. In visualizing the spot, he remembered a turn-of-the-century cathedral-like church dominating the corner. If memory served him right, across the street from the church and halfway down the block toward Washington Avenue was Joe's Automobile Parts, a junkyard surrounded by an eight-foot high chain-link fence. He had quipped to Mick that the fence was there to keep intruders out and the two huge German shepherd guard dogs in. The need for the guard dogs and the high fence were also indications of how the neighborhood had gone downhill in recent years. "Are you sure that's where it is?" he asked Stephanie.

"I'm positive."

"Isn't there a church on that corner?"

"Yes, but the candy factory took over the building."

"Okay, I understand." Howie pictured the brownstone structure. "When did the place stop being a church?"

"I don't know when that happened, but the candy factory opened up three years ago. My brother told me that the building had been vacant for quite some time before Mr. Gilbertson came into the picture."

"Gilbertson? Who's he?"

"He's the man who bought the church building." Stephanie's eyes softened. "LaMar said that it was because of Mr. Gilbertson that he decided to get a job there."

"What do you mean? I'm not sure I follow."

"You had to have known my brother. Don't ask me why, but he always seemed to have a thing for church architecture ever since he was a kid. Even though Mr. Gilbertson renovated the inside of the church, LaMar liked that the stained glass windows were kept. He said it gave him a feeling of peace." Stephanie's eyes shifted to the box of tissue on Howie's desk, staring at it for quite some time before speaking. "I hope he's at peace now."

Howie waited as his client continued to gaze at the tissue box. "Nothing was done to the outside of the building?" he asked when she finally looked up.

Her face registered puzzlement at his question.

"You said that the inside of the church was renovated," he pointed out. "Was anything done to the outside to change its appearance?"

Stephanie shook her head. "No, Mr. Gilbertson wanted the building to remain looking like a church. That's why they decided to name it 'The Chocolate Angel Candy Factory.' He also told me that he didn't want the candy factory to draw any attention."

"So you have met Gilbertson?"

"Yes, he was very helpful to me when LaMar died." She hesitated for a moment as a flicker of guilt flashed in her eyes. "You see I wasn't in town at the time."

Howie leaned forward, but said nothing.

"I was out of the country traveling in Europe with a girlfriend." Stephanie paused and wet her lips. "It was a trip that we had planned nearly a year ago. We both needed to get away and have a vacation, but I should've..." Her eyes turned downward.

"You should've what?"

When Stephanie made eye contact, her eyes reflected a deep sadness. "It's important that you understand that the trip was something I needed for my own sanity." As she gave her explanation, her fingers slid back and forth along the arm of her chair. "The plan was to travel with no agenda or schedule, to decide each morning where we wanted to go that day. We traveled by train; sometimes we rented a car. We both were rebounding from failed relationships and needed time to heal without interruptions." She paused, her eyes searching for understanding. "We just needed to be free spirits for a while."

"I can understand that," Howie said, trying to be supportive while anticipating what she was leading up to.

"The time away was everything it was meant to be, but when LaMar died..." Stephanie closed her eyes for a moment and took a deep breath. "When he died, there wasn't any way to get in contact with me." She closed her eyes again. Her lip quivered as she confessed in a tone that begged for absolution. "I got home two days after my brother was buried. I...I didn't even know that he had died."

"That must've been hard," Howie said. The woman needed a counselor rather than a detective. If Adam had been there, he would have turned her over to him. His partner was more sympathetic with these things and could better help her work through her feelings while offering counsel. "Who then handled the arrangements?"

"Mr. Gilbertson. He took care of everything." A hint of a smile crossed Stephanie's face. "He was wonderful. He even paid for the funeral."

"He paid for the whole thing?"

"Yes, he said that since LaMar's death happened at his factory, he felt responsible. When I offered to pay him back, he wouldn't hear of it." Stephanie took a deep breath. "I owe so much to that man."

Howie was curious as to why Gilbertson handled the arrangements. He would, however, save that question for another time. "Can you tell me now why you think your brother's death wasn't an accident?"

Stephanie nodded. "For one thing, the business about him stumbling and falling into that vat of chocolate can't be true. LaMar wasn't clumsy like that," she said with conviction. "He played sports in high school and was very athletic. I just can't see my brother tripping and losing his balance. I just know it wasn't an accident."

"I'm afraid accidents happen to the best of people." Howie turned to another page in his notepad. That the woman believed that her brother was immune from accidents wasn't in her favor. Accidents happen, and some are deadly. A couple of years ago, one of his high school classmates was killed falling off the roof of his house. "You've got to give me something more than that for grounds for a murder. What else have you got?"

"About a month before LaMar died, he told me that he was suspicious of a fellow worker."

"Suspicious? Of what?"

"I don't know." Stephanie paused. "The only thing my brother said was that this man was always acting strange around the place."

Howie raised his eyebrows. "What did he mean, strange?"

"Mysterious like. LaMar told me that he was planning to follow him some night after they got done with work. He wanted to find out what this man was up to." Stephanie's tone softened. "I guess he liked playing the role of a detective."

"And did he follow him?"

"Yes, and he called me and said he was on to something. When I asked him what, he wouldn't tell me except to say that he needed to get some proof." Stephanie waited until Howie finished jotting down whatever he was writing. "He knew I was going on my trip and told me to enjoy it. He said that he'd call me when I got back."

Howie flipped a page in his notepad. "This guy that your brother talked about. Do you know his name?"

"Ken."

"And his last name?"

"Lamar always referred to him as Ken. He never told me his last name, and I...I never thought to ask."

Howie wrote down the name and put a question mark behind it. "And when did you have that conversation with your brother?"

"It was two days before I left on the trip." When Stephanie's voice broke, she reached for a tissue. "Please, excuse me. LaMar was the only family I had left."

"So, there's nobody else?"

"We had a younger sister who died when she was three years old. Both sets of grandparents have died. Our parents were killed in a car accident three years ago." Stephanie shook her head as though even she couldn't believe her story could be so tragic. "It's like our family has been cursed. When our parents died, my brother and I drew close together. We had no other relatives to speak of. He walked me down the aisle when I got married. If I ever get married again and have a son, I'll name him, LaMar."

"I'm sure he'd like that." Howie's comment drew a smile. "Now, besides this guy, Ken...is there anything else that leads you to believe your brother's death wasn't accidental?"

Stephanie shook her head.

"Do you remember anything else from the telephone conversation you had with your brother that day?"

"What do you mean?"

"Did you talk about anything else? Anything at all?"

"I don't...wait a minute." She put her finger to her lips; her gaze turned inwardly as though searching for a memory. "He did ask me if I knew the name of a good dentist."

"A dentist?"

"Yes. He was having some kind of problem and needed to see one."

"Did you suggest any?"

"Yes, a Doctor Filmore. Why do you ask?"

"I just might pay him a visit." JD's advice to follow all leads, no matter how insignificant they may seem, echoed in his head. "Where's his office?"

"On Broadway and Girard."

Howie jotted it down. When he looked up, Stephanie's face had a puzzled expression. "Maybe your brother said something while at the dentist's office that could prove helpful," he explained. "We have to investigate every angle. It's a long shot, though."

They talked for another fifteen minutes. When he asked where her brother had lived, she said that LaMar had shared an apartment with another man. He wrote the address down along with the name of the roommate, knowing that he would want to talk with him. After discussing and agreeing upon the fee, he walked her to the door. "I'll be in touch with you," he said as he opened the door for her.

"I know I haven't given you much to go on." Stephanie bit her lip. "I'm sorry."

"Don't worry." Howie offered a smile that he hoped would be reassuring. "You've given me enough to start on."

After Stephanie left his office, Howie called Mick, filled him in on their new case, and asked him to come with him the next day to pay a visit to the candy factory. He also called Adam and asked him to come, but Adam wouldn't be able to make it. Howie shared with each of them his doubts about Stephanie's claim that her brother's death wasn't accidental. Even though Mick and Adam shared his skepticism, they expressed excitement, as well as apprehension, at the thought of investigating a potential murder case. Adam, being ever so cautious, suggested that they contact JD, their police detective friend, and get his take on it.

"If this is a murder case, we need to get the police involved," Adam argued.

"They had their chance," Howie said. "Now, it's ours."

"But, at least call JD."

"I will if there's a need." After nearly a year in the business, Howie felt confident that they could handle this case without any outside help.

# Chapter 5

MICK ARRIVED AT Howie's office around four in the afternoon. After
Howie briefly reviewed the information that Stephanie Turner had shared
the previous day, they headed down the stairs and across the street to his
car. On the way to the Chocolate Angel Candy Factory, Mick agreed that
they should start with Gilbertson, the owner, and then get his permission to
talk with the other employees. "We might as well get this done all at once
while we're there," he said. In contrast to Adam's careful one-step-at-a-time
approach to cases, Mick preferred a do-it-now, action-orientated one. It
wasn't that he was careless in his investigations; he just liked to get things
done.

Howie favored Mick's approach, but also considered Adam's style
helpful in providing a balance. At times, he would intentionally play his
partners off against each other, and then sit back and observe. If, after the
fact, either accused him of manipulating them, he would simply point out
that it was a way of teaching them about the detective business and how
vital it was to look at things from different angles. It was also a way to
observe how well they each stood up to challenges and didn't back down on
things they strongly believed in. Although he never openly admitted it, he
would rather have them going at each other than joining forces against him.
"It should be only a couple more blocks," he announced as he turned the
corner onto Fifteenth Street.

"It's sure sad to see a church go out of business," Mick said.

Howie slowed down for a kid retrieving a ball that had rolled out into the
street. "Well, maybe the people just got tired of God, kicked him out, and
closed the place."

Mick gave his boss a sideways glance. "Why don't you save that remark
for Adam? The two of you can bring it up with his professors at the
seminary."

"There it is up ahead." Howie pointed to the brownstone building. He
had no interest in meeting any of Adam's professors nor did he care what
they would have to say on matters pertaining to God. He bitterly
remembered the day his mother had died. The minister had offered to have
a prayer, but he would have none of it after he had asked and was told that

the prayer wouldn't bring her back to life. When Adam entered seminary last year, Howie let him know that he didn't want any lectures about religion. "I had my fill of church and God-talk when I was young," he told Adam, making sure his partner got the message.

"Hey, it still looks like a church to me." Mick pointed toward the roof of the building. "Except it doesn't have a cross on top."

"God probably hocked it to get some traveling money." Howie glanced over at his friend, wondering if his sarcasm was proving to be too much. Mick and his fiancée attended church on a regular basis and their wedding later on this year would be held in a church. "Aren't you going to tell me that I'm being sacrilegious?"

"I didn't say a word."

"I know, but you gave me that 'better be careful what you say' look." Howie glanced over at Mick. "If there's a big guy upstairs he's got to have a sense of humor, too."

"And if God doesn't have a sense of humor, you're in big trouble." Mick grinned. "And when he comes looking for you, I'm going to tell him exactly where to find you."

"That's fine because there are a few questions I'd like him to answer." Howie pulled up and parked across the street from the front entrance of the church. The building wasn't as massive as he had remembered. The structure was huge, all right, but it looked as if it had been squeezed onto the corner. A five-foot strip of lawn that needed cutting separated the building from the sidewalk. Unlike the benefit of having large parking lots of the suburban churches, those who had once attended this church must have been content with on-street parking.

"Do you think it's open?" Mick asked as he peered through the windshield.

"Let's go and find out." Howie got out of the car and waited for his partner to join him. They walked across the street and stood for a moment, taking in what once must have been, in years past, a magnificent church structure. He glanced at his watch. "It's only a few minutes after four. There's got to be somebody here."

"Are you sure? It looks deserted."

"Yeah, I'm sure. Stephanie told me that her brother went to work around six, an hour after the others went home."

"So Jones and that other guy worked the same hours?"

"Pretty much so." Howie started up the cement steps that led to the arched double doors of the front entrance.

"Man, I feel like I'm going to church," Mick said as he caught up to Howie.

"If it's still a church, God better stop skimming the offering plates," Howie said. "These steps are in need of cement work." He pointed to some pigeon droppings. "They could also use a cleaning."

Mick gestured toward the corner of the building. "Looks like that stonework could use some repair."

Howie nodded. "Yeah, and a good scrubbing as well. Gilbertson sure didn't spend any money on the outside." He glanced around. "There's not even a sign advertising that this place is a candy factory."

"Look at that." Mick gestured to a small, hand-printed sign to the right of the door. *Help wanted. Apply within between eight and five.*

"Forget it. You've got a job, already." Howie tried the door but it was locked. He felt a nudge on his arm. Mick was pointing to a buzzer to the right of the door. Howie pushed the white button and waited. He was about to push it again when the door opened and a brute of a man appeared. Thick, black-cropped hair covering a head as massive as a cinder block along with sunken eyes and a nose so hooked-shaped that it could be used for a bottle opener, transformed any likely description of him as a friendly giant into a misnomer of monumental proportions.

"Are you looking for a job?" the giant asked, his voice rough and deep.

"I'm afraid not," Howie replied, momentarily taken back by the man's size. "We're from the MAC Detective Agency. I'm Howie Cummins. This is my partner, Mick Brunner. We'd like to ask a few questions about LaMar Jones. If we could—"

"We've already talked to the police about that matter!" the giant snapped, and then proceeded to close the door.

Howie grabbed the door. Rude people and doors being shut in his face were two of his pet peeves. "Wait a minute. Can we see Mr. Gilbertson?"

"He has nothing more to say."

"Did he tell you to say that?" Mick took a half step forward. If the giant was intimidated by a man nearly as big as he was, his eyes didn't reflect it. Mick put an edge to his tone. "You'd better have specific instructions about that, because if you don't, you just may lose your job."

The man's eyes narrowed. "It was the boss who told me to tell that to snoops like you," he said with a sneer and then pulled the door shut, nearly taking Howie's hand with it.

"Not too friendly, is he?" Mick said.

"You can say that again." Howie tried the door again with no luck. "The guy looks like he's a reject from a monster movie."

"Yeah, I know what you mean. And as big as I am, I still wouldn't want to meet the guy in a dark alley."

"Dark alley?" Howie rolled his eyes. "That guy is the dark alley." He stared at the door for a moment. "Did you see that honker of his?"

Mick's eyebrows rose. "How could you miss it?"

Howie looked around for a moment. "Come on. Let's get out of here before old Hooknose decides to come out and eat us for a snack."

"Got any ideas about how we're going to get into this place?"

"Yeah, that Help Wanted sign."

"Oh, sure," Mick said as he and Howie trotted down the steps. "Why don't we go back and ask Hooknose for a job application. You know how far we'd get on that."

"Maybe not us..." Howie glanced back at the Help Wanted sign. "But what about Adam?"

"What are you talking about?"

"Wasn't he just saying the other day about needing to find some extra work for the summer months?"

"Yeah, but do you think he'd go for it?" Mick asked as they crossed the street to Howie's car.

"What do you mean?"

"You know what I'm talking about." Worry lines appeared around Mick's eyes. "If he doesn't like interviewing people under false pretenses, how is he going to feel about deceiving people every day when he works undercover? The poor guy struggles so much with whether he's cut out to be a minister. This isn't going to help him."

"We don't have any other choice. He may not like it, but I'll persuade him to do it." Howie recalled a conversation he and Adam had a couple months ago.

"I don't like doing stuff like this," Adam had said after he and Howie had interviewed a person under the guise of being claims adjustors for a car insurance company. "It just doesn't seem right. We're lying to people."

Howie had had to hold his temper. This wasn't the first time the issue had come up between the two of them. "We're not telling big lies that hurt anyone," he had replied calmly.

"It doesn't matter whether they are big or little lies. Lying is lying, period." Adam had grown silent, but his brooding eyes had flickered with intensity. "I feel like a charlatan when I lie."

"Look, I know you haven't agreed with me and Mick in the past about this, but there are times when the end justifies the means." As far as Howie was concerned, the end almost always justified the means if it meant solving a case. "Remember, we represent victims who are seeking justice. Doesn't that count for something?"

Adam never did answer his question and as far as Howie knew, his partner still struggled with it. Adam's dilemma was that he found detective work exciting and, whether he cared to admit it, the work suited his personality. On more than one occasion, Howie had told Mick that their partner had the makings of a good detective if only he would come down out of that pulpit and into the real world.

"So, when are you going to talk to him?" Mick asked after he and Howie got into the car.

Howie turned the ignition, put the car in gear, and pulled away from the curb. "I'll call him as soon as we get back."

"Do you think he'll go for it?"

"If he wants to continue in this kind of business, he'd better."

# Chapter 6

WHEN HOWIE AND Mick got back to the office, Howie told Mick to get himself a bottle of pop from the refrigerator while he called Adam. "Get me one, too!" he yelled as his partner headed for the kitchen. He had a six-pack of beer in the frig as well, but Mick didn't drink. A cold brew would've hit the spot, but he didn't want one in his hand if Adam was coming over. After he dialed Adam's number, he doodled on a piece a paper.

"Here's your pop," Mick said, setting the bottle on the desk.

"Thanks." Howie took a sip just as Adam answered. "Hey, Adam. It's Howie. Can you come over for a few minutes? Mick's here and we want to talk to you about something."

"About what?"

"I'll tell you when you get here."

"Can't you just tell me now?"

"No, you need to come here." Howie always liked to talk to people in person. That way, he could charm them into doing things he figured they might not want to do. "I don't want to talk over the phone. It's too impersonal."

"I don't know. Why can't you just—"

"Come on. It won't take long. You're just down the block." Howie looked at Mick and gave him a knowing wink. "It's not like you have to get in your car and drive over here." He took another sip of pop while he waited for Adam's reply.

"Okay, I'll be right over," Adam said, a note of hesitancy in his voice. "But this better be worth my while."

"Trust me. It will be. See you in a few minutes." Howie hung up the phone and took another sip of pop. After his partners left, he would fix himself a sandwich and have a beer.

"That 'just down the block' gets Adam every time," Mick said. "You sure know how to push the right button. I have to admit that you're one clever but devious boss." He held up his bottle in a mock salute.

"How can you say that?" Howie replied as he raised his bottle in return. "Don't you know that it's my charming personality that makes people want to do things for me?" He took a sip, pulled out a phone book from his desk drawer, and started paging through it.

"What are you doing?"

"I'm looking up the phone number of that dentist that Stephanie Turner recommended to her brother."

"Do you think you'll get much from him?"

"I doubt it, but I'll call him when I get a chance and see if I can stop by some time and ask a few questions." Howie preferred interviewing face-to-face. It was always better to question someone in person than over the phone. A person's body language could tell you a lot. He copied down the phone number and then shared with Mick about his experience at the nursing home.

"That Nana sounds like a fireball."

Howie rolled his eyes and nodded. "You'd better believe she is." He was about to ask Mick if he wanted to go with him the next time he went to see her when the office door opened and Adam walked in.

Adam stopped in front of Howie's movie poster, straightened it, and then took a seat next to Mick. He stretched out his legs and clasped his hands behind his head. "Okay, what's so important that you have to talk to me in person?"

"I've got a job for you."

Adam sat up straight and looked at Mick. "What's he talking about?"

"He's the boss. I'll let him tell you."

"We went to the candy factory to interview Gilbertson." Howie took a sip of pop and then set the bottle to one side. "But this goon wouldn't let us get past the front door. The guy was bigger than Mick and had a nose on him that you could use as a fishing hook for whales."

"Did he answer any questions?"

"We didn't get a chance to ask any. He told us that they had nothing more to say about the case and then shut the door in my face."

"Friendly, eh?"

"Oh, yeah, real friendly," Mick said.

"So what has this got to do with me?" Adam looked at Howie and then at Mick and then back at Howie. "If you guys couldn't get in, how am I supposed to?"

"There was a Help Wanted sign by the front door," Howie said. "I figure if you go over and apply, you might get the job. Even if you don't, at least you'll get in the place. Once you're in, you can check it out. Maybe you'll even get a chance to talk to Gilbertson, the owner."

"What if they don't hire me?"

"Don't worry, they will."

Adam breathed deeply and let out a puff of air. "I knew as soon as you said you wanted to talk to me in person that I was in trouble."

Howie was surprised that Adam hadn't raised any objections. To work undercover meant living a life of lies and deceit; not exactly attributes you expect to find in a person studying to become a minister. "Then you'll do it?" he asked.

Adam nodded.

"You will?" Mick's tone reflected the astonished look in his eyes.

"I said I would." Adam turned to Howie. "When do you think I should go and apply for this position?"

Howie checked the time. "It's too late now, but how about bright and early tomorrow morning? We don't want to take any chances that someone else could get the job."

After Adam left, Howie and Mick finished their drinks in silence. That their partner had accepted the assignment without so much as a protest was mystifying.

# Chapter 7

AT A FEW minutes past eight in the morning, Adam climbed the steps of the Chocolate Angel Candy Factory. He had surprised Howie and Mick by immediately agreeing to take on the assignment without so much as an argument. If he got the job, he would be working at the place under false pretenses. That was okay. He needed to see if he could work undercover without feeling so guilty that he found it difficult to sleep at night. His sleeplessness for the past several weeks had been due to his indecision about whether to go back to seminary in the fall. If he didn't go back it would be hard on his mother. She had helped put him through college and had been so proud when he entered the seminary. Hopefully, she would understand. More than likely she wouldn't. Perhaps undercover work would help him finally decide whether being a detective was his true calling.

After trying the entrance doors to the building and finding them locked, Adam pressed the buzzer. While he waited, he breathed in the fresh spring air of the June day and thought about what his opening line should be to whomever answered the door. *Hello, I'm Adam Trexler*, he would say with a smile and then extend his hand for a friendly handshake. *I'm here for--* The door suddenly opened, startling him so that he involuntarily took a step back. He immediately recognized Hooknose from the description his partners had given him. Although Howie had a reputation for exaggerating, he certainly hadn't done so this time. Adam, at six feet, found himself staring up into eyes that glared back from a face that looked like it had never experienced a smile. *Fee, Fi, Fo, Fum. I smell the blood of...* The words of the giant from the story *Jack and the Beanstalk* echoed through his mind.

"What do you want?" the giant asked in a not so friendly tone.

"I, ah..." Adam pointed to the Help Wanted sign.

Hooknose looked him over, obviously wanting to know whom this person was who wished to enter his domain. Adam extended his hand, but it was brushed aside with a cold glance. Once the guardian of the gate seemed satisfied, however, he stepped back and allowed Adam to enter.

"Wait here!" He shut the door behind Adam, the harshness in his voice unabated.

Adam watched as Mr. Personality walked toward a desk where a young woman with short, curly, black hair sat typing. She appeared to be in her twenties, was quite attractive, and looked very soft and cuddly in her light-blue, fuzzy sweater. When she smiled as Hooknose approached, Adam wondered if she received one in return. Of course she would. Even the giant wouldn't be able to resist returning her smile.

While Hooknose and the young woman talked, Adam glanced around at what once had been the narthex of the church. Dark oak, floor-to-ceiling-paneled walls surrounded him. Other than a brightly lit floor lamp next to the desk where the young woman was typing, the ornately decorated wall lamps poorly illuminated the space. Elaborately carved arched doors stood directly in front of him. The doors no doubt led into what would have been, at one time, the sanctuary. Pamphlet racks, to the right of the doors, that once held religious tracts and daily devotionals stood empty. To his far left were stairs going down.

"Hey, you!"

Adam looked toward his right.

A scowling Hooknose waved him over. "This guy wants to apply for the job," he said as Adam walked up.

The woman looked even more attractive close up. Her stunning, unblemished complexion complimented the whitest teeth Adam had ever seen. "Please have a seat," she said in a pleasant tone of voice. "I'll be with you in just a moment."

"Do you want me to stay?" Hooknose asked the woman as he glanced at Adam.

"No, Leo, that's fine."

Adam sat and watched as her long slender fingers flew over the keys of the typewriter. He didn't see any wedding or engagement ring; not that he was looking for any relationship. With college and seminary, the past several years had been devoted mainly to his studies. The few women he had dated had trouble dealing with his brooding, introspective personality. Besides, how could he devote any energy to a relationship when his own inner struggles had been consuming so much of him?

"Thank you for waiting," she said after finishing her typing. Her smile came across as warm and soft as her sweater. "I understand that you wish to apply for the job."

"I sure do, if it's not too late."

"Oh, you don't have to worry about that."

"Why's that?"

"I was afraid we wouldn't get any applicants." Her eyes revealed a vibrant, energetic personality, a person in love with life. "You see, my father doesn't believe in advertising in the paper."

"Your father owns this place?"

"Yes, but don't get the wrong idea. The size of the building isn't an indication of the size of our operation. We're known as a candy factory, but the word 'factory' is misleading." As she talked, her eyes continued to sparkle. "We're a small, family-owned business. Our specialty is—oh, please forgive me." A hint of pink appeared in her cheeks. "I forgot even to introduce myself. I'm Rachel Gilbertson."

"Hi. My name is Adam Trexler."

"You'll have to excuse me," Rachel said. "I'm not used to hiring people, but around here everybody does a little bit of everything." She folded her hands on the desk. "My father told me I should do this because I'm a good judge of character." With a smile she extended her hand. "As far as I'm concerned, you're hired."

"Just like that?"

"Just like that."

"That's great." He liked the touch of her hand, wishing there was some reason he could hold on to it longer. "I don't know what to say. Thank you."

Rachel smiled. "I suppose I should have you fill out an application form to make it official." While she got the form from her desk drawer, Adam glanced in the direction of Hooknose. The big guy was standing at the stairway, glaring at the two of them.

"You can start next Monday evening." Rachel handed Adam the application form and a pen. "Your hours will be from six until midnight, and you'll do a variety of jobs: cleaning, packaging, assembling of boxes, shipping, and running some errands. It's pretty much anything that comes up. Ken will show you the ropes; he works those same hours. I'll let him know we've hired someone. He'll be looking for you that evening."

Once Adam filled out the necessary paperwork and was informed of the wages and benefits, Rachel invited him to go on a quick tour of the place. She took him through the doors leading into the former sanctuary. Although the pews had been removed, the vaulted ceiling and stained glass windows imbued the space with reverence and a feeling of peace. Besides having the pews removed, the only other major renovation was that the chancel area had been partitioned off into what appeared to be a large office.

About a third of the way into the work area, a half dozen women sat at two rows of long wooden tables. All of the women appeared to be in their fifties, and most looked as if they had sampled more than their share of chocolate over the years. Adam's presence didn't seem to bother them. Considering what had happened here, the atmosphere seemed normal. Perhaps things were too normal.

"All of our candy is individually wrapped by hand," Rachel explained as they walked up to the long tables. Each of the workers had trays of neatly stacked chocolate angels next to them.

Adam watched as one of the workers quickly, but with a practiced expertise, wrapped an angel with gold foil and gently placed it in a candy box already half full. "They really handle the candy with care," he said.

Rachel smiled. "My father takes pride in the personal touch given to each box of candy." She introduced Adam to each of the women and then moved on to another area. Near the front and off to the right, in a space that must have been for the choir, were several other women; they were pouring thick, dark chocolate into molds. A large vat stood off in the corner. The vat reminded Adam of a witches' caldron, except it was stainless steel and it looked new. "What's that used for?" he asked.

"To mix and heat the ingredients." Rachel moved closer and whispered. "My father has a secret ingredient that he stirs in when no one else is around."

As a way of giving her an opening to say more, Adam thought about remarking that the vat was large enough to take a bath in, but decided not to say anything, afraid that she might get suspicious.

"That is the holy of holies," Rachel said, laughing gently, and pointing to the partitioned area up front. "What used to be the chancel area is now my father's office and workroom." Her smile faded for a moment. "It's off limits to everyone, including me. I would introduce you to him, but he's not here today."

As they walked back into the narthex area, Hooknose was still standing by the stairway. "We'll go downstairs now," Rachel said.

"Who's that guy by the stairs, anyway?" Adam whispered. "He never introduced himself to me."

"I'll introduce him to you," she whispered back. "Leo's really a nice guy once you get to know him."

The scowl on Hooknose's face told Adam that the guy didn't like the idea that he and Rachel were whispering.

"This is Leo Rappaport," Rachel said after they had walked up to him. "We wouldn't know what to do around here without him. He's a jack-of-all-trades." She touched the giant on the arm. "Leo, this is Adam Trexler. He'll be working here starting Monday."

"Hi," Adam said. "Remember me?" He had meant it as a joke, but Hooknose only glowered back as though Adam was an intruder.

"I'm giving Adam a quick tour of the place," Rachel said.

As Adam followed Rachel down the stairs, the hairs on his neck prickled; he didn't have to turn around to know why.

# Chapter 8

MICK PARKED HIS car on the side street across from Kass Drugstore and sat for a moment gazing up at Howie's apartment windows. Twenty minutes earlier Howie had called him.

"Can you come up to the office?" Howie had asked. "I need to talk to you about something in person."

"I'll be there shortly." Howie no doubt had some kind of assignment for him. That was okay; it was good timing. Several days earlier, he had finished teaching for the school year and now had more time and energy to give to investigating their cases. Although his fiancée, Mary, had concerns about him working as a detective, he enjoyed having the part-time work and considered it a diversion in his life. Even his experience last fall one night in the cemetery while working on their first case had not dampened his enthusiasm. He still tried to live by Will Roger's philosophy about never meeting a man he didn't like. There were, however, a few exceptions. "Well, let's see what the boss has planned for me this time." He got out of his car, making sure it was locked. Even during daylight hours on the North Side, you locked your car unless you wanted to take a taxi home. He trotted across the street, opened the entrance door to the apartment building, and climbed the stairs two at a time. When he got to the top landing, he looked back down the two flights of stairs with a triumphant smile. Even though it had been eight years since he played football in high school, he was still in good shape. He opened the door and strolled into the office. Howie was leaning back in his chair with his feet propped up on his desk and, as usual, paging through one of his *Police Gazette* magazines.

"Have you heard from Adam yet?" Mick asked as he walked over, plopped down in his favorite chair, and stretched out his legs.

"Nope." Howie set his magazine aside.

"Maybe that's a good sign." Mick glanced at the clock. "It's past ten. You'd think that he'd be back by now if Hooknose wouldn't let him in."

Howie nodded. "Let's hope he got that job." He took out his notepad, and then gave his partner a winsome smile. "There's something I need you to do."

"I figured you did. So what have you got?"

"I want you to interview Jack Miller."

"Sure, but who is he?"

"LaMar Jones' roommate."

"Okay, I can do that." Mick shifted in his chair, getting more comfortable. "I'll be interested to meet the guy. Where does he live?"

"Over on Central Avenue near Lowry." Howie paged through his notepad. "Stephanie said that Miller and her brother shared an apartment above some used clothing store." He tore a page from his notepad and handed it to Mick. "Here's the address. Miller works evenings till about midnight. So, he should be up by now."

Mick looked at the address, folded the paper, and then stuffed it in his shirt pocket. He appreciated Howie trusting him to do these interviews alone. One of the things he liked about working as a detective was the interesting people he met. "Any particular questions you want me to ask?"

"Yeah, feel him out as to whether he thinks LaMar's death was an accident or something else."

"Anything else?"

Howie glanced at his notes. "Stephanie told me that her brother was suspicious of somebody named Ken."

"What's his last name?"

"She didn't know, but her brother and Ken worked together." Howie rocked in his chair for a few moments before continuing, a sign that he was processing any other advice he wanted to give. "Without giving too much away, find out if LaMar ever talked about any of the people he worked with at the factory, especially this guy Ken."

"Okay, will do." Mick stood up. "Is that it?"

"Just come back to the office when you've finished. By then Adam should be here and we'll all compare notes."

Mick headed for the door, opened it, and paused. "Do you think this Miller guy will provide us some good leads?"

"I don't know, but we'll find out, won't we?"

# Chapter 9

MICK DROVE ACROSS the Broadway Bridge over the Mississippi River, past the Grain Belt Brewery Company in northeast Minneapolis, and turned left onto Central Avenue. Within ten minutes he spotted the address Howie had given him for Jack Miller. He was lucky and managed to find a parking place around the corner.

The entrance to Miller's apartment building was nestled between a second-hand clothing shop and a corner grocery store. As soon as Mick opened the entrance door, a dry musty odor confronted him. The old building could use a spring airing. In the entry, to his right, were four mailboxes. Even though light came through the glass window in the entry door, he had to squint to read the names on the mailboxes. Apartment number one listed Jack Miller. The name below Miller's had been crossed out with a black marker. "Bingo," he said, and started up the stairs.

Miller's apartment was the first door on the right at the top of the stairs. Mick knocked, waited, and was about to knock again when the door slowly opened and a young man wearing jeans and a wrinkled, blue-knit shirt appeared. The man, who looked like he had just woken up, appeared to be in his late twenties. His tousled, blond hair along with a muscular physique gave him the appearance of an ancient Greek athlete.

"Yeah, what do you want?" the man asked as he yawned.

"Are you Jack Miller?"

"The last time I looked in the mirror I was." He scratched his chin; the blond stubble indicated a couple of day's growth. "And who are you?"

"Mick Brunner. I'm with the MAC Detective Agency located over on Broadway and Third across the river."

If Miller was surprised that a detective was at his door, he showed no indication. "So what do you want with me?"

"We've been asked to look into the death of LaMar Jones."

Miller's eyes widened at the mention of his former roommate. He crossed his arms in front of his chest, but remained silent.

"The two of you shared this apartment, didn't you?"

"Yeah, so?"

"If you don't mind, I'd like to ask you some questions."

Miller hesitated and for a moment Mick thought he was going to brush him off.

"Sure, come on in," Miller said as he glanced behind the detective as though he expected to see someone there. "The place is sort of messy," he said as he closed the door behind his visitor. "I haven't had a chance to clean it this morning."

The man was right about the place being a mess. At least half-dozen socks were scattered around the living room floor. A pair of jeans lay crumbled over the end of the couch, and a lounge chair in the corner looked as if it served as a clothes hamper. A faint odor of stagnant beer permeated the air. The room, like the building, needed an airing. If there was any semblance of order in the room, it was in the one corner by the television where several cardboard packing boxes were neatly stacked.

"Those are LaMar's clothes," Miller said, having noticed that Mick was looking at the boxes. He cleared newspapers and an empty pizza box off the end of the couch and motioned for Mick to sit. Several empty beer bottles sat on the coffee table. A crumpled bag of potato chips and a slice of dried-up pizza on a greased-soaked napkin lay next to the beer bottles. In the ashtray were several butts, two of them having a faint trace of lipstick. Miller grabbed the pile of clothes in the chair, tossed them on the floor, and sat down. "Laundry day is tomorrow," he explained with a smirk.

Mick nodded, but said nothing. Howie always suggested allowing people to ramble for a few minutes before asking the first question. He always told them they'd be surprised at what people reveal in those first few minutes.

"His sister told me she didn't want those clothes," Miller said, gesturing to the boxes. "So I packed them and was going to take them to Goodwill." He massaged his face for a few moments and then ran his hands back through his hair. "I've been going to do it for days now, but haven't gotten around to it yet." He took a deep breath and let it out slowly. "LaMar's death really was a shock to me."

"I'm sure it was." Mick didn't sense any grief behind Miller's words, nor did he see it in his eyes. "How long did you guys share this apartment?"

"Going on a couple of years."

"How did the two of you meet?"

"We knew each other from high school. Graduated the same year. Both of us were in gymnastics." Miller felt the pocket of his shirt, giving Mick the impression that he was reaching for a pack of cigarettes. "After we graduated, we made it a point to keep in contact. A couple of years ago, he and I decided to get this apartment, you know, as a way of cutting down on our expenses."

"It sounds like you knew him pretty well. What kind of guy was he?"

"He was pretty serious, kept to himself, and only had a few friends. He was the type of guy that if you were his friend, however, he'd do anything for you." Miller stifled a yawn. "He was getting close with his sister again. Too bad he had that accident."

"Yeah, too bad." It would serve no purpose to ask Miller if he had any suspicions about LaMar's death now that the guy was making it quite clear that he thought it was an accident. "Did he say anything about work, anything unusual going on there?"

"What do you mean?" Miller shifted in his chair and then crossed his legs. "I'm not sure what you're trying to get at."

"Just trying to piece together what was going on in his life before he died." Mick intentionally kept his tone calm. "Nothing more than that."

"Well, maybe you should be talking to Rosie."

"Rosie? Who's that?"

"That's his girlfriend, Rosie Carpenter. She was supposed to have been down at the factory the night he died."

"Is that so? Why was she going to be down there?"

"I don't know. You'd have to ask her. LaMar just said that she was coming. Maybe they were going to have a party or something." Miller smirked. "You know what I mean?"

"Do you know where I can find her?"

"Just a minute, I think I've got her address."

While Miller was gone, Mick picked up one of the cigarette butts with lipstick, examined it, and then put it back just as Miller returned.

"Yeah, here it is," Miller said. "She lives over on the North Side. You want me to copy her address and phone number down for you?"

Mick nodded, and then watched as Miller tore off a piece of cardboard from the pizza box, scribbled the information on it, and handed it to him. "Thanks." He slipped the address in his pocket.

Miller settled back in the chair. "So, do you think LaMar's death was something more than an accident?"

"We don't think anything at this point. We just want to check everything out and tie up loose ends." Mick paused. "You know, for insurance purposes." By mentioning insurance, he hoped that Miller would be thrown off track. Unlike Adam, he had no problem fabricating a falsehood. One of the conclusions that he had come to since working as a detective was that in catching the bad guys the end almost always justified the means.

"So, who's your client?"

"Sorry, but I can't tell you that. You understand...confidentiality." Although Miller nodded his understanding, Mick had a gut feeling that he already knew the name of their client, and for that matter, wasn't buying the phony inference that he was asking questions for insurance purposes. Miller knew more about the case than he was letting on.

# Chapter 10

WHEN THE PHONE rang, Howie hoped it would be Adam. "MAC Detective Agency." The voice at the other end screeched her name so loudly that he had to hold the phone away from his ear. "Oh, hello, Nana," he said, wondering how she got his number.

"I've got a plan to catch those crooks."

"You've got what?"

"Didn't your mother ever tell you to clean the wax out of your ears?" Nana scolded. "I said I've figured out how to catch those diamond thieves!"

"You have?" Howie was almost afraid to ask. "And how are you going to do that?"

"Can't tell you."

"What? Why not?"

Nana lowered her voice. "Because the phone is buggy."

"Your phone is what?" Howie wondered if he was having a bad dream.

"Not mine! Yours!"

"My phone is buggy?"

"That's what I just said!" Nana yelled. "You're a detective, you should know about how crooks can listen in," she chided. "That's why I'm paying you." She grew silent for a moment. When she continued, her tone was calmer. "Even my grandson, Jerome, knows about such things. Maybe you should talk to him."

"But this phone isn't bugged."

"How do you know?"

"I...ah...had the phone company check it out only last week." It was a lie but Howie wasn't about to spend time arguing whether his line was tapped. And he certainly wasn't in a mood to talk to her precious grandson.

"Did you ask to see the man's ID?"

"What man?"

"The man who checked your phone."

"No, but—"

"Your phone is buggy! I just know it."

"Okay, if you say so." Howie opened his desk drawer to look for something to take for the headache he felt coming on. "So what do you want me to do?"

"Get down here pronto!"

"I don't know if—"

"And do it before lunch, you hear!"

"Look, I— Hello? Hello?" Howie stared at the receiver in disbelief. To call Nana back would be to no avail since she was convinced that the line was *buggy*. He scribbled a note for Mick and Adam, asking them to wait in the office until he got back. After taping the note to the outside of his office door, he headed down to his car. He decided he would also leave word with Kass just in case his partners stopped at the drugstore.

Kass gave him an understanding smile when he learned where he was going. "Ah, that Nana reminds me of my own grandmother," he said with a note of nostalgia. "Old Grandma Zelda was something else. She would drive the family crazy with her active imagination." The parting advice he gave to Howie before he left to see Nana was to be sure and keep a sense of humor. "And good luck," Kass added.

The drive to the nursing home took Howie longer than last time. In addition to hitting every light just as it turned red, a fender-bender tied up traffic. When he finally arrived, the only parking space he could find was nearly a block and a half away. He made up his mind that he would get in and get out fast. He had a real case to work on waiting for him back at the office.

Nana was waiting by the aquarium that sat on a table in the corner. She waved him over as soon as she saw him walk in. "What took you so long?"

"I got here as fast as—"

"Come on! Let's go down to my room." Nana whipped her wheelchair around and headed down the hallway.

Howie stood there for a moment, glanced at the goldfish staring at him, and then started after her.

As soon as they got to her room, Nana told him to shut the door. "Hurry up and sit down!" she ordered. "We've got things to discuss."

Howie looked around. The chair next to the small writing desk had several boxes sitting on it. The only other chair was a wheelchair sitting in the corner.

"Go ahead and sit in the wheelchair," Nana said. "The thing isn't going to bite you." Her chuckle sounded more like a cackle. "You'll get a touch of what it's like to sit in one of these things all day long." She shifted in her chair and wrinkled her nose. "It gives you a mighty sore butt."

Howie sat down, finding it more comfortable than he had thought. He moved closer to Nana. "Okay, what's this plan you have?"

Nana put her finger to her lips. "Shhh." She wheeled to the door and checked to make sure it was closed. "Can't be too careful," she said as she scooted back to Howie. She leaned forward and whispered, "Gertrude agreed to help us set a trap."

"Who's Gertrude? And what kind of trap are you talking about?"

"To catch those diamond thieves!" Nana shot back in a raspy, high-pitched tone of voice. "Gertrude lives down the hall." She eyed him closely. "You're not too bright for a detective, are you?" she asked, and then continued without giving him a chance to reply. "I reckon you've still got some learning to do."

"I'm learning something new every day," Howie said through gritted teeth. "Now, why don't you tell me about your plan?"

"Gertrude has this diamond ring. She said it's worth a G." She eyed Howie again. "Do you know what a G is?"

"I believe it's—"

"A thousand smack-a-rues!" Nana said as her eyes nearly doubled in size. "I know because I watch those cop shows." She inched forward. "I'm not just an old biddy, you know. I keep up with everything."

"I'm sure you do." This time, Howie's smile was genuine. "So this ring that's worth a thous...a G. What do you two plan to do with it?"

"I'm getting to that!" Nana snapped. "Don't rush me! Gertrude's ring is only worth a half of G, but don't tell her I said that. She got it from her second husband...or was it her third?" She paused, closed her eyes, and sat motionless. The antique wall clock slowly marked the passing of time.

Howie waited while listening to the ticking of the clock. He leaned forward to make sure Nana was still breathing. Kass told him that older people had the tendency to nod off in the middle of a conversation. Just as he was about to loudly clear his throat, Nana's body jerked and her eyes popped open.

"What were we talking about?" she demanded.

"Ah...about your friend, Gertrude."

"What about her?"

Howie needed to take some aspirin. "You were wondering which husband gave her the diamond ring."

"Just a minute, I'll call her to find out."

"You don't have to do that. It doesn't—"

"Got to get the facts straight for detective work, don't you?" Nana wheeled over to the telephone and began dialing. As she waited for her friend to answer, she played with one of her pigtails. "Is that you, Gertrude?" she yelled into the receiver and then turned to him. "Poor old thing is hard of hearing."

Howie glanced at his watch. "Maybe we—"

"It's me!" Nana yelled into the receiver. "I'm with that detective I told you about."

Howie watched as Nana's head nodded in agreement.

"Yes, I know that the toast was cold this morning."

He looked at his watch again as he listened to Nana talk about lukewarm oatmeal and runny eggs.

"We want to know which husband gave you that diamond ring," Nana finally said. "So, it was George." She looked at Howie and gave him a thumbs-up. "He was your third husband, wasn't he? Good, that's what I thought. That's all we want to know. I'll come down to talk to you after I'm done here. What's that?" She moved the phone to her other ear. "What's that you say? No, we don't have raisin toast tomorrow. Tomorrow is Thursday. We have raisin toast on Fridays. That's right, dear." She hung up without saying good-bye and wheeled back to Howie.

"So it was her third husband?"

"Yep. He was the cheapskate. It's a big ring but not worth a G." When Nana's thin eyebrows knotted, the bridge of her nose wrinkled. "I'm not going to tell her that, and don't you be telling I said that!" she warned, wagging a bony finger at him

"Don't worry, I won't." Howie shifted in the wheelchair. He hoped he didn't have to sit much longer; the chair was beginning to become uncomfortable. "Why don't you tell me about this plan you have?"

"Gertrude is going to place her ring on her dresser tomorrow and then leave the room. I'll be down the hall pretending to be asleep in my wheelchair, but I'll be watching and waiting." Nana stopped and eyed Howie. "I'm not going too fast for you, am I?"

"No. I think I'm keeping up with you."

"That's a good boy." Nana's eyes flickered with excitement. "Every time someone goes in and out of Gertrude's room, I'll check to see if the ring is still there."

"Aren't you afraid of being noticed?"

"I told you I'd pretend I'm sleeping!" Nana said with a note of irritation. "What's the matter with you? Do you need to borrow one of Gertrude's hearing aids?"

Howie shook his head, wishing he had never asked the question.

"I may even snore for effect. I can do that pretty good." Nana eyes lit up. "Do you want to hear me?"

"No, I trust you do it well."

"Don't you think it's a good plan?"

"It sounds like it," Howie replied. It seemed harmless enough and it might keep her out of his hair for a day. "Just be careful," he said and then added with the intention of providing some drama to spice up Nana and Gertrude's big day. "You never know about those diamond thieves."

"You're right." Nana's eyebrows rose. "Do you think I should pack a rod, then?"

"A what?"

Nana narrowed her eyes, cocking her head in a way to indicate that she wasn't too sure about this guy who claimed to be a detective. "A rod's a crook-shooter."

"I know what you're talking about, but I don't think you'll need one." Howie chastised himself for opening his big mouth.

"But I can get one easy," Nana whispered as she looked toward the door. "I have my connections, you know."

"I'm sure you do, but it's really not necessary," Howie said. He had a feeling that it wouldn't take much urging to get her to get in touch with her connections. "I would just forget about it if I were you."

"Oh, fiddle." Nana sat and tugged at her pigtail for quite some time. "Okay, if you say so," she finally said, scrunching her nose in an obvious display of her disappointment. "But you're taking all the fun out of detectiving."

Howie got up from the chair, wanting to leave before she changed her mind about packing a rod. "I have to get going."

"So soon? Don't you want to meet Gertrude?"

"Maybe next time. I really have to go."

"Okay, but just a minute." Nana wheeled to the door and put her ear against it. She listened for a long time before opening it slowly and peeking out, looking both ways. "Go ahead, the coast is clear. Twenty-three skidoo."

# Chapter 11

HOWIE'S PARTNERS WERE waiting for him at his office when he got back from meeting with Nana. Adam was relaxing in his usual spot, the leather chair closest to the window. Mick, however, was leaning back in Howie's chair.

"Hey, big guy," Mick said, giving his boss a huge grin. "Welcome back." He got up, stretched, and then patted the chair. "I just had to try it out to see how it feels."

"Yeah...and?"

"And I've got to tell you that I felt like I was back in Anderson's office waiting for him to start drilling away." Mick gave the chair a spin. "Why you took this dentist chair when Anderson moved out, I'll never understand."

Howie sat down and stroked the arm of his chair. "This thing has proven to be a great conversation piece." He looked around. "I'll have you know that someone once described my office as being eclectic."

Mick glanced around the office. "I won't argue with that."

"Personally, I think it's more reflective of my free spirit."

"Not to mention our limited cash flow," Mick said with a smirk.

"That, too." Howie leaned forward and addressed Adam. "Okay. Let's get down to business. How did it go at the candy factory? Did you get the job?"

"I start Monday night."

"Great." Howie slapped his hands together and rubbed them back and forth. He thought about asking Adam if he had any concerns about working undercover, but he didn't want to take a chance on getting a lecture on ethics. "Now we're cooking."

Mick took his place next to Adam. "Like I was telling Adam before you came in, he must've really wowed them with his charming personality."

"What are you going to be doing?" Howie asked.

"Sweeping floors and doing odd jobs." Adam had always told his partners that it wasn't beneath him to do manual labor. Life seemed simpler doing that than having to deal with the demons of his inner struggles. "But get this, though; I'll be working with that Ken guy."

Mick leaned toward Adam. "Did you meet him?"

"No, but I will Monday."

"Good." Howie took out his notepad. "Maybe then we can begin to find out what he's up to and why LaMar was so suspicious of him."

"Tell him about the tour of the place," Mick said.

"Wait a minute." Howie opened his top desk drawer and took out a pen. From the beginning of opening the agency, he had decided that he would keep notes. Although he had a pretty good memory, he didn't want to take any chances of letting anything slip by. Cases could remain unsolved by losing track of small details. Also, with each entry, he dated it; and when he remembered to do so, recorded the time of the entry. "Okay, go ahead."

"The inside of the place still gives you a sense of being in church," Adam began. "The narthex has the feel and look of a narthex, but they made it into a reception area with a desk and stuff like that." He waited while Howie flipped a page in his notepad. "The sanctuary was converted into their main work area." As his boss made notes, he briefly described the women at the long tables wrapping and boxing the candy. "And off to where the choir must have sung, there were other women pouring the chocolate into molds."

Howie looked up from his notepad. "Did you see the vat they used to heat the chocolate?"

"Yeah, but I'm pretty sure it wasn't the same one. It looked new."

"That doesn't surprise me." Howie chewed on the end of his pen for a moment. "Let's assume that the vat is new and is the same size as the old one." He tapped the pen on his chin a couple of times and then pointed it at Adam. "So tell me; did it seem like somebody could stumble and fall into it?"

Adam shook his head. "It doesn't seem likely where it is now, but I was told that it was recently moved."

"Where was it before?" Mick asked.

"In a section where you had to step down into the space. I suspect the church organ had been there at one time." Adam brushed back a shock of hair. "I suppose there's the chance a person could've stumbled and fallen into the vat then, but it would've been a mighty freaky accident if you ask me."

"LaMar's sister doesn't think it was an accident." Howie leaned back and drummed his fingers on the arm of his chair for a few moments. "Anything else about that space?"

"Yeah. I didn't like that they partitioned off the chancel area and made it into an office." A look of disapproval swept over Adam's face. "It's not right, and I know that Professor Karsten would have a fit about what was done to the chancel."

Mick tapped Adam on the arm. "Who's Karsten?"

"He's the professor of church history at the seminary. He takes a special interest in church architecture."

"Did you get a look inside the office?" Howie wouldn't have cared if the area had been converted into a pool hall.

"No, it was off limits. Nobody's allowed in there except Gilbertson, the boss. Not even Rachel can go in."

Howie looked up from writing his notes. "Who's she?"

"Gilbertson's daughter."

Mick's eyebrows rose. "The boss' daughter, you say? So you charmed her with your good looks and personality. No wonder you got the job."

Adam shot Mick a stern look signaling that any kidding about Rachel and him wasn't going to be an option.

"Anything else about the building?" Howie asked, suspecting from Adam's reaction to Mick that his partner was attracted to Gilbertson's daughter.

"We went downstairs to what used to be the fellowship room and Sunday school classes. That whole area is now used for storage. They have some of the pews down there." Adam paused as a pensive expression swept over his face. "What's really interesting is that there's also a sub-basement."

"And what's down there?"

"I guess more pews. We didn't go down there and when I asked about it, Rachel just shrugged it off, saying that she avoids the area because it reminds her of a dungeon."

"Tell him about Hooknose," Mick urged

"His name is Leo Rappaport and he's very protective of Rachel." Adam chewed on his lip for a moment. "I don't think he liked that she was so friendly toward me."

"You better watch yourself, then," Howie warned, recalling that Hooknose was a big brute. "Okay, anything else?" When Adam shook his head, he turned his attention to Mick. "How about you? Any luck with LaMar's roommate?"

"He told me that LaMar had a girlfriend."

"You don't say." Howie wondered why Stephanie hadn't mentioned that bit of information. "What's her name?"

"Rosie Carpenter." Mick leaned forward. "And get this. According to Miller, she was supposed to have been down there at the factory the night LaMar died."

"Is that so? Hmmm." Howie drummed his fingers on the desk. "Well, I think we need to have a little talk with her. Did you get an address?"

Mick handed him the piece of cardboard with Carpenter's address and phone number. "I hope you're not hungry; it smells like pepperoni pizza."

Howie copied the information and then tossed the cardboard into the wastebasket under his desk.

"There was something, however, about that guy that didn't quite jive."

Adam looked over at Mick. "What do you mean?"

"I got the distinct feeling that he was holding back, that he knew more about the case than he was letting on." Mick stroked his chin. "He kept referring to Jones' death as an accident, but I'm not sure he believed it himself."

"We'll just have to keep an eye on him," Howie said. "I think—" The office door opened and Stephanie Turner walked in. Mick offered her his chair and then went over and sat on the window ledge. After introductions were made, Howie shared with her that they had touched base with LaMar's roommate and had been told about his girlfriend.

"Girlfriend!" Stephanie let out a forced laugh. "My brother was planning to dump her. He had gotten sick of them fighting all the time."

Howie and his partners exchanged glances. "What would they fight about?" he asked.

"Her jealousy. She didn't want him to even look at another woman, and when she thought he had, she'd go into a rage."

Mick glanced at Howie and then asked Stephanie. "Do you think that she could get jealous enough to kill him?"

Stephanie appeared stunned by the question. She opened her mouth but didn't say anything for several seconds. "I...I...don't know. I hadn't thought of that."

Even though Howie felt an important break had been made in the case, he deliberately kept his voice calm. They may have just identified their number one suspect. "I think we should have a talk with Rosie Carpenter."

"Good," Stephanie said. "For your information, I happen to know that she's a waitress and works afternoons and evenings. I know where she works, but I don't know where she lives."

"We do," Howie said. "And we'll pay her a visit tomorrow morning."

# Chapter 12

"JUST A FEW more blocks," Howie announced as he and Mick drove to the address Jack Miller had given them for Rosie Carpenter. Anxious to talk to her about being at the candy factory the night LaMar died, Howie wanted to hear her version of what took place. That is, if she was even there. Perhaps Miller was lying. Could he trust him? Should he? No, but he trusted Stephanie Turner and if she's right about Rosie, jealousy could very well be a motive for murder. If the Carpenter woman had anything to do with LaMar's death, he would pursue her until he got the answers. "What time is it?"

"A few minutes past noon." Mick looked at Howie with a pleading expression in his eyes. "It's time for lunch. Can't we stop and have a quick bite to eat?"

"Later."

"Have a heart. I didn't have breakfast."

"We'll eat afterwards. I don't want to risk missing her." Howie took his notepad out of his shirt pocket with his right hand while keeping his left hand on the steering wheel. He flipped a few pages in the notepad, and then took a quick glance at what he had written. "According to this address Miller gave you, she lives on Penn Ave."

"It must be right off Broadway," Mick said. "Miller told me that she lives above a shoe store on the corner of Penn and Broadway."

Howie slipped the notepad back into his shirt pocket and stepped on the gas to just make it through the intersection on the yellow light. "That's got to be it up ahead on the right hand side," he said, gesturing to a three-story brick building on the corner. He slowed the car as they approached the intersection and rolled to a stop just as the light turned red.

"There's the shoe store and the apartments are above it," Mick said.

"Where do we go in?"

"The entrance must be right around the corner on Penn." When the light changed, Howie made the right-hand turn. "Yup, there it is," Mick said, pointing to the entrance door. "And we're in luck, there's even a parking place. Do you see it? It's up about three or four cars, ahead of that blue-and-white Chevy Impala."

After parking the car and getting out, they paused to admire the Impala. "This is one classy car," Mick said as he slid his hand across the right front fender. "And it's a brand new '67. Wouldn't you love to own it?" He took a peek through the windshield at the interior. "I wonder how much this baby cost."

"A lot more than you and I can afford." Howie's own car, a blue Ford, needed new tires and a paint job. The eight-year-old car had been left to him when his father died. "Let's go," he said to Mick who was still admiring the car's interior. They walked to the entrance of the apartment building, went in, and after checking the mailboxes in the entryway, headed up the flight of stairs.

"Do you smell that?" Mick asked as they got to the top of the stairs. "Someone's cooking a pot roast." He sniffed the air. "And they're frying onions. I can almost see them sizzling in the pan. Oh, man, that makes my mouth water."

"Put your tongue back in," Howie said. "I told you that I'd feed you later." He motioned to his partner. "Come on. Her apartment has got to be in the back."

As Howie and Mick walked past the first apartment door, Mick suddenly stopped and turned his head.

"What's the matter?" Howie looked around, wondering if his partner had seen or heard something.

"Do you smell that?" Mick sniffed and pointed to the door they had just walked past. "It's coming from back there." He inhaled deeply. "What do you say that we go back and ask for a handout?"

"Come on, get serious. We've got work to do."

Mick took one last sniff and rubbed his stomach. "Okay, but remember you promised to feed me later."

Once they located Rosie Carpenter's apartment, Howie knocked on the door. As they waited, Mick whispered, "Don't forget."

The door opened before Howie could respond. Even though the young woman was dressed in a plain-blue waitress uniform, her curves were revealed quite well. With eyes the color of emeralds and naturally blond hair, her present waitressing job was probably only temporary. She seemed to be the type of woman who was probably passing the time working as a waitress while waiting for some Hollywood agent to come along and discover her. And with her knockout looks, she wouldn't have to wait long.

"Can I help you?" the future starlet asked in a voice that seemed perfect for the big screen.

"Yes, ma'am." Howie wondered why such an attractive woman would be jealous of anyone. Stephanie had to have been mistaken in her assessment. "Are you Rosie Carpenter?"

She shifted her eyes between the two of them. "Yes," she replied hesitatingly. "And who are you?"

"I'm Howie Cummins and this is my partner, Mick Brunner. We're from the MAC Detective Agency down on Broadway and Third." If people knew they were from the area, they would be more receptive to answering questions. Those who lived on the North Side always seemed to have this inherent mistrust of others from outside the area. "Could we talk to you for a few minutes?"

"What about?"

"LaMar Jones." When she rubbed the corner of her eye, Howie couldn't be sure if she was brushing away a tear. Even if she wasn't tearing up, her eyes revealed pain, or maybe fear. "We understand that the two of you were friends."

"I was devastated when LaMar died," Rosie said. "Yes, we were friends." She took a deep breath. "More than friends."

"May we come in?" Howie had no intentions of conducting the interview standing in the hallway. "It won't take long."

Rosie looked at them for several long seconds. "Okay, but I only have a few minutes and then I have to go to work." She invited them into the living room. He and Mick were directed to a light-blue upholstered couch while she made herself comfortable in a matching chair.

"When did you last see LaMar?" Howie asked, taking note that the furnishings in the apartment appeared to be a few steps above the salary of a waitress.

"Late that afternoon of the day he died. He came into the café where I work." Rosie brushed a lock of hair from her eye. "He used to come in every day to have a cup of coffee before going to his job. That's how we first met."

"Did you ever meet any of his friends?"

Question marks appeared in Rosie's eyes. "Why are you asking these things? I thought his death was an accident."

"It was," Mick said. "We're here to get as much information as we can so the case may be settled with, ah, the insurance company."

"My partner's right," Howie quickly added, pleased that Mick was comfortable using that phony line. Adam would have balked at being part of such a deception. "These are just some routine questions we have to ask." He considered taking out his notepad, but decided it would make her more nervous than she already appeared to be. "How long did the two of you know each other?"

"Nearly a year. We had many of the same interests. He and—" Rosie looked toward Mick as a low rumbling came from his direction.

Mick shifted on the couch as he gently patted his stomach. He gave Howie a sideways glance before offering an apology. "Sorry, ma'am, but I haven't eaten lunch yet."

"What were you about to say?" Howie asked.

Rosie shifted her gaze between the two of them. "That LaMar and I dated on a pretty steady basis, but I suppose you already knew that." She crossed her legs and folded her arms. Her tone turned edgy. "Is that why you came to see me?"

Howie nodded. "We knew the two of you were close so we figured you knew what was going on in his life." He waited for a response, but none came. "Did he ever talk to you about his work? What was going on there? The people he worked with?"

Rosie continued to glance between the two of them. "I wish I could help you, but I'm afraid that LaMar never talked to me about his work."

"He never said anything about his work at all?" Howie had a gut feeling that the woman was lying through her pretty white teeth.

"I already told you he didn't," Rosie replied sharply as she uncrossed and crossed her legs. "I don't see what this has to do with any insurance claims."

Mick's stomach rumbled again. "Sorry," he said. He glanced at Howie, shrugged, and offered a weak grin.

Howie cleared his throat. "If we could just ask a few more questions."

"I've told you all I know." Rosie stood up abruptly. "I need to leave for work." Before either of them could respond, she headed toward the door. Howie and Mick exchanged looks, got up, and followed her.

"Thank you for your time," Howie said as he stood at the open door. "But we may have to come back for another visit." The look he received told him that Miss Carpenter wasn't in favor of giving them any more of her time.

As they headed down the stairs, Mick turned to Howie. "Sorry about my stomach. I couldn't help it."

"Don't worry about it." Howie offered a half smirk. "But next time I'll know it's better to feed you before we go on an interview."

"I don't think that woman was telling us everything," Mick said once they were out on the sidewalk. "What do you think?"

"I agree. And do you know what else I think?"

"What?"

"I think I'd better buy you a donut and a cup of coffee at the bakery across the street. That should keep you until we get back to the office."

The two detectives crossed the street and entered the bakery. After ordering donuts and coffee, they stood by the window and looked out at Carpenter's apartment across the street.

# Chapter 13

ROSIE CARPENTER'S PHONE rang within minutes after the two detectives left. At first, she thought it was one of them phoning, wanting to ask more questions. She debated whether to answer the phone, but decided that if it was one of them, she would just hang up.

"Hello."

"I noticed that you just had some visitors," a man said. His low raspy voice, sounded as though he had been the victim of too many cigarettes.

The thought of someone watching her apartment made Rosie uncomfortable. She glanced at her door to make sure she had bolted it. "Who is this?"

"A friend of LaMar's."

"What is it that you want?"

"We need to sit down and discuss some things."

"What are you talking about? What things?"

"Things concerning LaMar's unfortunate accident."

"I don't believe it was an accident."

"Neither do those two detectives."

"What do you mean?"

The man laughed. "Haven't you figured out why they talked to you? They think you're involved in LaMar's death."

"That's absurd," Rosie said, trying to keep her voice calm.

"Is it? I think we need to talk…in person."

"You mean right now?" Rosie looked at her watch. She didn't need to be at work for a couple of hours. Whoever this was, he knew things about LaMar's death that she wanted to know. "I can meet you now, but where?"

"There's a coffee shop on the corner of Broadway and Washington, across from the liquor store."

"Okay, I know where that is," Rosie said, relieved that they were meeting in a public place. If the man made her too uncomfortable, she could just get up and leave.

"I'll be waiting for you."

"But how will I know— Hello...hello?" Rosie slowly hung up the receiver. She stood staring at the phone and then grabbed her purse and car keys.

"That Carpenter woman is definitely hiding something," Mick said after he and Howie finished off a couple of donuts and were having a second cup of coffee at the bakery. "Did you notice the more questions you asked the more defensive she got? And when she crossed her legs, her foot started wagging a mile-a-minute. Isn't that a tell-tale sign of being anxious?"

"It sure can be." Howie sipped his coffee. He liked the idea that both his partners were learning to pick up clues about people as they became more experienced in the business. "She seemed more frightened than anything else."

"But of who or what?"

"I don't know." Howie took another sip of coffee. "But it's something we're going to find out."

"That means we're going back to talk to her again."

"That's right."

Mick set his coffee cup on the window ledge. "Well, I hope she's friendlier than...hey, there she is now."

Howie looked just as Rosie stepped out onto the sidewalk. She glanced around and then began walking in the direction that his car was parked.

Mick nudged Howie. "Where's she going?"

"She said she was going to work." Howie, however, watched with interest as the Carpenter woman got into the blue-and-white Impala and drove off.

"Wow!" Mick exclaimed. "Did you see what she's driving? How can she afford something like that?"

"That's what I'd like to know." When Mick's stomach growled, Howie took him by the arm. "Come on. Let's get back to the office. You can fix yourself something to eat." As they left the bakery, he looked in the direction Rosie had driven, knowing that she didn't make that kind of money doing waitress work, no matter how good the tips.

ROSIE WALKED INTO the coffee shop realizing that she didn't know the name of the man who had called her. She looked around, feeling conspicuous in her waitress uniform. Two men sat on stools at the counter. One of them, a balding man in his late forties, looked at her and smiled. That wasn't unusual; she often got looks from men. When she didn't return the smile, however, the man shrugged and turned away. An older couple sat in the nearest booth, three teenagers occupied the next booth, and the farthest three booths were empty. Her caller had said that he would recognize her when she came in. She didn't think to ask what he looked liked or what he would be wearing. Just as she decided that she would sit in the booth next to the one with the teenagers, a stocky, dark-haired man came from the door in the back that led to the rest rooms. The man looked in her direction, nodded in a way that told her he was the person who had phoned her, and then motioned her over as he sat down in the end booth. She took a deep breath and walked toward him, very aware of his unwavering smile and his stone-cold eyes. When she sat down, there was a cup of tea already in her place. She felt unnerved at the thought that the man knew that she preferred tea to coffee.

"I'm afraid I've forgotten your name," she said.

"That's because I didn't give it." He gestured toward her cup. "If it's not hot, I'll call the waitress over."

Rosie took a sip of her tea, holding the cup with both hands. The tea was barely warm. "It's fine," she said, setting the cup down.

"Would you like something to eat?"

"No, this is fine. I just want—"

"What did you tell those detectives?" His thin lips curled into a tight smile.

"I didn't tell them anything." She wondered if she had made a mistake in coming. The man gave her an uneasy feeling she couldn't explain. "Who are you, anyway? Are you really a friend of LaMar's?"

"I am and I know that he talked to you." His eyes narrowed as his sneer became more pronounced. "Let me give you some advice." His tone turned threatening. "Don't talk to those detectives again, and don't even think about going to the police."

"I...I don't know what you're talking about." Rosie hoped that the man couldn't sense the fear she was desperately trying to control. "LaMar didn't—"

"Don't give me that." Although he kept his voice low, the tone was as ice-cold as the look in his eyes. "I know that he talked to you, so don't try to play cute with me. He told you his life was in danger, didn't he?"

She made a move to leave, but he grabbed her wrist with such a powerful grip that she was afraid it would leave bruises.

He waited until one of the teenagers walked past their booth, heading toward the rest room. His eyes narrowed and he lowered his voice. "You can leave in a few seconds, but there's one more thing you need to know, Miss Carpenter."

Rosie swallowed, but couldn't say anything.

"Be careful out there in the world."

"Wha...what do you mean?"

"It's a dangerous place out there. I read someplace that most accidents happen right in a person's home. So just be careful." He loosened his grip. "Accidents can happen anyplace, at anytime. LaMar, himself, would tell you that now...if he could."

# Chapter 14

THE RINGING OF the telephone greeted Mick and Howie when they walked into the office. Howie rushed over, grabbed the phone, nearly knocking it off the desk. "MAC Detective Agency."

"It's about time you answered!" yelled a high-pitched, screechy voice. "Have you caught those crooks yet?"

Howie closed his eyes, squeezed the bridge of his nose using his thumb and forefinger, and then exhaled slowly. "No, Nana, but we're working on it." He squeezed the bridge of his nose again hoping it would stop the headache that no doubt soon would be coming on. "And how are you doing?"

"How do you think I'm doing?" Nana shrieked. "My arthritis is acting up again and I hardly slept a wink last night."

"I'm sorry to hear that." Howie eased into his chair.

"Don't be sorry about me. I'm in better shape than Agnes. That old gal has arthritis so bad that her hands look like snarled tree roots." Nana cackled. "It's a wonder she can hold a fork to eat her food."

"That's too—"

"And Louise is always complaining about her gout. She thinks she has it worst, but she's just looking for sympathy. In my book, she's a pansy. Why, just the other day at breakfast she was whining about the..."

"Who is it?" Mick whispered.

Howie wrote Nana's name on a slip of paper and showed it to Mick. His partner grinned and nodded his understanding.

Nana continued her litany of complaints. "It might rain today and that always makes the joints in my fingers ache. It's going to be hard to wheel my chair."

"Just take it easy, then."

"Take it easy, nothing. I won't be able to race Selma up on second floor. When you get to my age, all your tired old bones begin to—"

"Nana...Nana...you need to tell me why you called." When she didn't reply, Howie envisioned her tugging at her pigtail in an effort to remember. "Why don't you call me later when you—"

"You've got to come here now!" she cried, her words bursting forth like a racehorse at the starting gate. "It's the crooks."

"Them again, huh?" Howie glanced at the clock. He had planned to eat something and then spend the rest of the evening relaxing and reading some articles in his *Police Gazette* magazines. "I don't know if I can—"

"I'll wait for you in the lobby. It's urgent. Something's happened!"

"Wait a minute, slow down," Howie pleaded as Mick looked on with bewilderment. "What's urgent? What happened?"

"Can't talk on the phone!" Nana shouted, her voice ringing with irritation. "Got to talk eyeball-to-eyeball!" She lowered her voice to a nearly a whisper. "They might be listening. Get down here."

"Right now?" Howie rubbed his forehead. "I suppose I can, but…hello? Hello?" The sound of the dial tone only served to aggravate his emerging headache. He hung up and sighed.

"What's going on?" Mick asked.

"Don't ask me. Nana wants me to come over now. She says that it's urgent." Howie put his elbows on the desk and buried his face in his hands. "It's always urgent with her," he muttered. "She's going to drive me crazy."

"Didn't you try to explain?"

Howie looked up and stared at his partner in disbelief. "Explain? Are you kidding? She tells me what she wants and then hangs up before I can say anything." He leaned back in his chair, placing his head gently against the headrest. "That woman is going to put me in a nuthouse."

Mick raised his hand to his mouth in a futile attempt to hide his amusement. "So, ah…what are you going to do?"

"What choice do I have? I'd better go and see what's so pressing or else she'll sic Jerome on me." Howie's tone softened as he eyed his partner, offering him a discerning smile. "Say, why don't you come with me? Then you'll get a chance to meet her."

"Oh, no," Mick said as he waved off the invitation. "I'm starving and you promised I could eat. I'm going to fix myself a couple of sandwiches." He settled back in his chair. "The only place I'm going is out to your kitchen. Besides, you don't need my help with that dear little old lady. You'll do just fine. I can meet her another time."

"Thanks a lot. Some partner you are." Howie got up and headed toward the door. "Don't use up all the bread," he said as he opened the door to leave. "I'll need it for sandwiches for later on…if I survive until then."

# Chapter 15

AS SOON AS Howie walked into the lobby of the Golden Years Retirement Home he spotted Nana sitting by the aquarium. He waved, but she was too preoccupied with the fish tank to notice him.

"Hi there, Sonny."

Howie turned toward the voice. Elmer, the former truant officer he had met on his first visit to the home, had positioned his wheelchair next to a small couch not far from the entrance. "So you remember me," he said as he walked up to Elmer, hoping that the man wasn't going to ask him to show his I.D. again.

"Of course I do," Elmer replied gruffly as though offended by any suggestion that his memory was faulty. "I never forget a face." He motioned for Howie to come closer. "Young fellow, I've been thinking about you ever since I saw you last time. I've got a question for you. Are you willing to answer it?"

"If I can. Go ahead and ask."

"If you're not in school, what kind of work are you in?"

"I'm a detective." The words came out of Howie's mouth before he realized what he had just revealed. He quickly crouched in front of Elmer so they could be, as Nana would say, eyeball-to-eyeball. "But that's a secret between you and me, okay?" he said quietly as he glanced around.

Elmer's bushy eyebrows shot up. "You can count on me," he whispered. "Do you know why?" he asked with a sly grin.

Howie shook his head.

"Because us two have something in common."

"And what's that?"

"Why, me, a truant officer and you a detective." Elmer reached over and patted the right side of Howie's sports coat. "Don't you carry a gun?"

"I'm afraid I don't."

"That's good. Neither did I. Didn't have to."

"Glad to hear that. We just have to outsmart the bad guys. Right, Elmer?" Howie stood up and glanced toward Nana. His client was tapping on the front of the aquarium. "I wish I could stay and talk longer, but I'm here to see someone."

"You don't have to apologize to me, Sonny. I understand." Elmer tried to wink, but couldn't quite get his one eyelid down without closing both eyes. "Do you want me to be on the lookout for any suspicious characters?"

"No, that's okay." As soon as Howie uttered the words, the corners of Elmer's mouth turned downward as disappointment swept over his face. "Wait a minute," Howie said. "Now that I think about it, there is a guy you can watch for."

"There is?" Elmer's eyebrows shot up again. He grinned so broadly that his upper dentures began to slip out.

Howie waited until his new "partner" pushed his dentures back in place, and then proceeded to give him a description of Mick.

"So this fellow's a big guy with black, bushy hair and eyebrows to match, huh?" Elmer scanned the lobby. "He sounds like a really mean character." His eyes narrowed, causing his eyebrows to knit together at the bridge of his nose. "I'll watch out for him." He inched closer in his wheelchair. "Should I arrest him on the spot? I can get some of my friends here to hog-tie him so he can't get away."

"No, just let me know if you see him," Howie said, suppressing a smirk. "We'll just keep our eye on him."

"That sounds like a good plan, Sonny." Elmer stuck out his bony hand for Howie to shake. "You can count on me."

"Thanks, I knew I could." Howie shook Elmer's hand. Adam's ethics professor might have problems with what he had just done. It didn't matter, however, what Adam and his professors thought. He had just made an old man happy and that was all that counted. He walked up to Nana. By now, the old gal had her nose nearly pressed against the front of the aquarium. "What's so interesting?" he asked.

Nana gave Howie a stern look and then pointed to a tiny, silver fish floating on the surface. "That's the way I want to go, belly up." She cackled. "Now, don't you fret. I'm only pulling your leg." Her smirk, however, quickly faded as she pointed to the dead fish again. "But it's terrible, just terrible, to have that poor thing floating there for all of these old people to see." She shook her head in disgust. "Someone ought to take that poor thing out of there."

Howie, hoping that this wasn't why Nana called, looked around for a nurse to see if he could borrow a couple of aspirins. Although he didn't have a full-fledged headache when he walked in, he was sure that he would have one before his visit was over. "When you telephoned, you said it was urgent." He gave a wary glance toward the fish tank. "What's so urgent?"

"We can't talk here." Nana wheeled her chair around. "Let's hightail it to my room. They may be watching."

"Who are they?"

"The crooks!" Nana cried, making it sound as if it should be obvious to anyone who *they* were. "Come on, let's twenty-three skidoo."

Before Howie could say anything, Nana took off down the hallway toward her room. He took one last look at the dead fish and started after her.

Every now and then she would look behind her to see if he was following. "Don't worry, I'm coming," he would assure her each time.

As soon as they got to her room, Nana shut the door and ordered Howie to sit on the corner of her bed. "Gertrude died last night," she announced matter-of-factly.

"Oh, no. I'm sorry to hear that." Howie had to make a conscious effort to erase any mental images of Gertrude floating belly up.

"She was a dear friend." Nana spoke with little emotion, like someone who has seen her share of death. "I'll miss her, but she went peacefully in her sleep. When my time comes, that's the way I want to go."

"What happened to her?"

"Her old ticker just gave out." Without saying another word, Nana wheeled over to the door, flung her pigtails out of the way, and placed her ear against the door. Several moments passed before she gave Howie a thumbs-up, and wheeled back to him. "It's too bad we never got a chance to pull that scheme off. Gertrude was so thrilled about using her diamond ring to set a trap for those crooks. She hadn't been that excited since winning three times at bingo last month...or was it four times?"

"Is this why you wanted to talk to me? To tell me about Gertrude's death?"

"Land sakes, no! I could've told you about that over the phone." Nana looked at him in a way that made him feel as though he had just asked the dumbest question possible. "I want you to find out what happened to her diamond ring."

"I suppose her family would—"

"She didn't have any living relatives."

"None at all?"

"Nope. They have all croaked. She was the only one of three sisters to marry. Her two other sisters made it very clear that they didn't need men in their lives." Nana's eyes twinkled. "Men aren't much good except for making babies and they're not always good at that."

"And there are no other relatives at all?"

"That's right. That's why I wondered what was going to happen to her ring." Nana's eyes narrowed and she scrunched up her nose. "She wasn't wearing it when they carted her out last night."

"How do you know she wasn't wearing it?"

"Because the nurses let me spend a few minutes with her after she passed." Nana shifted in her wheelchair. "That diamond has got to be around here someplace. I know that she wanted to be buried with it."

"So, what do you want me to do?"

"Do some detecting!" Nana shouted. "You know how, don't you? Or should I get my grandson to help you?"

"No, you don't have to do that." Howie wished he had a handful of aspirins. "I'll do some checking."

"Good, but be careful." Nana wagged her finger at him. "Remember, they're watching." When Howie got up to leave, she went to the door with him. "Now, don't you fret," she said.

"About what?"

"About catching those crooks." Nana's eyes emitted a look of determination as she stuck out her pointed jaw. "I'm going to figure us out a new plan." She wagged her finger at him again. "And don't you worry. I'll think of something."

"I'm sure you will."

After he left Nana's room, he headed toward the nurses' station. A woman in her mid-twenties sat at the desk, writing in a chart, as he walked up. Only after he cleared his throat did she take notice of her visitor.

"Yes, may I help you?" she asked.

"I hope so." He took note that the attractive blond wasn't wearing a wedding or engagement ring. "Is there anybody I could talk to about a missing item?"

"Did you lose something?"

"No, one of the people who lives here did." Howie wasn't about to disclose that he was a detective. The less people knew about his identity, the better. "She's a friend of mine and asked me to see if I could track it down."

"I'd suggest you talk to Pete Larson."

"And who's that?"

"Pete's the head of housekeeping," she replied in a voice as appealing as her looks. "He also takes care of lost and found, and handles security."

"Where can I find him?"

"Downstairs. His office is right next to the snack machines. There's a sign on the door that says *Housekeeping/Security*." She smiled. "You won't miss it. You can take the elevator, or if you like, the stairway."

"Thanks." Howie took the stairs. When he opened the door to the bottom level, he looked one way and then the other. Once he spotted the snack machines, he started in that direction. The door to Larson's office was closed. He knocked, hoping the guy was in.

"Come on in," a husky male voice said.

Howie opened the door to find a heavy-set man in his early forties with hair and a mustache the color of dark chocolate sitting behind a cluttered desk. As soon as he saw Howie, he got up and came around to greet his visitor.

"Hi, I'm Pete Larson." He extended a pudgy hand. "What can I do for you?"

"I'm Howie Cummins. One of the nurses told me that you might be able to help in locating a missing ring."

"I'll do what I can. Have a seat."

While Larson went back to his chair, Howie sat down and glanced around. Other than the desk, a couple of chairs, and a file cabinet in one corner, there wasn't much else in the office. Except for a small landscape print of the ocean, the walls were nearly as bare as the room.

"So, what's the story?" Larson asked.

"I've a friend who lives here. She's concerned that her friend down the hall who just died may be missing a diamond ring."

"Is that so? And who's this friend of yours?"

"Anabel Peterson. Do you know her?"

"Everyone knows Nana. She makes life around here rather interesting." Larson stroked his mustache. "And believe me, that old gal is one person who speaks her mind. That woman approaches life like a tornado going through a town made of playing cards."

"That's her, all right."

"Nana's always crusading for one thing or another." Larson's voice took on a more sober tone. "Unfortunately, she's been going downhill the past year. Becoming more forgetful, if you know what I mean." He paused as though waiting for Howie to confirm his assessment. "And whose ring is she concerned about?"

"I don't know the last name, but her first name is Gertrude."

"Oh, yes. That would be Gertrude Anderson." Larson placed his elbows on the desk and interlaced his fingers. "So what's the story?"

"Apparently, some time ago this Gertrude told Nana that when she died, she wanted to be buried with her diamond ring. Nana's just concerned about the ring and that nothing has happened to it."

"Can't nothing happen about nothing."

"I'm not sure I understand."

"It's simple. There's no diamond ring."

"What? What happened to it?"

"There was no ring in the first place." Larson briefly looked at a sheet of paper he had in front of him. "According to the records, Gertrude never had a diamond ring."

Howie leaned forward, wondering what Larson had looked at. "But Nana said she did."

"I know, but Nana says a lot of things. Like I told you, she's been getting more confused lately."

"Are you sure there's no ring?"

"Positive. Part of my job is to check with each new person when they come in as a resident. I go through their valuables with them, list them on a sheet of paper, and then have them sign it." Larson picked up the sheet of paper in front of him. "I was just checking Gertrude's listing now. Do you want to take a look?"

"Sure." Howie took the paper. No diamond ring was listed. In fact, there was nothing of much value listed. The document was dated and signed. Gertrude Anderson's signature was clearly legible. "Thanks, I appreciate you sharing this with me," he said as he handed the paper back.

"Anything else I can help you with?"

"No, that was it." Howie stood up to leave. "I guess I've wasted your time. Sorry."

"Don't worry about that. Nana doesn't mean any harm." Larson got up, walked around his desk, and extended his hand to Howie. "As I said, she just gets confused at times."

Howie left Larson's office wondering if Nana, herself, even had a diamond ring. If she had a ring at all, she probably just misplaced it in one of her dresser drawers. For that matter, the ring could even be at the bottom of that fish tank in the lobby. He was convinced more now than ever, that they didn't have a case to investigate. The problem, however, was how to explain that to Nana.

# Chapter 16

ON MONDAY EVENING, Adam trotted up the steps to the Chocolate Angel Candy Factory. Although he wasn't scheduled to begin work until six, he hoped to make a good impression that first night on the job by arriving a half hour early. He also hoped that Rachel Gilbertson hadn't left for the evening. That she had made an impression upon him was undeniable. In the past several years, because of his schooling, he hadn't had much time for relationships. Besides, the few women he had dated found it difficult to deal with his introspective personality. Rachel seemed different, however. For reasons he couldn't explain, she had touched something deep within him. He felt attracted to her and that troubled him for two reasons. First of all, he wasn't sure he wanted to start a relationship that might require sharing something of himself. And secondly, he felt guilty spying on her and her father. He rang the buzzer and waited, wondering what Rachel would think of him if she found out that he was coming to work there under false pretenses. Before he could speculate on his own question, Leo opened the door.

"Hi, there...ah, Leo," Adam said, almost letting the name "Hooknose" slip from his tongue. He kept his tone casual, hoping that the big guy might be friendlier than the last time they met.

Leo hardly looked at him, acknowledging his presence only with a grunt. "Follow me!" he ordered. "And make sure you shut the door tight behind you."

Adam stepped inside and glanced toward Rachel's desk. A white, cardigan sweater was draped over her chair. He hesitated for a moment while looking for her, but then turned to follow Leo who was already several steps ahead and moving in the direction of the stairway leading to the lower level.

"So, you're early," a friendly female voice called out from behind just as Adam caught up to Leo.

When Adam turned, he was pleased to see Rachel. Dressed in a mauve, short-sleeved blouse and a bluish-gray skirt, she looked even more attractive than the last time they had met. "Hi," he said as she walked toward him. "I didn't see you when I came in."

"That's because I wasn't at my desk," she replied teasingly. "I was just talking to my father." She glanced back at the double doors leading into the work area. "He's in his office now. Would you like to meet him?"

"Well, I..." Adam looked at Leo and decided that he wasn't going to let the man's scowl intimidate him. "Sure, I'd like that."

Rachel took Adam by the arm and then smiled at Leo. "I'll bring him right back," she promised in a playful tone. "Is that okay?"

Leo nodded, but didn't look happy about the two of them going off together. "I'll wait here," he mumbled.

To Adam's disappointment, Rachel let go of his arm when she opened the door to the work area. The late afternoon sun, filtering through the stained glass windows, cast a soft hue into the former worship space. No doubt, earlier that day, the workers would have been gloriously bathed in such hues while they wrapped and boxed the chocolate angels. Although the space showed evidence of the work activities of that day, it now rested peacefully. He surveyed the vaulted ceiling and breathed in the security of the thick stone walls.

"This place sure gives off a tranquil feeling," Adam said, wishing that somehow he could find that peace for himself.

"Yes, I know what you mean." Rachel slowly looked around. "That's why I love to come in here."

Adam walked with Rachel to the front and waited as she knocked on the office door. He glanced around, taking in the beauty of the stained glass windows. That LaMar could have been murdered in such a setting was ironic.

"Daddy, it's me, again. Can you come out?" Rachel offered Adam a coy smile." There's someone here I want you to meet."

"Just a second," a man's voice answered.

"He used to sing baritone in a barbershop quartet," Rachel whispered. "Even though he doesn't do that anymore, he still has a wonderful voice." She paused. "I want him to sing at my wedding."

"Your wedding?"

A hint of a blush swept over Rachel's face. "Oh, that is when and if I ever get married. I just haven't met the right man yet."

The door opened and a tall, distinguished-looking man with dark, wavy hair appeared. Dressed casually in slacks and a short-sleeve, plaid shirt, he looked as though he had just come in from the golf course. He closed the door behind him but not before Adam caught a glimpse of a small black kettle sitting on a table inside the office.

"Adam, this is my father, Charles Gilbertson."

"Hello," Adam said, not sure whether he should call him Charles or Mr. Gilbertson. Chuck or Charlie didn't seem appropriate.

"So you're the fellow my daughter has been telling me about." When Gilbertson stepped closer, Adam noticed the graying around his temples. "I understand that you're going to be a second-year student at the seminary."

"Yes, sir." Adam hoped Gilbertson wouldn't ask if he was excited about his studies and future vocation.

"I almost became a preacher when I was your age," Gilbertson confessed. "Everybody said I had a stained-glass voice and would do well in the pulpit." He shrugged. "But worldly things got the best of me, and here I am."

"Don't let him fool you," Rachel said, interlocking her arm with her father's. She patted his hand. "My father's a very religious man. And I'll have you know that he sings solos in church whenever he can."

Rachel's father sighed. "And I'm afraid that isn't as often as I'd like." He extended his hand to Adam, his grip firm and strong. "Welcome," he said. "We're a small-time business with a big-time heart." After shaking hands with his new employee, he turned to his daughter. "Are you showing him around?" She nodded, letting go of his arm. "You have a good guide, here," he said to Adam. "She used to guide me through the woods every fall."

"Oh, Daddy, stop. You're the one who took me hunting."

"Yes, and you were the one who always got a deer." When Adam gave Rachel a puzzled look, her father went on to explain. "Rachel and I have gone hunting a number of times. Let me tell you, she's an excellent shot. I could tell you lots of stories about her."

"I'd like to hear those some time."

Gilbertson laughed. "Maybe we'll get a chance to do that in the future." He cleared his throat. "Anyway, it's a pleasure to have you working here." He glanced at his daughter before turning his attention back to Adam. "If you like working here, perhaps we could arrange for you to work part-time once school starts in the fall."

Adam felt the glow of Rachel's smile at her father's offer. "Mr. Gilbertson, I...I don't know what to say."

"I'm sorry; forgive me. I know I must be putting you on the spot. We can talk about it after you've been here for a couple of weeks." Gilbertson checked his watch. "Now if you'll excuse me, I have some things I need to finish."

"Daddy, will you be home for supper?"

"I'm afraid not. The angels are calling me."

Rachel sighed. "Okay, I understand, but you be sure and eat when you get home. I'll have something for you in the refrigerator. Don't forget."

Gilbertson gave Adam a look that said *I'd better not argue with her.* "Ever since her mother died, my daughter has taken it upon herself to make sure I'm eating properly."

"Well, somebody has to make sure you eat," Rachel said and then gave him a hug before he went back into his office.

Even though Rachel's father opened and closed the door quickly, Adam caught a glimpse of a person's shadow inside the office. The shadow moved when the door opened, as if the person had stepped back so as not to be seen. "What did your father mean when he said that the angels were calling him?" Adam asked as they walked back through the work area.

"That's his way of saying he's going to make some candy tonight." Rachel stopped to pick up an empty candy box off the floor, setting it on a table stacked with other boxes. "Every now and then, he'll stay late and make up several boxes of chocolate angels to send to friends. He does it all from scratch."

"I'm not sure what you mean."

"My father begins by heating and preparing the chocolate. When it's ready, he hand pours it into the molds." Pride filled Rachel's eyes. "Once the chocolate sets, he removes the angels from their molds, wraps, and boxes them."

"That sounds like a lot of work." Adam recalled the shadow he had seen in Gilbertson's office. "Does anybody ever help him?"

"Oh, no," Rachel said, shaking her head. "He insists on always doing it alone."

"Really?"

"Yes, he says it reminds him of when he first started in the candy business and had to do nearly everything himself." She glanced back at her father's office. "He tells me that it keeps him humble and in touch with his roots."

"And who are these lucky people getting the candy that your father makes?" Adam asked, wondering if she knew that her father wasn't alone tonight.

When Rachel hesitated, Adam considered that perhaps he was asking too many questions. He was about to apologize for being so nosy when she replied.

"He sends them to friends around the country. His personal touch makes it a very special gift." She reached for the door but didn't open it. "I want you to know that I'm really glad you applied for the job here."

"So am I," Adam said, hoping his eyes wouldn't reveal the growing guilt he felt about deceiving her.

"I suppose you should be getting back. I've kept you away from Leo long enough."

At the mention of Leo's name, the magic of the moment was broken for Adam. "Speaking of Leo...is he always that unfriendly or is it just because I'm the new kid on the block?"

Rachel's smile faded for a moment. "Don't mind Leo, he's...he's just a little protective of me. When he gets to know you better, he'll warm up." She touched Adam on the arm before opening the door.

# Chapter 17

LEO, HIS ARMS folded and leaning against the wall next to the stairway, had the look of a mid-summer storm cloud as Rachel and Adam came back from seeing Rachel's father.

"He's all yours," Rachel said.

"Good," Leo replied, nodding to her, but shooting Adam a threatening look, as though warning him to stay away from Rachel.

"Thanks for introducing me to your father," Adam said, not wanting her to go. "He seems to be a really nice man."

"I think so, too. You have a good night, now." When Rachel glanced toward Leo, Adam detected a momentary flicker of concern flash across her face. "I'll see you tomorrow," she whispered to Adam and then headed toward her desk.

"Come on, let's go!" Leo said, his tone, harsh. Without waiting for Adam, he turned and trotted down the stairs.

Adam took one last look at Rachel before heading for the stairway. By the time he caught up, Leo was already downstairs talking with a slender-built, dark-haired man who appeared to be in his mid-thirties.

"This is Ken," Leo said when Adam joined them. Ken nodded, adjusting his black-rimmed glasses. "He'll show you what you have to do." Leo's tone remained as unfriendly as it had been from the first time they met. "Remember, you work until midnight and you only get one break. You got that?"

Before Adam could reply or ask any questions, Leo turned and headed upstairs. He waited until Leo was out of sight and then extended his hand to Ken. "Hi, in case he didn't tell you, my name is Adam Trexler."

"Don't let Leo get to you," Ken said as he shook hands. "He told you my first name. My last name is Pritchett." He motioned for Adam to follow. "Come on, I'll show you what needs to be done. It's not that hard to learn."

Ken explained Adam's duties to him, showing him the cleaning equipment he needed, the areas that required attention, and the location of the storage rooms. Adam's duties were simple: sweep and mop the floors on both levels (Mr. Gilbertson insisted that it be done every night), clear and then wash all the tables in the work area, and make sure to restock the necessary supplies for the workers who come in the next day. He would also be responsible for cleaning the rest rooms.

"The women are especially fussy about the bathroom," Ken noted, a hint of a smile on his thin lips.

Adam assured Ken he would make sure the rest room was spotless. "How about the sub-basement?" he asked. "Do I do any cleaning down there?"

"Nope. You don't have to worry about that area. Nobody goes down there. And Mr. Gilbertson's office is off-limits," Ken added. "The boss likes to do his own cleaning." After he took Adam through the areas he was responsible for cleaning, they returned to where they originally had met.

"Where do I start?"

"As far as I'm concerned, it's up to you." Ken appeared anxious to leave now that he had done his duty and shown the new man the ropes. "If you have any questions, I'll be around."

"I do have one question."

"And what's that?"

"I hope you don't mind me asking, but I'm just curious. What kind of things do you do around here?"

Ken studied Adam for quite some time, appearing to be sizing up the inquisitive new man. He offered a half smile. "I'm what you call the night watchman, but the only thing I really have to watch is that vat of chocolate upstairs."

"Oh, yeah?" Adam kept his voice casual. He didn't want Pritchett to become suspicious the first night. Whereas he had felt guilty when he had been with Rachel, he now felt an adrenalin charge talking with their prime suspect. "What do you have to do with the chocolate?"

"I make sure it remains heated and I stir it every half hour or so. When I leave, and I'll leave shortly after you leave, I'll turn the heater off so that the chocolate cools by morning."

"So you're the last one out?"

"That's right. And before I leave, I check all the doors to make sure the building is secure." Ken took off his glasses, wiped the lenses with a handkerchief, and then slipped them on again. "Anything else you want to ask?"

Adam shook his head, worried that he had pushed him too far. Howie told him not to rush it with Pritchett. "No, I was just curious."

"Then I'll be going."

The next couple of hours Adam swept and mopped the floor on the lower level, emptied the trash, and straightened out the storage rooms. It was after nine when he decided he would start on the main work area upstairs. He wondered about Ken. He hadn't seen him since the guy had left him alone. Based on his initial encounter with Pritchett, however, he would have to report to Howie that their suspect hadn't come across as mysterious and sinister as LaMar's sister portrayed him to be.

When Adam got to the top of the stairs, he surveyed the carpeted reception area as he tried to remember where Ken had said the vacuum cleaner was stored. As he walked toward Rachel's desk, a photograph on her desk caught his attention. The photograph, encased in a small oval-shaped, gold frame, sat on the right-hand corner of the desk. It was a picture of Rachel and her parents standing in front of Excelsior Amusement Park. She appeared to have been a teenager at the time the photograph was taken and was already showing that she had inherited her mother's beauty. He was still admiring the photograph when a noise startled him. The door to the work area was just swinging shut as a man came out carrying a candy-box-size package wrapped in brown paper.

"Can I help you?" Adam asked, noting that the man seemed just as startled as he was at the two of them meeting.

"No, I'm just on my way out," the man said, looking at Adam with eyes so piercing that they could penetrate steel plating. "You're new around here, aren't you?"

"It's my first night."

"Is that so?" When he walked over to Adam, the ring of keys on his belt jingled with his every step. He offered a crooked smile and then stuck out a hand for Adam to shake. "Good luck, then."

"Thanks."

"Don't work too hard," the stranger said, and then walked away without uttering another word.

Adam watched him leave by the front entrance, wondering who he was and what was he doing in the work area at this time of night. Adam stared at the entrance door, puzzled by how the man got in. Did the guy have a key to the place? And who was he to have a key? What was his connection to Gilbertson? For the time being, he wouldn't be able to answer any of these questions, but he was determined to do so. He had just set the photograph back on the desk when the doors to the work area opened again and Rachel's father walked out.

"Hello, Mr. Gilbertson," Adam said, consciously keeping from chewing his lip. "I, ah, can't remember where Ken said the vacuum cleaner was stored."

Gilbertson gave him a questioning look and then pointed in the direction of the hallway to the right of the stairway. "There's a closet around the corner in the first room. You'll find the vacuum there."

"Thanks." Adam picked up Rachel's wastebasket. "After I empty this, I'll vacuum this area and then I'll do the main work area."

Gilbertson glanced at the front entrance doors. "I hope you haven't spent too much time looking for the vacuum cleaner."

It was an odd statement, and Adam suspected that Gilbertson really wanted to know if he had been there long enough to have seen the other man come through the reception area. "Oh, no. I just got up here."

"Well, don't worry about not remembering where the vacuum is stored." He offered Adam a warm smile. "Once you work here for a while, you'll get familiar with all the nooks and crannies of this place."

"I hope so." Adam picked up a piece of scrap paper that he spotted by Rachel's chair and made a show of tossing it into the wastebasket, hoping his action would validate why he had been caught by Rachel's desk. "By the way, your daughter told me earlier about those boxes of chocolate angels that you make up."

"She did, huh?"

"Yes, and I think that's great. Were you able to finish any of them tonight?"

"No, I'll finish them tomorrow," Gilbertson quickly replied.

"If you should ever need help, I'll be glad to assist."

"Thank you, Adam, but this is one of those things I prefer to do by myself. I hope you understand."

"Yes sir, I do."

"I thought you would." Gilbertson looked around. "Well, I trust that you'll enjoy working here."

"I'm sure I will."

"That's good because my daughter spoke very highly of you." When Gilbertson glanced at Rachel's desk, Adam realized that he had placed the framed photograph on the opposite corner than where it had been originally. "We'll see you tomorrow," Rachel's father said, giving no indication that he had noticed that the picture had been moved. "Good night."

After Gilbertson left, Adam wondered about the identity of the other man and if the package he had with him contained chocolate angels. If he did have chocolate angels in that package, why would Rachel's father lie about not finishing any tonight? And what was so special about Gilbertson's chocolate angels, anyway?

# Chapter 18

"PERFECT TIMING," HOWIE said as Adam walked in and sat down.

Adam scanned the office. "Perfect timing? For what?"

"Can't you tell? I just finished cleaning." Howie opened the bottom drawer of the file cabinet and tossed in the torn tee shirt he used as a dusting rag. Every Tuesday morning (or, at least, a couple times a month) he gave his office its ten-minute once over. He closed the drawer, leaned against the file cabinet, and folded his arms across his chest. "How did it go last night?"

Adam shifted in his chair but didn't reply.

Howie had seen that troubled look before, but wasn't in the mood for dealing with Adam's internal struggles of right and wrong. His partner could deal with his ethical issues on his own time. He had told him on more than one occasion to leave his preacher's standards in his dresser drawer whenever they were working on a case. Ethical behavior in detective work, however, was a continued source of disagreement between the two of them. "Look, I know you don't like doing undercover work, but you agreed to do it. If you really didn't want to take this assignment, you should've said something."

"I know. It's just that…"

"Just what?"

Adam got up, moved over to the window, and stood gazing out. Several minutes passed before he turned to face Howie. "It's just that I have trouble deceiving people. I thought I could do it, but…there are some decent people there."

"There could also be a murderer there. Think about that."

"Yeah, but—"

"But nothing!" Howie said as he slammed his hand against the side of the file cabinet and locked eyes with Adam. "I know this is a crummy assignment for you." His tone softened. "If there was any other way we could have done this, we would have."

A look of resignation swept over Adam's face. "You're right." He closed his eyes and took a deep breath. "Don't worry, I'll handle it," he said as he sat back down.

"I hope you will," Howie said, almost adding *you damn well better handle it.* Mick would have been his first choice if Hooknose hadn't had contact with him.

"So do you want to hear about last night?" Adam asked, sounding and looking repentant.

Howie walked over to his desk, opened the top drawer, and took out a pen and notepad. "You can tell me about it on the way."

"Where are we going?"

"To the nursing home."

"What? Why?"

"Nana called."

"Again?"

"Yeah, again." Howie slipped on his sports coat. "That woman is driving me nuts with all of her schemes."

"What is it this time?"

"I don't know." Howie checked to make sure his car keys were in his jacket pocket. "She wouldn't tell me because *they* might be listening."

"They?" Adam's brow wrinkled. "Who are they?"

"You can ask her that when you see her." Howie went to the door and waited for his partner. "I'll drive. My car's parked in front."

Adam got up slowly and joined his partner at the door. "Howie?"

"Yeah?"

"Thanks."

"For what?"

"For putting up with me."

Howie nodded. "Hey, it goes both ways. Come on, let's go."

Within a few minutes the two detectives were downstairs and into Howie's car. During the ride to the nursing home, Howie asked questions and listened as Adam filled him in on what Adam seemed to think had been a fairly routine evening on his first night of work at the candy factory.

"Well, there's nothing routine about that shadow you saw in Gilbertson's office." Howie always told his partners that the smallest of details could be an important clue. And it was certainly no small detail that Gilbertson had lied about being in his office by himself. "Do you think it could have been that guy you saw later?"

"I don't know. Maybe." Adam grew silent for a moment. "But remember that it was over three hours between seeing that shadow and meeting that guy with the package."

Howie tapped his finger against the steering wheel. "The question is, what was he doing in Gilbertson's office all that time?"

"My guess was that he was helping Gilbertson make the chocolate angels."

"And you say Pritchett just kept to himself most of the night?" Howie asked as he slowed down for a young woman crossing the street in the middle of the block.

"That's right. As far as I know, he did. He didn't do anything suspicious that I could see." Adam glanced over at Howie. "But like I told you, I didn't see too much of him."

Howie turned the corner on Queen Avenue. After parking the car across the street from the nursing home, he and Adam headed toward the entrance. Several of the residents greeted Howie by name. Two ladies in wheelchairs giggled when he told them they were looking very attractive in their spring dresses.

"Who are they?" Adam whispered as they walked past them.

"My fans," Howie replied with a smirk.

Adam tapped Howie on the shoulder and directed his attention toward a nearly bald gentleman with bushy eyebrows the color of snow. The old guy, leaning dangerously forward in his wheelchair, was furiously waving his cane at them. "Is he another one of your fans?"

"That's Elmer." Howie waved at the one-time truant officer. "Come on," he said to Adam. "I'll introduce you. He's my undercover agent here at the home."

"Your what?"

"I'll explain later."

"Hello, young fella," Elmer said to Howie, but eyed Adam suspiciously. "Can we talk in front of him?" he asked, pointing his cane at the newcomer.

"Don't worry about him. He works with me."

Elmer squinted as he checked Adam out before turning his attention back to Howie. "I've been keeping my eyes open for that big fellow you described the other day, but I ain't seen hide nor hair of him."

"You just keep watching," Howie said. "I'm sure he'll show his face around here."

"Do you think he could be wearing a disguise?" Elmer scratched the stubble on his chin as his eyes shifted between the two young men. "You know, a fake beard or something like that. I've heard of crooks doing things like that."

"I don't think you have to worry about that."

After listening to Elmer's endless descriptions of the strangers who had come and gone that morning, Howie and Adam excused themselves. On their way to Nana's room, Howie explained how Elmer happened to get involved doing undercover work for them.

"And you gave him Mick's description?"

"That's right, but don't mention a word of this to Mick."

"I won't, but I'd like to see what happens when Elmer spots Mick."

As Howie and Adam walked passed the nurses' station, Howie looked for the blond nurse he had talked to last time. To his disappointment, however, she was nowhere in sight. They passed several residents, each of them greeting the two of them with friendly hellos and smiles. "Here's Nana's room," Howie announced as they stopped in front of her door.

"Do we just go in?"

"I wouldn't advise that." Howie knocked a couple of times, waited for several seconds, and then knocked again.

"Hold your pants on!" a woman's voice screeched from inside.

"That's Nana," Howie said. "If you go in there unannounced, you just might find a bedpan flying through the air at you."

After a couple of minutes, the door slowly opened and Nana peeked out. She acknowledged Howie but when she saw Adam, her eyes narrowed and her button-shaped nose wrinkled. "Who's he?"

"My partner, Adam Trexler."

"Well, don't just stand out there!" Before closing the door Nana peered down the hallway in both directions. "Just want to make sure you boys weren't followed." She closed the door and ordered them to sit down.

"What did you want to talk to me about?" Howie asked as he sat on the edge of the bed. Adam sat on the chair in the corner.

"Don't rush me! I'll get to that!" Nana motioned to Adam. "Go check the door."

"What?" Adam looked to Howie for an explanation.

"She wants to know if anybody could be standing outside and eavesdropping. Isn't that right, Nana?"

"Right as apple pie," Nana replied, adding, "It's about time you're learning something." She waited until Adam got to the door. "Put your ear against it real tight-like and listen," she directed and then spoke to Howie in a tone that was meant to be a whisper. "He must be new to the detectiving business."

Howie caught a glimpse of Adam glancing back at them. "He's new all right, but he's a fast learner."

"I don't hear anybody out there." Adam waited until he got the okay from Nana to come back and sit down.

"Okay, now, why did you call?" Howie asked again.

"I found one of my old diamond rings. It's not worth much, but it can serve as bait." Nana rubbed her hands together and snickered. "I'm sure they'll fall for it."

Adam gave Howie a quizzical look.

"Go ahead, ask her."

"Who are *they?*"

"*They* are the crooks!" Nana snapped. "What kind of detective are you, anyway?" She glanced at Howie and then cocked her head toward Adam. "You know about crooks, don't you?" Before Adam could reply, she went on. "I'll leave the ring on Hilda's dresser."

It was Howie's turn to ask a question. "And who's Hilda?"

"She's a friend of mine who lives in the room down the hall." Nana leaned forward and lowered her voice. "Hilda doesn't have all her marbles. The poor woman will probably think it's her own ring." She chuckled. "That old gal's as blind as a bat and just as dingy."

"I'm confused," Howie said. "If this woman is blind, how is she going to know if the ring is gone?"

"She won't!" Nana cried. "That's where I come in." Her eyes, brimming with mischievous intrigue, shifted between Adam and Howie. "I'll leave my door partly open. That way I can see who goes in and out of her room for the next twenty-four hours." She scrunched her nose at the two detectives. "Haven't you ever heard of a stake-out?"

"Isn't that a long time to stay awake?" Adam asked.

"Humph! I'll just drink more coffee. I don't have to pee every few minutes like some of these other people around here do." Nana leaned toward the two of them. "And as far as getting some shut-eye, when I'm in the bone yard, I'll have plenty of time then for that."

Howie suppressed a grin, but noted with amusement the concerned look on Adam's face. "Are you sure you want to do this?"

Nana stuck out her chin. "Of course I'm sure!"

"Okay, but let us know if you find out anything," Howie said, realizing that it would be impossible to talk her out of her plan. He and Adam got up to leave, said their good-byes, and walked out into the corridor.

"Don't you think we should tell her to be careful?" Adam said.

"Careful of who? The crooks?"

"I know there're probably no crooks and that it's all in her head."

"It's in her head all right."

"Okay, so she might be a little confused. I'm just concerned that she might overdo it." Adam waited until a resident in a wheelchair went past. "I wouldn't want her to get sick or worse yet, have a heart attack."

Howie made a sweeping gesture toward Nana's door. "Go right ahead and be my guest. You go in and tell the nice little old lady then."

"Me?"

"Why not? It's your idea."

After Adam opened the door and walked in without knocking, Howie smiled to himself. He expected his partner to be clobbered over the head with her cane for breaking and entering. When he didn't hear anything, he moved closer and was about to put his ear against the door when Adam came out, shutting the door behind him quietly.

"So, what did she say?" Howie asked.

"Not a thing. Our detective is sitting in her chair, sound asleep."

# Chapter 19

BACK AT THE office Howie and Adam chatted about their visit with Nana over a cup of coffee. Howie leaned back in his chair and sipped his coffee.

"That Nana is sure some sparkplug," Adam said.

"You don't have to tell me that. That old gal has got more energy than she knows what to do with." Howie raised the cup to his lips just as the phone rang. He eyed the phone with suspicion, letting it ring. If it was who he suspected, he would have to take some aspirin with his next sip of coffee. "Why don't you answer it," he said. "And if it's Nana, tell her…tell her I've gone to the moon."

"I'm not going to tell her that."

"Tell her anything you want, then. Just as long as you tell her I'm not here." He didn't care if Adam heard the irritation in his voice. He was in no mood to go trotting back to that nursing home and listen to Nana's wild schemes for catching crooks.

Adam picked up the phone. "MAC Detective Agency." He shot Howie a concerned look. "Sure, just a minute. He's right here."

Howie leaned forward and set his coffee down. "Who is it?"

"I don't know, but it doesn't sound like Nana," Adam whispered as he handed the phone over to his boss.

"Hello, this is Cummins. Who?" Howie fumbled in his shirt pocket for his notepad and pen. "Of course I remember." He glanced at the clock. "When did this guy contact you? And he said what? Wait a minute, slow down." He flipped a page in his notepad. "Yeah, I can understand why you'd be upset. Sure. Just hang tight. My partner and I will be right over."

"Who was that?" Adam asked as soon as Howie hung up.

Howie drummed his pen on the notepad. "Would you believe, Rosie Carpenter?"

"LaMar's girlfriend? What did she want?"

"To talk to us."

"What about?"

"She wouldn't tell me over the phone, but she says it's urgent."

"Did she sound scared?"

"Oh, yes. She has good reason to believe that LaMar's death wasn't an accident." Howie closed his notepad and slipped it into his shirt pocket. This might just be the break they needed. And the fact that it didn't sound like the Carpenter woman had contacted the police was good. It would be great if they could get the case solved without the cops being involved. "Some guy contacted her yesterday."

"Who?"

"She didn't say, but whatever they talked about, it upset her so much that she couldn't go to work today."

Adam set his cup on the desk. "Let's go then."

Within seconds Howie and his partner were out the door. They flew down the stairs, hopped in Howie's car, and took off. Howie pushed the pedal to the floor as much as he dared, weaving in and out of traffic. Although Rosie's apartment was only ten minutes away, it took twice that long because of a traffic tie-up. They parked the car, scrambled up the apartment stairs, rushed to her door, and knocked.

"Maybe she's left," Adam said when no one answered.

"I don't think so."

"What makes you think she's still here?"

"Because that was her car we parked behind." Howie knocked again. As they waited, a door opened at the end of the hallway and a middle-aged woman dressed in black slacks and a beige sweatshirt came out. She walked toward them carrying a handful of letters. When she saw the two of them, she hesitated as though she might retreat back to the safety of her apartment.

"Excuse me, ma'am," Howie called out.

"Yes?" She looked at them with apprehension. "What do you want?"

"Is there a manager or someone we could talk to about unlocking this door? We have to see if Miss Carpenter is okay." When the lady still seemed apprehensive, Howie explained further. "You see, she called us and said she was feeling faint."

The woman walked up to them, apparently having lost her uneasiness about the two strangers in the hallway. "You know," she began, peering at them over the rims of her glasses. "I wondered about Rosie. I just saw her."

"How long ago was that?"

"She left her apartment not more than ten minutes ago. And it looked like she really needed the help of the man who was with her."

"Did you know the man?" Adam asked.

"No, I never saw him before." The woman lowered her voice to a whisper. "But she didn't appear to be feeling very good."

Howie spoke up. "Why do you say that?"

"Because this man had a pretty good grip on her arm." She took hold of Howie's arm for a moment and squeezed it hard. "Just like that. I figured he must've been holding her up because she looked a little flushed."

Howie exchanged glances with Adam. "What did this guy look like?"

"I didn't take a good look." The woman paused, turned up her nose slightly, and sniffed out her next words. "I try to mind my own business."

"I understand, but can you tell us anything at all about him?" Howie asked, taking out his notepad.

"He was taller than you," she said to him and then eyed Adam. "But not as tall as you. He had dark, shaggy hair and had on a light-colored jacket...I think, blue, or it could have been gray."

Howie jotted down the description. "Anything else about him?"

"Not that I can recall. I was looking more at her."

"And Miss Carpenter looked pretty ill?" Adam asked.

"Lands sake, yes. And she looked frightened." The woman's mouth dropped open. "Oh dear!" she exclaimed as she clutched her hands to her breast. Several of her letters felled to the floor. "Do you think he could've been taking her to the hospital?"

"Maybe," Howie said as he picked up the fallen letters and handed them to her. *But I don't think so.*

# Chapter 20

ROSIE CARPENTER HAD answered the knock on her apartment door only when the man identified himself as being from the MAC Detective Agency. She realized her mistake immediately. It had been too soon after her phone call to Howie Cummins; he and his partners couldn't have made it over that fast. What confirmed her fears, however, was the way the man was dressed, scuffed tennis shoes, baggie trousers, and a black turtleneck under a dusty-gray jacket. In contrast to the two clean-cut, young detectives who had talked to her the other day, this guy looked like he hadn't shaved for days. He reeked of stale cigarettes and beer. Shaggy, oily hair hung over his ears. She tried to shut him out, but he forced his way in, closing and locking the door behind him. With the only way out now locked, she retreated into the living room. On the coffee table lay a pair of scissors; she picked them up and waited, her breathes coming in gulps. Footsteps on the wooden hallway floor served noticed he was coming. She clinched her free hand into a fist to keep it from trembling. Her heart pounded. When he came into the room, he stopped and glared at the scissors she held.

"Don't you come near me," she threatened, thrusting her weapon at him and praying that her voice wasn't revealing how terrified she felt. The man just stood and scowled. She hoped that her ploy had worked and that maybe, just maybe, he would leave. When his scowl became a sneer, though, she realized that he wasn't going to back down. Before she could say a word, he pulled a gun from inside his jacket.

"Don't play cute with me!" he said. "Put those scissors down and do exactly what I tell you if you don't want trouble."

"Wha...what do you want?"

"I told you. Put those scissors down and then we're going out the door, walk down the steps, and out to my car." His voice sounded raspy as though he had a sore throat. "If you try anything, just remember I have this." He turned the gun so she could see it from the side. "It's brand new and hasn't been used...yet."

"You're not going to shoot." Where she had gotten the nerve to speak those words, she didn't know. "As soon as my neighbor hears the gunshot, she'll call the police."

The man's eyes narrowed and he reached into his pocket. In one swift motion, he pulled an object out, pressing the side of it with his thumb.

"Oh, my God!" Rosie had seen switchblades before, but not one with such a long blade. She swallowed hard as she backed up a step.

"Okay, so I'm not going to shoot, but I'm going to put my calling card on that face of yours if that's what it's going to take to convince you to come with me." He put his gun away and took a step toward her, slowly waving the knife back and forth in front of him. "Is that the way you want it?"

Rosie bit her lip and shook her head. With every ounce of energy, she fought back the tears. She thought about screaming for help, but didn't want to take the chance of him using that knife.

"That's better," he said after she lowered the scissors. "Now just put them on the table there." He watched as she laid the scissors on the coffee table. "That's a good girl. Let's get moving now and don't even think about calling out for help. I can slice you in a second."

When they left, the man held her arm so tightly that she knew it would later form a bruise. Mrs. Bromwell, the woman who lived in the apartment down the hall, was coming up the stairs just as they started down. When they passed, Rosie hoped that her neighbor would see the fear in her eyes and call the police. She even hoped that they might meet the detectives on the way out. Her hopes were dashed, though, when they stepped out onto the sidewalk and the man motioned to another man sitting at the wheel of a car that was double-parked in front of the entrance. The driver reached over and opened the passenger door.

"Get in!" her abductor ordered. After she got in, he slid in after her. "Isn't this cozy, now," he said, pressing his body against her.

They drove across the Broadway Bridge into northeast Minneapolis. When they got to Central Avenue, they took a left. For the next ten minutes, they rode in silence. Her mind filled with questions that she dared not ask for fear of antagonizing either of them. As they pulled into a motel whose neon sign sputtered *Vacancy*, her only thought was that they were going to rape her. She was convinced of that when they took her into the room, tied her hands and legs, threw her on the bed, and then put tape over her mouth. She struggled, but was slapped and threatened with the knife. When the driver of the car sat down on the bed and stroked her breasts, however, the other guy told him to knock it off.

"The boss doesn't want any of that stuff going on."

Toward evening, they let her have a bathroom break and even offered her something to eat. She declined the food, saying she wasn't hungry. When she asked what they were going to do with her, they just looked at each other and smirked. The driver eventually left, telling his friend that he would see him in the morning. The man who stayed watched television and ate and drank his way through a couple of bags of potatoes chips and a six-pack of beer. It was nearly midnight when he turned the television off. Before he lay down on the other bed, he used another rope to secure her already tied hands to the bed frame.

"Don't try anything during the night," he warned, and then took out his knife and ran the blade lightly over her cheek. "Not if you want to keep your face nice and pretty."

It was mid-morning when someone knocked on the motel door. Rosie naively hoped it might be the motel manager. When the man opened the door, however, a middle-age woman in a nurses' uniform came in. Without saying a word, she walked over to the bed and set down the large black purse she carried. Rosie watched in horror as the woman snapped open the purse, took out a bottle of clear liquid and a white hand towel. The woman unscrewed the bottle cap and poured nearly half of the liquid onto the towel.

"Just breathe it in, honey," she said as she placed the towel over Rosie's nose and mouth.

# Chapter 21

HOWIE'S FACE WAS partially buried in his pillow when the ringing woke him. Still groggy, he slowly opened one eye and tried to focus on the telephone sitting on the bed stand. He couldn't tell if the light coming through his bedroom window was from the streetlights on Broadway or from an early morning dawn. It didn't matter. Either way, he just wanted to go back to sleep and finish his dream about that gorgeous blond nurse at Nana's nursing home. Groping for the telephone, he nearly knocked over the reading lamp. He nestled the receiver next to his face on the pillow. "Hello," he managed to mumble even though his mouth felt like he had sucked on cotton all night. The all too familiar high-pitched voice at the other end, however, made him want to unplug the telephone, stuff the cotton in his ears, and pull the covers over his head.

"Nana, why are you calling me at..." with great effort he lifted his head off the pillow and squinted at his alarm clock. He blinked a couple of times to make sure he was reading the clock right and then let his head flop back on the pillow. "Do you realize what time it is? It's not even six. The roosters haven't even gotten up yet."

"Don't you know that the early bird gets the worm?"

"Yeah, and do you know what that bird can do with that worm?" he mumbled.

"What? What did you say? Speak up!"

"I...ah, said that it's a lucky bird that gets the worm so early." Howie closed his eyes. "Nana, why are you calling at this hour?"

"The crooks didn't fall for the bait."

"What?"

"My ring's still on Hilda's dresser."

"That's too bad. Maybe next time you'll—"

"Just wanted you to know that. I'm going to get an hour of shut-eye now before breakfast. We get waffles and bacon this morning, my favorite."

"Sounds good to me." Howie lay there, waiting for her to say more when he realized the droning sound in his head was the dial tone. He hung up the receiver, but then picked it up again. "And good-bye to you, too," he mumbled and pulled the covers over his head.

Howie rolled over and came face-to-face with the alarm clock. He blinked a couple of times and rubbed the sleep out of his eyes as the clock's face came into focus. *Nearly eight-thirty.* He sat on the edge of his bed for a while before finally standing up. After washing and dressing, he fixed some toast, poured himself a cup of coffee, and settled down at the kitchen table. Adam had promised he would call sometime that morning to report in about his second night of work. Howie wasn't expecting too much. If Adam had come across anything significant, he would have called by now. That was okay. They had other concerns for the moment. He and his partners were puzzled and worried about the whereabouts of Rosie Carpenter. *What had she wanted to tell them? And who was the guy the neighbor lady saw with her?*

Yesterday afternoon, when Mick had come up to the office just before Adam left for his job, they had all agreed that the Carpenter woman had been taken against her will. The problem was they had no leads. They checked at the restaurant where Rosie worked. The owner told them that, as far as he knew, she had no family in the area. "She moved up here from some small town in Iowa over a year ago," the owner said. When asked if she had ever mentioned the town's name, he replied that if she did, he couldn't recall. Howie left his name and phone number. "If you do hear from her, give me a call." Afterwards, out in the car, he shared with Mick and Adam that he would like to track her down.

"I have to admit, though, that I've no clue where to begin."

"Neither do we," Mick said.

"Well, I guess all we can do then is to wait and see if she contacts us."

Now, as Howie finished his breakfast, he wondered if something else could have been done to get a lead on Rosie. "Don't start second-guessing yourself," he told himself, thinking that he might go back and talk to her neighbor again. He got up, poured himself another cup of coffee and headed for his office with the intention of going over his notes from the past couple of days.

An hour passed and Howie was still reviewing his notes when the phone rang. He hoped it was Rosie Carpenter calling. "MAC Detective Agency. Howie Cummins, here."

"Hi, Howie, it's Adam. Just calling to check in."

Howie took out his notepad and picked up a pen in case his partner had something to report. "Anything happen last night on the job?"

"No, things were pretty quiet."

"Well, that's okay." Howie set the pen down. "Just be patient. Something is bound to turn up sooner or later."

"I hope so."

"Just hang in there." Howie wasn't sure if Adam sounded down because nothing happened or because he was still struggling with working undercover. "Maybe we'll talk to you later. If not, keep your eyes and ears open tonight."

After hanging up the phone, he went back into the kitchen, poured himself a glass of milk, scrounged the cupboard until he found a couple of gingersnap cookies, and headed back to his desk. He looked forward to relaxing and reading an article in his *Police Gazette* magazine. The magazine, one of his collector's issues from the late 1800's had just the kind of bizarre stories he enjoyed reading to relax. The article that drew his attention this morning was from the February 18, 1882, issue; its headline read *How a Coterie of Villains Amuse Themselves in Prison*. He had just turned to the article and dunked a cookie into his milk when the office door opened and Jerome, Nana's grandson, strolled in. The dunked portion of his cookie broke off, leaving him only with what he held in his fingers. Not wanting the kid to see what had happened, he quickly moved the glass to the side and let the remaining cookie he held drop undetected to the floor.

"How come you're not in school?" he asked as Jerome walked toward him.

Jerome looked at him as if to say *and what planet do you live on?* "Because school got out two weeks ago. I'm on summer break."

"I knew that, kid. I was just testing you. So, what can I do for you?"

Jerome sat down in the chair, opened his spiral notebook, and took a pen from his pocket. "I came for a status report."

"A what?"

"A status report on the case. Have you—" Jerome's attention was drawn to Howie's glass of milk. His nose wrinkled at the cookie floating on top. He glanced at Howie and then back at the glass.

"I like my cookies soft," Howie explained, pleased to see the pained expression on Jerome's face. "So tell me, what were you going to say?"

"Have you gotten any leads yet?"

"None to speak of." Howie disliked the idea of answering to some kid, and even if he had information, he wasn't about to divulge it. Jerome technically wasn't his client. To get him out of his hair and to humor him, however, he would give the kid a bone to chew on. If he didn't give him something to leave with, Jerome would go running to his grandmother, and Howie didn't feel like getting any more early morning phone calls. The idea came to him in a flash. Adam would consider it underhanded, but as far as he was concerned, it was brilliant. Besides, the little twerp had it coming. "Wait a minute. Now that I think about it, we do have one lead."

Jerome's eyes widened as he leaned forward. "Really! What is it?"

"Just hang on. Let me check my notes." Howie took out his notepad and flipped pages until he came to a page he had written the telephone number of a pizza parlor he and Mick had ordered from last week. "Ah, here it is. Let's see, what do I have written here?" *Large pepperoni, heavy on the cheese, no olives.* "Give me a minute. I'm having trouble reading my own writing." He continued to take his time as Jerome inched closer to the edge of his seat. "Okay, now it's making sense," Howie said, stretching the time even further. Finally, he closed his notepad, leaned back in his chair, and let out a low whistle.

"What?" Jerome whispered excitedly.

"Hmmm, just as I expected. It's the lead that may break the case wide open." Howie took pleasure at seeing Jerome's mouth drop open. "Your grandmother suspected that *they* might fall for a trap she had set using one of her diamond rings. It didn't work this time, but she says she's on to them." He leaned forward. "Your grandmother is pretty sharp so *they'd* better watch out."

"*They?*" Jerome's eyes widened even further. "Who are *they?*" He hurriedly turned the page in his notebook. With pen in hand, he appeared eager to write down whatever new information the detective had.

Howie smiled, hoping that the kid wouldn't notice the smirk behind it. "Well, you're going to have to ask your grandmother that one. I think she'll be better able to fill you in on the details."

"Okay, I'll ask her." Jerome swallowed hard and then jotted something in his notebook. "Thanks." He closed his notebook and slipped the pen back into his shirt pocket.

"Are you hungry?" Howie asked as he reached for the glass of milk. He set the glass in front of him. "Hey, the cookie is just the way I like it." He slowly slid the glass toward Jerome. "Go ahead. Have some. I'll be glad to share."

"No...no thanks." Jerome looked like he had just been asked to take a spoonful of castor oil. "I...I need to go now."

"So, soon? Too bad. Next time you come we'll share cookies and milk together."

After Jerome left, Howie picked up the glass of milk, walked out into the kitchen, and dumped it in the sink. He poured himself a cup of coffee, headed back to his desk, and planned to resume reading about how the villains amused themselves in prison. It was nearly ten and he was looking forward to having some time to himself. He had no sooner read the first paragraph than the phone rang.

"MAC Detective Agency."

"Get over here pronto!" the voice shrieked

"Nana, I don't know if I can get away." He picked up his magazine. "I was just going over some important stuff right now. I—"

"This can't wait!"

"Are you sure it's that urgent?"

"I got us a witness!"

"You have a witness? A witness to what? Hello... hello?" Howie slowly put the phone down, ran his hand through his hair, and looked over at his movie poster. "Bogie, what am I going to do with that old gal?" He leaned his head back on the chair and closed his eyes. He was determined to set some boundaries with Nana. That wouldn't be easy, though, for two reasons. The first was because of her screwball, but strong-willed personality. The second, however, was because she was beginning to grow on him. If there was such a thing as adopting a grandmother, he had to admit that Nana would be at the top of his list.

# Chapter 22

HOWIE TURNED THE hallway corner and walked toward Nana's room. His client was up ahead, just outside her doorway, sitting in her wheelchair. Although she looked in his direction, he wasn't sure if her eyesight was sharp enough to distinguish who was coming. Just as he was about to raise his hand in a friendly wave, she lifted her arm above her head, clenched her hand into a fist, and pumped her arm up and down as though lifting weights. "Hello, there," he said as he walked up to her, feeling sorry for the woman, thinking that she might be doing some new kind of exercise for her arthritis. He knelt on one knee so that they could have direct eye contact.

"What's wrong with your arm?" he asked. "Is your arthritis acting up again?"

"What in sam blazes are you talking about?" Nana leaned forward until her face was less than a foot from his nose. She had remarkably smooth skin for a woman her age. "There isn't anything wrong with my arm. It's you!"

"Me?"

"That's what I said! You!" Nana's face scrunched into a wrinkled question mark. "What's the matter? You got beeswax in your ears?" She made a fist and pumped her arm a couple of times. "See that?"

Howie nodded, but still didn't understand what she was getting at.

"Don't you recognize the signal for double-time when you see it?"

"So that's what—"

"You're going to have to learn to move faster." Nana leaned back and wagged a bony finger at him. "I like you, but an old lady like me can't afford to sit around and wait forever. At my age, every second counts." She leaned forward, pressing her face even closer than before. "You'll come to know that in a few years, yourself."

"I'm sorry, but I—"

"Apology accepted!" Nana swung her wheelchair around brushing Howie just enough to make him lose his balance and causing him to land unceremoniously on his backside. "Now, don't you just sit there!" she chided. "Come on into my room and make it snappy! We've got some talking to do."

The hairs on the back of Howie's neck prickled. When he turned to see who might be watching, he discovered to his chagrin that it was the blond nurse whose name he had been hoping to find out. The attractive woman-of-his-dreams stood at the nurses' station with a hand covering her mouth; her eyes filled with merriment. He smiled sheepishly, picked himself up, and followed Nana into her room. This was no time to ask her name.

As soon as he entered the room, Nana closed the door and then checked to make sure it was shut tight. After listening for any noise outside the door, she wheeled up to Howie, who was sitting comfortably on the corner of the bed. "It's safe to talk now."

"So what's so urgent?"

"It's Morris."

"Who's Morris?"

Nana clasped her hands together in front of her chest. Her eyes widened, and when she spoke, her voice trembled with excitement. "He just moved in last night from another nursing home over in St. Paul. I met him at breakfast." Her eyes sparkled like a lovesick teenager. "He is such a nice gentleman. Do you know what he did for me?"

"I can't even begin to imagine."

"He gave me a slice of his raisin toast." Nana sighed. "Wasn't that nice of him, considering that was the first time we had breakfast together?"

"Oh, yeah. Very nice." Howie hoped that Nana didn't call him to come over just to tell him that her newfound gentleman friend had been kind enough to share his raisin toast with her. "But what does Morris have to do with the case?" he asked, wondering if the blond nurse had any aspirin.

"Hold your pants on! I'm coming to that." Nana inched closer. "It happened when we were eating our tapioca pudding."

"You mean, you and Morris?"

"No!" Nana cried. "Isabelle and me. After she left, Morris sat down." She gave Howie a disapproving look. "You're not too swift for being a detective."

"Go on. I'll try to keep up."

"You do that!" Nana tugged at her pigtail. "Now where was I?"

"You just finished eating tapioca pudding."

"Oh, yes." Nana twisted her pigtail around her finger. "That's when Morris sat down." She sighed. "He and I talked about how many people kicked the bucket every week. It was a delightful time. We spent nearly an hour together. And do you know what?"

Howie shook his head. "I don't even want to venture a guess."

"When I told Morris that I had a diamond ring stolen, he said that where he came from..." Nana paused, looked toward the door, and then lowered her voice, "a couple of women there told him about their diamond rings being missing."

"They did, huh?" Howie closed his eyes for a brief moment in an effort to relieve his headache. "Is he sure they said missing or misplaced?"

"Missing!" Nana exclaimed with a tone of annoyance, her eyes flashing with indignation. "Morris knows what he heard!"

"Did these women report that their rings were missing?"

"He couldn't remember, but he told me that the man in charge of security over there knows all about it." Nana reached over and patted Howie on the knee. "You go over to that place and talk to that security fellow. He might be able to give you some pointers on how to track down diamond crooks."

"And what's this security man's name?" Howie reluctantly took out his notepad.

"I forgot to ask, but Morris would know."

"I might as well go and talk to him. Where is he now?"

"That's a good idea." Nana patted his knee again. "He lives four doors down, room 113. His roommate is an old coot by the name of Charlie." She squinted at the clock on her nightstand. "Bingo doesn't start for another hour, so Morris should still be in his room." Her eyes flickered with anticipation. "And you're going to see him now?"

Howie nodded as he slipped his notepad back into his pocket.

Nana reached out and took Howie's hand. "I can't tell you how happy this makes me." She squeezed his hand gently. "I just know you'll find out something at that other nursing home."

When Howie noticed a tear forming in Nana's eye, he felt guilty about the nasty thoughts he had had about her when she had made the inference that he needed to get some pointers on doing detective work.

"Land's sake!" Nana blurted out as she reached up and rubbed her eye. "What kind of shaving lotion do you have on?"

"Why?"

"Because whatever it is, it's making my eyes water." Nana shook her finger at him. "Don't you be wearing that smelly stuff the next time you come. You hear? And don't forget, I'll expect you to report on what you have learned about detective work."

Even though the blond was at the nurses' station when Howie walked out of Nana's room, he was in no mood to talk with her at the moment. "Keep your cool," he muttered, reminding himself again that Nana was just trying to be helpful. He decided that it wouldn't take that much time to drive over and talk with the security person at the other nursing home. If it would keep a little old lady happy, he could do that. Besides, with Nana happy, maybe she wouldn't be calling him all the time.

The door to Morris' room was closed. Howie could hear a television blaring from inside. Someone was listening to a game show. A woman on the game show shrieked with delight at having just won the grand prize of a new 1967 red convertible. He rapped on the door as loudly as he could, but no one acknowledged his knocking.

"Hello, anybody home?" he asked as he opened the door a crack. The noise from the television was so overwhelming that he was sure that his chest bones would start vibrating. Upon opening the door wide enough to see inside, he saw that a curtain divided the room. He couldn't see who was on the other side of the curtain, but the gentleman closest to the door sat in a wheelchair at the foot of the bed, his eyes fixed on the television.

"Are you Morris?" Howie shouted as he stepped into the room and waved his hand at the man in an effort to gain his attention.

The fellow flinched and turned toward Howie. "What did you say?"

"Is your name Morris?"

"Speak up! I can't hear you!"

Howie moved to the television and motioned to the guy if he could turn it off. Once he got the man's approval, he shut it off and the room became serenely quiet. "Are you Morris?" he asked, intentionally keeping his voice raised.

"Don't have to yell! I ain't deaf, you know."

Howie didn't want to linger in the room too long. Beads of sweat formed on his forehead, and he wondered at what temperature the thermostat was set. "Are you Morris?" he asked again.

The man shook his head and gestured with his thumb to the other side of the curtain. Howie thanked him and peeked around the curtain. Someone was huddled under the covers. "Morris?" When the covers didn't move, Howie raised his voice. "Morris?"

"You ain't going to wake him," the roommate said. "He's all tuckered out from the move from that other place."

Howie excused himself, but was reminded that he needed to turn the television back on. Once outside the room, he decided that he would stop at the nurses' station and inquire about Morris. He also looked forward to finding out that blond nurse's name and maybe even her telephone number. When he got to the station, however, the hoped-for-answer to his lack of female companionship was nowhere in sight.

"Hello," another nurse greeted him. With gray hair and bifocals, this nurse didn't seem that many years away from becoming a resident herself. "May I help you?"

"I hope so." Howie offered her a winsome smile. "Could you tell me what nursing home Morris in room 113 came from? He asked me to go there to get some personal items he left behind." When the nurse gave him a questioning look, he added, "I asked him, but he forgot. He said it was some place in St. Paul." He offered another smile. "I'm doing it as a favor. He and my father were best friends."

"I see. Just a moment, please." The nurse went into the charting area. Within seconds, she came back with a chart. "I'll have it for you in a moment." She flipped a couple pages. "Here it is. Morris came in yesterday from the Rest Easy Retirement Center in St. Paul."

Howie took down the address and within minutes was on his way to Morris' former place of residence. He parked and walked to the main entrance of the three-story brick building. The reception he got from residents sitting inside was not unlike that which he received from those living at Nana's nursing home. Many of the residents, especially the ladies, smiled and greeted him with cheerful hellos. He stopped at the information desk and asked the woman if he could see the person in charge of security.

"You're in luck," the receptionist said. "He just happens to be in today. You just go down the hall and to the left."

Howie easily found the door labeled *Housekeeping/Security.* He knocked and a voice from inside asked him to come in. When he opened the door, he momentarily stopped in his tracks.

"You're that detective fellow, aren't you?" Pete Larson said and then invited Howie to have a chair.

The office appeared to be nearly an identical twin to Larson's office at the other nursing home. Howie sat down, but said nothing.

"I suppose you're wondering what's going on with me being here?" Larson asked with a look of amusement bordering on smugness.

"I, ah, sure am. But first I'd like to know how did you find out that I was a detective?"

"It was easy enough." Larson leaned back in his chair and clasped his hands behind his head. He looked like he could rest his feet on his desk any minute. "After you left, I went up and asked Nana."

"Oh, I see." Howie would have to have a little talk with his client. "And so how do you happen to be here?"

Larson laughed. "Those of us doing this kind of work aren't going to become rich. You ought to know that." He stroked his mustache a couple of times and then folded his arms in front of his chest. "Don't you work part-time in a drugstore?"

Howie nodded, wondering how he knew that and what else he knew.

"See what I mean?" Larson may have meant his tone to sound confident, but it came across as being cocky. "I also have to work a couple of jobs to make ends meet." His manner and tone turned collegial. "In the work we do, it goes with the territory." He glanced around his office. "So I divide my time between this place and the other. The owner has been pretty good about that."

"So, the two nursing homes are owned by the same person?"

"That's right. And he's planning to purchase a third home near Lake of the Isles."

Howie visualized the area Larson was referring to. "That's in a classier neighborhood, isn't it?"

"A lot classier than this one." Larson leaned forward, folding his hands on the desk. "Now, what can I do for you?"

"It has to do with a fellow who recently moved in over at the Golden Years retirement home. He came from here."

"Is that so? And who might that be?"

"Morris...ah..." Howie chided himself. "Sorry, but I don't know his last name. But he just moved in yesterday."

"That must be Morris Wilson. He's been talking about moving for months." Larson chuckled. "He always complained about the food here, but the trouble is he forgets what he eats from day to day." He paused to scratch behind his ear. "So, what's the deal with him? Did he hire you to investigate the cooks here?"

"Nothing like that, but he told Nana that there's been some stuff stolen around here."

The smile on Larson's face disappeared. "I'm afraid that happens all the time. It's surprising what gets taken. A woman told me that her afghan was stolen a couple of days ago." He picked up a sheet of paper from his desk. "I've just got a report here about a guy up on second floor who claimed his roommate stole his false teeth."

"According to Morris..." Howie cleared his throat. "Some women are missing diamond rings."

Larson shook his head. "Not as far as I know. A couple of women claimed their diamonds were stolen, but neither of them had diamond rings when they came in."

Howie didn't want to go back to Nana without something to report. "Would it be any problem if I talked with them?"

"It could be."

"Why's that?"

"One of them, Gladys, went to visit her daughter out east. She'll be gone for a week or longer. There's even a possibility that she may not return if the daughter decides to have her live in a home out there."

"How about the other woman?"

"I'm afraid that's not going to be possible."

"I don't understand."

"She died three weeks ago of a massive heart attack." Larson paused for several seconds as if out of respect for her passing. "It was for the better, however. She was in constant pain and not very happy."

"I don't suppose there's anybody else who lives here who is claiming their diamonds rings are missing?"

"Nope. And if there was, I'd surely hear about it."

"I'm sure you would." Howie stood up to leave. "Thanks for your time."

"Sure, no problem." Larson got up and came around his desk, shook hands with him, and then saw him out the door.

Howie walked down the hallway and headed toward the entrance door. As he passed the receptionist, she waved him over. "How did your visit go?" she asked.

"It went fine. He was very helpful."

"That Pete Larson is certainly a nice guy," she offered. "I sure wish we could see him more often around here. He really makes an effort to get to know the residents."

As soon as Howie Cummins left, Pete Larson picked up his phone and dialed. It rang several times before his partner answered. "Hey, this is Pete. I'm here in St. Paul. We've got a woman at the other place who's been yakking with some private detectives. That's right. And I'm afraid she'll stir up the pot too much." He drummed his fingers on the desk. "Sure, I know who she is and I'm going to have to do something about her." He opened his desk drawer to get his pack of cigarettes. "Yeah, I know it's only been three weeks since the last one. Listen, no one questioned that one, and no one will question this one. After all, people die in nursing homes all the time. Don't worry, you just handle things at your end and let me take care of them at this end." After hanging up, he plucked a cigarette out of the pack, lit it, and took a long, deep drag. He had some planning to do.

# Chapter 23

VERNA ODDEGAARD FINISHED her notations in the chart book, set her pen down, and took note of the time. Nearly midnight. "You can have the chart now," she said to Sally, a nursing assistant, who happened to be walking by her workstation.

"I'll put it with the others," Sally said. "Do you want me to bring you Louise's chart while I'm there?"

"No, I'll get to that one later."

In the nearly thirty years Verna had worked as the night duty nurse at the Golden Years retirement home, she thought she had written notations in resident's charts on just about everything that could happen in a nursing home. Like the night during a routine room check she had come upon Clarence Johnson trying to climb into bed with Louise Larson. Both in their nineties, they were as naked as the day they were born. "Clarence, what are you doing and why aren't you in your room?" she had exclaimed, and then nearly burst out laughing when he whined, "Shucks, can't a guy have a little fun around here?" In the meantime, Louise had pulled the covers over her head and giggled like a teenager. Verna recalled another night, however, that wasn't so humorous: the night Sophie Carlson had suddenly decided that "strangers" were keeping her locked up against her will. Eighty-three-year-old Sophie, determined to break out of her "prison," had stormed up and down the hallway yelling obscenities at anybody who happened to cross her path. When she began to get uncontrollably violent with staff and then with other residents, Verna had found it necessary to call the police. It took two husky police officers with the help of a male nursing aide to subdue the two-hundred-plus-pound woman before Verna could sedate her. As the two officers had walked away, Verna overheard the one say to the other, "Man, we're sure going to get a ribbing when they find out that we needed help to take down some old lady." The other officer shook his head and replied, "Don't worry about it. We're not putting that part in our report."

As far as Verna was concerned, however, what had happened earlier tonight was something quite out of the ordinary. Neither humorous nor scary, it was just plain heart wrenching. Two hours ago, she had gotten a phone call from Lucy, the night receptionist.

"I thought you'd like to know that they're just bringing a woman into the lobby on a gurney," Lucy said. "And she's going to be admitted to your floor."

"What! Whoever heard of admitting someone at ten o'clock at night?"

"I agree, but I've got papers here signed by the administrator."

"What room is she going into?"

"351," Lucy said, and then whispered, "she's even got a private nurse."

Verna had waited at the elevator, curious as to who would be receiving such special attention. Room 351 was scheduled to go to a person coming in the next night. In all of her nursing days, she had never experienced anything like this. She wasn't happy with what was happening, and was prepared to tell that to whoever was bringing this person in. When the elevator doors opened, however, she was shocked at what she saw. Lucy hadn't told her that the woman was young. "What's wrong with her?" she asked, noting that the woman looked like she was comatose. The two men accompanying the gurney glanced at the nurse they had come with, apparently with the expectation that she would handle whatever questions might be asked. The stern-looking woman with short, steel-gray hair, though, simply brushed Verna's question aside, explaining that she wasn't at liberty to comment. Verna was also informed that under no circumstances was other staff to enter the room.

"And just who's going to clean the room and change the linens?" Verna asked, her anger rising.

"All of her needs will be taken care of by private staff," the woman briskly replied.

Verna had gone back to the nurses' station that night muttering to herself. "Now, I've seen everything." Several things bothered her, however. *Why did they bring such a young woman here? What was wrong with the poor girl anyway?* That the regular staff wasn't allowed to help in her care had irked Verna more than anything. She decided that she would let Betty, her replacement, worry about those things. After tonight, she was leaving on a three-week vacation that she had been looking forward to for months.

# Chapter 24

WHILE VERNA ODDEGAARD waited out the hours of her final night before vacation, Stephanie Turner, LaMar Jones' sister, waited in her parked car and kept an eye on the front entrance to the Chocolate Angel Candy Factory. Although she had hired Howie Cummins and his partners to investigate her brother's death, she wasn't about to idly stand by and do nothing. It just wasn't part of her temperament to observe the action from the sidelines. Even in grade school, a teacher had called her "tenacious" after she voluntarily stayed in from recess two weeks in a row to work on an extra credit project. It was a label that she strove to live up to all of her life. She had called Howie yesterday and asked if he had found out anything about the man her brother had been suspicious of at work.

"Only that his name is Ken Pritchett," Howie had said and then went on to explain that it was still too early in the investigation. "You've got to give it some time," he suggested. "I'll call you when we find out anything."

Stephanie rolled her car window down. If she hadn't been watching for Pritchett, she would have enjoyed taking a walk on this warm moonlit night. In the past, she had taken many late night walks on such an evening as this. LaMar, however, had been livid when he found out about her evening strolls. "I don't want you going out walking so late at night by yourself," he had scolded. She had listened patently as he played the role of a protective older brother. After he had finished lecturing her, however, she had smiled, thanked him for his concern, and then pointed out that she was perfectly capable of taking care of herself.

Now, as she sat watching the entrance to the candy factory, she recalled the night a car had slowly followed her as she began one of her late night walks. She had gone less than a block and then stopped, waiting for the car to pass. When the driver had pulled over to the curb and rolled down the window, she had discovered it was LaMar.

"I'm only watching out for you," her brother explained.

She had gotten so angry with him that she kicked a dent in his passenger door, spraining her ankle in the process.

LaMar had got out, examined the dent, and burst out laughing. "Okay, Sis, you win. I won't follow you anymore. My car can't take it. Now, come on and get in," he had pleaded, flashing the engaging smile he always used when he knew he had overstepped the line with her. "I'll treat you to pie and coffee, and then take you home."

Now, a car turned the corner and headed in her direction. Stephanie quickly leaned sideways until her face nearly touched the ribbed vinyl of the car seat. She remained motionless as the illumination from the headlights washed through her car. For a moment, it seemed as though the oncoming car had slowed down. She shut her eyes and held her breath. After the car passed, she exhaled, thankful for the sheltering shadow of the large oak tree she had parked under. She straightened up, smoothed her skirt, and glanced at her watch. Twelve-fifteen. Forty-five minutes had gone by since she first arrived. *Where is that man?* She would stay there all night if necessary. Convinced that Pritchett had something to do with her brother's death, she was determined to get some answers. The first step was to follow him and find out where he lived. What came after that, she wasn't sure. All she knew was that she had to be doing something.

It was half-past midnight when the entrance door to the candy factory opened and a slightly built man wearing glasses came out. He walked down the steps, stopped under the corner streetlight, and lit a cigarette. Her brother had described Pritchett and one other guy who sometimes stayed late. LaMar said that the other guy, Leo, was as big as a building. Pritchett, in contrast, was lean and medium height, and wore glasses. *This had to be Pritchett.* She watched the man walk across the street and get into a dark-color, late model car. When he pulled away, she started her car and followed, staying back far enough so he wouldn't get suspicious. He took a left on Broadway. That was good. Traffic was just heavy enough for her car to blend in, and yet light enough so that she could tail him without losing him. Ten minutes later, Pritchett pulled over and parked in front of an all-night café that was wedged between a clothing store and a gift shop. As Stephanie drove past, she saw him heading toward the café. *What's he doing?* She turned at the corner and parked. On impulse, rather than waiting until he came out, she decided to go into the café.

The café was less than a third full, mostly couples. Pritchett had taken a seat at a table near the back. Stephanie paused for a moment and then sat at a table by the café's front windows, positioning herself so that she could observe Pritchett. After ordering coffee, she took out a paperback book from her purse and opened it randomly in the middle. Every so often, she would sneak a glance at Pritchett. For the next fifteen minutes, Pritchett did nothing but sip coffee and look at a newspaper. Whenever the entrance door opened, however, he would look up. *So, he's expecting someone. Who?* Within a matter of minutes, she got her answer. A well-dressed, older gentleman came in, paused for a moment, and went directly to Pritchett's table. She watched as they greeted each other like old friends. The man ordered coffee and appeared to be doing most of the talking. Every now and then Pritchett would nod his head.

"Would you like anything else?"

"What?" Stephanie hadn't noticed the waitress come up, and nearly jumped with fright. "Oh, I'm sorry," she said and then pointed to her coffee cup. "I'll just have another refill."

As soon as the waitress left, Stephanie shifted her eyes back to Pritchett's table just in time to see the well-dressed gentlemen slide a brown envelope across the checkered tablecloth. Pritchett smiled, picked up the envelope, briefly examined its contents, and tucked it away in his pocket. The two men talked for a few more minutes and got up to leave. As they came toward her, Stephanie opened her purse and pretended to be searching for something. She was relieved when they walked past without bothering to notice her. After they left, she realized that by the time she paid for her coffee and got to her car, Pritchett would be long gone. That was okay. She didn't need to follow him home tonight. Seeing that brown envelope was payoff enough. She took a sip of her coffee. Tomorrow she would pay a visit to Howie Cummins.

# Chapter 25

Mɪᴄᴋ sᴛᴏᴏᴅ ʙʏ the window gazing down at the street while Adam sat quietly, paging through one of Howie's *Police Gazette* magazines. Only the ticking of the wall clock punctuated the silence. Howie leaned back in his chair and pondered the phone call he had received that morning from Stephanie Turner. It was now mid-afternoon and he and his partners were waiting for her to arrive. She had called in an urgent tone of voice requesting to meet with all of them. When he inquired as to the purpose of the meeting, she said only that she had some important information that could help their investigation of her brother's death. He pressed her to say more but she declined, preferring to wait until she could talk to them in person. As soon as he hung up, he called his partners. Luckily, both were in and available to meet at the time she had requested.

Howie checked the time. They still had twenty minutes to wait. Stephanie said she would be there at three or shortly thereafter. He leaned forward and drummed his fingers on the desk. The ticking of the clock was beginning to become unnerving. When Mick and Adam had arrived ten minutes earlier, he asked Adam if anything of significance had happened at the candy factory last night. His partner just shrugged saying that there wasn't much to report. They planned to talk further about Adam's night after their meeting with LaMar's sister, but Howie needed to do something to make the time go faster. He opened the top drawer of his desk and took out his notepad. "Why don't you fill us in on what's going on at the job?" he asked Adam. "We might as well make use of this time."

"That's a good idea," Mick said as he walked over and sat down, stretching out his legs. "I'd like to know how old Hooknose is doing, anyway."

"I haven't seen too much of the guy since I started." Adam placed the magazine on the desk. "Every time I do see him, though, he's not very friendly towards me. The man hasn't said more than five words to me since I started." He shifted in his chair. His partners knew that although he had a tendency to be a loner, it still bothered Adam if people didn't like him. "I don't understand what he has against me."

"I wouldn't worry about it." Mick picked up a rubber band from Howie's desk and playfully shot it at the wall clock, missing it by a foot. "The guy probably treats everybody like that." Howie tossed Mick another rubber band. This time, he hit the clock dead center.

"Speaking of Mr. Personality," Howie said. "I know you told me his last name yesterday, but I forgot to write it down." He opened his notepad to a page labeled, "Suspects." "Give me Leo's last name again."

"Rappaport," Adam replied, spelling it out.

Howie jotted the name down, writing in parentheses, "Hooknose." If Stephanie's brother had been murdered and Howie still wasn't convinced that LaMar had been, Rappaport might have been involved. And if the death wasn't an accident, then everybody at the candy factory could be considered a suspect. Although he hadn't mentioned it to Adam, the list of suspects would also include Rachel Gilbertson and her father, both of whom Adam had spoken of with high regard. For now, however, they would concentrate on their client's suspect. "How about Pritchett? Has he done anything suspicious?"

"So far, nothing."

"You sound frustrated," Mick said. "Are you?"

"A little," Adam replied. "Pritchett doesn't usually show his face in the areas where I'm working. I don't know what the guy does with all his time. As far as I've seen, there's just not that much work to keep him busy."

"Anything else?" Howie asked.

"No, that's it." Adam sighed. "I just wish I had something more substantial to report."

"You will, just be patient," Mick counseled. "If Pritchett did away with LaMar, he'll make a slip." He looked to Howie for agreement. "Isn't that right?"

Howie nodded. "Bad guys always do."

"See what I mean?" Mick said. "Even the boss agrees. If this guy's guilty, we'll nail him eventually." He patted Adam on the shoulder. "Remember, you've only been there a couple of nights. Don't be so hard on yourself."

"I hear you, but I think I'm going to have to take initiative and do some more snooping around."

"If that's what it takes, you'll do it," Mick said. "And you'll do a good job at it."

"I agree, but just be careful." Howie appreciated Mick's attempt at bolstering their partner's confidence. Adam had the makings of a top-rate detective, if only he could get some of his inner struggles worked out. He hoped that Adam's resolve to take some initiative at the candy factory didn't come from his desire to get the job done as quickly as possible so he wouldn't have to continue living a lie doing undercover work. "Anything else about last night?"

"No, I'll just keep working at it."

Mick looked to Howie. "It's your turn now."

"What are you talking about?"

"What else? The Nursing Home Caper."

"The what?"

"You know, the case of the missing diamonds over at the nursing home." Mick's eyes twinkled. "From what Jerome tells me, his grandmother has just about wrapped up the case for you." He winked at Adam. "Who knows, if Nana's as sharp as Jerome tells me, Sam Spade here should make her an offer to come in with us."

"If I do, she'll be your partner."

Once the bantering settled down, Howie brought his partners up-to-date on his visits with Nana. He also told them about Pete Larson and how the guy worked security at both places to make ends meet. The reference to making ends meet initiated a discussion about the future and how much money each of them might be making in ten years. Mick thought that he'd probably still be working with Howie to earn extra cash since teaching salaries weren't all that great. "I'll be glad to have you with me," Howie said.

"And I suppose you'll still be working at Kass'," Mick replied.

"I hope not." Once his detective agency became financially established, Howie planned to quit the drugstore job. Being a soda jerk didn't fit his image of a private investigator. He and Mick were kidding Adam about the big bucks preachers make when they heard the downstairs entrance door open and bang shut.

"That's got to be Stephanie," Mick said, "and she's right on time." He poked Adam in the arm. "Wait until you see her. She's a knock-out."

The three detectives listened as the two flights of stairs leading up to the office creaked with every step taken. When Howie first moved into his apartment, his partners had pleaded with him to do something about those stairs.

"Get me a can of oil, and I'll oil them for you," Mick had offered.

Adam had also agreed to help. "And while we're at it, we'll fix that downstairs entrance door as well. It's always banging shut."

"We're not going to do either of those things," Howie had said. "That door and those stairs let me know when people are coming."

"And I suppose you can tell whether it's a male or female and how old they are," Mick had said, his eyes and voice teeming with mischief.

Now, as they waited, Howie cocked his head and listened to the creaking of the stairs. "It's a woman all right, and she's wearing high heels."

"Get out of here," Mick said. "You're guessing."

"Just wait and see." When the creaking stopped, the three of them waited in silence for the door to open.

"Why doesn't she come in?" Mick whispered.

"Because she's taking a few minutes to compose herself," Howie replied. Within seconds the office door opened and Stephanie Turner walked in. As anxious as she had sounded on the telephone that morning, she appeared calm and very much in control of herself. "Welcome," he said, taking personal satisfaction that she was wearing high heels. "Let me get you a chair from the other room."

"Wait a minute." Mick stood up. "She can have mine. I'd rather stand."

Stephanie walked over to Mick's chair, but seemed reluctant to sit down. "Are you sure?" she asked.

"Oh, yeah. Go ahead and sit down. I need to stretch a bit, anyway." Mick moved over to the file cabinet and leaned against the wall, resting his arm on top of the cabinet.

Howie gestured toward Adam. "This is Adam Trexler, my other partner."

Stephanie smiled. "Nice to meet you."

"You said you had something important to share with us," Howie said.

"I do." Stephanie sat down, crossed her legs, and smoothed her skirt over her knee. "Thank you for being here as well," she said to Mick and Adam, her eyes warmly acknowledging them before turning her attention back to Howie. "I suppose you're wondering why I wanted your partners here."

"I'm sure you have a good reason."

"I do," she replied with conviction. "I believe the more people involved in the case, the better the chance of proving that my brother's death was no accident." Stephanie paused, taking time to make eye contact with each of them. "What I witnessed last night only confirmed my suspicions about Pritchett." She took a deep breath before sharing her story about waiting outside the candy factory for Pritchett to get off work. "I followed him to a restaurant. This man dressed in a three-piece suit came in and joined him at his table."

"Did you recognize the guy?" Howie asked.

"No, but he and Pritchett chatted like they were old friends, and then this man slid a brown envelope across the table to him." A hint of a smug smile crossed her lips. "They didn't think anybody was watching, but I was."

"I don't suppose by any chance you saw what was in that envelope?"

Stephanie shook her head. She leaned forward and gripped the edge of Howie's desk with both hands. When she spoke, it was with the intensity of a prosecuting lawyer making a case-deciding point to a jury. "It had to be money and it must've been a lot because Pritchett seemed pleased when he checked it."

"So you're thinking all of this had something to do with your brother's death?" Howie said. His partner's skeptical looks reflected his own nagging question. Why would Pritchett want to kill LaMar Jones? In a court of law, the jury would need to hear something called a motive. And so far, they had none.

"Do you know why your brother was suspicious of Pritchett?" Adam asked.

"No." Stephanie settled back in the chair. "I just know, though, that that man is up to something no good. I don't know what, but my brother found out about it and..." Her voice trailed off as she looked toward the floor.

"And he murdered your brother to keep him quiet," Howie said. "Is that what you were going to say?"

Stephanie shuddered and rubbed her arms as if a chill had come into the room. "I just couldn't bring myself to say that. It still sounds so awful."

"It is awful," Mick said, and then added, "If it's true."

"It is true!" Stephanie cried, casting Mick an angry look.

"And that's what we want to find out," Howie quickly added. "I appreciate you bringing us this information, but I'm concerned about the risk you took." He leaned forward to emphasize the importance of his plea. "I'd suggest that you not take any further risks. After all, that's what you're paying us to do." When Stephanie seemed unmoved, he said in a stern voice, "If your brother was murdered, and if Pritchett is the killer, then your very life could be in danger. Have you thought about that?"

Stephanie said nothing, but her eyes narrowed, revealing defiant determination.

"He didn't recognize you, did he?" Adam asked.

"Oh, no," Stephanie said. "I don't think he even knows who I am. He attended LaMar's funeral, but I wasn't there."

"Here's what I'm going to do." Howie hoped that his course of action would deter her from doing anything further. "I'm going to talk to this guy tonight after he gets off work. I'll put a little heat on him."

"I'm not sure what you mean," Stephanie said, her face registering puzzlement.

"I'm going to tell him he's under suspicion in LaMar's death. I'm also going to let him think that I tailed him to that restaurant and saw him receive an envelope of cash." Howie noted the surprised looks his partners were giving him. "If I can rattle his cage a little, maybe he'll get nervous and make a mistake."

"I hope so," Stephanie said. "Please, let me know what happens." After Howie promised he would, she got up, and walked to the door. "Good luck," she said and then left.

As soon as the downstairs entrance door banged shut, both Mick and Adam questioned Howie as to why he hadn't shared his plan earlier about confronting Pritchett.

"Because I just thought it up as I was talking to her."

"I should've known," Mick said.

"Do you think he'll fall for it?" Adam asked.

"I don't know, but it satisfied Stephanie for the time being. I didn't want her to think we're twiddling our thumbs on this case." Howie picked up a rubber band and shot it at the wall clock, missing it by two feet. "We'll just have to see what happens tonight. Maybe we'll get lucky and he'll confess."

# Chapter 26

IT WAS CLOSE to midnight and Ken Pritchett decided to leave work a few minutes early. Even though he was supposed to be the last one to leave the building at night, he trusted that the new guy, Adam, could make sure the door locked behind him when he left. He wasn't certain what to think of Adam, having heard that he was studying to become a minister. He had no problems with that as long as the preacher-to-be didn't start on him with that religious mumbo-jumbo stuff. He still reeled from having religion pushed down his throat when he was a kid. When he went to look for Adam he found him downstairs straightening up a storeroom.

"I need to leave early tonight," Ken said.

"Okay, so what do I have to do to close up the place?"

"Nothing. Just make sure the entrance door locks behind you when you leave. If it doesn't, just push on it until you hear it lock. See you tomorrow night."

When Ken stepped into the night air, he took a deep breath. It wasn't as warm out as it had been last night, but he didn't care; he felt great. He couldn't help but smile to himself as he walked down the steps. His plan had worked just like he had hoped it would. Mr. Gilbertson had been there earlier that night, working in his office. Ken had knocked on his door and asked if he could borrow his set of keys to open one of the storage rooms. When Gilbertson asked about his own keys, he had lied and said that he had misplaced them and hadn't found them yet. Actually, he put them in the wastepaper basket by his desk. That way, he could use the excuse that his keys must have dropped into the basket by accident and were found only when he went to empty it. Gilbertson gave him his set of keys and told him to bring them back as soon as he was done with them. Ken hurried to his office and shut the door.

It had taken him less than five minutes to make wax impressions of the keys, doing it in just the way Benny had instructed. Benny would charge him an arm and a leg for making duplicate keys from the impressions, but it would be worth it. Besides, he had dealt with Benny before and the guy was someone who could be trusted to keep his mouth shut. Once he got the duplicate keys from Benny, then it would only be a matter of finding the right one to Gilbertson's office. Benny had told him the keys would only take a few days to make. Ken smiled to himself, knowing that once he had access to Gilbertson's office, he could get his hands on what he originally began working there to find.

As Ken now walked to his car, he stopped to light a cigarette. He had just taken his first drag when he noticed the man coming toward him. *Where did he come from?* Ken quickened his pace, hoping to get to his car before the guy cut him off, but it was too late. *If he wants my wallet, I'll just give it to him.*

"You're Ken Pritchett, aren't you?" the man asked as he intercepted him.

"Yeah. Why do you ask?" Ken breathed easier. This stranger in the night looked too clean-cut to be a mugger.

"I'm Howie Cummins from the MAC Detective Agency. If you don't mind, I'd like to ask you a few questions."

"Now?" Ken tossed his cigarette away. "What about?"

"LaMar Jones."

Ken kept a calm outward appearance as his stomach twisted into knots. "What's there to talk about? The poor guy had a freak accident."

The detective took a step closer to him. "I don't believe it was an accident and I've got to tell you, Mr. Pritchett, that you're under suspicion."

"Me? You're out of your mind." Ken needed a cigarette.

"Is that so? Then tell me what were you doing at that restaurant last night up on Broadway." The detective paused, but Ken held his ground, refusing to take the bait. "You didn't see me, but I was there."

He scrutinized the detective's face. "If you were there, then you'd know I was sharing a cup of coffee with a friend."

"And I suppose that was sugar in that brown envelope he passed to you."

"I don't know what you're talking about."

"Do you want to know what I think?" The detective moved closer, his eyes narrowed as his tone turned ominous. "I figure it was some kind of payoff and that it was connected in some way with LaMar Jones' death."

"Look, I don't have to talk to you." Ken began to walk away.

"I guess I'll just have to go to the police with what I witnessed."

Ken stopped, turned, and came back. That was one thing he didn't want to hear. "Look, I don't want to get into trouble." He lowered his voice. "That guy you saw me with was my bookie and I just hit it big in a horse race. He was paying me off. I wouldn't want the police to know about that."

"Do you expect me to believe that?"

"It's the truth, and if you want to talk to my bookie, I'll have him call you." Ken suspected the detective was fishing for leads. "If you're so suspicious about LaMar's death, I suggest you do some checking on Leo Rappaport."

"Who's he and why should I talk to him?"

"Leo works at the place, too. He has a thing for the boss' daughter. When LaMar started coming on to her, Leo got very jealous. He and LaMar even got into a fight about it one night." Ken could see that the information had taken the detective by surprise. "Can I go now?"

"Okay, but just know that I'm going to be checking on this, and if it's not true, we'll be seeing each other again."

After Ken got in his car, he took out his pack of cigarettes, lit one up, and watched the detective slip away into the shadows of the night. He took a drag off his cigarette and smirked. *I wonder if he believed the story about the money.* He chuckled. *Hell, it sounded so damn convincing that I almost believed it myself. There was no harm telling him about Leo and LaMar. At least, that part was true, and maybe it'd give that nosey detective something to work on...and leave me alone.* He took another drag of his cigarette. *That detective was bluffing when he said he saw me at the restaurant. He wasn't there. I'm sure of that. But who could've tipped him off about me being there?* He turned the ignition and sat there, letting the car idle. He went to take another puff, but stopped just as the cigarette touched his lips. *Of course, it had to have been Lamar's sister. She thinks I didn't recognize her sitting there last night. We may never have met, but her brother showed me enough pictures of her that I'd recognize her anyplace. If she stirs up any more trouble, I'll have to have a little talk with her.* He took one last drag of his cigarette, rolled down the window, and flipped it out. *Once she finds out about her dear innocent brother, she'll drop the case.*

# Chapter 27

"THERE'S SOMETHING FISHY going on up on the third floor." Nana's voice came over the telephone in hushed whispers as if to underscore that mystery and intrigue filled every nook and cranny at the Golden Years Retirement Home.

Howie, familiar with Nana and her *they* paranoia, took her call in stride. As soon as he recognized her voice, he eased back in his chair, closed his eyes, and silently berated himself for answering the phone.

It had been nearly one that morning when he had gotten home after his encounter with Ken Pritchett. Although exhausted, he hadn't gone to bed right away; he'd stayed up for another hour. During that time, he had jotted down notes from his confrontation with Pritchett and reviewed previous ones on the case. And then, deciding he was hungry, he'd had a couple glasses of milk and munched on a slice of week-old pepperoni pizza he'd discovered on the bottom shelf of the frig. When he had finally got to bed, he'd tossed and turned for what seemed like hours. He wasn't sure if his restlessness had resulted from the pizza or Pritchett's surprising revelation about the bad blood between Leo Rappaport and Stephanie's brother.

His alarm had gone off at eight. Although he could have slept for another couple of hours, he'd dragged himself out of bed, washed, dressed, and made a pot of coffee. He'd just poured himself a third cup of coffee and sat down at his desk to go over his notes when the phone rang. That it was Nana on the other end of the line made him want to go back to bed and pull the covers over his head. He had heard her opening words, but didn't respond.

"Did you hear what I said?" Nana demanded

"Yeah, you said something about the fish up on the third floor." Howie's attempt at early morning humor didn't go over well, and he had to hold the phone away from his ear as she yelled that he should clean the wax out. "There must be static in the line," he said and then asked her to repeat herself. When she did, he replied in a more serious tone. "So, what's going on up there?"

Nana lowered her voice. "I can't tell you over the phone because—"

"*They* might be listening and this phone might be bugged." Howie took satisfaction that he had beaten her to the punch. "Am I right?" he asked, and then waited. "Am I right?" The only response he got was the dial tone. He slammed the phone down. When he picked up his coffee to take a sip, the movie poster of Bogart caught his eye. "Okay, Bogie, so I don't have to be so tough on the old gal. Well, I'm not dropping everything at her beck and call just because she snaps her bony little fingers." He took a sip of his now lukewarm coffee. "She's just going to have to wait until I get done talking with Adam." He picked up the phone and dialed his partner's number. It rang several times before Adam answered.

"Hey, it's Howie. Can you come over now so we can touch base...I know, but I'm in a rush. Something has come up...good, I'll see you in ten minutes." He hung up the phone and sat quietly for several minutes, his head resting against the back of the chair. It was only when his stomach growled that he decided he should grab something to eat. He picked up his coffee cup and headed towards the kitchen.

Howie had just buttered his third piece of toast when he heard the office door open. "I'm out here in the kitchen," he yelled. He had left the door open from his office leading into his living quarters. From his office, it was a straight shot through the hallway into the kitchen. The eight-foot-long hallway connecting the kitchen to the office had a door on either side: one leading to his bedroom, the other leading to the bathroom. "Don't look at my bedroom, it's a mess!" he yelled as Adam came through the doorway into the hallway.

"It's not any messier than usual," Adam remarked as he walked by the bedroom on his left. "When was the last time you cleaned it?"

"My maid comes in every other Tuesday," Howie quipped as Adam came into the kitchen. "Take a load off your feet." He pulled out a chair for him. "We'll talk in here." He held up his piece of toast. "Do you want some?"

"Nah I've eaten." Adam settled in the chair. "So how come we're meeting earlier than we'd planned?"

"One word: Nana."

Adam smiled. "Okay, say no more. I understand." His smile faded. "So tell me, how did it go with Pritchett last night? Did he fall for it?"

"Not exactly." Howie sat down at the table and glanced out the window. He liked the idea of having his kitchen table pushed up against the windows. Sometimes, at night, he would sit in the darkened kitchen and observe the street life on the sidewalks below. "Pritchett put a new wrinkle into the case."

"What are you talking about?"

For the next several minutes Howie went over in detail his midnight encounter with their prime suspect. Adam was just as surprised about Leo Rappaport's name entering into the picture as Howie had been.

"That does add a new wrinkle," Adam said as he shifted in the chair. "Do you think Leo could've killed LaMar?"

"Jealousy has always proven to be a pretty strong motive." Howie pointed his piece of toast at Adam. "You're going to be a preacher. You ought to know that. Isn't there some story in the Bible about one sister killing another sister because she was jealous of her looks or something?"

Adam shook his head. "It wasn't two sisters. It was two brothers, Cain and Abel. And the story had nothing to do with looks. It was about one being jealous of the other because his offering was more acceptable to God."

Howie shrugged. "Well, whatever. It's the same principle." He got up, went to the refrigerator, found a jar of grape jelly, came back and sat down. "Didn't you tell me that you and Rachel Gilbertson hit it off right from the beginning?" he asked as he spread the jelly on his two half pieces of toast.

"Yeah, so?"

"So, I got to thinking." Howie put the top back on the jelly jar. "With what Pritchett told me, that could be the reason that Rappaport hasn't been too friendly to you." He stood and picked up the jar of jelly. "He's jealous of you," he said as he headed toward the refrigerator.

"That's hard to believe." Adam waited until Howie sat back down. "Isn't it possible that Pritchett was just saying that to throw you off base?"

"Maybe, but I don't think so." Howie took a bite of toast. "It's easy to check out," he mumbled as he chewed.

"How're we going to do that?" Adam grabbed the other half piece of toast off Howie's plate and took a bite. "Besides Pritchett, the only two people who witnessed this alleged fight were the ones involved in it. One is dead, that's LaMar." Adam picked up Howie's cup and took a sip, and then paused as his partner got up and headed toward the coffee pot. "We sure enough can't approach Rappaport on it. First of all, he'd get suspicious. And secondly, we wouldn't get anywhere with him. He'd simply stare at us with those stone-cold eyes and then walk away without saying a word."

"That's for sure." Howie set a cup in front of Adam and poured him some coffee. "There is, however, one other person we could talk to who probably knows something about it."

"Who's that?"

"Rachel Gilbertson." The troubled expression that flooded Adam's eyes signaled Howie that his partner knew exactly what was coming next.

"And you want me to talk to her, don't you?"

"You're the logical choice," Howie said, aware of the awkward position he was putting his partner in. "But you're going to have to do it without blowing your cover."

"I know, but I hate playing games with her." Adam gnawed at his lip. "She's such a nice person and she trusts me."

"So much the better."

"But what's she going to think when she finds out that I've been deceiving her all this time?" His eyes shifted toward the floor for a moment. "I don't suppose I could let her in on who I am and why I'm there?"

Howie shook his head. "Sorry, but that's the way it is."

"That's what I figured, but I had to ask anyway."

Howie took note of the time. The image of Nana sitting and impatiently waiting for him flashed through his mind. "I've got to be going soon. Tell me about last night. Anything out of the ordinary with Pritchett?"

"No, same as usual." Adam took a sip of coffee. "There was something, however, that happened around ten that was different."

"What was that?"

"I was sweeping the main area when Gilbertson comes out of his office and calls me over. He hands me a box of chocolate angels and tells me to wrap it and get it ready for shipping."

"Isn't that sort of late to be doing that kind of thing?"

Adam nodded. "That's what I thought. I didn't say anything, but he must've read my mind because he tells me that a good friend of his is giving the box of candy to his wife, and his friend needs it by tomorrow evening."

"Why the rush?"

"Apparently, the wife raves about these chocolate angels. It had to have been an anniversary gift or something." Adam shrugged. "Gilbertson didn't go into detail about that. He then tells me that a courier should be there in a half hour, and that I'm to meet him at the door and give him the package. After I finished wrapping it, I realized that he hadn't given me any name or address to put on the package."

"Did you go and ask him?"

"I thought about it but decided not to bother him; he seemed too preoccupied. I figured if the courier didn't know where to deliver it, then I'd talk to him."

"So what happened?" Howie asked as he finished off his toast.

"The courier came some twenty minutes later. It was some kid with bushy, red hair whose uniform looked two sizes too large."

Howie took out his notepad and jotted down the description of the courier. "Did you catch what outfit this kid worked for?"

"Yeah, he wore a shirt embroidered with the logo *Roadrunner Courier Service.*" Adam waited until Howie wrote the name down before continuing. "Anyway, he asked me if I had the package. I said I did, but it didn't have any address on it."

"Was he surprised about that?"

"No, he said that he knew where it was going. He also told me that it's going to be one expensive box of candy. When I asked him where he was delivering it to, his answer blew me away."

"What do you mean?"

"He said he was taking it to the airport."

"To the airport?" Howie's curiosity shot up a couple of notches. "Is that where Gilbertson's friend works?"

"No, get this." Adam's eyes flickered with intensity. "He was taking the package there because it was going to be shipped air express on a midnight flight."

Howie put his pen down. "Did you ask where it was being shipped to?"

"I did, and at first, he wasn't going to tell me because of company rules or something like that." Adam took a sip of coffee. "I was never quite sure what the problem was, but then he whispered to me, 'It's going to Chicago.'"

"Chicago!" Howie moved his cup aside. "Why in the world would someone be sending a box of candy via air express in the middle of the night?"

"You've got me."

"Well, I can't believe it's just because some guy wants to surprise his wife with a box of chocolates." Howie opened his notepad to a new page. "Did you get the name and address in Chicago?"

"I asked, but the kid didn't know. He said that all he was supposed to do was to deliver it to the Air Express representative. Gilbertson must've called ahead and arranged everything."

"Anything else?"

"No, that's about it."

"Okay, thanks." Howie finished jotting his notes down, making a special notation to call Leon, his contact at the airport. Leon had worked at the airport as a baggage handler close to thirty years; long enough that, according to Leon, everybody there owed him a favor or two. If anybody could get the information, Leon could. At least it would be worth a phone call.

He and Adam talked for a few more minutes, and then Howie said that he had to get going or else Nana would hire a detective tutor for him. "When you go to work tonight, make a special effort to observe Pritchett if you can," he said as they got up from the table. "I want to know if he seems nervous or jumpy now that I've turned up the heat."

"I'll do that." Adam waited until Howie put the dishes in a sink full of other dishes, and then they walked back into the office area.

"Keep an eye on Rappaport, also," Howie said, adding, "And be careful."

"Don't worry, I will." Adam gnawed at his lip.

"What's bothering you?"

"Is...is there anyway I could leave Rachel out of the picture?"

"I'm afraid not. You're going to have to talk to her."

After Adam left, Howie slipped on a sports jacket and picked up his car keys. Nana was waiting for him.

# Chapter 28

NANA MET HOWIE at the entrance door. After chastising him for being nearly an hour late, she dragged him to her room and shut the door. The only shining moment had been just before they had reached her room and were passing the nurses' station. The blond nurse had exchanged glances with him and he was positive that she had given him a provocative smile.

"Okay, Nana, tell me what's going on." Howie hoped to ask a few questions, listen to her story, jot down some notes, and get out. As soon as he was done with her, he planned to stop at the nurses' station and work his charm on a certain blond. If things worked out, his social life was about to dramatically improve. "So what happened?" he asked. "Don't tell me another diamond ring is missing."

"Nope, the crooks have been laying low."

"They have?"

"You're darn right they have. And do you know why they haven't shown their mugs?" Nana stuck out her chin. "Because they know I'm on to them."

"So, why did you send for me?"

"I've got a job for you."

"What do you mean you've got a job for me?"

"They've got somebody hidden away in a private room up on the third floor." Nana lowered her voice to the point that Howie strained to hear her. "The door's always shut. I hear tell that only certain staff can go in."

"What's so strange about that? Maybe the person likes privacy, or maybe is sick and doesn't want visitors."

"I don't think so." Nana's eyes narrowed. "Eleanor knows who it might be."

"Who's Eleanor?"

"She's my contact up on third. She's a good friend, but..." Nana tapped the side of her head with a bony finger. "She doesn't always have it up here."

"Did she see who was in that room?" Howie asked as he took out his notepad and pen.

"No, but she's sure it's somebody important."

"Like who?"

"The President."

"The President!" Howie looked up to see if Nana was kidding. She wasn't. "You mean of the United States?" When Nana nodded, he closed his notepad and slipped it back in his shirt pocket. "And you believe her?"

"Of course not!"

"Then why do—"

"Because I just know that something mighty peculiar is going on up there."

Howie closed his eyes for a moment, wishing he were back at the office reading one of his *Police Gazette* magazines and having a cup of coffee, or better yet, having a drink with the blond nurse, and then inviting her back to his apartment. "What has this got to do with me?"

"You're a detective!" Nana huffed. "I want you to investigate it." She wagged her finger at him, a gesture that was happening all too frequently. "That's why I'm paying you!" she chided. "It's probably some rich person who has lots of diamonds." Her eyes glistened with intrigue. "Eleanor can be our spy. She'd like that."

"I don't know if that's a good idea."

"Humph! You don't have any other real leads yet, do you?" Nana's tone had an accusatory ring to it.

*Maybe if this was a real case, I might.* "Not at this point."

His client scooted closer. "Isn't it the code of detectives to track down every possible lead?" After Howie reluctantly agreed, she placed her hand on his and patted it. "Now, if you need help with this I could call my grandson, Jerome. He's a good boy and would be glad to lend a hand."

"Oh, no," Howie said, and then cleared his throat to give himself enough time to calm down. He wondered if little old ladies could cause high-blood pressure; they sure enough caused headaches. "What I mean is that there's no need to bother your grandson. Your friend's help will be enough. Believe me, more than enough."

"Good." Nana patted his hand again. "Now, here's my plan."

"What do you mean? Your plan?"

"Just what I said!" Nana's tone dared him to challenge her. "I figure you're going to need me to get you up there."

"I don't know about—"

"You can't just go wandering around this place without bringing attention to yourself." The wagging finger again. "You ought to know that!"

Howie massaged his forehead. "What have you got in mind?"

"You push me in my wheelchair." Nana's eyes danced with excitement. "If anybody stops us, just tell them that I'm all tuckered out and you're taking me to see my friend on the third floor."

"And who am I suppose to be?"

"One of my grandsons." Nana leaned forward and studied Howie's face. "You and Jerome could pass as being related. You both got the same light eyebrows, button noses, and dimples. Let me see your choppers."

"My what?"

"Your choppers!" she cried, pointing to her teeth.

"Nana, I don't know if—"

"For heaven's sakes, open your mouth and quit yakking!"

Howie hesitated for several moments before complying.

Nana leaned forward. "Hmmm. Good. You and Jerome have nice straight white teeth." She nodded her approval. "Yes, I think you could pass for his older brother."

"I'm so glad to hear that," Howie said, not caring if she picked up on the sarcasm in his voice. The only way he would have that precocious little rug rat as a younger brother was if Jerome's older sister was a blond nurse. And even then, it would be a toss-up. "So, what happens when we get up there? We still can't get into the room if someone's watching it."

"Simple as apple pie," Nana said, brushing Howie's concern off with a wave of her hand. "I'll just get everybody's attention. When I do, you take a peek in the room."

"And just how are you going to get their attention?"

Nana offered a sly smile. "Never mind, I will." She wound a pigtail around her finger. "Once you get a good look, you come get me and we'll scram."

"It sounds like a good plan," Howie said, biting his tongue for lying. Even his preacher-partner, Adam, would be tempted to lie given this scenario. "What do you say we carry it out two weeks from today?" he suggested, hoping by then she would've forgotten about it.

"That's too far away. Right now is as good as ever." Nana arched a thin eyebrow. "Don't look so shocked. We might as well do it while I can. At my age, you can't wait too long." She leaned so close to him that he could smell mint, either residue from her toothpaste or mouthwash. "Did I ever tell you my favorite saying?"

"No, but I'm sure you're going to tell me now."

Nana straightened up in her wheelchair as if she was about to recite the Pledge of Allegiance. "When you live, live in clover. For when you're dead, you're dead all over." She wheeled her chair around and headed toward the door. "Come on. Let's go and live in the clover while we still got the chance."

As Howie pushed Nana out of the room, the blond at the nurses' station smiled at them. *Just stay right there. Don't go away, I'll be right back for your name and phone number.* He pushed Nana to the elevator and pressed the button for the third floor. While they waited, a man using a walker shuffled up, stopped, and eyed the two of them. "Who's this?" he asked Nana, jabbing Howie in the arm.

"My grandson. He's taking me up to see Eleanor."

"Eleanor!" The man's laugh sounded like a pig snorting. "That old bitty?" He looked at Howie. "Do you know what that woman did last week? She called the police. She claimed that she was being held against her will. I tell you, she's crazier than a loon."

Howie closed his eyes for a moment, positive that he was going to need some aspirins soon.

"Now, Harold!" Nana snapped. "Don't you be calling my friend any names. She can't help it if she gets confused sometimes."

"Confused!" Harold snorted again. "That's a polite word for loony."

Before Nana could reply, the elevator door opened.

Howie quickly got Nana into the elevator. "Good-bye, it was nice meeting you," he said to Harold, and then repeatedly pressed the button to close the elevator doors. After the doors closed, he took a deep breath and leaned his head against the side of the elevator. He hoped that the elevator's motion might sooth his aching head. If he hadn't separated Nana and Harold, they might have gotten into a heated argument or worse yet, knowing her, a brawl, and he would have gotten caught in the middle of it. The thought of trying to convince that blond nurse that he had just been an innocent bystander made him shudder. "Maybe today isn't a good day to see Eleanor," he said as the elevator moved past the second floor. "It's right after lunch. She could be taking a nap." *Or maybe having tea and cookies with the President.*

"Don't you fret, there's nothing to worry about. I called her before you came."

"You did?"

"She told me that she'd wait by the elevator. You should've heard her. She was so excited about being in on this that she had to go and take a pee."

"Really?" Howie closed his eyes, wishing he were someplace, anyplace, else. "That excited, huh?"

"You bet your bottom dollar she was. Why, this is the most thrilling thing that has happened up there since Clarence went streaking buck-naked down the hallway in his wheelchair." The elevator came to a stop and the doors opened. "Get ready," Nana said and then wheeled out before any reply could be made.

Howie stepped out and looked around. Two elderly gentlemen were asleep in the chairs across from the elevator; their chins were resting upon their chests. To the right of the chairs, a woman wearing a wide-brim, scarlet hat sat in a wheelchair talking to a teddy bear she held in her arms. Another lady in a wheelchair looked in their direction and smiled, motioning for him to come. He took a step toward her.

"Where're you going?" Nana asked.

"Isn't that Eleanor?" Howie pointed at the woman who had begun to inch toward him in her wheelchair.

"Heavens sakes, no! That's Lillian. She's just going to ask you if you're married. You better be careful, she flirts with all the men." Nana took off to the right and just before she turned the corner to go down the corridor, she called to Howie. "Come on! You don't have time to talk with her."

Howie nodded and then smiled at Lillian who, by now, was picking up speed. He waved good-bye to her, and started after Nana. By the time he caught up to Nana, she had parked herself next to a heavyset woman asleep in her wheelchair.

"Eleanor, wake up!" Nana shouted, tugging on the sleeve of the woman's floral dress. "Come on, wake up!"

The sleeping lady slowly lifted her head, smacked her lips a couple of times, and looked around before settling her eyes on the person right in front of her. "Oh, hello, Dearie."

Nana pointed to Howie. "This is the young man I told you about."

The woman shifted her eyes toward Howie and smiled. "Hello, Dearie."

"Hi." Howie heard a noise behind him. Lillian was inching her way around the corner. The woman was smiling and with a gleam in her eyes, motioning for him to come. *Oh, man, what am I doing here?* He wanted to get this over with as soon as he could and get out. "Eleanor, Nana said you have something to tell me."

"She did?" A puzzled expression swept over Eleanor's face as she turned to Nana. "What was I going to tell him?"

"About that room where no one can go in."

Eleanor's eyes doubled in size as she put her finger up to her lips. "They've got the President in there," she whispered and then glanced around as though looking for enemy agents. "Do you think we should we call the police? I know their number."

"He's a detective," Nana said, pointing to Howie.

When Eleanor's mouth dropped open, her bottom dentures slid out. "These things are no good," she mumbled as she pushed them back in and clacked her teeth a couple of times.

Howie moved closer to Nana. "Don't you think we should try this some other day? Maybe you and Eleanor should go play bingo. I saw a poster that says it begins in a half hour."

Nana shook her head. "Which room is it?" she asked Eleanor. Her friend didn't answer, however, because her eyes were closed and she was snoring. Nana reached over and tugged at the sleeve of her dress again. "Eleanor!" she yelled.

Eleanor's eyes popped open. "Wha...what?"

"I asked what room is that person in?"

"What person?"

"You know. The President."

"Oh, yes. It's down at the end of the hall, across from the back exit." Eleanor placed her hands on the wheels of her chair. "I'll go with you to rescue the President."

"No, you better stay here," Nana said.

"But I want—"

"You stay here and be the lookout." Nana gave Howie a knowing wink. "We need a lookout, don't we?"

"Yeah, that'd be very important." Howie sensed someone behind him. Lillian was now only ten feet away. "See that woman coming?" he said to Eleanor. "Ask her if she wants to be your assistant lookout."

Eleanor beamed with delight. "Oh, she'll be so happy about that." She took off in Lillian's direction.

Nana tugged on Howie's coat jacket. "Wheel me down close to the nurses' station now and then give me a few minutes. When I get their attention, you take a peek into that room." She glanced around and then lowered her voice. "And while you're in there ask the person if they have lots of diamonds."

"Sure thing." Howie had no idea what Nana was up to. For that matter, he wasn't sure what he was doing either. Getting in and out of that room and away from this place as soon as he could was his goal. He wheeled Nana to within ten feet of the nurses' station and then walked over to a painting on the wall, pretending to examine it while he waited for Nana's plan to unfold. Her scream startled him. He turned just in time to see Nana slip from her chair onto the floor.

"My heart!" Nana cried. "My heart! Help!"

"She's having a heart attack!" shrieked a housekeeper who had rushed over and knelt down beside Nana. The housekeeper, a blue-tinted haired lady in her sixties sounded as if she could have a heart attack herself.

Several staff persons suddenly appeared from various rooms and rushed toward the stricken woman. Howie fought the urge to check on Nana to make sure she really was okay, but he remembered her advice. "When the crowd gathers around me, get yourself into that room." While the commotion centered on Nana, he moved quickly to the end of the hallway just as a nurse came out of the room where the President was supposedly being held.

"What happened?" she asked.

"I think you're needed down there." Howie pointed toward the crowd. "One of the residents just had a heart attack." The nurse ran toward the commotion. As soon as she was a safe distance away, Howie went to the room, opened the door, and slipped in. The curtains were drawn and the overhead lights were off. Only two lamps were on: one by the bed, the other by a lounge chair. He moved closer to get a better look at the person in bed. His mouth dropped opened and he couldn't believe his eyes. *Rosie Carpenter! What's she doing here?*

# Chapter 29

MICK POPPED THE last of a glazed donut into his mouth and washed it down with a gulp of milk. "I just can't figure it out," he said to Howie and Adam as the three of them met in Howie's office. "What in the world was that Carpenter woman doing at that nursing home? Who could've brought her there and why? It doesn't make sense."

"I agree," Adam said.

"Well, it doesn't make any sense to me, either," Howie confessed. "And those are the same questions I spent half the night trying to figure out." He opened the bag of donuts and took one for himself, his second. As soon as he had gotten back to the office yesterday, he had called Mick and Adam. When his partners heard that he found Rosie Carpenter and where, they were stunned. It didn't take any convincing for them to see that they needed to meet this morning to talk over a plan of action. Except at the moment, Howie had no plan.

Mick took a couple more gulps of milk and then set the nearly empty glass on Howie's desk. "This whole thing's bizarre. One minute the Carpenter woman calls and tells us she wants to talk. The next minute, she's conked out in some bed at a nursing home." He shifted in his chair, stretching his legs out. "And you said that you couldn't wake her?"

"That's right."

"She must've been doped up," Adam said, the concern in his voice evident.

Howie appreciated Adam's feeling of empathy for people; his partner had enough for the three of them. Adam's compassion for others, however, sometimes presented a problem since he was too quick to trust in the intrinsic goodness of people. That was something Howie would never do. "When I tried to get her to respond, she didn't even open her eyes," he said.

Mick reached over and picked up his glass. "And I suppose you didn't get a chance to search the room for clues?"

"I wanted to, but I was afraid the nurse would come in and find me. I'm just glad for the time I had, thanks to Nana."

"She's sure one smart little lady," Adam said. "I can't believe she pulled that whole thing off."

"Neither can I." Howie took a bite of his donut. "For a minute, though, she even had me worried the way she was carrying on. I was beginning to think she was having a real heart attack." He wiped the glaze from the corner of his mouth. "She's just lucky she didn't get bruised more than she did when she slipped onto the floor." He couldn't get out of his mind the image of Nana lying on the floor. "I thought for sure she broke a bone."

Adam sipped his coffee, declining a donut when Howie offered the bag. "How bad did she get hurt?"

"She had a cut on her elbow. It didn't look all that good to me, but she said it was nothing. I overheard one of the nurses tell her that she'd have some nasty black-and-blue marks." Howie finished off his donut and took a couple swallows of lukewarm coffee. "Do you want to hear something amazing? That cut on her elbow? When I finally got her back to her room, she told me that she hoped it'd leave a scar."

"You're kidding," Mick said. "Why would she want a scar?"

"She said it'd give her something to remember the day."

Adam put his elbow on the arm of the chair and placed his chin in the v formed by his thumb and forefinger "She is one tough old cookie."

Mick nodded. "She sure must be." He drank the rest of his milk, waving off Howie's offer of a refill. "So during this whole time, the staff never caught on?"

"I think they were suspicious, especially when she recovered so quickly." Howie overheard a couple of nursing aides questioning Nana's behavior. "They made her see a doctor, however."

"That must have been worrisome for you not knowing if she was really hurt," Adam said.

"It sure enough was. I paced the hallways while the doctor examined her." Howie recalled how the time had dragged until Nana appeared. "The doc told her she was fine but that she should cut back on her activities for a while."

Mick shifted in his chair. An old high school football injury sometimes made it difficult for him to sit comfortably. "What did she say about that?"

"She told him in no uncertain terms that she'd continue to do the things she has always done." Howie smiled to himself as he remembered the look of determination in Nana's eyes. "And that if he insisted, she'd change doctors."

"Wow!" Mick slapped the arm of his chair. "Now, I know I've got to meet this woman. She's one lady who doesn't take any guff from anybody."

"That's for sure," Howie said. Nana had also warned him not to even think about putting any roadblocks in her way.

"I'm not cutting back on anything, including this case," she had told him. "And don't you get any notions in your head about asking me to do so, not while we're so close to catching those diamond thieves." She gripped his arm. "I just know those crooks are around here someplace. And I aim to be in on the bust."

Adam stood up, stretched, and sat back down again. After the first night on the job, he had told his partners that he wasn't used to mopping floors and that his body ached in places he never thought possible. "Did you tell her you knew the person in the room?"

Howie shook his head. "I didn't want her to know that we're working on another case. If she found that out, she'd want to help solve it."

"So what did you tell the old gal?" Mick asked.

"That it was somebody who just wanted to be left alone and that there were no diamonds involved." Howie's next words were for Adam's benefit since his partner often questioned his habit of lying to people. "Hey, if I would've told her the truth, she would've enlisted some of her loony friends to break Carpenter out."

Mick straightened up in his chair. "You know, that's not such a bad idea."

"What are you, nuts or something? That's all I need, Nana and a group of her friends storming the third floor in their wheelchairs."

"No, no, no." Mick waved his hand back and forth as if erasing one of the blackboards in his classroom at school. "That's not what I mean. What I'm saying is that we have to figure out some way to get Rosie out of there." He looked to Adam for support. "That's the only way we're going to get a chance to talk to her and find out what she wanted to tell us."

"He's right," Adam said. "And it could have something to do with LaMar's death. We need to talk to her, and we can't do it while she's being held at that nursing home." He fixed his gaze on Howie. "Her life may be in danger, and we just can't sit around and do nothing."

"I agree with everything you guys are saying." Howie picked up a pencil and rolled it back and forth between his thumb and forefinger. "Believe it or not, I've been thinking the same thing myself." He let the pencil drop onto the desk. "Except that I haven't come up with any workable plans as to how we could get her out of there."

"How about we just go up and sign her out?" Mick said. "We can say we're her relatives."

"I considered that, but the problem is that the woman's unconscious. She wouldn't be able to get up and walk out with us."

"How about a wheelchair?" Adam asked.

"I thought about that, too, but we'd probably have to tie her in. And staff would still question why we're taking an unconscious woman out of the building, not to mention asking for identification to prove that we were relatives."

Mick slumped lower in his chair. "I see what you mean." He shrugged and then offered Howie a half smile. "I suppose we could always wrap her up in a blanket and carry her out."

"What did you say?" Howie felt as if an electric current shot through his tired brain.

"That we could wrap—"

"Not that part, the last part."

"Carrying her out?"

"Yeah, that's it! That's the answer!" Howie slapped the top of his desk. "Why didn't I think of that last night? It's perfect. We'll just carry her out."

Mick looked to Adam for an explanation, but he just shrugged. "I'm not sure what you're talking about," he said to Howie. "If we can't take her out in a wheelchair without raising eyebrows, how in the world are we going to carry her out wrapped in a blanket without drawing a crowd?"

"Just bear with me for a moment." Howie felt energized. "Nana told me the other day that the only reason many of her nursing home friends take all the pills they take is to keep them on this side of the sod." He looked at his partners for understanding, but their faces registered question marks. "What she's saying is that if you don't take your pills, they'll carry you out in a pine box."

"So, we're going to carry Rosie out in a pine box?" Adam deadpanned, glancing at Mick, who looked just as perplexed.

"Not exactly, but you're close." Howie, pumped-up by his idea, felt ready to go ahead with his plan. Even though it might sound bizarre at first hearing, he was convinced it could work. "Nana told me that they have so many deaths at that place that the residents know the funeral directors by their first names. The coming and going of these morticians and the bodies they're taking out is pretty common. It happens on a weekly basis."

"I think I know where you're going with this," Adam said. "And you're serious about doing it, aren't you?"

"I sure am." Howie took out his notepad, wanting to jot down the ideas while they were still fresh in his mind. "If you can think of a better plan, let's hear it," he challenged Adam.

"Wait a minute, you two." Mick straightened in his chair. "Maybe I'm a little dense this morning, but what are you guys talking about?"

"We want to get Rosie out of that nursing home, don't we?" Howie said, flipping open his notepad to a blank page and printing at the top "Operation Pine Box." He then showed it to Mick and Adam. "This is going to be our plan. We just have to work out the details."

"I still don't understand." Mick leaned forward and read again what Howie had printed. "It sounds like you're talking about Rosie as though she were dead."

"That's what we hope people will think." Howie paused, counting that his partners were up for the next part of his plan. "We're going to dress up as funeral directors and—"

"What?" Mick's mouth dropped open. "We're going to do what?"

"You're kidding, aren't you?" Adam asked.

"No. We'll dress in black suits and ties like funeral directors, go up to the third floor, place Rosie on a cart, toss a sheet over her, and get out before anybody is the wiser." Howie waited for Mick's response, but he simply sat there with a stunned look. "You want me to go over it again?"

Mick ran his hand back through his hair. "No, I think I understand it now. I...I just can't believe that we're going to try and pull something like this off." He looked at Howie as though his boss had just announced that they were going to the moon. "I've known you since junior high and I've got to tell you this is one of the wildest schemes you've ever planned."

"Do you have a better idea?" After Mick indicated he didn't, Howie turned his attention to Adam. "Didn't you tell me that you had some connections with a funeral home?"

"Yeah...indirectly. There are a couple of the guys from school who work part-time in one over in Northeast Minneapolis. Why?"

"Because we're going to need a hearse to pull this off."

Adam let out a puff of air. "Oh, man!" He grew silent as though processing the feasibility of Howie's request. "Okay, at least, I can ask. These guys do owe me a favor since I helped them with Greek last year."

"Assuming we get one, how're we going to get past the nurses' station?" Mick asked. "Won't they recognize Rosie?"

"No, remember she'll be covered by a sheet." Howie amazed himself at how easily his plan was unfolding. "And as far as the nurses' station, we'll just have to figure out a way to keep the staff occupied. If we can pull this off two days from now, it'll be the weekend. That'll be good."

"Why's that?" Mick asked.

"Because there's not as many staff working then. Nana always complains about how the place is short-staffed on the weekends." Howie took a sip of coffee and then pushed the cup away. He didn't need any more caffeine. "We can do it at lunchtime when the staff is busy in the dining room with the other residents."

"That makes sense," Mick said. "What happens once we get past the nurses' station?"

"We'll get the cart on the elevator, go down to the first floor, and then out the entrance. If anybody asks, we'll just say we've already filled out the papers on the third floor." Howie continued to be amazed at how freely his ideas were flowing. "If they see the hearse parked out in front, they'll just assume that it's legit. And even if someone gets suspicious, by the time they check, we'll be long gone." He jotted more notes down. "Do you think we can get the hearse this weekend?" he asked Adam. "Let's say, Saturday morning around eleven?"

"I don't know."

"Why don't you give your friend a call and find out if it's possible?" Howie pushed the phone toward Adam and then got out the phone book.

After looking up the number of the funeral home, Adam picked up the phone and dialed. "Hello, is Jim Lang there? Okay." He put his hand over the receiver. "We're in luck. They're getting him. I've known the guy ever since—hello, Jim? This is Adam. How're you doing?"

While Adam and his friend exchanged small talk for several minutes, Howie drummed his fingers on his desk. "Ask him about the hearse," he whispered.

"Say, ah, Jim, I need a favor." Howie listened as Adam explained why he was calling. Adam frowned. "Are you sure you can't make an exception? I know, but you owe me. Remember that Greek exam I helped you with?"

Howie and Mick listened as Adam used his persuasive powers on Jim.

"Yes, we'd take good care of it," Adam said, giving his partners thumbs-up. "Great. We'll pick it up Saturday morning. Okay?" He nodded to Mick and Howie. "Oh, I'd say for a couple of hours. Around eleven. That's perfect. Yeah, I'll understand if things change. Thanks. I'll be in touch." He hung up the phone. "We're in business."

Howie leaned back in his chair. "I feel that we have a pretty good chance to pull this off. After all, what could go wrong?"

# Chapter 30

PETE LARSON HESITATED before he knocked on Nana's door. He wasn't overly anxious to see the woman, but he was curious as to why she had called that morning and asked him to come to her room. When he inquired as to the reason she wanted to see him, she told him that it was a matter not to be discussed over the telephone and promptly hung up before he could reply. He had heard about her episode on the third floor yesterday and was still trying to figure out what that was all about. When he had asked about it, one of the nurses told him that Nana's grandson had brought her to see Eleanor, and that Nana somehow slipped out of her chair when she thought she was having a heart attack. The doctor didn't think it was a heart attack and that she probably just had indigestion. "Nana must've become overly excited when she thought it was her heart," the nurse speculated. The story sounded innocent enough, but when it came to Nana, Pete had a growing suspicion of everything she did.

"Well, let's see what the old bag wants," Pete muttered and then knocked. He felt for his cigarettes. A smoke would be nice right now, but Nana would have a fit. He was about to knock again when the door opened a crack and two eyes peeked out at him.

"It's about time you got here!" Nana swung the door open. "Come on in. You can sit on the bed."

Pete sat down and waited for her to close the door. "You're looking quite nice today," he said after Nana wheeled up to him. She really didn't look all that great, but he made it a habit to compliment the residents even when they didn't deserve it. The flattery was one of the ways he used to gain their favor. "What can I do for you?" he asked cheerfully.

"I told you that I hired a detective, didn't I?"

Although Pete nodded, her blunt question took him by surprise, and he wondered if she was laying some kind of trap for him. If she had plans to confront him, he felt confident that he could talk his way out of anything. He had done it many times in a variety of situations with other people; it was a gift he had. When he was a teenager, his mother told him that because he had been blessed with what she called a "golden tongue," she believed that someday he would become a minister. Now, until he knew Nana's intentions, he smiled and cleared his throat, deciding to play it straight. "I met Mr. Cummins the other day," he began. "He seemed to be a very nice man, although he appeared quite young to be a detective."

"I know and that's why I wanted to talk to you." Nana inched closer to him and lowered her voice. "I sent him to check on Gertrude's missing diamond ring and he came back and told me that she had no ring. I know he's wrong."

Pete noticed a hint of sadness flicker in Nana's eyes as she spoke of her detective's fallibility. "Mr. Cummins is just short on experience," he offered.

"I know that, and that's why I'm wondering if he did a thorough enough investigation."

"Well, he's right about there being no ring," Pete replied, thinking that the snoopy old bat should mind her own business. "Gertrude never came in with any diamond ring."

Nana's eyes nearly doubled in size. "What are you saying?" she asked. "She always talked about her ring."

The golden tongue went into action. "Did you ever see the ring?"

"No, but I know she had it. She wouldn't have lied to me."

Pete's tone became as patronizing as his smile. He liked playing with the minds of the residents. "Now, Nana, you and I both know that Gertrude could, at times, be confused." He reached out to pat her hand but she pulled it away. "I'm afraid she was confused about the ring as well," he continued, feeling a note of triumph when it appeared as if he had Nana second-guessing herself. "When people come in, they sign a paper listing all their valuables." He paused. "You signed one didn't you?"

Nana nodded.

"Gertrude also signed one. I showed Mr. Cummins the paper she signed." Pete paused again. "I can assure you that Gertrude's signature was on it. Her signature was as clear as the nose on my face."

"Her signature!" Nana cried. "That couldn't have been her signature."

"And why not?" Pete asked, his words squeezing through a fixed plastic smile.

"Because Gertrude was paralyzed on her right side from a stroke. She couldn't write. I know that because she asked me to write letters for her."

"Is that so?" Pete's muscles tensed up, but he kept his smile and spoke calmly. "Well, I think you may be a little mixed-up. Gertrude had the stroke after she'd been here for a couple of weeks." He looked for any hint of self-doubt on Nana's part, but saw none. "You probably started writing letters for her after that. You have to remember that was a long time ago, nearly two years."

Nana stared at him for quite some time before she spoke. "You may be right," she said. "I must not have been thinking clearly." She turned her wheelchair and wheeled up to the door, opening it. "Thank you for coming."

"Sure, anytime." Pete left and headed toward his office, feeling certain that the old busybody didn't buy his story. It didn't matter whether she did believe him. Her day was coming, and soon. He got to his office, went to his desk, grabbed the phone, and started dialing. On the third ring, his party answered. "It's me," Pete said. "I just got done talking with that old bat I told you about before. She's becoming too suspicious...yeah, I know. I told you I'd take care of her. When? Maybe some time next week. I first have to take care of the problem on the third floor." He listened as his partner explained that putting Rosie Carpenter in that room was only meant to have been a temporary solution. "I know it was. We'll get her out and take her over to the other place. And don't worry. I'll handle it personally. Tomorrow is Saturday, and there's less staff around. We'll get her at noon when the staff's busy feeding the residents." Pete hung up the phone, pulled out his cigarettes, and lit one up. He sat down in his chair, leaned back, exhaled, and watched the smoke curl upwards.

# Chapter 31

"THESE PANTS ARE too short for me," Mick complained to Howie. "Look at what happens when I sit down."

Howie got up from his chair, leaned over his desk, and peered at Mick's feet. When his partner sat down, the cuffs on his pants rose a couple of inches above his ribbed black socks.

"See what I mean? I look like a clown."

"I wouldn't complain if I were you." Adam pushed up his sleeve. "My jacket's got to be at least two sizes too big for me." He stood up and let his arms drop to his sides. The jacket sleeves extended beyond his knuckles.

"We look more like the three stooges than funeral directors," Mick lamented. "They're going to laugh us out of that nursing home. We should've insisted on getting these suits altered."

"Hey, look, I tried but they said they couldn't on such short notice." Howie sat back down and rolled up the cuffs of his pants one notch, thankful that his jacket fit reasonably well. "The manager of that rental place told me that we were lucky to get what we got. When you call on Friday afternoon and want to pick up the stuff that evening, you have to take what they have in stock...and they didn't have much." He brushed lint off his sleeve. "Supposedly, there are a lot of weddings going on this weekend." When the manager had asked why the last minute rush to rent the black suits, Howie replied, "A friend of ours is involved in a quickie shotgun wedding."

Mick shifted in his chair, plainly uncomfortable with his tight fitting jacket and pants. "What time do we pick up the hearse?" he asked Adam.

"Jim told me any time after eleven."

Howie glanced at the clock. They would need to leave soon. He wanted to get the hearse no later than eleven-fifteen. By getting the hearse then, they would have some time to spare in case of any unforeseen circumstances. "Are there any wakes going on at the funeral home this morning?"

"No. Jim said that for a Saturday, it's pretty quiet. I guess they'll have one later this afternoon, though." Adam pushed up his jacket sleeves again. "I think he's nervous about doing this. It'll be his neck if his boss ever finds out. He's counting on us having the hearse back within a couple of hours."

"That shouldn't be a problem." Howie took out his notepad and flipped to the page he had marked "Operation Pine Box." He had made a list of things they needed to do. "What do you say that we go over the plan once more?" He didn't wait for them to agree. "After we pick up the hearse we'll drive right to the nursing home."

Mick leaned forward and looked at Howie's list. A puzzled look came over his face. "What about your car? What do we do with that?"

"Once we pick up the hearse, we'll park my car on some side street a couple blocks away from the funeral home." Howie turned to Adam. "Why don't you drive the hearse and follow Mick and me until I ditch my car?"

"Will do."

"Now, we should get to the nursing home around eleven forty-five. We'll park right out in front." Howie paused, realizing that somebody should stay with the hearse. "Why don't you guys stand up for a minute?"

"What for?" Mick asked.

"Because I want to see which of you look worse." As soon as his partners stood up, Howie pointed at Mick. "You win."

"Does that mean I'm excused from this caper?" Mick said with a hint of hopefulness in his tone as he and Adam sat back down.

"No, that means you stay with the hearse," Howie said. "But you'll have to help get that gurney out of the back of it. And have the motor running when we come out. You're going to be the driver."

"That's okay with me." Mick gave a sideways glance at Adam and winked. "I've never driven a getaway hearse before."

"Okay, we've got that part settled." Howie turned his attention to Adam. "While Mick stays with the hearse, we'll go and get Rosie. By the time we get up there, it should be just about noon. That's good because most of the residents and staff should be in the dining room. We'll slip into her room, place her on the gurney, get to the back elevator, and—"

"The back elevator?" Adam said. "Doesn't that mean when we get to the main floor, we'll be at the opposite end of where the hearse is parked? Why don't we just take the front elevator and get off on the main lobby?"

"Because then we'd have to go past the nurses' station up on third," Howie explained. "I don't want to take that chance. That's why we're taking the back elevator. Besides, it's not that far away from her room." He checked his notes. "Now, once we get off the elevator, we'll head for the main lobby, take Rosie out through the entrance, and load her into the hearse." He pointed to Mick. "When you see us coming, make sure you get the hearse's back door open."

"No problem."

"And what do we do if some staff person stops us?" Adam asked.

"I'm counting that we don't run into anybody on the third floor."

"How about on the first floor?"

"We'll just say all the paperwork has already been filled out. They won't question that. " Howie closed his notepad. "I think that about covers it. Any questions?" He waited for a moment. "Good. Let's get going."

"I'LL MEET YOU guys at the back entrance at eleven forty-five and don't be late," Pete Larson said and then hung up the phone. He had it all arranged. The nurse they hired to take care of the Carpenter woman would give her another shot at eleven. That shot would be good for three or four hours; enough time to transport her. He told the nurse that she should leave as soon as she gave the shot. "Make sure you disappear and never show your face around here again," he warned. The warning, however, was unnecessary since she would lose her nursing license if anyone found out what she had done. Besides, she shouldn't have any gripes since she was so well paid.

He picked up the phone again and dialed his partner's number. While he waited, he plucked the last cigarette from his pack, crushed the empty package, and tossed it into the wastebasket. He had just lit his cigarette when his partner answered. "Hi, it's me," Pete said. "I was just calling to tell you that things are all set. Yeah, don't worry. Everything should run like clockwork." He took a drag off his cigarette. "Okay, I'll call you when the problem is solved." He hung up, took another drag, and checked the time. Eleven-fifteen. In less than an hour, they would have Rosie Carpenter out of this place. Once that was done, he would turn his attention to Nana.

# Chapter 32

ADAM'S FRIEND, JIM Lang, was waiting for them as they pulled up to the rear entrance of the funeral home. They got out of the car and Adam introduced Howie and Mick to his lanky, dark-haired classmate who had come up from one of the southern states to attend school. As Jim shook hands, he slowly looked them over.

"Y'all sure enough could pass for funeral directors. If y'all ever got tired of the detective business, I know of a couple of places looking for help." Jim's eyes twinkled with amusement as he again took note of their attire. "Before we got y'all a job, though, we'd have to have a little sit down talk with your tailor."

"No thanks," Adam said.

"I suppose I shouldn't ask just exactly what kind of case y'all are working on that y'all need a body wagon."

Howie smiled. "It's better that *y'all* not know."

Jim chuckled. "Okay, I get your drift."

"Now don't worry about the hearse," Howie said. "We'll have it back by one. Thanks for letting us use it."

"Sure enough." Jim handed Adam the keys, wished them good luck, and headed back toward the building. Before he went in, he waved at them and flashed a broad smile.

Adam got behind the wheel of the hearse and started the engine. Howie motioned for him to roll the window down.

"Just follow me and Mick," Howie said. "I'll turn right out of the driveway and then..." he looked down the street. "I'll take a left at the next block. When I park, pull up behind us and keep the engine running." He motioned to Mick and the two of them got into Howie's car. Once Howie made sure the hearse was behind him, he pulled out of the parking lot.

"Maybe we should turn on the headlights," Mick said.

Howie glanced over at his partner. "Y'all only do that when y'all got a body." Although they were joking around, he knew that it was just a way of handling the nervous tension; like doctors joking during an operation, or cops sharing dark humor after a shoot-out.

Within a few minutes, Howie parked on a quiet, residential side street. The hearse pulled up behind him. It seemed to be a perfect spot to handle the transfer once they got Rosie. Mick had asked why didn't they just leave the car at the funeral home and make the transfer there. "The reason is simple," Howie explained. "We would've drawn too much attention doing the transfer at the funeral home."

"Yeah, I guess that wouldn't look too good, would it?" Mick acknowledged.

"You've got that right. Adam's friend wouldn't appreciate people seeing a body being moved from a hearse to a car. It'd be bad for business."

Howie and Mick joined Adam in the hearse. Mick insisted on having the window seat leaving Howie no choice but to sit in the middle. "It smells like a flower shop in here," Mick said. He turned around and peered through the glass panel.

"What are you looking at?" Adam asked as he pulled away from the curb.

"I'm just making sure it's empty back there."

"It's eleven thirty," Howie noted. "We're right on schedule."

Adam turned the corner and got onto the main street. "What if the receptionist questions us when we come in?"

"Don't worry, I'll handle that," Howie said.

"What are you going to say?" Mick asked.

"I'm not sure yet."

PETE LARSON TOOK a sip of coffee and glanced at his watch. Eleven thirty-two. He was to meet his friends at the rear entrance in less than fifteen minutes. Everything should be set. He had gone to the supply room and gotten a wheelchair. If he had to, he would strap the Carpenter woman in the chair and take her out that way. He wasn't worried about anyone questioning him since he had made it a habit every now and then to give residents a ride in their wheelchairs. While pushing the old fools in their chairs, he was endearing himself to them and gaining their trust.

He leaned back in his chair and glanced around his office. If things went right, in a few more years he would be out of his crummy surroundings and living in style in some luxurious pad in Florida. The thought of warm weather, sunning himself on the beach, and young women in skimpy bathing suits brought a smile. He took another sip of coffee, closed his eyes, and allowed himself a few moments to daydream.

# Chapter 33

THE THREE DETECTIVES pulled up to the front entrance of the nursing home. Adam turned off the ignition and sat quietly, glancing around the area.

"How are we doing on time?" Mick asked.

Howie checked his watch. Eleven forty-eight, three minutes behind schedule. "We're doing okay," he said, aware that Mick and Adam's nervousness was evident by how quiet they had been on the ride over. "Let's go and get it done with." They got out of the hearse, walked around to the back of it, opened the door, and slid out the gurney.

"Okay, I know I'm staying with the hearse and I'll keep my eyes open for anything suspicious," Mick said as he shut the door. "But what if someone asked me who died?"

"Just say you don't know," Howie said. "Tell them your partners have the paperwork and that you're just the driver."

"Okay. Good luck, guys."

"Thanks," Adam said. "We'll need it." He helped Howie roll the gurney up the sidewalk toward the main doors. Several residents were sitting out in front; more were inside, peering out at them from the windows.

As they approached the entrance, one of the residents, an elderly gentleman with a white mustache and goatee to match, waved them over. "I sure hope that thing ain't for me," he said, using the stem of his unlit pipe to point to the gurney.

"Fred, you don't have to worry," a man sitting next to him said.

"And why's that?" Fred asked.

"Because you're too darn ornery to die. God isn't ready for you and the Devil doesn't want you." The man raised his cane and pointed to a fellow across from them sitting in a wheelchair and snoring. "Why don't you take Henry over there? He sleeps all the time, anyway."

Fred snickered. "Yeah, and he wouldn't even know the difference."

Howie offered a half smile. "Maybe next time." He held the doors open as Adam pushed the gurney into the lobby.

The receptionist looked up. Her eyes widened as she gave the two young men dressed in dark suits pushing the gurney a startled look. "Oh, my dear! No one notified me that there's been a death. Who died?"

"I've got the name right here," Howie said. "Just a minute." He made a show of checking the inside pocket of his suit coat, and then turned to Adam. "Have you got the slip?"

Adam shook his head.

"I must have left the slip back at the office," Howie said to the receptionist. "But I know it's someone on the second floor." He hoped that his little lie would further confuse the issue and give them some extra time for their getaway. "You don't have to give us directions, we've been here before," he continued, not giving the woman a chance to reply. "We'll take the back elevator."

"If you would like, I could call up to second and find out," the receptionist said. Just as she reached for the phone, it rang. She looked at the phone and then at Howie.

"Go ahead and answer it," Howie said. "Don't worry about us." He pointed to the gurney. "They'll know why we're up there."

The receptionist nodded and then picked up the phone. "The Golden Years Retirement Home. May I help you?"

"Let's get going," Howie said to Adam. They moved through the lobby and into the corridor that led to the elevator at the back of the building. "Our luck is holding," he said as they moved quickly past empty rooms. "Most of them must be in the dining room." Halfway down the hallway, a housekeeper coming out of a resident's room with her cleaning cart saw them and quickly moved to one side to let them past.

"Blessed Mary, Mother of God," the housekeeper uttered as she crossed herself.

Howie acknowledged the housekeeper's presence, but her eyes were fixed on the gurney. When they got to the elevator, he pushed the button. As they waited, a middle-age couple walked up and stood beside them. Howie noticed the woman glancing down at his rolled-up pants cuffs.

"We'll wait for the next one," the woman said after the elevator doors opened. Howie helped Adam push the gurney in and then pressed the third floor button. Just before the doors closed, the woman whispered something to her husband while pointing to Howie's pants cuffs.

"Wow!" Adam blew out a puff of air as he leaned against the wall of the elevator. "I'm glad we got past that first part."

"So am I, but now comes the challenging part." Howie checked his watch. Three minutes to twelve. So far, so good.

"DAMN IT! THEY should have been here ten minutes ago," Pete Larson said to no one in particular as he stood at the back door, looking through the glass panels at the parking lot. Just as he thought he was going to have to get the Carpenter woman by himself, the dark-blue van pulled in and his two associates got out. "It's about time!" Pete opened the door. "Hurry up!" he snarled. "We've got a job to do."

As soon as the elevator doors opened, Howie stepped out and looked toward the nurses' station. "I don't see anybody. Let's go." He and Adam rolled the gurney out and headed toward Rosie Carpenter's room. They opened Rosie's door, went in, and positioned the gurney along side of her bed. After lifting her onto the cart, they used the sheet from the bed to cover her.

"Look in the closet," Howie said. "See if any of her clothes are in there."

Adam opened the closet doors. "Nothing." He moved to the small dresser and opened a couple of the drawers. "Nothing here, either."

"Well, we're not going to worry about that now. Let's get out of here." Howie slowly opened the door and peeked out. "Okay, it's clear." He and Adam pushed the gurney into the corridor and headed for the elevator.

"Push the third floor button," Pete said as he wheeled the empty wheelchair into the elevator. "And Sam, you stay here and wait. Jerry and I will go up and get her."

Sam grabbed the elevator door, preventing it from closing. "Why do I have to stay here?" he asked with a hurt look on his face.

"Because, stupid, if anybody comes and wants to use this elevator, I want you to tell them it's out of service."

"But what if they want to go up another floor?"

Pete's hand curled into a fist. He felt like smashing some common sense into the dope. "Tell them to take the elevator in the lobby or use the stairs. We need this one so we can get out of here fast. Understand? Now, let go of the door! We're wasting time."

Howie and Adam wheeled the gurney to the elevator just as a housekeeper came around the corner. When she saw the sheet-draped body, her eyes widened but she walked past them without saying a word.

"I bet the first person she sees, she's going ask who died," Howie said. "Let's hope she doesn't talk to anyone until we get off this floor."

Adam pointed to the indicator lights above the elevator doors. "Somebody's on the way up."

"Quick," Howie said. "Duck around the corner and hope they go the other way when they get off." He and Adam pushed the gurney around the corner just as the elevator doors opened. Howie peeked and saw Pete Larson and another man get off. He felt a tug on his coat.

*Who is it?* Adam mouthed.

Howie put his finger to his lips. "Shhh." Only after the two men headed in the other direction was he able to breathe a sigh of relief. "Come on," he told Adam. They moved the gurney to the elevator again and as soon as Howie pressed the button, the doors opened. "Hit that *close door* button," he said. After the doors closed Adam pressed the first floor button and then took a deep breath. "That was close," Howie said, giving Adam a nervous smile. His partner swallowed hard and nodded his head.

"WHAT THE--" PETE couldn't believe his eyes when he and Jerry walked into Rosie Carpenter's room.

"Maybe she's in the bathroom," Jerry said.

Pete gave him a disbelieving look and then rushed out of the room. He wanted to find the nearest staff person and find out what the hell was going on.

"WE'RE NOT OUT of the woods, yet," Howie said as he waited for the elevators doors to open onto the main floor. "We still have to go through the lobby and hope that no one stops us." When the doors opened, the stocky man standing facing them with a startled look took both him and Adam by surprise. "Excuse us," Howie said. The man didn't move. "Excuse us," Howie repeated. "Ah, we have to get this body to the funeral home…" He glanced around and then spoke in a hushed tone as though sharing a secret. "It needs to be embalmed before…well, you know."

The man eyed the gurney and then looked at the two men in black suits, his eyes shifting from one to another. He stepped aside and then removed his baseball cap as the gurney moved past him.

"Thank you," Howie said as he and Adam moved down the corridor. They had nearly gotten to the main lobby when they heard a commotion behind them. "Oh, no," Howie muttered, looking back. The man in the baseball cap was talking with Pete Larson and another guy, and was pointing in their direction. Immediately, the three men rushed toward them.

"What are we going to do?" Adam asked.

"I don't—" Howie spotted the firebox alarm on the wall. As soon as he pulled it, the fire doors behind him closed, bells rang, and lights flashed. "Let's go!" he yelled. They rushed toward the entrance doors, thankfully observing that the receptionist was too busy with the switchboard to even notice them.

"Hey, look!" Adam cried as he pointed to the scene at the curb. An elderly man, sitting in a wheelchair and wheeling a cane, had Mick backed up against the side of the hearse.

"Oh, man! Not Elmer!" Howie and Adam moved quickly toward the hearse.

"I've got him cornered!" Elmer the one-time truant officer declared as Howie and Adam came up with the gurney.

"Will you tell this guy I'm with you?" Mick said, his arms in front of his face to shield himself from his would-be attacker.

"Elmer, I don't have time to explain, but he's one of my partners."

"Is that so?" Elmer lowered his cane. "Well he looks like that guy you described."

Howie took a glance back at the entrance. "Look, Elmer, the bad guys are after us. You can help us if you slow them up at the entrance door."

"Roger that. You can count on me." Elmer spun his wheelchair around and charged toward the entrance door.

"Come on!" Howie yelled to his partners. "Let's get her in and get out of here!"

Mick ran to the back of the hearse and opened the door. "What's going on?" he asked as his partners wheeled up with the gurney.

"I'll fill you in later," Howie said. The three of them picked up the gurney and slid it into the hearse. Howie slammed the door. "Let's go now!" They piled into the front seat. Mick stepped on the gas and pulled away with the wheels squealing. In the distance, they heard the wail of sirens. "That must be the fire trucks," Howie said. He glanced back at the front entrance and smiled. Elmer had parked his wheelchair directly in front of the doors and had slid his cane through the door handles to prevent them from opening.

On the way back to the funeral home, Howie shared with Mick what had happened. "Wow!" Mick kept repeating as he heard the details. When they got to where Howie had parked his car, Mick pulled along side of it. Opening the back of the hearse, they slid the gurney out and placed it on the ground. While Howie opened the door to the backseat of the car, Mick and Adam threw back the sheet and lifted Rosie. An older gentleman on the other side of the street walking his dog stopped and stared at them. A car pulled up and the woman driver rolled down her window.

"What's going on?" she asked.

"The hearse broke down," Howie replied.

The woman gasped, her mouth dropped open, and her eyes doubled in size as she watched Mick and Adam struggle to place Rosie's body into the back seat of Howie's car. The woman sped off without saying another word.

After they had covered Rosie with the sheet, Adam turned to Howie. "The hearse broke down?"

"Hey, what else was I suppose to say?"

Mick tapped Howie on the shoulder. "We better get going."

"I'll drive the hearse back," Adam said. "I'll meet you guys there."

After they picked up Adam at the funeral home, they drove to Howie's apartment, and parked in front of the entrance. They got out of the car, opened the back door, and lifted Rosie out, draping her arms around Mick and Adam's shoulders as they carried her in. Once they got upstairs, they laid her on Howie's bed, shut the door to the bedroom, and went out into the office.

"I'm sure glad that's over," Mick said as he plopped down in a chair.

Adam collapsed into the chair next to Mick. "The question is what do we do now?"

"The only thing we can do is to wait until she comes around," Howie said.

"How long is that going to take?" Adam asked.

"I don't know. Probably a couple of days for the drugs to wear off." Howie turned to Mick. "Can you do me a favor?" he asked. "Would you ask Mary to come over and help?"

"Sure, no problem. I know she'd be happy to do that for us."

"Great, but tell her as little as possible." Although Howie trusted Mick's fiancée, the less she knew, the better. "Just say Rosie's a key witness in a case we're working on."

PETE LARSON STORMED into his office, slammed the door, and lit up a cigarette as he paced back and forth. He couldn't very well call the police about Rosie being taken, and he just finished explaining to the third floor staff that she wasn't dead; that the family just wanted her to be taken to another facility. He picked up the phone and dialed. The person on the other end answered on the second ring. "Someone took the Carpenter woman before we got to her. You heard me right." He took a couple drags of his cigarette and then snuffed it out in the ashtray. "It was that nosey detective I've told you about. I've a pretty good idea where he may have taken her. Don't worry. I'll take care of it."

# Chapter 34

HOWIE YAWNED. ONLY nine o'clock on a Sunday evening, but he felt so exhausted that it could just as well have been midnight. In the nearly thirty-six hours since they had rescued Rosie Carpenter, he had barely slept. Sitting at his desk, reviewing his notes, he now had a hard time keeping his eyes open. Last night he had tried to sleep on the lumpy couch in his office. What a joke that had been. Besides tossing and turning trying to find a comfortable position, he couldn't stretch out without his feet hanging over the end of it. His partners would have found that amusing. Since his junior high days he had always told them that he hoped to grow another seven inches to hit six feet. While Mick and Adam both hit six feet or better by the end of high school, he only managed to add a couple of inches. Before he became a detective, he worried about his height until he discovered that he and Humphrey Bogart were equal in stature.

After stifling a yawn, he tossed his pen on the desk and rubbed his eyes. It was time to get up and move around. He walked into his living quarters, went into the bathroom, turned on the cold water, and splashed his face a couple of times. After drying off with a towel, he looked in the mirror. Blue eyes that were usually bright and sparkling were as faded as an old pair of jeans. Before heading back to his office, he stopped to listen at his bedroom door. No sound. He opened the door a crack and peeked in. Rosie Carpenter appeared to be resting comfortably in his bed. Mick's fiancée, Mary, had been over yesterday and brought some nightclothes, a bathrobe, and some personal items. "I think she can also wear these," Mary said as she put a pair of tan slacks and a light-mauve sweater on the chair next to the bed.

It had been close to eleven last night when Rosie came around enough to mumble a few words. Howie assured her that she was safe and that she should rest. "We'll talk in the morning after you get some more sleep," he said.

This morning, Rosie had been awake enough to eat a half piece of toast and have a little hot tea while sitting up in bed. Mary had stopped over, and with the help of Howie, took Rosie into the bathroom. At Mary's suggestion, he had changed the bed sheets while she and Rosie were occupied. Once they had gotten her back to bed, he again had told her to get some sleep and that they would talk when she felt up to it. Mary had stayed for a few minutes longer and then left. "If you need me, don't hesitate to call me," she had said before leaving.

As Howie now gazed upon Rosie in his bed, he wondered what information she had wanted to share with them. He quietly closed the door, went back to his desk, got out his notepad, and began reviewing his notes. *Let's see, what do we have? The sister of LaMar Jones says she believes her brother was killed. Okay, assuming he was, who are the possible suspects? Leo Rappaport.* He chewed on the end of his pen for a moment and then wrote the word *motive* and underlined it. *Jealousy; Leo was jealous because LaMar was coming on to Rachel, the boss' daughter.* He turned the page and jotted down the name of Ken Pritchett. *What's this guy's racket anyway? Whatever it was, LaMar was on to him. If he killed LaMar, what would be his motive, though?* He drummed his fingers on the desk. *Blackmail? It could be, but for what? Maybe LaMar caught Pritchett stealing from the place. Stealing what? Chocolate Angels?* He wrote the word *motive*, put a question mark behind it, and flipped the page. He swung his chair around until it faced the door leading into his living quarters. *What about Rosie Carpenter?* He put a question mark behind her name. *If she killed LaMar, why would someone want to kidnap her? What is she hiding?* He glanced at the clock, massaged his eyes, and decided that he was too tired to go on. He hoped he would sleep better tonight. If he didn't, he thought that he might have to start sleeping in his chair. "Maybe tomorrow, we'll get some answers," he muttered as he headed for the couch.

# Chapter 35

HOWIE WOKE TO the ringing of the telephone. Thinking he was in his bed, he reached in the direction of where he thought his nightstand would be and promptly tumbled onto the floor. If it hadn't been for the telephone continuing to ring, he would have stayed there. At least, he could stretch out. He slowly picked himself up and stumbled over to his desk. The light coming in through the window told him it was morning. Early morning, but morning.

He blinked a couple of times as he focused on the wall clock to make sure he was reading it right, wondering who would be calling at such an ungodly hour as ten after six. "MAC Detective Agency," he mumbled and then wet his lips so they wouldn't stick together. "Howie Cummins speaking."

"Have you caught those crooks yet?"

Howie resisted the urge to hang up. "Hello...Nana," he said with little enthusiasm as he settled into his chair. "What can I do for you?"

"Have you tracked down those rocks?"

"Rocks? What are you—"

"What's wrong with you?" Nana yelled. "Have you got cobwebs in your head this morning? Haven't you learned crook-talk by now?"

It took Howie a moment to realize what she meant by *rocks*. "We haven't tracked down the diamonds yet, but we're still in the process of checking some leads." It was a lie, but he didn't have the heart or the energy to admit that he had no leads. After all, how can you have leads on missing diamonds when there are no diamonds in the first place? He rested his elbow on his desk and supported his chin in the palm of his hand. With his eyes slowly closing, he half listened to her go on about some person that she needed to discuss with him. "Who did you say it was?" he asked, stifling a yawn.

"Pete Larson, the security guy!" Nana shouted. "Didn't I tell you to clean the wax out of your ears?"

"Howie sighed. "I'm working on it."

"Good. Now what time are you coming?"

Larson must have talked to her about what happened on Saturday. "Look, I just can't come over today."

"Why not?"

"I just can't."

"Then come tomorrow!" Nana said, her tone indicating that she wasn't about to take no for an answer.

"Okay, tomorrow for sure."

"Today's better because it's urgent"

"Yes, I know." *It's always urgent.* Howie yawned just as she mentioned Larson's name again. He didn't hear what she said about him, but wasn't about to ask her to repeat it. "We'll talk about it tomorrow, okay? I'm just too—" She had already hung up.

Howie headed back to the couch. At first, he lay on his stomach with his feet draped over the end of the couch. When that didn't work, he curled up on his side, and then after awhile, he lay on his back. After repeatedly trying various sleeping positions, he finally decided that he wouldn't be able to get back to sleep. He lay staring at the ceiling for a long time. With effort he brought himself to a sitting position and stayed that way for several more minutes. He finally stood up and headed for the kitchen, first stopping and listening at his bedroom door. Nothing.

After making a pot of extra strong coffee, he poured himself a cup and then rummaged through the cupboards until he found a crumpled bag with a couple of plain donuts that were so hard that they could be used to hammer railroad spikes. Grabbing the bag of donuts and picking up his coffee cup, he found his way back to his office and sat down at his desk. He picked up his notepad, looked at what he had written last night, and put it aside. While he gnawed at a donut, he began reading an article in his *Police Gazette* magazine. Halfway through the article, the words began to merge together. When he found himself reading the same sentence for the third time, he gave up. Using his forearms as a pillow, he laid his head on the desk, telling himself that it would be only for a few minutes and then he would finish reading the article, whatever it was. At that point, he was too sleepy to remember.

IT WAS NEARLY eight when Howie woke up. His neck was stiff and his arms ached from being used as pillows, but it was a small price to pay for a couple more hours of sleep. He stretched and then reached for his cup of coffee only to discover part of his donut floating in it. He took a quick shower and got dressed in clothes he had set aside the night before. The clothes he slept in were stuffed in a cupboard under the kitchen sink. After making himself a fresh cup of coffee, he headed back to his desk.

Around mid-morning, he heard noises coming from his bedroom. He got up and stood in the doorway and listened. The bedroom doorknob slowly turned and Rosie came out wearing the robe that Mary had brought over. Even with uncombed hair and no makeup, she appeared quite attractive. She first looked toward the kitchen and then at him.

"Good morning," Howie said. "Come on in and sit down."

She took a shaky step, placing her hand against the wall for support. "I...I...don't know...if I can."

"Just hang on." Howie walked over and took her by the arm to steady her as they moved into his office. He got her to a chair and pulled up the other chair to sit next to her. "How are you doing?" he asked.

She didn't answer right away. "I'm...ah, still groggy, but..." She slowly looked around at her surroundings. "But I, ah...I think I'm okay."

"Would you like something to eat?"

Rosie shook her head but changed her mind. "Maybe...ah, some toast and hot tea."

"Anything else?"

"No, thank you."

"Okay, coming right up."

"Where is your, ah..."

"My bathroom?"

"Yes." Rosie's eyes reflected a note of concern as though she had suddenly become aware of her circumstances. She clutched the top of her bathrobe, gathering it at her neck. "Oh, dear. I don't have anything with me."

"Don't worry about that," Howie said, reassuring her with a smile and sharing that his partner's fiancée had bought some items for her. Mary had purchased a comb, toothbrush, and some other things that she thought Rosie would want to have. "They're in an overnight case," he said. "Just stay here, I'll get it for you." After he got the case, he helped her to the bathroom, gave her a clean towel and washcloth, and closed the door. "I'll wait until you come out before making the toast. That way, it'll be nice and warm."

Twenty minutes went by and Howie began to get concerned. He went to the bathroom door and knocked. "Everything okay?"

"Yes, I'll...be out in a few minutes," she said, her voice sounding stronger. "You can make my toast now."

By the time the toast popped up, the bathroom door opened. Although still pale, Rosie had combed her hair and applied makeup. Howie was impressed at the transformation. The woman had gone from just being attractive to gorgeous. He helped her to the chair and then brought in the toast and hot tea. After she finished her toast and was sipping her second cup of tea, she seemed more relaxed. Color had come back into her cheeks and her eyes had a little more of a sparkle to them.

"I think, ah...I'm ready to talk now." Rosie put her teacup down and rubbed her forehead with the back of her hand. "My brain...it feels...a little...a little..."

"Jumbled?"

"Yes...jumbled."

"We can wait if you'd like." Howie hoped, however, she would say no. He was anxious to get some answers from her.

"No, I...ah...want to talk." Rosie spoke slowly as if it was an effort to string words together to express thoughts. "You...ah...must have questions."

Howie took out his notepad, wondering if she had forgotten that she had contacted him because she was so frightened. "Why don't you tell me about LaMar," he said, deciding to take it slow and see where it goes. He opened his notepad. "I hope you don't mind if I take a few notes?"

Rosie shook her head. She picked up her teacup, took a sip, and set the cup down. "His death..." She began to rock ever so slightly in her chair. "I...ah...don't believe was an accident."

"What makes you think that?"

"Because he, ah...called me the day...the morning of the day he died." The pain in Rosie's voice was obvious, matching that in her eyes. "He said he had found out something."

"About what?"

"I...don't know. He...ah...didn't want to talk over the phone. He said that his roommate...I...forget his name..." She closed her eyes for a moment. "I should know it..."

"No problem, we have his name."

"Good." Rosie took a deep breath as though relieved that she didn't have to remember the man's name. "He was in the other room and LaMar, ah...didn't want to risk the chance of being overheard." She took another sip of tea.

Howie waited until she set the teacup down. Her movements were as slow as her speech. "Are you saying you don't think he and his roommate shared things about their personal lives?"

Rosie nodded. "They only roomed together to share expenses."

"Why didn't you and LaMar get together that day he died?"

"He had some doctor's appointment." Rosie paused. "Or maybe, ah...a dentist's appointment...one of the two. I'm sorry. I'm...I'm not thinking very clearly. After the appointment he was going to work." She closed her eyes for a second. "He said he'd call me the next day and...ah, we'd get together and talk." Her hand shook as she picked up her teacup. "Excuse me," she said as she put her cup down and took a tissue from her pocket to dab the corner of her eyes. Her next words were spoken in a whisper. "But we...ah...never got together."

"How did you happen to end up at the nursing home?"

Fear replaced her tears. "I...don't remember. They must've..." She chewed on her lip while staring at her teacup. As the clock ticked off several minutes, she sat silently, wringing her hands. "I'm sorry," she finally said. "But I...I don't remember."

"Whom are you referring to when you say *they?*"

Rosie avoided his eyes.

"Look," Howie began gently, wanting to put her more at ease. "If you want us to help, you have to cooperate." He felt bad about pressing her, but didn't want to miss this opportunity. "Believe it or not, we're the good guys."

"I...I know." She handed him the teacup. "Can we talk later? I...ah, need to lie down again."

"I'll tell you what. I'm meeting my partners for an early lunch. I'll bring something back for you and then we'll talk some more. Okay?"

Rosie got up from the chair without assistance, but needed help to the bedroom. Once Howie got her in bed and covered her up, she reached out and gripped his hand, surprising him by the strength of her grip. "LaMar was murdered. I'm convinced of that. And I'm...I'm so afraid."

"Don't worry. You're in safe hands now. Nobody knows where you are. You just get some rest. I'll be back shortly. Once you eat some solid food, you'll feel better."

# Chapter 36

HOWIE CHECKED ON Rosie before he left to have lunch with his partners. Although still asleep, she seemed quite restless. He went back to his office and dialed Mary's number, hoping that she could come over and stay with the Carpenter woman while he was gone. After the eighth ring, however, he hung up, drummed his fingers on the desk, and got up to leave, locking the office door behind him.

It took him ten minutes to cover the four blocks to the Rainbow Café. He didn't mind the walk; the warm June day and the bright sunshine gave him a chance to get his mind off the case for a while. After this case, he would perhaps take a few days of vacation. Maybe he would go up north to Duluth and spend some time on the north shore. When he entered the café, Mick waved at him from the back booth.

"How's the Carpenter woman doing?" Mick asked as Howie slid in next to Adam.

"She's doing okay." Howie motioned for the waitress to come over. Although he felt that Rosie was safe, he still didn't want to be away from her too long. The woman had a mind of her own, and just might decide to take off. When the waitress stopped, he and Adam each ordered a hamburger and a cup of coffee. Mick ordered a couple of burgers and a large glass of milk. "Oh, and I'd like a hamburger to go," Howie said. "And would you give me some fries with it?" he added thinking that Rosie might be hungry by the time he got back.

"Did you get a chance to talk with her?" Adam asked Howie after the waitress left.

"A little. She's still weak, but she told me that she doesn't think LaMar's death was an accident."

"She doesn't?" Adam gnawed at his lip. "So what does she think happened?"

"We didn't get that far." Howie recounted the phone call she received from LaMar the morning he died. "Although she didn't come out and say it, I got the impression that she doesn't trust Jack Miller, his roommate."

"I don't blame her," Mick said. "Miller seemed a little suspicious to me. Does she think that he had something to do with LaMar's death?"

"That's..." Howie paused when the waitress came up. After they were served their drinks, the waitress left. He waited until she was out of earshot. "That's one of the questions I want to ask her."

"What about what happened to her?" Adam took a sip of coffee. "Did she tell you why she called you in such a panic and how she ended up in the nursing home?"

"No, she was very vague about all of that." Howie couldn't forget the fear in her eyes. "She's terrified for her life. When I asked her who took her to the nursing home, she said she couldn't remember."

"What do you think?" Mick asked. "Do you believe her?"

"I don't know. She's too scared right now to talk." Howie waited as a customer walked by. "I'm convinced she knew who it was, but didn't want to tell me...or wouldn't tell me."

"I'm not sure if I follow you," Adam said.

"What if she and an accomplice killed LaMar? Or what if she hired someone to do it?" Howie looked on as his partners exchanged glances. "And now this other person is concerned that she might talk."

Mick took a sip of his milk. "So that would mean she couldn't very well name that person without fear of being implicated herself."

"Exactly."

Adam frowned. "But why drug her and stick her in a nursing home? That just doesn't add up."

"You don't have to tell me that." Howie glanced out the window at the traffic on Broadway. The more he got into this case, the more confusing it became. "It doesn't make much sense to me either when I hear myself trying to explain it. I hope to find out more when I go back and talk with her after we eat." He took a sip of coffee.

"Are we finished with Rosie for now?" Mick asked Howie.

"I guess so. Why?"

"I'd like to change the subject."

"Go ahead."

Mick nodded. "Any luck with Jerome's grandmother?" he asked, his tone sounding apologetic, as though the mention of Jerome and Nana might spoil his boss' lunch. "I'm asking because I saw him the other day and he asked if there was anything new to report."

Howie toyed with the saltshaker for a moment. "I'm getting nowhere with that. I haven't even been able to prove that any diamonds were missing."

"Didn't she say her diamond ring was missing?" Adam asked.

"Yeah, but there's no proof."

"He's right," Mick said. "Jerome told me that he never actually saw her ring, but he believes every word his grandmother says."

The waitress brought their food, asked if there was anything else they wanted, and hearing no other requests, she left.

When Mick bit into his medium-rare hamburger, the juices dripped onto his chin. "Do you guys remember when we use to come here when we were in high school?" he asked, using his napkin to wipe his chin.

Adam squirted catsup on his burger and handed the bottle to Howie. "Yeah, that seems like a long time ago."

Mick set his hamburger down and gestured at Howie while directing his words at Adam. "Our boss here really cooked up some schemes in here, didn't he?"

"Adam's right," Howie said. "That was a long time ago." He wanted to leave that image of him behind, buried and forgotten. Whenever he saw former classmates now, he made sure they went away thinking of him as a detective who took his work seriously, rather than being remembered as having been voted the class clown.

The three young men continued to reminisce about the days gone past while they ate. Mick was in the middle of sharing a story when Howie took note of the time. "Hey, I better get going. Why don't you guys come back with me?"

"You don't think having the three of us there will intimidate her, do you?" Adam asked.

"I don't think so. It'll make her feel more secure knowing that there are three of us around to watch over and protect her."

After paying their bill, they walked back to Howie's office, stopping at Kass' Drugstore. Howie needed to find out when he was scheduled to work again.

Much to Kass' surprise, they turned down his offer of free banana splits. "What's the matter, are you boys sick or something?"

Howie explained that they didn't have time and that they would have to take a rain check on his offer. If Kass had his way, the whole world would be eating banana splits.

"Well, just remember," Kass said. "I have an ulterior motive."

Mick asked, "And what would that be, as if we didn't know?"

"I just want to be nice to the detectives who someday I know will be famous," Kass replied with a twinkle in his eyes. "When that day comes, then my drugstore will become a famous landmark and I can retire."

Howie and his partners were still musing about Kass' remark when Howie abruptly stopped as they reached the top of the stairs to his office.

"What's the matter?" Mick asked

"The door," Howie whispered as he pointed to his office door that was ajar. "I locked it before I left." He tossed the bag containing Rosie's food to Adam and rushed toward the open door of his bedroom. The tipped-over lamp and the bed covers flung in a heap on the floor told him that he didn't need to search the apartment. Rosie Carpenter was gone and she didn't go of her own free will.

# Chapter 37

"I'M GLAD YOU two could make it," Howie said as Mick and Adam sat down and got comfortable. Mick took his usual place on the left, having claimed that over time the old leather chair conformed to the contours of his body. Howie had asked his partners to drop by the office so that the three of them could discuss what if anything could be done about finding Rosie Carpenter. "It's been nearly a week since Rosie's disappeared and I've no idea as to where she might be," he reluctantly confessed, feeling guilty that he had left her alone that day.

"Are you still sleeping on the couch?" Adam asked.

"Oh, yeah."

"How much longer are you going to do that?"

"For as long as it takes to find her. Every time I lay down in my own bed, it reminds me that she's still missing and then I lie awake trying to figure out what can be done. After a couple of hours, I end up on the couch." Howie ran his hand through his hair a couple of times. He was tired and his body ached, but most of all, he was angry at himself for not having stayed with Rosie that day. "I still toss and turn most of the night, though."

"It sounds like you're not going to get much sleep until she's found," Mick said.

"That's the way it goes." Howie rubbed his forehead in an attempt to ward off a headache he felt coming on. "Now, how about you?" he asked Mick. "Did you find out anything new?" He hoped that his partner had turned up a lead.

"Not a thing." Mick settled back in the chair, stretching his long legs out until his feet disappeared under Howie's desk. "I've checked her apartment every day. I even wedged a match between the door and the casing, near the bottom of the door like you told me." He shrugged. "The last time I looked, though, the match was still there."

"Just keep on it." Howie felt good that his partners used some of the tricks of the trade he had taught them. The match in the door had served them well in the past. "How about that neighbor lady down the hall?" he asked as he opened his notepad. "Anything from her?"

"Nope, she hasn't seen Rosie since she saw her coming out of the apartment with that guy. When I asked if she's heard any noises coming from the apartment in the past week, she said that it's been as quiet as a church mouse in there." Mick waited until Howie finished writing in his notepad. "And she's the type of snoopy neighbor who'd know things like that." He straightened in his chair and leaned forward. "And get this. She tells me she's been taking in Rosie's mail so it won't pile up in the mailbox."

"Maybe she's just trying to be a good neighbor," Adam pointed out.

"I doubt that," Mick said. "I think she's more interested in getting an eyeful of what sort of mail her neighbor gets."

Howie had also considered how he might get his hands on Rosie's mail. A letter could easily be steamed open and resealed; a practice that Mick would tolerate for the sake of the case, but not Adam. One of the lessons that Adam had to learn was that being a preacher and being a detective were two entirely different things. His partner's inner struggle came from trying to live having a foot in each world. "Perhaps I should also have a look at her mail," he said to Mick, ignoring Adam's look of rebuke.

"That's a good idea," Mick said, settling back in the chair again. "Who knows? It just might produce a lead."

Howie jotted himself a reminder to check on it. "Anything else?"

"Yeah. That neighbor asked me if she should notify the police."

Adam gave Mick a questioning look. Of the three of them, Adam was most in favor of involving the police whenever possible. "What did you tell her?"

"That Rosie's whereabouts is being looked into and for the present time, it isn't considered a police matter." Mick looked to Howie. "Is that okay I said that?"

"Of course. If we have to contact the police, we'll do it, but don't worry, I'll handle that." Howie wasn't thrilled about the cops being notified. While concerned that outside involvement might compromise the case, he was determined to solve the case on his own. If the Carpenter woman didn't show up soon, however, he'd leak the word that she was missing to Detective Jim Davidson, his contact within the police department. That would satisfy Adam. JD might ask some questions but would keep it confidential as a favor. "What did you find out at the place where she works?" he asked Adam.

"Not much." Adam's tone indicated a hint of discouragement. "The manager told me that they haven't heard from her and that if she doesn't call him within a couple of days, she's going to be out of a job."

"Really?" Mick said. "That's being pretty tough on her."

"I know. According to her boss, she has always been a good worker and seldom missed. You'd think he'd be a little more understanding." Adam's eyes flashed with anger. His partners knew that he didn't like injustice in whatever form it took. He had told them several times that one of the things that drew him towards becoming a minister was that he could work at helping correct some of the injustices he saw within society. "Taking her job away without giving her a chance to explain isn't fair."

"That's the way the world operates," Howie said, not impressed with his partner's social conscience. "Get used to it."

"Maybe you can!" Adam snapped. "But I can't!"

Howie opened his mouth but didn't say anything. He and Adam, however, locked eyes.

"Come on, guys," Mick said. "We're here to talk about the case." He turned to Adam. "What do you think may have happened to her?" he asked in a gentle tone meant to defuse the showdown.

Adam continued to glare at Howie. "I don't know," he finally said, his eyes shifting toward Mick. "But I hope she's okay."

"If we only had a lead," Mick said. "It sure is frustrating. We don't know anything more today than we did last week."

Mick's words hit Howie like a sledgehammer. "I shouldn't have left her alone!" he cried, slamming his fist on the desk with such force that a pencil bounced and rolled off the edge onto the floor. Mick and even Adam were startled by his outcry, and for quite some time the only sound in the room was the clock ticking off the passage of time.

"Don't be so hard on yourself," Mick said, using the same tender tone he had used with Adam. "How could you've known? And besides, you weren't gone that long."

"But I shouldn't have left her alone." Howie's headache had come on full-blown. "It was an amateur mistake."

Mick sat up and leaned forward as if he was about to underscore a point to one of his students at school. "Let's think about this some more. Weren't we going to do some brainstorming about this case?"

Howie nodded. Even with his headache and his hand hurting from slamming the desk, he felt better having let off his pent-up frustrations. Some of his frustration, however, resulted from Adam's self-righteous sense of justice. But this wasn't the time to knock heads with him on that.

"Try this one on for size," Mick said. "Is it possible that Rosie had a change of heart about talking to us and that she took off on her own?"

"He might have a point there," Adam said, his edgy tone having disappeared. His partners were well aware that his mood swings changed like the weather in Minnesota. "We've been working on the assumption that somebody came in and kidnapped her. Maybe she just walked out."

"I don't know about that." Howie intentionally kept his tone neutral. They had checked the door and couldn't tell if it had been jimmied. "What about the lamp that was tipped over?" he asked, unwilling to accept what his partners were saying until he heard more.

"Okay, the lamp's a problem," Mick agreed. "But she could've knocked it over herself to make it appear as if there had been a struggle."

Adam spoke up. "Mick has a point. This whole thing could've been staged to look like she put up a fight. You know, to throw us off track. It's a possibility."

Howie wasn't buying it, and by the tone in his partner's voices, they weren't fully convinced either. "But what about the clothes that Mary brought for her to wear?" he asked. "We can't forget that little detail." His partner's faces were already conceding defeat. "Those clothes were still in the closet. She wouldn't have gotten too far wearing the bathrobe. I know people on Broadway have seen some strange things, but someone walking down the street in a bathrobe and slippers in broad daylight...I don't think so. Someone would've told us about that." He gave his partners a knowing half-smile, appreciating their attempt to lessen his guilt. "Look, I understand what you're trying to do, but if you could have seen the fear in her eyes, you wouldn't be saying the things you are right now."

"Okay, but consider this angle," Mick said, seemingly unwilling to give up his suspicions about the Carpenter woman. "Doesn't Rosie hope to be an actress some day? Who's to say that the fear you saw in her eyes was real or a put-on?"

Howie opened his mouth to reply, but didn't. He had forgotten about her aspirations to be an actress. "If she was acting, then she's got my vote for an Academy Award," he said, adding, "And we won't know until we find her, will we?" His mind was spinning and he wanted to explore another aspect of the case. There was nothing more they could do about this part for now. "Look, can we move on?" His partners nodded. "Good." He turned to Adam. "Anything happening at the candy factory?"

"Not much. It's been pretty quiet. Either Pritchett is laying low or he's outsmarting me." Adam's voice revealed frustration. "I've been keeping an eye on the guy as much as I can. The only thing he's done that seemed a little odd happened a couple of nights ago."

"And what was that?" Howie asked.

"I had just finished cleaning up in the main work area upstairs and had put my stuff away when Pritchett came in." Adam shifted in his chair, appearing uncomfortable with what he was about to say. "He didn't see me because I ducked in an alcove. Luckily, only a few lights were on and I was in the shadows."

Mick patted Adam on the shoulder. "Very sneaky. I'm proud of you. You're really taking this undercover work to heart."

"No, I'm not!" Adam's eyes darkened. "And I hope I never do!"

"So what did you see?" Howie quickly asked, not wanting another flare-up.

Adam hesitated before replying. "This is going to sound bizarre, but Pritchett took some chocolate out of that vat."

"You're kidding," Mick said.

"No, he used a dipper and just dipped into the chocolate and poured it into what looked like a coffee can," Adam replied, and then turned to Howie. "He was wearing gloves so he wouldn't burn himself. He must've filled his container about half-way and then left."

Howie rubbed his forehead, took a deep breath and blew it out slowly as he turned to a new page in his notepad. "What do you think he was doing?"

"Maybe he's got a sweet tooth," Mick quipped and then added in a serious tone, "He could be taking it home as an added benefit."

"What are you getting at?" Adam asked.

"Just this. Maybe this guy wants to make his own chocolate angels. From what I hear, the chocolate they use is very expensive." Mick turned back to Howie. "Pritchett could even be selling it on the side. I read someplace that a high percentage of people steal from their employers. It's the national pastime."

"Keep an eye on him," Howie said. "I can't believe the guy's doing that just to satisfy a chocolate craving or to make a little extra dough on the side. There's got to be another reason." He rubbed his forehead again, hoping the throbbing would go away. As soon as his partners left, he would take a couple of aspirins...maybe a whole handful the way his headache was progressing. "Anything happening with Hooknose?"

"Not a bit. The only time I see him is when I'm talking with Rachel. It's sort of creepy the way he always shows up unannounced." Adam chewed his lip as he stared at the edge of Howie's desk.

"What is it?" Howie asked, having seen that reluctant look before.

"Well..." Adam looked toward the window for several long seconds as though trying to decide how to share whatever he was going to say. "You guys should know that the two of us are going out to eat before I go into work tonight."

Mick's eyebrows shot up. "Wow! Going on a date, huh? You must be getting soft on her."

"It's nothing like that!" Adam snapped, showing a rare display of anger at Mick. "I just want to get to know her better."

"That's good," Howie said, surprised at Adam's outburst. "And while you're at it, see if you can get anything from her about LaMar's death. Be casual about it and—"

"I wasn't looking at our having supper together in that way." Adam's eyes revealed his irritation at Howie's suggestion.

"Look, you're there because we've been hired to investigate a possible murder." Howie intentionally kept his tone level, but set his jaw to make sure his partner knew that he saw the situation differently. He seldom played the *boss* card, but if he had to with Adam, he would. "If you want to start something with her, that's fine...but you do your romancing after we've finished with the case."

"Maybe I'm finished with it now!" Adam said as he stood up.

"Maybe you are!" Howie shot back.

"Calm down, you two." Mick flashed a concerned look at Adam. "Come on, sit down. Howie didn't mean it the way it sounded. He's only thinking about the case."

"Mick's right." Howie softened his tone. "You know that the case always comes first with me. The crack about romancing wasn't called for...sorry."

Adam stood silently gazing at nothing in particular. Finally, he took a deep breath and sat down. "What do you want me to do?" he asked without looking at Howie.

"You don't have to push her hard. When the timing is right, feel her out about LaMar. And also about Pritchett if you can."

"I doubt if she knows anything."

"You're probably right," Howie said, concerned that Adam was getting too emotionally involved with Rachel. "But just try to find out some information that would be helpful in this case. I know it feels underhanded, but there's no one else to handle this except you."

Adam was silent for a minute before he spoke. "I know, and you guys are right. I haven't had any problem spying on Pritchett because he may have murdered LaMar. When it comes to Rachel, she's just so innocent...and she trusts me." He let out a deep sigh. "I'll do what I can, though."

"Sorry about the crack about going soft on her," Mick said as he reached over and touched Adam on the arm. "It was a dumb thing to say."

"It's already forgotten."

Howie closed his notepad. "Okay, is there anything else that we need to talk about?"

"How's Jerome's grandmother?" Mick asked. "I hear she's been sick."

"Yeah, there's some bug going around at the nursing home. I went over to talk to her, but the lady at the reception desk said that they weren't allowing visits for a few days." Howie slipped his notepad into his shirt pocket. "When I got back to the office, I called the nurses' station and was told that Nana was down with the bug. I called today and she's better, but isn't up to having visitors."

"Do you have any idea why she wanted to talk to you about that security guy?" Mick asked.

"I suspect it might've had something to do with us taking Rosie out of there." Howie could just hear Nana bawling him out in that screechy voice of hers. "She's probably ticked off at me for not asking her and her friends to be in on our scheme."

Howie and his partners chatted for a few more minutes, and then agreed to meet again tomorrow. "Hope it goes well with Rachel," he said as Adam got up to leave.

Adam nodded and left without saying a word.

# Chapter 38

IN PREPARATION FOR taking Rachel out to eat, Adam had talked to Pritchett the night before. He informed him that he would be late to work the next evening, offering as an excuse that he had some important errands to run.

"It shouldn't be a problem," Pritchett said. "Just don't be too late."

Rachel told Adam that their supper together would be their own little secret and that she wouldn't mention it to her father. "He tends to be a little over protective," she said, and then added, "But I know he'd be okay with you."

"Why would that be?"

"Because you're going to seminary." His questioning look caused her to explain further. "My father's a very religious person. When he was a young man, he considered becoming a minister." Rachel offered him a warm smile. "You studying to be a minister is a plus in his eyes. He likes that and he likes you."

"That's good." Adam wondered, however, what she and her father would say if they knew that he was working under false pretenses at their factory. Would they still like him if they found out he had lied to them right from the very beginning? From the first time he met Rachel, his guilt in deceiving her and her father had caused him more than a couple of sleepless nights.

Adam took Rachel to the Café Antonio. With card-sized tables covered with red-and-white checkered tablecloths, the café wasn't as fancy as its name, but the ambiance was what had attracted him. On the walls hung turn-of-the-century photographs of the cities and countryside of Italy. Flickering candles in small, rose-tinted glass jars served as centerpieces on each table. Background music coming through speakers mounted on the walls featured the Italian opera. He had eaten there once before and had enjoyed both the food and the atmosphere. The café had a reputation for the best spaghetti in northeast Minneapolis. They arrived shortly after five and discovered, much to Adam's delight, that they had the place nearly to themselves. An hour later and the place would be half full. By seven, Antonio's would be packed, and with people waiting in line to get in. They requested a table toward the back, away from the other customers. He seated her and then sat across from her.

"Oh, my, this place certainly has character." Rachel glanced around. "I like it." She reached over and touched his hand for a moment. "I'm glad you picked it."

"Thanks, I was hoping you'd like it." Adam wished her touch had been longer.

Before they could say anything further, the waiter appeared. He was a young man with black curly hair and a smile that would make any customer feel special. He gave each of them a menu and asked if they would like something to drink. Rachel deferred to Adam, and when he ordered a glass of red wine, she did also. Upon the recommendation of the waiter, they both ordered the house specialty.

"It might be a little early for supper, but I hope you're hungry," Adam said.

"I can always eat," Rachel replied with a gentle laugh, her eyes reflecting the flame from the candle. "How do you like working at the factory?" she asked.

Adam cleared his throat, intentionally keeping his smile. "It's not bad. I don't mind it at all," he said, hoping that she couldn't see the guilt he felt. "How long have you and your father worked in the candy business?"

"Not as long as you might think. Daddy owned a larger candy factory fifteen years ago, but things went bad after a few years."

The waiter brought their wine. Adam took a sip and waited for Rachel to continue.

"Daddy had a business partner who was dishonest." Rachel paused as though trying to decide whether to reveal the details. She looked at him with eyes so trusting that it made him uncomfortable. "The man embezzled huge sums of money."

Adam set his glass down. "That must've been awful."

"It was." Rachel's eyes reflected the pain heard in her voice. "By the time Daddy found out, it was too late. The financial reserves of the partnership had been nearly cleaned out. Creditors called day and night. He had to let people go who were not only employees, but over the years had become friends of the family."

"What happened then?"

"The whole thing finally ended up in bankruptcy. There was so much tension during those months that..." Rachel looked away for a moment. "My mother died of a heart attack six months after we sold our home and moved into an apartment. Although the doctors thought differently, Daddy was convinced it was because of all the strain."

"I'm so sorry."

Rachel took a sip of her wine. She seemed more relaxed now that she had shared her family's secret. "At the time of my mother's death, I was barely sixteen. It took Daddy seven years to scrape up the money to open up this candy factory."

"That had to have been a terrible time in your lives."

"It was." A determined look appeared in Rachel's eyes. "I never want to go through something like that again. Daddy was working two, sometimes three jobs, and I had to work after school and summers. He vowed that he'd make it up to me. The poor man felt ashamed that my senior high years had been disrupted."

"What happened when your mother died? I mean, do you have other sisters or brothers?"

"I'm the only child."

"So am I."

"Really? Tell me more."

"There's not much to tell. My parents divorced when I was less than a year old. My mother raised me. From what my mother tells me, my father remarried and lives in another part of the country. I've never talked to him, since he's never bothered to contact me." Adam took a sip of wine. Although he seldom talked about his past, he felt comfortable doing so with Rachel. "I bet your father was happy to have you around."

"Oh, yes. He's always said that if it hadn't been for me, he didn't know if he would've survived it all. He's a very loving father."

"I can tell that." Adam chewed on his lip. He needed to start probing for information that Howie might find helpful to the case. Although he seldom drank, he took another sip of wine. "And when did you say he opened up the candy factory?"

"Four years ago come this winter."

"Who thought of the name, the Chocolate Angel Factory?"

Rachel raised her hand. "I did."

"You did? How did you come up with that name?"

"Easy. Since it had once been a church and we were going to specialize in chocolate candy, I thought, why not make chocolate angels?"

"That's pretty clever."

"Thank you," Rachel said, smiling. "Daddy immediately liked the idea. The molds for the angels were expensive, but the angel design proved to be a hit. That along with the old family recipe makes them the best chocolate angels around."

The waiter brought their food. Aromas of savory peppers, onions, and garlic intermingled with the steam rising from the huge plates of spaghetti placed in front of them. Adam offered Rachel a slice of warm Italian bread that had been served wrapped in a white cloth and nestled in a wicker basket.

"What kind of interests do you have?" Rachel asked as she picked up her fork.

"I enjoy reading and going to movies." He was amazed at how comfortable he felt sharing with her. "How about you?"

"Art and geography are my passions."

"Geography? You mean, maps and stuff like that?"

Rachel shook her head as she finished chewing. She dabbed at the corner of her mouth with her linen napkin and took a sip of wine before replying. "I like reading about places like Paris and London, but what I'd really love to do would be to visit those cities."

"Maybe someday you'll get a chance."

"Can I tell you a secret?" Rachel's eyes sparkled.

Adam nodded as he took a sip of wine, not wanting to make eye contact.

"Last month my father said he'd take me on a trip around the world next year." Rachel picked up her bread and broke it apart. Her face glowed with excitement. "I'll be able to visit all the famous art museums."

"That's great." Adam enjoyed watching Rachel eat. She seemed to approach her food with the same enthusiasm as she approached life.

"You know what's wonderful?" Rachel asked.

Adam shook his head.

"This place, this food…and being here with you."

As they continued to enjoy their meal and each other, the conversation turned to the building Rachel's father had purchased and renovated for the candy factory. Adam got the impression that the price for the old church had been a bargain too good to pass up. He was surprised to learn that in the church's sub-basement there were a couple of room-like cells where years ago priests and monks would come and stay for week-long contemplative retreats. Rachel's father, who had an interest in such things, had done research on the church's history. He told her that the silent retreats were meant to help the priests and monks re-center themselves on the things of God, and for that reason, they would stay inside their rooms nearly the entire time, only coming out to use a community bathroom.

"I've ventured down there a couple of times, but that was when we first bought the building," Rachael said.

"What's down there?"

"Nothing but cobwebs, some old altar furnishings, and a stack of pews."

Since Adam had never seen the sub-basement, he made a mental note to check it out at the earliest opportunity.

It was after dinner while having a cup of coffee that Adam felt that it was time to do the probing, having put it off long enough.

"Ken and I were talking the other night during a break," Adam lied, his stomach knotting up. He and Pritchett never shared breaks together and very seldom talked. "He mentioned something about a guy who died at the factory not too long ago. I think he said something about it being a freak accident."

"It was." A hint of sadness crept into Rachel's tone. "We all took it very hard, especially Daddy." Her gaze turned inward for a moment. "He wasn't himself for days after the accident. LaMar was such a nice man."

"Was that his name? LaMar?"

"Yes. LaMar Jones."

Adam took a sip of coffee. He needed to calm himself and concentrate on what Howie wanted him to find out. In order not to raise any suspicions, he also needed to ask the questions in a casual manner. He took another sip of coffee, hoping it would settle his stomach. "You say he was a nice guy?"

"Very much so. He was always polite, a good worker, and he got along with most everybody at the place except..."

"Except who?"

"Oh, it's so silly. Do you really want to know?"

"Yes," Adam said, keeping his smile.

"Well, since you already know all about my family history, I suppose I can share this as well." She leaned forward slightly and lowered her voice. "He and Leo got into a terrible fight one night."

"Over what?"

"I shouldn't be telling you this because Daddy wanted it played down." Rachel reached across the table and touched Adam's hand again. "But I feel I can trust you."

"Excuse me." Adam pulled his hand away and rubbed his eye as if something had gotten in it. He was sure that Rachel could sense his lies simply by touching his hand.

"Are you okay?"

"I'm fine." He forced a smile. "It was just a speck of dust. Please go on."

"Leo started with my father at our first candy factory. Even after he was let go because of the bankruptcy, he remained a good friend to our family." Rachel's face glowed as she talked. "He's been around so long that I think of him as an older brother. His only fault is that he's very protective of me."

"When you, ah...say they got into a fight, you mean a real one or just an argument?"

"I'm afraid a real one." A frown appeared on her face. "Leo got a black eye out of it and I was concerned that LaMar's jaw was broken."

"You say his jaw was broken?" Adam asked, remembering that Howie mentioned something about LaMar having gone to the dentist.

"We thought it was, but thank goodness, it wasn't." Rachel shuddered. "But let's not talk about this. Not tonight."

They talked about other things over a second cup of coffee and made plans to go out for supper again. Adam, however, couldn't help but wonder about what Rachel had shared. *If Leo is jealous and protective, could he have killed LaMar if he thought the guy was making a pass at Rachel?* After he took her home, he would make a brief stop at Howie's office before going to work.

# Chapter 39

LEO RAPPAPORT CLINCHED his fists, his fingernails digging into his skin. He had followed Adam and Rachel from the time Adam picked her up at her house. At one point, just as they entered Antonio's, he considered going up to Rachel and telling her that he didn't trust Adam and she shouldn't either. He thought back to a year ago when he had finally gotten up enough courage to ask her out for a date. She declined, saying, "You're just like a brother to me. I can't date my brother." At the time, Leo laughed, but inwardly felt the pain of rejection. He wasn't good-looking and was nearly ten years older than Rachel, but he loved her. He fell in love with her the very first time he met her; she was only a teenager at the time, but that didn't matter. She had been friendly and kidded around with him a lot. He liked that and he liked to make her laugh. "I'll wait," he vowed to himself that day. He waited for years, and even though she had turned him down for a date, he didn't give up hope. When LaMar Jones started to make passes at her, he got angry. One night, he warned the man to keep away from her, but LaMar only laughed. "Says who? You?" All that Leo remembered next was that his fist smashed into LaMar's jaw. The fight had lasted less than a minute, but it was enough time for LaMar to get in a good punch to Leo's right eye.

Leo remembered that black eye now as he stood on the corner watching the restaurant where Adam and Rachel had gone. Although LaMar was no longer in the picture, there was now this new guy and Leo vowed to find out as much as he could about Adam. A younger man walking by quickened his pace when he saw Leo. Leo liked that. He didn't mind if people were afraid of him.

When Rachel and Adam came out of the restaurant, Leo got into his car, and followed them as Adam drove Rachel home. Although he parked far enough away so that they wouldn't notice, he was still close enough to see their heads coming together. "Why, that creep's kissing her," he muttered as he opened his car door, planning to go tell him to keep his dirty hands off of her. Just as quickly as he had opened the door, he closed it, knowing that Rachel wouldn't approve of his interference. He glared at the two of them embracing. "His time will come," he said as Adam walked back to his car.

His plan now was to follow Adam back to the factory and have a little talk with him. He put his car in gear as soon as Adam pulled away from the curb.

When Adam's car turned right on the next block instead of going in the direction of the candy factory, Leo wondered what he was up to. He followed for several more minutes before Adam turned off Broadway and parked on the side street by Kass' Drug Store. Leo pulled his car over and watched as he got out of the car, walked to the apartment entrance along the side of the building, and went in. Leo started his car, and drove by the entrance, noting with surprise the sign by the door: *MAC DETECTIVE AGENCY.*

# Chapter 40

HOWIE LEANED BACK in his chair and put his feet up on his desk. It was only a few minutes after nine; he had the whole day to follow up on any possible leads on the case concerning the alleged murder of LaMar Jones. The trouble was that he had very few leads. And all of the leads concerning the disappearance of Rosie Carpenter had also come to a dead end. She was still missing and he was still sleeping on the couch. Trying to sleep, that is.

The only thing new on Ken Pritchett was that he apparently was stealing chocolate out of the vat at the factory. What the man was doing with the chocolate, they had no idea. Howie had tried to find out more about Pritchett, but his efforts were in vain. It was as though the guy had come out of nowhere. Wherever Pritchett had come from, he had covered his tracks well. Howie turned his attention now to what Adam had shared with him yesterday. His partner had just come from dropping Rachel off after their dinner engagement, and by the look on his face, they must have had a great time. He had listened with interest as Adam told him about the altercation between LaMar and Leo.

"So Rachel thinks that Hooknose is just a little over-protective, does she?" Howie opened his notepad to jot down the information.

"That's right, but I have a gut feeling that the guy doesn't just want a brother-sister relationship."

"I can't agree more with you." Howie wondered how that bit of information struck Adam. If his partner was bothered by it, he wasn't showing it. "But the question is, was he over protective enough to kill LaMar?"

Adam shifted in his chair. "That doesn't seem like a good enough motive for murder, does it?"

"Motives come in all shapes and sizes, and jealousy is right up there at the top." Howie had briefly considered suggesting to Adam that he spend some time reading Howie's *Police Gazette* magazines and a little less time with those preacher books he got at school. Although the magazines might not offer the kind of sermon material Adam wanted, they certainly offered a more realistic view of the world, even if it was of the 1890's. As far as he was concerned, the stories in the magazine could just as well have been written about events going on in the 1960's. Times change, but people don't.

Howie leaned back, interlaced his fingers behind his head, and looked toward the window as he now thought about the conversation he had had with Adam yesterday. He was glad he hadn't suggested any *outside* reading to his partner, since it probably would have set him off, and the two of them have already had their share of conflict.

After a while, Howie put his feet down, scooted up to the desk, and took out his notepad. Leo Rappaport, alias Hooknose, just moved up to the number one suspect spot. He was writing a note to himself about looking into Leo's background when the phone rang.

"MAC Detective Agency," he answered.

"Where in blazes have you been?"

"Hello, Nana," Howie said, happy to hear from her. He had been concerned about her health. Although sounding weak, there was still the old spunkiness in her voice. "I'm glad you're feeling better. I was worried about—"

"Don't try to sweet talk me! Where have you been?"

"I've been busy."

"Too busy to see me?"

Howie visualized Nana's eyes narrowing as she thrust his chin out in determination. "I tried to see you, but the nurses told me not to come. You were pretty sick."

"Well, I'm better now."

"That's good to hear."

"I want you here tonight."

"I don't know if—"

"It's Beatrice's birthday! She's expecting you!"

Howie had no idea of who Beatrice was. "I'm not sure if I can make it," he said, hoping she wouldn't ask him what else he had planned. If she did ask, he would have to make up something.

"You have to come!"

"Why?"

"It's her ninetieth birthday!" Nana's tone sounded demanding as usual. "The old gal might not make it to the next one. You could live to regret it for the rest of your life if you didn't show up. Old folks don't live forever, you know. She may—"

"Okay, okay," Howie said. "But I can only stay for a little—"

"Bring some booze!"

"Some what?"

"Booze! Do I have to spell it out for you?" Nana shouted. "I've told you before. Clean the wax out of your ears. You're getting as bad as Agnes."

"I didn't think they allowed you to have...ah, booze."

"What they don't know won't hurt them. Besides, it's for medicinal purposes," Nana argued and then added with a wicked cackle, "It'll spice up the party a bit for the old folks."

"I'll see what I can do. Is that okay? Nana? Nana?" He hung up and looked over at his poster. "Bogie, how did I ever get myself involved in a case like this?" For a split second, he thought Bogart's thin lips formed a hint of a smile.

As far as Howie was concerned, the entire morning had been a bust. He was actually looking forward to the birthday party, if for nothing else, to see how Nana was doing. He was also hoping that the blond nurse would be there. After talking to Nana, he had called the dentist that LaMar had gone to, but was informed that the man was vacationing in Hawaii and wouldn't be back for a couple of weeks. The only progress he had made in gaining information on Hooknose was getting his address from the phone book.

Howie checked the time. Since he still had a couple of hours before going to the nursing home, he decided to take a drive over and see what kind of place Leo lived in. The drive to south Minneapolis took a little more than a half hour. Huge oak trees lined the street Leo lived on. The houses and yards were small but well kept up. Leo lived in a canary-colored rambler with white shutters and an unattached garage. Howie pulled up across the street from the house. He was confident that even if Leo did see him, he wouldn't remember him. Leo had barely looked at him that day at the candy factory when he wouldn't let them in to talk to Gilbertson. As he sat there studying Leo's home, wondering what it had to say about its owner, an elderly woman came out of the house where he was parked. Hoping she might provide some information on her neighbor across the street, he got out of the car and approached her. He had not taken more than five steps when he detected a hint of apprehension in her eyes.

"Hello, I'm Howie Cummins," he said as he got closer, putting on his best smile and hoping that his boyish looks would dispel any fears she might have.

"You're not selling anything are you?" Her tone was cold, untrusting. "Because if you are..."

"Oh, no, ma'am. You don't have to worry about that." Howie could see that his charm was beginning to work. "I'm here on behalf of the, ah..." He took note of her floral housedress. "The Daisy Realtor Company."

"Not interested," she said. "I've lived in my house for sixty-two years now and I'm not planning on selling."

"I'm not here for that," Howie quickly said, concerned that she would turn around and go back into her house. "I would just like to ask some questions about one of your neighbors. It won't take long. I promise."

"I suppose," she replied, her tone softening, no doubt relieved that she wasn't being asked to sell her home. "Which neighbor are you talking about?"

"Leo Rappaport." Howie pointed in the direction of Leo's house. "He lives in that yellow rambler across the street."

"Oh, yes. Mr. Rappaport is such a nice man." The woman smiled, but her eyes reflected a look of concern. "I hope he's not planning to move."

"No, ma'am. We are, ah...a new company and looking at several houses we'd like to display on our brochure. Our motto is, ah, *This Could Be Your Next New House*." Howie gestured to Hooknose's house again. "Since Mr. Rappaport's house is yellow, the color of daisies, and our company's name is *Daisy*...well, you know, we thought it might be appropriate."

"Oh, Mr. Rappaport's house would be perfect."

"I agree, but we have to make sure that the house owner is a reputable, upstanding citizen of the community. You see, we must keep the reputation of our firm in mind." Howie glanced around and then lowered his voice. "The last time we did this, our brochure was at the printer when we found out that the owner of the house was a lady of the night...if you know what I mean."

The woman's mouth dropped open. "Oh, dear. Well, you won't have to worry about Mr. Rappaport. He's a fine, upstanding citizen."

"So what you're saying is that he must be a pretty good neighbor?"

"The best!" the woman gushed. "I can't tell you the number of times he has come over to shovel my sidewalk in the winter. In the summer, he mows my lawn. And the dear man not only does it for me, but also for a couple of other older people in the neighborhood." She clasped her hands together as though she was about to offer a prayer. Her eyes glowed with sincerity as she spoke slowly and reverently. "He's one of the kindest, nicest persons I have ever met."

"How well do you know him?" Howie wondered if they were talking about the same person.

She beamed. "Quite well. He has come over to my house for tea and cookies every month for nearly ten years. We've been neighbors for twelve and he brings me roses from his garden in the back of his house." Her eyes glowed with admiration. "Mr. Rappaport loves flowers, and he raises such prize-winning roses. He's won several blue ribbons from the State Fair. His roses are absolutely breathtaking."

This time, it was Howie's mouth that dropped open. "Ah...ah...that's wonderful."

"He'll be so thrilled about having his house on your brochure."

"On what?"

"The brochure your company is making up." The woman gave him a puzzled look. "Are you all right? You look a little dazed."

"No, ah...I'm okay. Ma'am, about the brochure?"

"Yes?"

"We haven't made our final decision yet, so I'm going to have to ask you to keep this conversation to yourself for now." The woman nodded her agreement. Howie thanked her for her time, declining her invitation to come in and have tea and cookies. "Sorry, maybe next time, but I'm on my way to see my grandmother at the nursing home." As he turned and walked to his car, he heard the woman say, "My, what a sweet young man."

AFTER A BRIEF stop at his office, Howie arrived at the nursing home shortly after five-thirty. Nana had told him to come early. He stopped at the desk and was informed that the birthday party was being held in the dining room on the second floor. He rode the elevator with a gentleman who was sitting in a wheelchair. The man had such a shock of flowing white hair and an elegant-looking goatee that he reminded Howie of Buffalo Bill Cody.

"Going to the shindig?" Buffalo Bill asked.

Howie smiled and nodded.

"Yup, me too," the distinguished-looking man said.

"How long have you known Beatrice?" Howie asked.

"Who's Beatrice?"

"She's the one having the birthday."

"Is that right? Well, I reckon I don't know the lady." Buffalo Bill must have seen the surprised look on Howie's face. "I just go for the grub." He grinned and then stroked his goatee. "Between all the birthdays and funerals around here, I get fed pretty good." He patted his ample stomach. "I've gained ten pounds since I've been here."

Howie offered to give Buffalo Bill a push to the party but the man politely declined, saying that he needed the exercise to build up his strength. "In case I run into any hombres," he declared with a wink.

When Howie entered the dining room, there had to be close to twenty residents, most of them in wheelchairs. Those without wheelchairs had walkers sitting next to their chairs. Several staff moved about serving punch. He looked for the blond nurse, but she was nowhere in sight. Nana came wheeling up to him as soon as he entered. She appeared to have lost some weight; her face was gaunt and she looked peaked.

"Did you bring it?" she asked.

"Bring what?"

"The booze," she whispered.

"Sorry, I forgot," Howie replied truthfully.

"Humph! I guess we'll have to be satisfied with that pink water they call punch." Nana wagged her finger at him. "You're getting as forgetful as some of the old people here!" she scolded. "Come on, I'll introduce you around."

Howie dutifully followed Nana as she wheeled up to a man who appeared to be asleep in his wheelchair. "Wake up, Gus!" she yelled.

"I'm awake," Gus lazily replied without opening his eyes, his chin still resting on his chest. He shifted in his wheelchair. "I'm just resting."

"Open your eyes!" Nana demanded. "I want you to meet someone." After Gus obeyed, she introduced her guest. "This is Howie, one of my grandchildren." After leaving Gus, she motioned for Howie to bend over so she could whisper something to him. "Thought I better not tell anyone you're a detective."

"Good thinking," Howie said and then obediently tagged along as she continued to introduce him to other residents and staff.

Beatrice, the birthday girl, swooned over Howie. She kissed his hand several times, leaving bright-red blotches of lipstick behind. "I wish I had a handsome grandson like him."

"Well, you can't have him!" Nana curtly replied. "He's mine!" Finally, she led him to a table where two other residents were sipping punch. "How's the case going?" she asked after they were served punch.

"The case?" Howie glanced at their tablemates; they were smiling and looking at him and Nana.

"Don't worry about them," Nana said with a wave of her hand as though she was shooing away a fly. "Both of them are so hard of hearing that they wouldn't hear a cannon if it was shot off right next to them."

"We're making some progress." Howie hoped she wouldn't ask how much. He was too tired to make up another story.

"What about that girl you broke out of the third floor?" Nana's eyes flashed with curiosity. "Did you give her the third degree and make her spill the beans?"

Howie debated whether to say anything, but since Nana was the one who gave them the tip, she deserved to know. He explained that they took the young woman up to his apartment, but then after returning from lunch the next day, found her gone. "I'm pretty sure that she didn't leave on her own accord."

"Is that so? Why didn't you put a guard on her?" Nana scrunched her nose in disapproval. "Don't you know that Sam Spade would never have done such a dumb thing as leaving a witness unguarded?" She crossed her arms and gave him a stern look. "Even my grandson, Jerome, would know better than to do a fool thing like that."

Howie took a sip of punch. He felt chastised and now wished he would have remembered to bring the booze.

# Chapter 41

WHILE HOWIE DRANK watered-down punch with Nana at Beatrice's ninetieth birthday party, Adam and Mick sat at the soda fountain at Kass' Drugstore drinking Cokes before Adam went to work. Their friend, Kass, had served them their drinks and then excused himself to run an errand.

"Have you come across any clues at the candy factory?" Mick asked.

"Not a one." Adam not only felt guilty about deceiving Rachel, but also about not having uncovered anything significant to the case. Although he hadn't shared his feelings with his partners, he felt as if he was letting them down. Howie and Mick had told him to be patient and that it could take time. It continued to trouble him, however, that with each day that he worked undercover, the longer he lived a lie with Rachel. This had been the first time he had met a woman he cared for, and he hoped to continue to see Rachel once the case was closed. That is, if she was willing to see him again. "There's a sub-basement that I haven't seen, yet," he said to Mick. "I'm going to try and check it out tonight."

"What's down there?"

"From what Rachel said, not much. It's used mainly for storage." Adam took a sip of his Coke. "I guess there are a couple of cell-like rooms down there."

"Oh, yeah? What are they for?"

"Years ago, they were used by priests who wanted to spend time in solitude." Adam finished his drink. "I'm curious to see what those rooms are like."

"You're not thinking about going on a retreat, are you?" Mick quipped.

Adam shook his head, appreciating that his friend was trying to cheer him up. "No, I just feel the need to take more initiative. That sub-basement might have some clues." Adam held up his empty glass in a mock toast. "As Howie always says, you never know what kind of clues may turn up in the most unlikely of places." An image of Rachel flashed through his mind. "The sooner this case is solved, the better."

"You sound determined."

"I am." Adam set his glass down. "I'm also going to try and get a look at Gilbertson's office," he said, wishing he didn't feel like he was betraying

Rachel and her father. "Howie is curious as to why it's off limits to everybody."

"Maybe Gilbertson just needs his own private space."

"That could be." Adam hoped Mick was right. Based on what Rachel told him about her father's interest with religious matters, Gilbertson might just consider his office as his own private retreat. He could understand that since there were periods in his life when he needed to have time by himself. He felt like that right now. The sooner he got this part of the assignment done, the sooner Howie would get off his back.

"You be careful, okay?" Mick said. "Don't do anything foolish."

"I won't." Adam slid off the stool. "I'd better get going if I'm going to make it to work on time."

"My car's out front. Do you want a ride?"

"No, I'll walk."

"See you tomorrow," Mick said.

Adam looked forward to walking the five blocks; it would give him some time to try and sort things out. *What would I say to Rachel if she ever found out that I was a detective? Would she understand? Would she be hurt that I deceived her and her father? Would she still want to see me?* He was still struggling with that last question as he walked up the steps to the candy factory. Just as he got to the top landing, the entrance door opened. Betty, one of the workers, came out.

"I've been waiting for you," Betty said, keeping the door from shutting with her hip. "I hope you don't mind being alone for a while."

"What do you mean?"

"Well, no one is here, but me. Leo said he had some important business to take of, and Ken Pritchett called in sick."

"How about Mr. Gilbertson?"

"He was here, but he rushed out about a half hour ago, saying he had an urgent errand to run and wouldn't be back for a couple of hours." Betty talked rapidly, no doubt anxious to get home. "Mr. Gilbertson was concerned about how you were going to get in since Leo was gone. He asked me if I could stay a few minutes longer and see that you got in." She glanced back into the building. "You're going to be in this old church all by yourself for a while. I hope you're not afraid of ghosts."

"If it's the Holy Ghost, then I'll be okay," Adam said, giving Betty a wink. After wishing her a good evening, he closed the door, making sure it locked. Now that he had the whole place to himself, he decided to first try for Gilbertson's office. If he had time, he would also check the sub-basement.

Moving to Rachel's desk, Adam opened the side drawer and found a paper clip. Howie had shown Mick and him how to pick a lock with a paper clip. He opened the doors to the work area and moved quickly to Gilbertson's office door. Glancing around to make sure he was alone, he straightened the paper clip and bent it at the end. Howie had referred to a bent paper clip as the *All-purpose Detective's Key*. Taking hold of the door handle, he was about to insert the paper clip into the keyhole when he discovered to his chagrin that the door wasn't locked. Gilbertson must have rushed off in too big of a hurry. He turned the handle, slowly opened the door, and flipped on the light. Gilbertson's desk was to the right; a long wooden table shared the other half of the room with a smaller card table. He went to the tables first. On the long table sat several stacks of empty candy boxes. Next to the empty candy boxes was a packing carton. He opened the carton and discovered metal moldings for the chocolate angels. On the smaller table sat a black cast-iron kettle on a hot plate. As he was examining the kettle, he heard a noise behind him. Before he had a chance to turn around, his head exploded in pain and everything went black.

"HURRY UP AND blow out the candles!" Nana yelled to Beatrice. "We're hungry for cake and ice cream."

"I will, but I've got to have some help." Beatrice looked in the direction of Nana and Howie. "Tell your handsome grandson to come over here."

To the applause of the others in the room, Howie got up, walked over, and stood next to the birthday lady. Beatrice motioned for him to come closer so that she could whisper something to him. "There are nine candles on the cake," she said. "One for each decade of my life." She kissed him on the cheek. "Now, on the count of three," she told him. "One...two...three." To the cheers of everyone, Beatrice and Howie blew out the nine candles with ease.

Howie brought ice cream and cake to Nana and the others at their table. After refilling everybody's punch, he sat down. He had no sooner taken his first bite of cake when Nana leaned over toward him. "Do you remember why I called you before I got sick?"

"No, you just said you had something to talk to me about," Howie replied, having forgotten about that phone call.

Nana twisted her pigtail around her finger. "I just know it had something to do with the case, but I just can't remember. Ever since I've been sick, I've become more forgetful."

"I'm sorry to—"

"Life's too short to be sorry!" Nana cried. "Just tell me what's going on with the case. It might jog my memory."

"Nothing much is going on. We don't really have any solid proof about anything yet." Howie spoke as gently as he could. "Other than yours, I don't know of any other reported missing diamonds." He couldn't bring himself to tell Nana that he had doubts about the whole case; he had grown too fond of her.

ADAM'S HEAD FELT as if it would explode. In addition to having a horrendous headache, his whole body ached. As he lay on the damp, stone floor, he became aware of a faint tapping coming from somewhere in front of him. He slowly opened his eyes, but it was too dark to see. It didn't matter; he would rather use his energy to listen and let his eyes rest. With great effort he opened his eyes again, but only for a moment. He wasn't sure how long the tapping lasted, but he didn't care. He was too drowsy to listen.

# Chapter 42

HOWIE OPENED ANOTHER box of paper clips, plucked one out, and added it to a three-foot-long chain. For the past fifteen minutes he had been working on his creation as Mick paced the office. Every few minutes, his partner stopped at the window, peered out at the street below, and then continued walking off his nervous energy.

"I wonder where he is," Mick said, finally plopping down in his chair. He shifted from side to side while rubbing his hands together.

"You're doing that again."

"What?"

"Cracking your knuckles."

"Sorry." Mick got up and went to the window again. "It's nearly five-thirty. I'm worried. That's not like Adam."

"You don't have to tell me that." Howie set his chain aside. Of the three of them, Adam was the most punctual, usually showing up early. He had told Adam yesterday that they were going to meet at the office at four the next day to compare notes on the case, and his partner agreed to be there. They had been waiting now for over an hour. If Adam were going to be late, he would have called. "Maybe he forgot." When Mick rolled his eyes at him, Howie just shrugged. He had called Adam's home, but there was no answer. Mick had even gone down to the hamburger shop where Adam's mother, Virg, worked.

"When I came home this morning, he was gone," she had told Mick. Virg worked the dogwatch as she called it, the eleven pm to seven am shift. "And when I got up this afternoon, he wasn't there. I'm such a sound sleeper, though, I couldn't tell you if he had been home or not." Her hazel eyes had flickered with apprehension. "There isn't anything wrong, is there?"

"Oh, no," Mick had replied. "We're just wondering if he was down here eating. You see, we forgot to tell him about a meeting we were having." He had kept his voice calm and casual. "If he comes in, tell him we're up at the office."

Howie checked the clock. "I'll tell you what we're going to do," he said, getting up from his chair. "We're going over to that candy factory and see if Adam's there."

"Won't that blow his cover?"

"No, we'll just make up something as to why we're there." Howie picked up his notepad and slipped it in his shirt pocket.

"So what kind of story are we going to make up?" Mick asked as he and Howie walked out and headed down the stairs.

"That we're there to...ah...give me a minute. I'll think of something." They were just going out the entrance door when the idea came to Howie. "I got it. We're there to question him on a hit-and-run case we're working on that he's a witness to."

The drive to the candy factory took five minutes. They parked the car, got out, trotted up the front steps, and pushed the buzzer. As they waited, Mick cracked his knuckles a couple of times, but Howie didn't bring it to his attention. Finally, the door opened.

"You guys again!" Hooknose said, scowling. "I told you before Mr. Gilbertson has already talked to the police."

"We're not here about LaMar Jones," Howie said. "There's another case we're investigating." He took out his notepad and flipped to a blank page, making sure Hooknose couldn't see it. "You have an employee here by the name of Adam..." He turned to Mick. "I don't have this guy's last name written down. Do you remember what that lawyer said it was?"

"Trexler."

"That's right. I remember now." Howie turned back to Hooknose. "We're looking for Adam Trexler." When Rappaport's face remained impassive, Howie continued. "We're working a case where we believe he's a witness to a hit-and-run. We need to talk to him."

A smug smile appeared on the big man's face. "He doesn't work here anymore."

"What do you mean he doesn't work here?" Mick grabbed hold of the door.

"Just what I told you!" Hooknose said, his smug smile transforming into a sneer as he frowned at Mick's hand on the door. "He quit last night."

"Are you sure about that?" Howie asked.

"Sure, I'm sure. He left a note on the desk."

"I don't believe you," Mick said. "Show us the note."

Hooknose's eyes turned stormy as he scowled at Mick. "I don't have to show you nothing."

"I know you don't," Howie said quickly but kept his voice even, not allowing the anger within him toward the human roadblock to spill out. "But if you don't, we'll just have to get a court order. Remember, this was a hit-and-run." He hoped that his bluff wouldn't be called. "I don't think your Mr. Gilbertson would want to be dragged into court, do you?"

Hooknose studied the two of them for a minute. "Okay, I'll show it to you. Just stay here." Without waiting for a reply, he shut the door.

"Adam wouldn't quit without telling us," Mick said. "Something's fishy."

"Something's fishy all right." Howie kept an eye on the door, expecting it to open any second. "That guy knows more than he's letting on."

"What do you mean?"

"It's just a gut feeling, but I get the sense he's playing with us. It's almost like…like he knows that we and Adam are connected."

Mick frowned. "Do you think he found out that Adam was a plant?"

"I can't be sure, but—"

The door opened and Hooknose appeared with the note in his hand. "Here, you can read for yourself that he quit." He held the paper in front of him but gave no indication that he was going to let go of it.

Howie leaned forward and read the note. *Mr. Gilbertson, Sorry for letting you know like this, but I decided to quit for personal reasons. Adam Trexler.* He looked at Mick and shrugged. "Well, that does it. We better go. I guess he doesn't work here anymore."

Mick didn't budge as he continued to glare at Hooknose. "I don't suppose you know where he went?"

Hooknose's lip curled into a smile. "You two should know better about that than I do."

"What are you talking about?" Howie asked.

"You're detectives, aren't you?" he replied with a sneer, and then slammed the door before they could reply.

When they got back to the car, Mick turned to Howie. "I've got to tell you. That wasn't Adam's handwriting."

"I know that."

Mick looked back at the entrance door. "Why don't we go back and search the place?"

Howie started the car. "First of all, we have no legal right to do that. Secondly, Hooknose would never let us in. And thirdly, we probably wouldn't find him there."

"What do we do, then?"

"I don't know…yet." Howie put the car in gear and pulled away from the curb.

CHARLES GILBERTSON PACED in his office waiting for the telephone call. As soon as the phone rang, he grabbed it. "Hello, Gilbertson here." He lowered his voice. "What should be done now?" He took out his handkerchief and dabbed at the beads of perspiration forming on his forehead. "No!" he cried as he glanced toward the door, fearful that someone might have heard his outburst. He lowered his voice again. "We can't have another accident. We already told those detectives that he quit." He moved around his desk and sat down. "What should we do? What do you mean, wait? For how long?" He winced when his partner told him not to be concerned and that he would take care of it. "Are you sure that's the only way?" After receiving his answer, he hung up and slumped in his chair.

He hadn't wanted to ask how or when it would happen. The less he knew, the better.

HOWIE ADDED ANOTHER paper clip to the chain he had started earlier as he watched Mick walk to the window and look down at the street. They had decided to wait at the office in case their partner showed up. "I don't suppose you see him?" he asked as he opened a drawer and put his chain away.

Mick shook his head. "I didn't expect to." He glanced out the window again. "Man, I feel as if we should be doing something, but I don't know what. Adam could be in real danger."

"Here's what I suggest," Howie said, also feeling the need to take some kind of action. "First, I'm going to call Adam's mother and tell her not to expect him to be home tonight. I'll tell her that he's staying with me."

"What if she starts asking questions?"

"Don't worry, I'll tell her that he's working late on a lead and that he'll be coming here to stay for the next couple of nights. He's done that before, so that shouldn't be a problem. And then, after I call her, I suggest we go back to that candy factory."

"Good! I'm with you on that." Mick slammed his fist into his palm. "And if Hooknose doesn't let us in, we'll bust down the door."

"We're not going in."

"We're not? Why are we going over there, then?"

"Because I think it's time to talk to Rachel Gilbertson." Howie checked his watch. "From what Adam told me, she usually works until six-thirty or so. If we hurry, we'll catch her when she comes out."

# Chapter 43

"WHAT TIME IS it now?" Mick asked Howie.

"Twenty after six." It was the second time in the past five minutes that his partner had asked about the time.

Parked a half block away from the candy factory, he and Mick had been waiting for the past fifteen minutes for Rachel Gilbertson to leave work. On the drive over, Mick had shared the conversation he'd had with Adam at Kass' Drugstore.

"He seemed so intent on becoming more aggressive in searching that place for clues," Mick said. "Do you think that led to his disappearance?"

"That's my bet."

"Oh, man." Mick cracked his knuckles. "I should've urged him to be more careful."

"He knew what he was doing," Howie said in an effort to counteract his partner's self-recrimination.

"I know, but..."

"Don't worry about him. He can take care of himself." Howie gave Mick a reassuring pat on the shoulder, even though he himself was worried about their partner. His concern, however, was that with Adam's aggressiveness, he may have slipped up and jeopardized their investigation. And he wasn't sure if their partner's desire to be more aggressive was a result of his wanting to solve the case or to resolve his own inner struggle as to whether he should be a detective or a preacher. "And listen, don't be so hard on yourself. You said exactly what I would've told him."

"Thanks, but I still think I should've cautioned him more." Mick sighed and then rolled down his window. The evening air brought with it the smell of rain. Thunderclouds in the distance reflected flashes of lightning. "Do you think we're going to get hit by the storm?"

"I don't know. Maybe." Howie looked toward the gathering storm. "I'd say it's going to the west of us."

The two detectives sat quietly, watching the lightning illuminate the sky and listening to the accompanying thunder. The air thickened with anticipation of the impending storm.

Mick stuck his head out his open window for a moment and took in a deep breath as he looked up at the sky. "Whenever my grandma heard thunder she would tell me that the angels in heaven were bowling."

"Is that right? Well, they must be rolling strikes right now."

Several minutes passed as they watched the storm move in their direction. Mick checked his watch. "Maybe Rachel didn't go to work today."

Howie considered what they would do if his partner was right. "If she didn't, we could go to her house. Either that or catch her on the way in tomorrow morning." Neither of those options, however, appealed to him. He was trying to decide what other options they had when the entrance door to the one-time church opened and a young woman stepped out. "She may be coming now," he said as he gripped the door handle. He waited until the woman started down the steps before opening his door.

"That's got to be her." Mick rolled up his window.

"Come on, let's go," Howie said. He and Mick got out of the car and walked quickly toward Rachel. By the time she saw them approaching, she had come down the steps and turned in their direction. When she stopped suddenly, Howie was afraid that she might turn around, run up the steps, and go back into the building. "We're friends of Adam Trexler," he called out, having now recognized her from the description Adam had given him. Although she stood and waited as they approached, a look of uncertainty flooded her face. "You're Rachel Gilbertson, aren't you?" he asked as they walked up to her.

"Yes," she replied, her tone cautious.

"Hello, I'm Howie Cummins and this is Mick Brunner. We're from the MAC Detective Agency over on Broadway and Third." He always liked to identify that they were from the area. That way, people were more apt to talk to them. "We would like to have a few words with you," he said as he handed her his card.

Rachel studied the card while glancing at the two men who stood before her. "What do you want?" she asked, still eyeing them with apprehension.

"As I said, we're friends of Adam." Howie had told Mick that they wouldn't tell her that Adam worked with them until it became necessary. "I know that you and Adam are friends. We'd like to talk with him."

"He no longer works here." Rachel slipped Howie's card into her purse. "He quit last night," she said with a touch of sadness in her voice.

Mick spoke up. "We don't believe he quit."

Rachel's eyes shifted between the two of them.

"We know Adam quite well," Howie said. "He's not the type of guy who would quit without telling us."

"What are you saying?" Flashes of lightning reflected in Rachel's eyes. Treetops swayed as the wind picked up. "Do you think something happened to him?"

"We're not sure, but it could be connected with the case we're investigating." Howie paused. "It concerns the death of LaMar Jones."

"LaMar? What has…" Rachel's eyes continued to shift between the two detectives as though sizing them up while processing what she had just been told. "I'm sorry, but this is just all very confusing."

The wind suddenly died down bringing an unnatural stillness, but then thunder followed on the heels of a flash of lightning and the treetops began to sway again. "Would it be possible for you to come up to my office?" Howie asked. "It isn't that far away."

"I don't know if—"

"Look, the storm is going to hit any minute. We can talk in my office."

"We'd really appreciate it," Mick said as raindrops fell. "We believe that you may be of some help to us in finding Adam."

"He may be in danger," Howie said.

Rachel glanced at the turbulent clouds above. "Okay, I'll come with you, but I'll follow you in my car."

In the five minutes it took to drive to Howie's office, the storm hit in full force. Even though Howie and Mick found a parking spot close to the entrance, they got drenched when they hopped out of the car and ran to the entryway of the apartment.

Mick wiped the storm's wetness from his face. Water dripped from his tousled hair and his normally curly locks were plastered to his forehead. "Didn't you say that the storm was going to miss us?"

"Hey, I'm a detective, not a weather forecaster." Howie combed his hand through his dripping-wet hair.

Mick pointed at Rachel when she got out of her car. "At least she's smart enough to have an umbrella. Where's yours?"

"In the trunk." Howie opened the entrance door for Rachel and the three of them climbed the stairs to his office. Outside, the storm boomed with intensity. As soon as he flipped the lights on in his office, his eyes went to what had served as his makeshift bed. "Excuse me," he said and quickly grabbed his pillow and blanket off the couch. "Let me put these things away."

"Get me a towel to dry off with," Mick said.

"Make yourselves comfortable." Howie opened the door leading to his living quarters. "I'll be right back." He rushed to the bathroom, tossed the pillow and blanket in the bathtub, and dried his head and face. After taking a moment to run a comb through his hair, he grabbed a clean towel and headed back to his office. Rachel was sitting in a chair. Mick stood by the window, gazing at the sky. Flashes of lightning illuminated the darkness outside as their thunderous claps rattled the window.

"Whew, it's getting pretty bad out there," Mick said as he moved away from the window.

"Can I get you a cup of coffee or something?" Howie asked Rachel.

"No thank you."

Howie tossed his partner the towel. "How about you?"

"I don't think so."

"Suit yourself." Howie took his place behind the desk. "It probably doesn't fit your image of a detective's office," he said to Rachel. "But it suits me."

Rachel glanced around, pausing briefly at Howie's movie poster. She took note of the modified dental chair he sat in, but said nothing.

"Now, Miss Gilbertson..."

"Call me Rachel...please."

"Thank you, I will." Howie wondered if she would be as friendly with her answers when he got to the tougher questions. "I'll get right to the point. We would like to know: when was the last time you saw Adam?" He already knew the answer, but wanted to find out how truthful she was going to be with them.

"Yesterday, we..." Rachel paused to wet her lips. "We went out for an early dinner," she said quietly.

"I see." Howie took out his notepad. "How did Adam seem at the time?"

"What do you mean?"

"Did he seem worried or anxious about anything?"

"What can I say? He seemed to be his normal self. At least, from what I know of him." Rachel crossed her legs. "He certainly didn't give me any indication that he was going to quit, if that's what you're getting at. Adam liked working there. That's why I was so surprised to see his note."

"Did he give you the note?"

"No."

Howie took out a pen and opened his notepad. "If he didn't give it to you, who do you think he gave it to?"

"I don't know."

"Does that mean that you didn't see him at all today?" Mick asked.

"That's right."

"And when the two of you were together last night, he didn't mention anything at all about quitting?" Howie asked.

"Not a word." Rachel uncrossed her legs, adjusted her skirt, and then folded her hands on her lap. "You said that you didn't think he quit. If that's true, why did he write that note?"

"We don't think he wrote it," Mick said. He moved away from the window and leaned against the wall.

Rachel stared at Mick for several moments before turning her attention to Howie. "I don't understand."

Howie took the lead. "We saw the note. That wasn't his handwriting." He leaned forward, clasped his hands together, and rested them on the desk. "Someone else wrote it. We think that Adam may have been..." He paused, searching for the right word. "He may have been *detained* against his will."

"What! By who?"

"We're not sure."

Rachel's eyes filled with questions. "What about the note? Who would write it and why?"

"We don't know, but we're quite sure that it was written by someone who wanted to throw off any suspicions that might come from Adam not showing up for work." If Howie's revelation stunned Rachel, her face didn't reflect it. "If everybody thought he'd quit, then no one would think anything of it when he wasn't around anymore."

"But why would someone want that?"

"That's what we're going to find out." Howie admired Rachel's poise and understood why Adam would be attracted to this woman. Someone at the candy factory must have written the note, but he wasn't about to point that out to her now. At the right time, he would bring it up and he hoped she would be able to identify the handwriting. First, he had to make sure she was on their side.

The lights flickered as the storm unleashed another bolt of lightning; the deafening clap of thunder sounded as if it had come from across the street. Mick glanced out the window. More lightning. The lights in the office flickered.

"Don't worry, if the lights go, I've got a flashlight," Howie said, and then remembered that it was in the car with his umbrella.

If the effects of the storm were unnerving to Rachel, it wasn't evident. She remained calm and spoke evenly. "You said this whole thing with Adam might be connected with LaMar's death. What did you mean by that?"

Howie shot a glance at Mick, giving him a quick nod. His partner nodded in return. On the ride back from the candy factory they had talked about coming to the point where they would tell Rachel the truth about Adam. That time was now. He wasn't sure how she would react. It was a gamble. She might feel betrayed, get up, and walk out. His instincts, however, told him that if they were going to get any leads on the whereabouts of their partner, they had to chance it. She could turn out to be their ace in the hole. Besides, it was obvious she had feelings for their partner. "Adam works with us."

Rachel's eyes widened, but she said nothing. Lightning flashed and thunder shook the windowpane. The young woman sat quietly, keeping her composure.

"We were hired to look into the death of LaMar Jones," Howie said. "It was my idea for Adam to get the job, not his."

"He's a detective?" Her eyes revealed the hurt of betrayal. "You mean everything Adam told Daddy and me about going to school is a lie?"

"Adam was telling you the truth," Mick said. "He does go to school and plans to become a minister; he only works part-time as a detective."

"He never liked deceiving you," Howie said. "But we had to find a way to get into the candy factory so we could investigate LaMar's death. We tried the normal channels, but nobody would talk to us. We couldn't even get past the front door." Rachel appeared to have recovered from the initial shock and was now listening intently. "When I saw the *Help Wanted* sign, I decided to go for it. The problem was that Mick and I had already identified ourselves as detectives. That only left Adam to apply." He paused to allow her to process what he had said. "You need to understand that we had no other choice. And we had a very good reason to do what we did." He wanted her to get the full impact of what he was about to tell her. "LaMar's death may not have been an accident."

Rachel's eyes flickered, but retained their strength. "What are you telling me...that he was...murdered?"

"That's a very likely possibility. And Adam may have come upon a clue that put his life in danger." Howie chose his next words carefully. "I know you care about him, don't you?"

Rachel stared at him for several moments before nodding.

"And I'm certain you want to do everything you can to make sure he's safe."

She nodded again.

Mick came over and sat in the chair next to her. "Can you tell us anything about LaMar and how he got along with the others at work?"

"Could I please have a drink of water?"

"Coming right up." Howie went into the kitchen. He liked Mick's question; it was a subtle way of finding out who might have had something to do with Adam's disappearance. When he returned he noted how calm Rachel appeared. She was some classy lady. If Adam hadn't been involved with her, he would have liked the opportunity. He set the glass down on the desk in front of her.

"Thank you." Rachel took a sip and then held the glass on her lap, holding it with both hands. "Leo and LaMar got into a fight one night."

"What was that about?" Mick asked.

Rachel took another sip. "It was over me," she said as she placed the glass on the desk. "Leo's always been protective of me."

"What do you mean...protective?" Howie asked. "In what way?"

"Like a big brother. He thought that LaMar was coming on to me."

"Was he?"

"A little...but it wasn't anything I couldn't handle."

"Could it be that Leo was acting out of jealousy?" Mick asked.

Rachel's eyes turned inward for a moment. "I hadn't thought about it in that way, but I don't think so."

Howie had warned Adam to be careful of Leo's jealousy. Although his partner had an athletic build, he would have been no match for Leo's brute strength. "How about Ken Pritchett? Did he and LaMar ever have problems?"

"Not to my knowledge. The month before LaMar died, they had gotten to know each other quite well." Rachel paused. "That surprised me."

"Why?"

"Because before that they weren't all that friendly toward each other." She reached for the glass of water, took a sip, and placed it back on the desk. "But now that I think about it, two or maybe three weeks before LaMar died, they went out to lunch together."

"Is that so?" Howie took a glance toward the window. With the rain subsiding, the storm seemed to be moving on. "Are you sure about them getting together?" he asked, finding that hard to believe based on what LaMar's sister, Stephanie, had told them about how her brother didn't trust Pritchett.

"Very sure," Rachel said, her tone strong and confident. "I was working one evening when I had to get something downstairs. Both of them were just around the corner at the bottom of the steps. As I came down I overheard them talking about having lunch the next day but..."

Howie looked up from his notepad. "But what?"

"I asked where they were going out to eat since I was taking Daddy out for his birthday, and I wanted to know if they had any recommendations."

"What did they say?"

"That I must have misheard them because they weren't going out for any lunch." Rachel frowned. "I know as sure as I am sitting here that they were lying, but I just let it go. It would've been silly to have made an issue out of it."

Howie glanced at Mick. They would have to have another talk with Pritchett. His money, however, was still on Hooknose as being the number one suspect. Pritchett, though, was fast becoming a close second.

"How does your father fit into all of this?" Mick asked.

"Daddy has been under so much pressure lately. He was terribly saddened by LaMar's death. I..." Rachel looked at Mick and then at Howie, her eyes widening. "You don't think my father had something to do with his death, do you?"

"Of course not," Howie quickly replied, wanting to relieve her of any fears that her father was under suspicion. If she thought they were investigating her father, she probably would clam up. Gilbertson, however, was still a suspect in his book. "You have to understand that we can't leave any stones unturned. It may be that whatever happened probably did so under your father's nose without him being aware of it." He noted Mick giving him a look that told him that his partner knew he was intentionally deceiving the woman. "Is there anywhere at the candy factory that Adam might have been checking for clues?"

"I can't think of any place."

"How about that sub-basement?" Mick asked. "What's down there?"

"Nothing," Rachel replied and then added, "I haven't been down there for a long time." She shifted in her chair. "There are no windows and the air is musty. It reminds me of a dungeon. There are a couple of rooms down there, but they're just for storage."

Howie had a hunch the sub-basement might hold a clue. He would have mentioned her father's office, but didn't want to upset her. He and Mick would deal with Gilbertson's office later. "Do you think you could check that sub-basement for us?"

"Check it for what?"

"Just find out what's down there. Check those rooms out, too. It might give us a hint as to what happened to Adam, and possibly some leads concerning LaMar's death." He paused. "It could reveal some clues as to what Adam was looking for."

"Are those rooms locked?" Mick asked Rachel.

"Yes, but I've an extra set of keys for everything in the building."

"I'd prefer that you do this without mentioning it to your father," Howie said. "Is that all right with you?"

"Oh, yes. He's under enough stress as it is now."

"Here's what I'd like for you to do." Howie explained how important it was for her to remember everything she saw. "Take a notepad and make a list of everything," he said, hoping that something would provide a clue as to what Adam might have found.

After Rachel left, Howie and Mick talked until nearly nine o'clock. When his partner left, Howie got a cup of coffee and sat down at his desk. He was sure that either that sub-basement or Gilbertson's office had to hold a clue to the case and to their partner's disappearance.

# Chapter 44

"CAN I HAVE my pills now?" Nana asked as she sat on her bed in her nightgown waiting for the nurse to leave.

The nurse, new to the facility, arched her eyebrow. "Dearie, you're certainly in a rush to get to bed tonight."

"That storm tired me out," Nana fibbed, wanting the woman to leave so she could call Howie. "And make sure you give me the right pills!" she warned, scrutinizing the nurse's every move. "I wouldn't want to get someone's horse pills."

"Dearie, you know we wouldn't do that."

"Oh, yes, you would!" Nana snapped. "It happened just last week to Mabel. That nurse with the big hips gave her George's laxatives by mistake. Poor Mabel had to sit on the pot all morning and couldn't watch her game shows." Satisfied that she had set the snooty nurse in her place, she took her pills along with some apple juice. "One more thing," she said as the nurse was about to leave. She gave the young woman a stern look. "Don't call me, Dearie. I'm not your Dearie. My name is Anabel."

The nurse's eyes nearly doubled in size. Without saying another word, she turned and left the room.

Nana picked up her telephone and dialed Howie's number. He answered on the third ring. "I'm calling for two reasons," she said.

"And what might those be?" Howie asked, his voice sounding hesitant.

"First, to remind you about my birthday party in three days. I expect you there."

"I look forward to it. I wouldn't think of missing it." Howie paused, his voice sounding even more hesitant. "And…what was the second reason you called?"

"I remembered now what I was going to tell you about the security man. We need to talk. Come over tomorrow."

"I can't tomorrow or the next day."

"Then we'll have to talk at my birthday party. You are coming to that, aren't you?"

"Yes, I told you that I—"

Nana hung up the phone. She was done with what she had to say.

Pete Larson lit up a cigarette and dialed the number. He had just taken his second puff when his partner answered. "It's me. Just called to tell you that it's all arranged. The old bag is having a birthday party in a few days and I'm sure her detective friend will be there." He took another drag of his cigarette, and then flicked the ashes off onto the floor. "Yeah, I know. Don't worry. She'll never get to blow out the candles on her cake. That's right. It's planned for the night before. Jack Miller's coming in to help." He picked a bit of tobacco off his tongue. "In a few days half of our problems will be taken care of, and then we'll take care of the other half."

# Chapter 45

THE THROBBING IN Adam's head wouldn't go away. He tried to swallow but his mouth felt as dry as the stale air he breathed. The tape over his mouth prevented him from wetting his parched lips. He had no idea how long he had been out. Minutes? Hours? The enveloping blackness he found himself in brought to mind another occasion. Years ago, he had visited Crystal Cave in Wisconsin. Halfway through the tour and down hundreds of feet, the guide had brought the tour group into one of the larger caverns and then informed them that the lights would be turned off. "I want you to experience what it's like being in a space devoid of light," he had said. "It can be pretty frightening." After the lights had been switched off, the guide told them that they wouldn't be able to see their hands if they held them in front of their faces.

Adam couldn't have held his hands in front of his face if he had wanted to. His hands and feet were securely bound. Whoever tied his hands behind his back had done it so tightly that his shoulders felt as if they were being slowly separated from their joints. With great effort he managed to stand up for a moment, but only to go down hard on his side. The resulting pain to his shoulder was so intense that he nearly passed out. For a long time he lay on his side until, with great difficulty, he managed to scoot himself into a sitting position, using the rough stone wall as a backrest. Now, as he gently rested his head against the wall, he thought about what had happened. *Who could've hit me? Leo? Maybe. Could it have been Pritchett? Betty said he had called in sick. But that could've been a ploy.* He shifted his body to ease the pain in his shoulder. His eyes searched the darkness for any sliver of light. He closed his eyes and thought about Rachel, imagining her in his mind. *I wonder what she's—*

His thought process was suddenly interrupted as something crawled across his forehead. Ignoring his pain, he shook his head, but the thousand-legged creature moved down his forehead, across his closed eyelid, onto his cheek, and stopped. He scraped the side of his face against the wall until he no longer felt the creature. He didn't want to think of where it had fallen or if it had friends. *Concentrate. Think about the case. Let's see, Rachel had said that her father personalized the boxes of chocolate angels he sent to friends. But making the angels from scratch? Something's not right here. What's he hiding?* The throbbing in his head increased. He breathed deeply through his nose a couple of times. Exhausted, he found it hard to focus. *Howie and Mick will be interested in hearing about Gilbertson's office.* The thought of his partners gave him a sense of hope, knowing that they must be looking for him. He closed his eyes and let his mind drift back to the Café Antonio and how beautiful Rachel looked sitting across from him, her eyes sparkling with life.

HOWIE GRABBED THE phone as soon as it rang, hoping that it was Adam, and not Nana calling again. It was neither.

"Hey, it's Mick. Have you heard anything from Adam?"

"Nothing, not a word."

"We've got to do something."

"I agree, but what?" Howie massaged his forehead as his partner vented his frustrations. "I'm frustrated, too," he told him. "But at least we've got the Gilbertson woman on our side." Rachel had said that the first chance she got tomorrow, she would check out that sub-basement. Both he and Mick, however, shared the hunch that her father's office might offer more clues. At this point, though, they hadn't figured out how they were going to get into it. "I'm going to be paying a visit to Ken Pritchett tomorrow morning."

"Do you know where the guy lives?" Mick asked.

"Some apartment building on Fremont near Lowry." Howie checked the address he had written in his notepad. "Do you want to come with me?"

"Sure. Count me in."

"Good. I'll see you around ten." Howie stayed up for a couple of hours reviewing the case and jotting down notes. It was nearly midnight when he headed for the couch. With Adam still missing, it would be another restless night.

ADAM WASN'T SURE how long he had drifted off, but the extra rest had eased the throbbing in his head. He opened his eyes to the same blackness and then closed them again to concentrate on his other senses. Howie always told Adam and Mick that what you smell and hear is just as important as visual clues. The only odor he could detect, however, was a musty, damp smell. He strained to hear any sounds, but there was nothing. He had just rested his head against the wall when he heard the sound of a door being unlocked. It had to be the door leading into his room.

The door opened and a beam from a flashlight blinded Adam. "I hope you've been comfortable," a male voice said. The man shut the door but kept the light shining in Adam's eyes. "What happened to the side of your face?" the man asked in mocked sympathy. "It's all scratched up. You'll just have to be more careful." He came closer, shining the light on Adam's arms and legs. "Just checking to see if you're okay. If you're good, I'll come back and bring you something to eat and drink. I'll even let you go to the can. How's that?"

*You creep, let me tell you what you can do with your hospitality.* Adam's words came out in muffled sounds.

"What's that you say? It doesn't sound like you're too happy with my kindness." Without warning, the man kicked him in the ribs. Adam moaned as he fell over on his side. "That's just a little love tap. Next time you speak a little nicer to me, you hear?" The man laughed and left, locking the door behind him.

Adam groaned. His ribs felt as if they were on fire and his breaths came in short, shallow spurts. He had survived this time and would the next time, but he prayed that his partners would find him soon.

# Chapter 46

HOWIE AND MICK parked in front of Ken Pritchett's apartment building. When Howie had looked for Pritchett's name in the phone book several days ago, he couldn't find any listing. Either the guy had no phone or had a private number. Howie guessed the latter. He had called the candy factory yesterday and got Pritchett's address from Rachel, assuring her that if Pritchett asked, he would keep confidential where he had gotten the information.

"This has to be the place." Howie turned off the ignition and compared the metallic black numbers above the entrance door with what he had written in his notepad.

"The owner doesn't believe in spending much money on upkeep, does he?" Mick said as he looked out at the reddish-brown, brick apartment building. Along both edges of the building at ground level, parts of the bricks had been broken off. It appeared almost like someone had decided to take a sledgehammer to the old building in an attempt to put it out of its misery.

The two detectives got out of the car and headed toward the front door. The apartment building, a narrow three-story structure, was squeezed between a small, corner food market and an older, two-story wooden-framed house with a sagging porch. Although the surrounding neighborhood was by no means well kept up, the apartment building looked like it could have been snuck in under the cover of night from one of the slum areas adjacent to the city. The patchy front lawn was less than five feet from the sidewalk to the front door and needed mowing. On both sides of the entrance sat shrubbery that needed to be given the last rites. The sign to the right of the entrance gave the name of the place but had letters missing. *Bel ir Ap rtme ts.* Although it was supposed to have been a locked entrance, the lock was broken. Once inside the entryway, which they found in surprisingly good shape, they looked for Pritchett's name among the dozen mailboxes.

"There he is," Mick said. "Apartment 301."

Pritchett's apartment was to the left at the top of the third flight of stairs. Howie knocked, wondering if Pritchett had been looking out his window when they had parked out in front. If he had seen them coming, he could have ducked out the back entrance. Howie knocked again, unsure of what his next move would be if there was no answer.

"Just a minute," a voice called from inside the apartment.

Howie gave Mick a knowing glance as they waited.

When the door opened, the shock at seeing Howie and his partner froze on Pritchett's face. Dressed in a white terrycloth bathrobe and non-descript slippers, he stood there speechless. "What are you doing here?" he finally blurted out. "How did you find me?"

"Save your questions for another time." Howie's tone was intentionally rough so that Pritchett understood that they meant business. "We've a few questions of our own." He pushed the door open and he and Mick brushed past Pritchett as they walked in.

"You can't come in here!" Pritchett's tone demanded his two uninvited visitors turn around and leave.

Mick flashed Pritchett a cocky smile. "What do you mean we can't come in? It looks like we're already in."

Howie liked that his partner could appear and sound tough when needed. He had always kidded Mick about being his hired muscle, and sometimes he wasn't kidding.

A sneer appeared on Mick's face. "So, why don't you shut the door, there's a draft. We wouldn't want you to catch a cold, now, would we?"

The look and feel of Pritchett's apartment was in sharp contrast to what they had experienced walking up to the building itself. The tastefully decorated living room had thick beige carpeting that complimented the rich look of the sandy-brown window drapes. The textured ceiling, the papered walls, and the oak woodwork showed no evidence of needing repairs. The furnishings, though not extravagant, were steps above the building itself.

"We want to have a little talk with you," Howie said.

"Look if you don't leave, I'll—"

"You'll do what?" Mick snapped.

"I'll...I'll go to the police."

"That's fine with us." Howie offered Pritchett a half smile. "We'll even drive you there. Go get your clothes." His smile faded as his tone turned icy. "And while we're there, we'll have you talk to a friend of ours, Detective Jim Davidson. He'd be more than happy to find out who you are and your connection with the death of LaMar Jones." He could see by the nervous tic in Pritchett's left eye that he was getting to him. "Then there's that little scene the other night at the restaurant when you received an envelope stuffed with cash. You told me that it was your bookie." He turned to Mick. "Isn't gambling illegal in this state?"

"Last I heard, it was."

Pritchett's tic became more pronounced. "What do you want?"

"Some questions answered," Howie said.

"About what?"

"Adam Trexler."

"What about him?"

Mick took a step toward Pritchett. "What did you do with him?"

"I don't know what you're talking about."

Howie's patience was growing thin. "Adam's our partner."

Pritchett's face registered shock for the second time in less than five minutes. "You mean to tell me that he's a detective?"

"That's right," Howie said. "And the last time we talked to him he told us that you've been snooping around the candy factory and taking some samples home with you." It was time to put the squeeze on Pritchett. "We think that you had something to do with LaMar's death."

Mick spoke up as on cue. "And if you had something to do with his death, then that means you had something to do with our partner's disappearance." He moved a step closer to Pritchett. "And that doesn't set too well with us."

"Look, you've got to believe me. I know nothing about the circumstances surrounding LaMar's death." Pritchett plopped down on the couch. "And I've no idea where you're partner is." He buried his face in his hands. When he finally made eye contact with the two detectives, he had the look of a person who had made a decision. "I'm taking a big chance in what I'm going to tell you, but I need to level with you to set you straight and get you off my back." He paused and took a determined deep breath. "I'm a private investigator."

# Chapter 47

"A PRIVATE INVESTIGATOR!" Howie glanced at Mick who stood wide-eyed staring at Pritchett. "I want to see some identification and then you'd better start explaining yourself."

"Surely, by all means." By the smirk on Pritchett's face, he was obviously pleased that he had taken Howie and his partner completely off guard. He walked over to a desk, opened the right-hand drawer, and came back wearing the same smirky look. He handed a business card to each of the detectives, and then settled himself on the couch. "If you think those cards are phony, I can give you some references from the Minneapolis Police Department. There are a couple of officers who can vouch for me. They think I'm rather good at what I do."

Howie slipped the card in his pocket. If necessary, he would contact JD to see if he had ever heard of Pritchett. "What are you doing at the candy factory?"

"I don't have to tell you, but since we're in the same line of work..." Pritchett continued to smirk. "Over a year ago, my services were retained by a certain individual who, himself, was representing another party."

"And who would that be?"

"I was never given that information. He just told me that it'd be best if I didn't know his client's identity." Pritchett spoke with calm confidence. "The man you saw me with at the restaurant hired me to find out as much as I could about the processing of the chocolate." He paused, appearing to be studying their reactions like any detective would do. "I was hired to find out Gilbertson's family recipe for the chocolate angels."

"His recipe?" Mick gave the guy an incredulous look.

"That's right. My client believes that there's a secret ingredient." Pritchett's left eyebrow rose slightly as a hint of a smile formed on his thin lips; the tick in his eye had long disappeared. "Personally, I don't think the chocolate in those angels is any different than other chocolate I've tasted...but, of course, I'm no expert."

Howie pulled up a chair and sat across from Pritchett. Mick found a spot by the stereo and leaned against the wall. "You mean to tell me you're some kind of...of candy spy?" Howie asked.

"I don't think of myself in that way."

Mick spoke up. "Isn't what you're doing illegal?"

Pritchett shrugged. "Technically, yes, but it's done all the time in the real world. Whether it's stereos, or food, or fashions, companies and individuals go after the ideas and innovations of their competitors. It's illegal to duplicate the product exactly, but there's no law in modifying it to suit one's own purposes, and I might add, profits."

Howie's head was pounding. He could use a couple of aspirins. "What was your connection with LaMar?"

"In the beginning, nothing. After a while, however, I realized that I could use him." Pritchett folded his hands in his lap. He was completely relaxed now that his identity had been revealed to peers who he no doubt assumed would be sympathetic to his style and ethics. He seemed to enjoy telling his story. "When I approached him, he jumped at the idea of making an extra buck. He was a savvy operator, though. He didn't come cheap."

"How much was he asking?" Mick inquired.

"Let's see, now..." Pritchett rubbed his chin for a moment, crossed his legs, and then rested his arm on the back of the couch. "I'm really not at liberty to divulge that, but let me say it would've been substantial for a man like himself. It's too bad what happened to him, however. I was growing rather fond of his greediness."

Howie ran a hand through his hair, massaging the back of his neck for a moment. Pritchett might be a private investigator, but one who walked dangerously close to the other side of the law. "Do you think what happened to LaMar was an accident?"

"I think so, but I can't be positive. He and Leo had some problems about his flirting with the boss' daughter." A wicked grin flashed across Pritchett's face. "Cute dame. Under different circumstances, I might've tried to do the same. I wouldn't mind having her shoes under my bed."

"Where were you the night he died?" Howie asked.

Pritchett chuckled. "Ah, always the detective, aren't you. Good, I admire that." Like the prima donna he was proving to be, he took his time before answering. "Sorry to disappoint you, but I wasn't working that night."

Howie had just about checked Pritchett off as a suspect, but not completely. "I suppose you have witnesses to back up whatever alibi you have?"

"Just an entire hospital." Pritchett's smile bordered on arrogance. "I was at North Memorial that night being treated for a bleeding ulcer. Nasty stuff. They kept me overnight. You may check it out, if you'd like."

Howie nodded. "We may just do that."

"Be my guest." Pritchett leaned forward. "So Adam was working undercover at the place, huh?" He stroked his chin; his eyes flickered with curiosity. "That means whoever hired you must think that LaMar's death wasn't an accident." He glanced at Mick and then turned his attention again to Howie. "Very intriguing case you're working on. What have you found out so far? Is Leo a suspect?"

"Do you know anything about Adam?"

"Okay, okay." Pritchett put his hands up in mock surrender. "I respect your professional ethics." He leaned back and crossed his legs. "What do I know about your partner? I was surprised to learn that he'd quit. I thought it was rather suspicious, but it wasn't my concern."

Howie's next words were spoken in a clipped tone. "We would appreciate it if you would make it your concern. I think it would be in your own best interests." He gave Pritchett a half smile. "If you know what I mean."

Pritchett's smile froze as his eyes shifted between his two visitors. "I think I do. Let me see if I understand. From what you're saying, if I don't make it my concern, Gilbertson might get a phone call. Is that it?"

"That's right."

"And if I do express some interest in your missing partner, I can continue to go about my business?"

"Right again."

"Well, since you put it that way, what do you wish for me to do?"

"We want to know what's in Gilbertson's office," Howie said, counting on Rachel to check out the sub-basement area.

"You'll have your answer tomorrow."

Mick moved away from the wall, his furrowed brow signaling that he was annoyed by Pritchett's quick and overconfident reply. "How can you be so sure of that?"

"Very simple." Pritchett rested his arm on the back of the couch again. He spoke casually as if entertaining guests at a cocktail party. "I'm going to get a peek into Gilbertson's office tonight."

"Is that right?" Howie was getting fed up with Pritchett's smugness. "And just how are you going to get in?"

"I've a duplicate key." Howie's puzzled look caused Pritchett to explain. "I've my methods. It's a trade secret, but I'm willing to share it with you. We could even exchange ideas. You must have techniques of getting into locked areas, don't you?"

Howie took out his notepad, tore off a blank sheet, and wrote down his telephone number. "Call me tomorrow morning at this number. I'll be waiting to hear from you. And the earlier the better."

"I'll call you as soon as I can." Pritchett took the paper, glanced at the number, and slipped the paper into the pocket of his bathrobe.

"Let's go," Howie said to Mick. "We're out of here."

# Chapter 48

ON THE WAY back from Pritchett's, Howie discussed with Mick what should be done next. "The first thing I'm going to do is call LaMar's sister," he said. "She'll be disappointed, but she needs to know that Pritchett's no longer a suspect."

"Are you going to tell her he's a private investigator?"

"I don't know, yet." Howie slowed the car to a stop for a red light. As he waited for the light to change, he drummed his fingers on the steering wheel. "I don't like Pritchett or the way he operates, but a deal's a deal." The light turned green and he stepped on the gas. "It gives me a royal pain to think that he's even in the same line of work as we are. If it wasn't for Adam, I'd love to blow his ship out of the water."

"I'm with you on that, buddy."

"Good," Howie said, a little surprised at Mick. His partner usually didn't think such vengeful thoughts. Pritchett must have gotten to him.

"What about Rachel?" Mick asked. "What do you think she'll find in that basement?"

"Probably nothing. My bet's on the office." Although he hated to admit it, Howie felt more confident in Pritchett if only because, as a private investigator, the guy would know what clues to look for. "But I'd better give Rachel a call, also. Maybe she'll have something for us by now." If Pritchett or Rachel didn't turn up anything, then he had no idea where to look next. The answer had to be at that candy factory. If only they knew what they were looking for. "Say, will you do me a favor?"

"Sure. What?"

"Stop and see Adam's mom. Tell her..." Howie rubbed his temple; his headache was killing him. "Just tell her that he's still busy working on a case and that's why he hasn't been home."

"And if she asks when is he coming home?"

"As soon as the case is over." Howie couldn't help but wonder what Adam and his ethics professors would think of his lying in this situation. Adam maintained that you should never lie, but what would he say about doing so to keep a mother from worrying about her son? "Let her know that he's with me and that she shouldn't worry."

"Anything else?"

"Nothing for now." Howie turned the corner by Kass'. Since there were no parking places in front of his apartment, he parked in the next block. As they walked back to his apartment, the warm sun and fresh air eased his headache. A nice walk around one of the Minneapolis lakes with that blond nurse would work wonders for him.

"After I see Adam's mom, I'm going to take a drive over to the hospital," Mick said as the two of them stood at the entrance of Howie's apartment building. "I know it's a long shot but I want to check on Pritchett's alibi just to see if it pans out."

"How are you going to find out if he was a patient?" Howie appreciated his partner's initiative. "That's confidential information."

"I've got a friend who works in medical records. She'll be able to verify whether Pritchett was there the night LaMar died."

Howie nodded his approval, but Mick would probably find that Pritchett was telling the truth. His partner, however, needed to be doing something. In their last case, Mick had been kidnapped and held for over twenty-four hours. He had shared with Howie and Adam that the only way he had gotten through his ordeal was that he knew with absolute certainty that they were doing all they could to find him, and that they wouldn't give up.

"Give me a call if you come up with anything at the hospital," Howie said. "If I don't hear from you, I'll assume you've struck out." He watched Mick cross the street and head toward Andy's Diner, the small hamburger joint where Adam's mother worked. "Well, let's see what I can do now," he muttered as he headed up to his office.

The first phone call Howie made was to Stephanie, LaMar's sister. She was disappointed that Pritchett was no longer a suspect. When she asked about other leads, he said they were working on a few. He didn't mention Adam's disappearance. To reassure her, he promised that he would stay in touch. Before he made the call to Rachel, he went out into the kitchen, got a glass of water, and popped down a couple of aspirins. After making a pot of coffee, he slapped together a peanut butter-and-jelly sandwich, poured himself a cup of the freshly brewed black coffee, and went back to his desk to make his phone call.

"Have you heard from Adam?" Rachel asked as soon as he identified himself. She sounded anxious and upset.

"I'm afraid not. We're hoping that you'll find something in that basement."

"I won't be able to do that tonight."

"Why not?"

"Because Daddy wants me to go out to dinner with him after work." She paused. "I suppose I could tell him no."

"Don't do that," Howie quickly replied, not wanting her father to get suspicious. He would ask Pritchett to check it out.

"I can do it tomorrow night. Is that okay?"

"Sure, but be careful."

"You'll call me if you hear from Adam?"

"Of course." After hanging up, Howie took out his notepad and reviewed his notes on the case. When he came to the name of Jack Miller, LaMar's former roommate, he reread what Mick had mentioned after his visit with the guy. *Miller knows more than he's letting on.* In parenthesis, Howie had scribbled, *Follow up!* He closed his notepad and slipped it into his shirt pocket. He quickly finished his sandwich, washing it down with gulps of coffee, and headed for the door, determined to find out what Miller knew. His gut told him that all of this somehow had to do with Rosie Carpenter and Adam being missing. There had to be a connection, but for the life of him, he couldn't figure it out.

PETE LARSON PUFFED on a cigarette as he waited at the café. "He'd better not keep me waiting too long," he muttered and then called the waitress over, asking her to refill his coffee cup.

"Anything else?" the waitress asked after filling his cup.

"That depends," he said, leering at her shapely figure. "What are you offering?"

"Not what you're thinking!" she snapped and walked away.

He chuckled and took another drag of his cigarette as he turned his thoughts to Nana. That bag-of-bones had been a thorn in his side for too long now. Besides, having that detective come around the nursing home so often was making him nervous. It was making his partner nervous as well. Pete was still angry that Howie and his partners had sprung the Carpenter woman from the third floor. He was confident, however, that they would never find her where she was now.

"Hey, what's cooking?" Jack Miller said as he slid in across from Pete.

"You're late!" Pete snapped, annoyed by Miller's cocky attitude.

"Just ten minutes. No big deal."

"I've got another job for you."

"Oh, yeah? What now?"

The waitress, a different one, a motherly-type, stopped and poured Miller a cup of coffee. When she asked for their orders, Pete said he was fine with just coffee. Miller, on the other hand, ordered a piece of banana cream pie. "And give my friend here the bill," he said with a smug grin.

Pete waited until the waitress brought Miller his pie. After she left, he spoke in low tones. "I want you to come over to the home on Wednesday evening and get a resident ready for her bath. Once you get her to the tub room, the one on the lower level, I'll take care of it." He paused. "Unless you want to take part."

"Not me. I'll let you handle those things." Miller slipped a forkful of pie in his mouth. "My price is double now."

"Double!" Pete wanted to reach over and smash Miller's teeth in. "Why you greedy little—"

"Hey, man, calm down. Remember, this is the second time around for me. I'm experienced now." Miller sneered. "Anyways, I know too much."

*The jerk is right; he does know too much.* "Okay, you'll get your damn money, but make sure you get her to the tub room."

Miller took a sip of coffee. "What if she gets suspicious about me?"

"Just tell her you're new on the job. Charm her like you did the other one."

HOWIE WALKED DOWN the steps from Pritchett's apartment. He had stopped to see if Pritchett would check out the sub-basement in addition to Gilbertson's office, but the guy wasn't home. He had stood and knocked on his door for ten minutes. Jack Miller hadn't been home, either. The afternoon had been a bust. The only thing he had gotten for his efforts was another headache. He planned to go home, take a couple more aspirins, call Mick, and wait it out until Pritchett contacted him tomorrow morning. He hoped for a good night's sleep, but with the disappearance of his partner gnawing at him, he would settle for a few hours.

# Chapter 49

"YOU'RE LOOKING TIRED," Howie said after Mick made himself comfortable in a chair. The two of them had agreed to meet at nine that morning in Howie's office.

"Anything on Adam yet?" Mick asked, his voice revealing his anxiety concerning the fate of their partner.

"Nothing." Howie had a sleepless night on the couch worrying about their partner. He had even gotten up at midnight, dressed, and drove around for a while as he tried to think of what their next step should be. "Did you find out if Pritchett was telling the truth about being at the hospital that night?"

"The guy wasn't lying," Mick said, sounding disappointed. "Pritchett was there all right." He yawned, stretching his arms for a moment. "From what my contact told me, he was a pretty sick man at the time of admittance. Apparently, the doctor left orders for the nurses to check on him every couple of hours. So there's no way that he could've slipped out that night."

"Well, I guess that scratches his name as a suspect." Howie closed his notepad and tossed it aside. "That leaves us with Hooknose and...who?" He hoped Mick had an answer because he didn't.

"Other than Hooknose, I don't know." Mick's tone matched the frustration on his face. "Right now, I just want to find Adam. I didn't sleep too well not knowing where he is or what's happening to him."

"I know what you mean." Howie felt frustrated, as well as responsible, for not having come up with any leads on their partner's disappearance. He picked up a pencil and rolled it between his fingers for several seconds before tossing it aside.

"What about Miller?" Mick asked. "Did you check on him?"

"Yeah, but he wasn't home." Howie tried to rub the weariness out of his eyes. He was bushed and his back ached from the couch. It was bad enough when Rosie disappeared and he took to the couch unwilling to sleep in his bed until she was found. Now, with Adam's disappearance, he wondered if he would even be able to get any sleep on the couch. "I thought we could try Miller's apartment again after Pritchett calls."

"Sounds like a good plan to me." Mick shifted in his chair, stretching out his legs. "When is he going to call?"

"I was hoping that he would've called by now." Howie settled back in his chair, clasped his hands behind his head, and stared at the phone, willing it to ring. After ten minutes of silence, he picked up the phone to make sure it had a dial tone. "Do you want a cup of coffee while we're waiting?"

"Sure, I need something to keep me awake."

"It'll do that, all right." Howie got up, stretched, and yawned. "I'm just going to reheat the pot I made last night."

For the next two plus hours, Mick dozed off and on in his chair while Howie sat at his desk and paged through several copies of *Police Gazette*. Neither one of them had been able to drink more than a cup of the bitter, black liquid. It was nearly noon when the phone rang. Howie grabbed it on the first ring. "Mac Detective Agency." *It's Pritchett*, he mouthed to Mick. "You did? Good. So tell—what? Well, don't answer it; tell them to go away. Can't you just—" He glanced at the clock. "Yeah, don't worry, we'll be here. See you then." He slapped the phone down.

"What's wrong?" Mick asked.

"Pritchett said he found something in Gilbertson's office, but get this..." Howie took a couple of seconds to settle down. "The jerk said he couldn't talk over the phone right now because somebody was at his door."

"Is he going to call back?"

"No, he wants to come over and talk."

"Is he coming now?"

"I wish, but he said he had to go someplace and check something out first." Howie dug his fingernails into his palms. "Something's going on with him, though."

"What do you mean?"

"I'm not sure, but he sounded scared."

"Of what?"

"I wish I knew." Howie checked the time. "Maybe he was just excited about whatever he found. He said he'd be here by two. We'll find out then."

The time passed more quickly than Howie expected, but two o'clock came and no Pritchett. He still hadn't shown up by half past two. Mick got up and stood by the window while Howie drummed his fingers on the desk as the clock continued to tick off the minutes. At quarter of three, Howie slammed his fist on the desk. "Where is that guy?"

"Maybe he's changed his mind."

Howie stood up so abruptly that his chair slammed against the wall. "Come on!" he said as he headed for the door. "If he's not coming to us, we'll go see him."

In less than twenty minutes Howie and Mick were at Pritchett's apartment. They moved swiftly but quietly up the two flights of stairs. "His door's ajar," Howie whispered as they approached Pritchett's apartment.

They stood at the door listening. "I don't hear anything," Mick said.

Howie pushed the door open. He thought about calling out Pritchett's name, but decided not to. The thought of possibly finding him dead crossed his mind.

Mick nudged Howie. "What should we do?"

"We go in."

The living room looked as though nothing had changed from the other day they were there. If anything could be said about Pritchett, it was that he liked everything in his apartment to be neat and tidy. They quickly checked the other rooms. If Pritchett had been taken against his will, there certainly was no evidence of a struggle. It was as though the man had just stepped out for a moment.

"Could he have skipped out on us?" Mick asked.

"I don't think so." That thought, nevertheless unnerved Howie. At this point, Pritchett was their best chance of finding Adam. "Let's give this place a going over," he said. "There's got to be something here that will help us."

For the next forty-five minutes Howie and Mick looked through closets, dresser drawers, under the mattress, behind furniture, and in the kitchen cupboards. They even looked in the refrigerator, which revealed that Pritchett had a preference for fine wines and choice cuts of meat. They walked back into the living room. Mick sat on the couch as Howie stood by the stereo and scanned the area.

"You know me pretty well, don't you?" Howie asked.

"Yeah, I would say so. Why?"

"Answer me this. Where do you think I'd hide something at my place?"

Mick rubbed the bridge of his nose, a trait that usually meant he was going through a thought process rather than scratching an itch. "You'd probably hide it behind your movie poster."

"You're right. I would. Too bad there's no..." The framed painting behind the couch caught Howie's eye. It wasn't the scene of a golden sunset over a tranquil ocean that drew his attention, but the fact that the frame was tilted slightly to one side. If there had been one thing they had noticed in Pritchett's apartment, it was how nothing had been out of place. Even the canned goods in the cupboard were arranged in rows and had their labels facing outward. "Do me a favor. Check out that picture behind you and see what's in back of it."

Mick turned around and peeked behind the frame. "Well, what do you know?" He took the painting off the wall and set it on the couch. "It's a notebook."

A thin black notebook had been wedged into the corner of the frame. Mick opened the notebook and paged through it.

"What is that thing?" Howie asked as he rushed over.

"It's some kind of daily journal." Mick flipped through it until he found the last entry. "Hey! Read this!"

Howie took the notebook and read the neatly handwritten entry. *Got into Gilbertson's office tonight. Chocolate angels not so angelic!*

# Chapter 50

ADAM'S RIBS ACHED. He could take shallow breaths but found it impossible to take deep ones without experiencing searing pain. With great effort, he managed to get into a sitting position, using the wall as a backrest. He wanted to just sit until the pain subsided, but knew that time wasn't on his side. The man would be back and that meant he had to somehow free his hands to have a chance.

At first, he worked his wrists back and forth, trying to loosen the rope. When that didn't work, he scraped the thick cord against the rough surface of the wall, hoping that it could be frayed to the point of allowing him to break free. Sweat ran down his forehead. His shoulders ached. His wrists stung from being rubbed raw. Exhausted, he slumped against the wall.

After resting for a couple of minutes, he tried to get loose again but it was of no use; the ropes were too secure. As he sat with his head against the wall, he considered other options. The only workable option was to somehow get on his feet, move over to the door, and try and knock the guy unconscious by slamming him against the wall when he came in. It was a long shot but worth the risk. After a couple of tries, he managed to stand up. Although his ankles were bound, he was determined to get near the door. As soon as the door opened, he would make his move.

He didn't get more than a couple of feet, however, before falling and cracking his head against the stone wall. As he lay on the floor, warm blood trickled into his eyes. He rolled on his side and tipped his head back so that the flow of blood found another path. Although his ribs were on fire, in a few minutes he would try again. He closed his eyes to rest. The sound of the door being unlocked, though, got his attention.

The light flooded in and a woman's voice cried out. "Oh, my god!"

With the light behind the person's back, Adam couldn't see who it was, but the familiar voice told him it was Rachel. He tried to call her name, but only a muffled sound came through the tape binding his mouth.

She rushed over and knelt beside him. "You're bleeding!" she cried as she looked around for something, and then used the hem of her dress to wipe the blood. "Let me take that tape off."

After the tape was removed, Adam had to move his jaw and wet his lips before he could speak. "Un...untie my hands...will you?"

It took Rachel several long minutes to untie the knots. Once his hands were free, Adam massaged his arms and then worked at untying his feet. "Let's get out of here before he comes back," he said.

"Who are you talking about?"

"I wish I knew." Adam stood, but was unsteady. He leaned on Rachel.

"Who did this to you?" Rachel asked as she helped him toward the door.

"I don't know that either." Although Adam suspected Leo was involved, he didn't say anything.

When they moved out of the room that had been his cell, he told Rachel to close and lock the door. As she did, he looked around. The sub-basement reminded him of a dungeon. There were two other doors, and no doubt behind each door was a cell-like room similar to the one he had been kept in. He couldn't imagine any sane person wanting to have a spiritual retreat down here.

"It's locked," Rachel said. "Let's go." She started helping him toward the stairs.

"Wait a minute!" he whispered. "Do you hear that?"

Rachel shook her head. "Please, let's go."

"It's coming from in there." Adam moved closer to the door leading into the room that was adjacent to his; a faint tapping could be heard coming from inside. He tried the door, but it was locked. He turned to Rachel. "Do you have—" He held his breath. The door at the top of the stairs opened and the stairs began to creak.

# Chapter 51

"IS THERE ANY other way out of here?" Adam whispered, knowing that it would be only a matter of seconds before they were discovered.

Rachel shook her head. She glanced around and then took him by the hand. "We can hide behind those pews back there," she said, motioning toward a stack of five or six pews near the back wall behind the stairway.

They moved swiftly but quietly. The stacked pews stood nearly six feet. Adam squeezed in first, brushing away the cobwebs. There was barely enough space between the pews and the wall for him as he inched his way with his back against the stone wall. Rachel followed. They moved in five or six feet. They couldn't be seen; which was good, but neither could they see anything.

Rachel stood next to him, their bodies touching. Adam, not wanting to take any chances, crouched, making sure his head was lower than the top of the pews. They stood silently, breathing in their dusty surroundings and listening to the creaking of the stairs as the footsteps got closer and closer to the bottom. By the sound of the footsteps, Adam was sure it was a man, probably the man who had knocked him out and put him in that cell, the man who took pleasure in kicking him in the ribs, the man he hoped to meet again, but on his own terms.

When the footsteps reached the bottom they stopped as if the man was looking around, checking out the area. Could their feet be seen? Adam hadn't thought about that. He could hear Rachel's breathing and wondered if the man heard it as well. What would the man do when he unlocked the cell and discovered his prisoner gone? Would he come looking for him? If he came back to where they were hiding...then what? They were trapped, and he was too weak to put up much of a fight. His ribs still ached from being kicked.

Adam recalled Howie's advice. "Devise a plan of action in every situation. You may not have to use it, but you'll be ready." Adam's mind raced. There was only one thing he could think of to do. He gently and very carefully pressed his body against the stack of pews. His heart nearly stopped when he thought he had pressed too hard and they moved, swaying slightly. At least, now he knew they could be toppled easily. That would be his plan, then. If the man came too close, he would push against the pews hopefully toppling them upon the man, and giving Rachel and him a chance to escape.

The sound of a door being unlocked caused Adam to gnaw at his lip until he nearly drew blood. This could be it. When the man discovered he was gone, he would come looking. Very carefully and slowly, Adam moved his head toward Rachel. At the moment his lips brushed her hair, he whispered his plan of action. Her response was to reach out her hand until she found his. She clasped his hand and then rested her head on his shoulder. He gently kissed the top of her head and squeezed her hand, not wanting to think of what would happen if his plan failed.

A door swung open, its hinges squeaking. Adam waited, straining to hear anything, but only aware of Rachel and his own breathing. Soon a man's muffled voice could be heard. It took Adam a moment to realize that the man had opened the other cell and was talking to whoever was in there. Suddenly, someone cried out in pain like an animal being beaten, causing Adam to have a flashback. Whoever was in that cell had been hit or kicked like he had been. Rachel's hand squeezed his and he squeezed hers in return.

"If he comes back here," Adam whispered. "When I push these pews over, you get out and go for help."

"I'm not leaving without you."

"You have to. I—" The sound of the cell door being closed and locked stopped Adam from finishing. It sounded as if the footsteps were now coming toward them. Adam pressed his body against the pews and got ready. He didn't dare breathe. It seemed like an eternity before he heard the creaking of the stairs and realized to his relief that the man was leaving. He and Rachel waited until the door at the top of the stairs closed. They didn't move from their hiding place for several minutes, wanting to make sure the man wasn't coming back.

"Who do you think that was?" Rachel whispered.

"I don't know." Adam's heart pounded so hard that he wondered if she could hear it. They moved from behind the pews and hurried toward the stairs. "Wait minute," he said, and went over to the door leading into the room where he had heard the tapping. "Do you have the key for this one?" he asked Rachel.

"No." She glanced at the door at the top of the stairs. "We need to go."

Adam rapped on the cell door. "Whoever's in there, don't worry. I'll come back and get you out. I promise."

# Chapter 52

"You look a whole lot better today than you did yesterday at this time," Howie said as Adam slowly lowered himself into the chair next to Mick.

"I should. I slept for nearly fifteen hours." Adam rested his head against the back of the chair. The left side of his face still showed bruising from where he had scraped it against the wall of his cell. An oversize Band-Aid covered the gash on his forehead. Dark circles under his eyes broadcasted his need for still more sleep.

"How are your ribs?" Mick asked.

"Sore and tender, but at least I can take a deep breath every now and then."

Mick had made Adam promise that he would see a doctor before going home last night. It being Saturday night, Rachel had taken him to the emergency room at North Memorial Hospital. "They're not cracked, are they?" Mick asked.

"No, they're just bruised."

Howie took out his notepad and flipped to the notes he had taken yesterday when Adam and Rachel showed up at his office. As soon as Adam came in, he and Mick had jumped up from their chairs and rushed over to him. Mick had been so overjoyed that he had wanted give their partner a bear hug, but Adam quickly put that idea to bed. After asking only a few questions about his ordeal, they had realized that Adam was too exhausted to provide any kind of detailed accounting. Adam had refused to go home or to the emergency room, however, without telling them about the person in the other cell and that he was determined to go back there today. They had agreed that they, including Rachel, would meet this afternoon in Howie's office to plan a course of action. Rachel was essential because she would be able to get them into the building. It being Sunday, there wouldn't be anyone working at the candy factory.

"I know we went over this a little yesterday, but I want to make sure I've got all my facts straight," Howie said. "We need to get at some things before Rachel gets here."

"What things?" Adam asked, his tone edgy as if suspecting that Howie didn't trust the woman.

"I don't want her to know anything about you being in her father's office." Last night Howie couldn't help but notice the way in which Adam and Rachel interacted; they certainly appeared to be more than just friends. That wasn't good. Adam couldn't let his feelings for her interfere with the case. Not at this point. And if they had to deceive Rachel for the time being for the sake of the case, so be it. "Is that clear about not telling her anything?" Howie asked, knowing that if his partner had trouble deceiving others, he would especially have a difficult time deceiving Rachel. When Adam didn't respond, he asked again, but this time in a sharper tone that demanded an answer. "Is that clear?"

Adam glanced at Mick before replying. "I guess so."

"Okay, now that we've got that settled, tell me what you saw in Gilbertson's office."

"Not much." Adam ran his hand through his hair. He took a deep breath, but not without wincing. "Besides a desk, there were a couple of wooden tables. On the larger table were stacks of empty candy boxes."

"Was there anything else on that table?"

"Yeah, a packing carton."

"What was in it?"

"Some metal moldings for chocolate angels."

"How about the smaller table? Anything on that?"

"A black cast-iron kettle on a hot plate."

"What was he using that for?" Mick asked.

"I'd guess to melt chocolate for the moldings. Rachel told me that her father likes to hand-make some of the angels to send to friends." Adam frowned. "Look, I've told you guys about that before."

Howie flipped to another page in his notepad, ignoring the annoyance he heard in Adam's voice. "Did you check his desk?"

"I didn't get a chance." Adam shifted in his chair, grimacing as he did. "I heard this sound behind me. Before I could turn around to see who it was, somebody hit me over the head. When I came to, my hands and feet were tied, my mouth was taped, and it was pitch-black in the room."

"And you didn't know where you were?"

"Not at the time. It was only after Rachel came in that I realized I was in the sub-basement." Adam waited for Howie to finish writing before adding, "I wouldn't be here now if it wasn't for her."

Howie drummed his pen on the notepad as he pondered whether he should set his partner straight that it was he and Mick who had contacted Rachel and persuaded her to check out the basement. He decided he would, however, inform Adam later of that detail since his partner seemed too edgy now. "And you didn't see who came down those stairs?"

"No."

"And you're positive that there was somebody in that other room?"

Irritation flickered in Adam's eyes. "Look, we were hiding behind a stack of pews. I couldn't see the stairs let alone see who came down them." His irritation showed now in his tone of voice. "And yes, I am sure there was someone in that other room." The muscles in his jaw tightened as he gripped the arms of his chair. "I heard him yell. Rachel was there. She heard him, too." His eyes flashed with anger. "Don't you believe me?"

"Calm down, buddy," Mick said, patting Adam gently on the arm. As usual, he served as mediator between the two of them whenever tensions flared. "Howie was just trying to get all the facts straight."

Adam stared at Mick for several seconds before leaning his head back and closing his eyes. "I know...I know. I'm just tired." He sat up and leaned forward. "I want to get that guy out because I know what he's going through."

"So you think it was a man?" Howie asked, having had thoughts that it might be Pritchett or perhaps even Rosie Carpenter.

"Ah..." Adam seemed surprised by the question. "I just assumed it was...why?"

"Nothing, just asking," Howie said, keeping his voice calm. "Are you sure no one saw you when you and Rachel slipped away from the place?"

"I can't be positive, but we didn't see anybody."

"And you came directly here?"

Adam nodded.

Howie closed his notepad. Even though Adam looked exhausted and needed to go home and get some more rest, there was no chance of talking him out of returning to that candy factory. Being held against your will in a cell-like dungeon was an injustice that his partner was determined to make right. "Why don't we just relax and wait for Rachel. She should be here any minute." He checked the time. Nearly four. Rachel had said she could make it by then. "Can I get you guys a cup of coffee or something?" Mick declined. Adam asked for a glass of water. By the time he came back with Adam's water, Rachel had come and was just closing the door. Mick got up, offered his chair to her and stood by the window.

Rachel sat down, leaned over and touched Adam on the arm. "How are you doing?" she asked, speaking with a tenderness that went beyond the boundaries of friendship.

"I'm doing okay." Adam looked like he wanted to take her hand. Under different circumstances, he probably would have, but he wasn't the type of guy that displayed affection in public, especially in front of his partners.

"Did you have to have stitches?" Howie asked.

"No." Adam touched the bandage. "There was a lot of blood, but the gash was small. The doc said that all the blood just made it looked worse than it was."

"I hope it doesn't leave a scar," Mick said, rubbing his chest. He had been left with scars from their last case. Although he later joked that the scars had been his baptism as a detective, it had been a traumatic experience. "What did your mom say when she saw you?" he asked.

"She was at work when I got home." Adam slowly shifted in his chair, his eyes reluctantly announcing that his body still needed healing. He wasn't the type of guy, though, who would tell you how much he was hurting. "I called and let her know I was okay and that I was going to sleep late this morning. When I finally got up, I found a note on the kitchen table saying that she'd gone to a movie with some friends."

Howie wondered how Adam's mother would have reacted if she had seen Adam last night. Over the years his mother had gotten to know most of the cops on Broadway since they were regular customers at the place she worked. If she had known about Adam, she would have wasted no time telling the cops all about her son and she would have asked them to do something about it. Howie's police detective friend, JD, would then also have found out and come storming into his office asking what the hell was going on, and demanding to be kept informed. If there was one thing Howie didn't need or want, it was police involvement. If they were going to make a name for themselves, they had to do it without being dependent upon outside help. JD would be angry for a while, but he would eventually come around. "You're lucky she hasn't seen you," he said to Adam, wanting to add *and lucky for us.*

Adam took a sip of water. After setting the glass on the desk, he drew in a deep breath and let it out slowly. His eyes narrowed. "Whoever was responsible for my stay in that place…I owe him."

"We owe him big time," Mick said.

"We've got to find out who it is first." Howie looked directly at Adam. "And then we'll go after him for some payback." He opened his notepad and then addressed his remarks to Rachel. "Adam said that neither of you could see who came down those stairs. Is that right?"

"Yes, we're just lucky that we weren't discovered."

"How about when the guy came into that cell with you?" Mick asked Adam. "Did you get a look at him then?"

"No, he always made sure he shined his flashlight in my face."

"Do you think it could've been Leo?" Howie asked, wanting to see how Rachel would react.

"Leo Rappaport?" Rachel's eyes flashed to his defense. "You've got to be kidding. He wouldn't do anything like that." She turned to Adam. The expression on her face asked for affirmation of her belief in Leo's innocence. "Tell them they're wrong."

Howie spoke up, keeping his tone gentle but firm. "Rachel, I'm not so sure if we agree with you." He had asked Adam last night if he thought the person who had kicked him was Leo.

"I don't think so," Adam had replied.

"Well, give it some thought after you get a good night's sleep."

Howie now felt that Rachel needed to be informed of their suspicions. He cast a knowing glance at his partners. Mick gave him a go-ahead signal, but he saw the reluctance in Adam's eyes. "We think you ought to know that we suspect that Leo may have had something to do with the death of LaMar Jones."

"You can't be serious," Rachel said, her tone incredulous.

"We're very serious," Mick said.

Rachel directed her attention to Howie. "I know you don't believe his death was accidental, but are you now telling me that you think Leo killed him?"

Howie leaned back and said nothing, letting the look in his eyes speak for him.

"You don't believe that, do you?" Rachel asked Adam.

When Adam winced, Howie suspected it wasn't from his sore ribs. "Rachel," Adam said, his tone pleading for understanding. "We can't be absolutely sure about Leo's involvement, but he is a suspect." He turned his attention back to Howie. "As far as I'm concerned, it wasn't him. The guy didn't sound like him, and was no where near his size."

"But he had to have been involved in some way," Mick said.

"Do you want to explain what you mean by that?" Howie said, glad that Mick spoke up when he did. He was in no mood to lock horns with Adam at this point. He stole a glance at Rachel. All this talk about Leo was upsetting her. That was too bad, but she needed to hear for herself where Mick was going with this.

Mick moved away from the window and sat on the corner of Howie's desk. He looked as if he was about to teach one of his classes at school. "Here's my take on this whole situation. For one thing, Leo hasn't liked Adam from the first day he started working there. We think that he may be jealous of..." He paused and rubbed the bridge of his nose.

Howie recognized the mannerism as an indication that Mick was considering how he might phrase what he was about to say.

Mick cleared his throat. "He may have been resentful that you and Adam had developed such a...friendly relationship." He paused again as though trying to read Rachel's reaction. She, however, gave no clue of her feelings. "After all, you've said that he was like a big brother, didn't you?"

"And big brothers like to protect their little sisters," Howie added to drive the point home.

Rachel glanced at Adam, no doubt looking for support. "But that doesn't prove anything."

"On that basis alone, perhaps not," Howie said. "But how did Adam end up in that room in the basement?" He waited for a reply, but none came. "Whoever took him there had to have had keys, not only to the building, but also to that room. It had to have been an inside job. If Leo didn't do it, then he probably let someone in."

"Does Leo have a set of keys?" Mick quietly asked in an obvious effort to lower the level of tension.

"Of course he does, but..." Rachel closed her eyes and slowly shook her head, apparently not wanting to believe the inference. "Again, that doesn't prove anything."

"I agree with her," Adam said and then checked his watch. "We're just wasting time. I need to go back to that place now." He turned to Rachel. "Can you get me a set of keys for the entire building?"

She hesitated. "I'm going with you."

"I don't know if that's a good idea," Howie said. "Mick and I will go with Adam. You don't need to be involved in this."

"But I'm already involved. This concerns my father's factory and I think I've every right to go." Her eyes were unflinching and her tone determined. "I also know where the keys are kept. Adam won't need to waste time looking for them. Besides, if he's seen going in with me, it won't be as suspicious as if he were seen going in alone. And if you two came, it'd be too much of a crowd."

"She's got a point there," Mick said.

"I don't know about this." Howie rocked in his chair and stared at the ceiling for a moment as he thought through the implications of what was being suggested. "Do you feel up to this?" he asked Adam, already knowing the answer. "Maybe I should just go with her. You and Mick stay here."

"Oh, no!" Adam cried. "I promised that person I'd be back, and I'm going back." He nodded toward Rachel. "Don't worry about her. We make a good team. We've been through a lot together already." He locked eyes with her before turning back to Howie. "We'll just go in and get out. There shouldn't be any problems."

"And if there are?"

"There won't be."

"But if—"

"There won't be!"

"Okay, you win." Howie closed his notepad. "But if you're not back within an hour, we're coming after you."

# Chapter 53

Howie got up from his chair, went over to the window, and scanned the street below. Rachel and Adam had only left twenty minutes ago, but he still wanted to check to see if they might be coming. Mick had left with them, explaining that he wanted to make a quick visit to his fiancée, Mary, who had not been feeling well all day. "I won't be gone long," he said. "I should be back within a half hour or so."

Not seeing any sign of Adam and Rachel, Howie sat down at his desk. He leaned back in his chair and closed his eyes. *Hooknose has got to be involved, but he can't be the leader. The guy has the brawn but not the brains. Could it be Rachel's father? Who else could it be? Is there somebody else at the factory that could be behind all of this? If so, who? Did we miss somebody? And who's locked in that other room? And why? What happened to Pritchett and where's that Carpenter woman? Is one of them locked in that room in the sub-basement? Maybe I should've called the police.* As quickly as that last thought came, he scratched it, attributing it to a moment of weakness. If he went to the cops, that would be like a death warrant for his agency. Who would hire detectives who had to depend upon the police? Even checking with JD, his police detective friend, wasn't something he would consider at this point. He leaned forward, took out his notepad, and wrote down the name Charles Gilbertson. After staring at the name for several moments, he put a question mark behind it.

The downstairs entrance door slammed and the stairs began to creak. Howie cocked his head. It wasn't Mick or Adam, but the footsteps sounded familiar. Before he could guess who, the door opened and in walked Jerome, Nana's grandson. At the sight of the kid, his first inclination was to reach for the aspirin bottle. "How come you're not in summer school?" he asked, hoping that the kid would get the message from his tone of voice that he didn't want him there at this particular time.

Jerome, however, merely looked at him as if he had lost his marbles. "Because I don't go to summer school and besides that, it's Sunday." He walked up and stood in front of Howie's desk. His tone and attitude was as confident as ever.

"How come you're not in Sunday School, then?" Howie wasn't about to let the kid get the better of him.

Jerome rolled his eyes. "At four-thirty in the afternoon?"

Howie offered a thin smile. "You may think those questions were dumb, but I asked them for a purpose. They're a test."

A flicker of uncertainly flashed through Jerome's eyes. "A test?"

"Yeah, to see if you're on the ball. It's a trick of the trade that us detectives use to test the reactions of people." Howie gave Jerome a thumbs-up. "You should be proud of yourself that you passed."

"I don't—"

"Sit down, kid, take a load off your feet. You're making me nervous standing there." Howie wasn't in the mood to hear Jerome's comments. "So, what brings you around here?"

"I'm here on orders of my grandmother."

"Is that so?" The thought that maybe he and his grandmother were going to hire another detective brought a genuine smile to Howie's face. "Okay, kid. Make it snappy. I'm in a rush."

Jerome dug out a lavender envelope from his pants pocket and placed it on the desk. "She wanted me to personally deliver this to you."

The envelope, with Howie's name handwritten in a spidery but legible scrawl, gave off such a strong lilac scent that he wondered if it had been soaked in a bottle of perfume. "What's this?" he asked.

"It's an invitation to my grandmother's birthday party tomorrow evening."

"Okay. Tell her thanks, and I'll be there." Howie hoped that Jerome would take off now that he had made the delivery, but the kid gave no indication that he was about to leave. "Is there something else or are you waiting for a tip?"

Jerome leaned forward to the point that he was sitting on the edge of his seat. "I've got something to discuss with you that is very important."

Howie slid the envelope aside. "Oh, yeah, and what's that?"

"I've figured out what's going on at the nursing home."

"Really? I can't wait to hear all about it," Howie said, but then quickly added, "Keep it short, though! Like I told you. I'm in a rush."

A smug smile came over Jerome's face. "The old people like my grandmother are being robbed of their diamonds by those who work at the place." The smile faded as he glanced back at the door.

For a minute, Howie thought that Jerome was going to jump up, rush to the door, and put his ear up against it. "Go on. I'm listening."

Jerome lowered his voice. "It has to be an inside job."

"You don't say." Howie opened his notepad, figuring that at least he would look like he was taking the kid seriously. "Do you have any ideas as to who it might be?" he asked as he prepared to write down Jerome's reply.

"The Mafia."

"The Mafia?" Howie looked up to see if Jerome was joking, but the intense look in his eyes told a different story. "You did say 'the Mafia?'"

"Yes, I've been going to the library and reading up on them." Jerome's nose twitched like a rabbit, causing his glasses to slide down. "I presume you're familiar with that element of organized crime?" he asked as he pushed his glasses up.

"I've heard of them."

"The owner of the nursing home should be checked out." Jerome waited but when no reply came, he continued. "I've deduced that if it is an inside job, the owner must be involved in some way." He leaned back and, looking like he had just outsmarted one of his teachers at school, triumphantly announced, "It's perfectly logical. Don't you agree?"

"I'm not sure if—"

"My grandmother agrees with me."

"She does, huh?" Howie didn't care if Jerome picked up on his sarcasm. "Then, by all means, it's got to be logical."

"Yes, and she'll want to discuss it with you further."

"Is that right? I better make a note of that then." Howie turned to a blank page in his notepad and wrote *this kid's nuttier than grandma.* "Anything else?"

Jerome twitched his nose. "If what I say is true, you'd have to agree that I've helped you in solving this case."

Howie gave the amateur sleuth a halfhearted nod.

"Good." Jerome pushed his glasses up. "Then you would agree that I've been a consultant to your detective agency."

"Okay, so you're a consultant."

"I'm glad you see it my way." Jerome looked like he had just checkmated his opponent. "And as a consultant, I think it's proper for me to receive a fee."

"What!"

The suddenness of Howie's outburst startled Jerome. When he spoke, his tone lacked the smug confidence that it had when he first came in. He cleared his throat. "Either that or a reduction in the fee we're paying you."

Howie didn't know whether to laugh out loud or strangle the scheming little rug rat. "This is something I'd have to discuss with my partners. Is that okay with you?"

"Of course."

After Jerome left, Howie got up and walked over to his poster. "Bogie, kick me in the butt if I ever...ever take another case involving a kid." On the way back to his desk, he stopped and looked out the window for any sign of Adam and Rachel. "I shouldn't have let them go alone," he muttered and then opened his desk drawer to get his bottle of aspirins.

# Chapter 54

ADAM PARKED RACHEL'S car in front of the candy factory, turned off the ignition, and handed her the keys. They had taken her car because she convinced him that it would draw less attention parked in front of the place on a late Sunday afternoon. She also made the argument that if someone happened to come by who worked at the factory, they would think that she probably just stopped in for a little while to get some stuff done for Monday morning.

"I just had a thought," Rachel said as they sat there. When she turned to Adam, her eyes reflected uncertainty. "What if no one's in that room?"

"What do you mean?"

"I mean..." Rachel paused. "Well, what if it was just our imaginations that we heard someone?"

"I don't know about you, but it wasn't my imagination," Adam said, puzzled by her question and wondering if it was an indication of apprehension. He glanced around, checking the neighborhood. Across the street, a middle-aged woman was walking her dog. She seemed to be paying more attention to her collie than the young couple parked in front of the candy factory. Halfway down the block two little girls were playing a game of hopscotch. Further past the two girls, a teenage boy mowed the grass. Adam waited until the woman and her dog had walked far beyond them before opening the car door. "Let's go," he said.

"Wait a minute...please."

"What's wrong?" Adam asked as he closed the door.

"Do you think we should be doing this?"

"What's the matter? What are you afraid of?"

"I just..." Rachel placed her hand on his arm. "I just don't want any harm to come to you." She leaned over and kissed him.

He kissed her back. "Come on. We'll just get in and get out."

NANA COULDN'T UNDERSTAND why she had been scheduled for a bath. For one thing, she just had a bath a couple of days ago. But the other thing that puzzled her was that it was Sunday. They didn't give baths on Sundays. And what was even more unusual was having the bath so late in the afternoon. It was past four-thirty and supper would be served soon. She had complained vigorously at the nurses' station. Although the nurse on duty admitted that it was unusual, she said that nothing could be done about it.

"Are you giving me my bath?" Nana asked.

"No," the nurse replied. "I was told that one of the aides would be doing it. He should be here any minute. He's on break right now."

"He?" Nana chuckled. "Well, I've never been given a bath by a man before."

"Do you have any problems with that?"

"Not if he's cute."

"Here he comes now, you can see for yourself."

Nana squinted at the young man coming toward her. His blond curly hair complimented his wonderful physique. When he got closer she could see that his bright smile revealed teeth that had been well taken care of, and that, as far as she was concerned, was in his favor. She didn't care for anyone, man or woman, who didn't take care of their teeth. "Teeth can tell you a lot about a person," she always told her grandson. She also advised Howie that the diamond thief would more than likely have choppers that were stained and crooked. "Crooks don't take care of their teeth," she maintained.

The young aide with the straight white teeth walked over and knelt down in front of her. "Hi, you must be Nana. I'll be giving you a bath as soon as I check out the tub room."

While his teeth and pleasant voice impressed her, it was his eyes that bothered her. His eyes were blue but not a warm blue like her grandfather's had been. This young man's eyes were so icy that even his broad smile couldn't thaw them. "And who are you?" she asked. "I don't remember seeing you around before."

"Oh, I've worked here a couple of times," he said. "They call me whenever they can use my services. My name is Jack...Jack Miller."

RACHEL UNLOCKED THE front door to the candy factory and she and Adam slipped into the building. Once inside, they stood and listened for a minute. "It sounds pretty quiet," she whispered.

"Let's get those keys," Adam replied, not wanting to spend any more time in the building than necessary.

They went swiftly to Rachel's desk, got a ring of keys from the second right-hand drawer, and then headed toward the door leading to the sub-basement. Rachel flipped on the basement lights and the two of them moved slowly down the stairs.

"Do you hear anything?" Rachel whispered as they walked over and stood in front of the door leading to the other cell.

"Not a thing," Adam replied as he strained to hear any sound of tapping coming from the locked room. "But let's open it."

Rachel began trying each key on the ring as Adam glanced around. As she was about to try the fourth key, the ring of keys slipped from her hands and clanged on the cement floor.

"Sorry," she whispered, adding, "I don't think any of the keys are going to fit."

"Let see what I can do." Adam bent down, picked the keys up, and began trying them. When none of the remaining keys fit, he decided to start from the beginning. The second key on the ring fit the lock and he slowly opened the door. Light from the basement crept into the dark room.

"Over there in the corner." Rachel pointed to a person curled in a fetal position. Adam could see by the clothes that it was a man, his hands and feet were tied just as his own had been. They couldn't see the face because of a black hood over his head. They stood for a moment waiting for some movement or sound.

"Do you think he's dead?" Rachel asked.

"I don't know." Adam took a deep breath, wincing from his bruised ribs. He hadn't anticipated finding a corpse. "I hope—"

The moan startled both of them. Adam moved quickly to the man, knelt down, and carefully removed the hood. "Do you know who he is?" he asked Rachel. When she didn't reply, he asked again.

"Yes, it's...it's LaMar Jones!"

# Chapter 55

HOWIE PACED HIS office, waiting for Adam and Rachel to return. He had just stopped at the window to see if they were coming when the telephone rang. He rushed to the phone, but when he grabbed for it, he nearly knocked it off his desk. "MAC Detective Agency!" he blurted out, trying to catch his breath.

"He's got nice choppers, but I don't like his peepers!"

"What?" It took Howie a split second to recognize the screeching voice on the other end of the line. "Nana, what in the world are you talking about?"

"The young man who's going to dip me into that tub."

"What about him?"

"Haven't you cleaned the wax out of your ears yet? I said he's got nice choppers, but I don't like the look in his eyes."

"And what's wrong with—"

"Get over here pronto and you'll see for yourself!"

"I can't come over now." Howie eased down into his chair. "I'm sure, though, everything will be fine."

"Humph! Says you!"

"Come on, Nana, you—"

"They don't give baths on Sundays around here! Something's fishy!"

"Why don't you just have your bath and you'll feel better," Howie replied, feeling guilty for putting her off. "I'm sure everything will be okay." He waited for a reply, but none came. "I'll see you tomorrow at your birthday party, okay?" When still no reply came, he switched the phone to his other ear. "I'm sorry, but I really have to go." He could hear a radio in the background. "Goodbye," he said, waiting again for some kind of response. "I really need to go. I'm expecting another call. Nana…Nana?" After reluctantly hanging up, he sat for a couple of minutes, staring at the phone. Just as he buried his face in his hands and was about to take a deep breath, the phone rang. He grabbed it before the second ring. "MAC Detective Agency!"

"If you don't see me at my birthday party tomorrow, it's because I'm dead meat!" This time Nana hung up without giving him a chance to respond.

# Chapter 56

JACK MILLER CHECKED the ground floor tub room. Even though he had been told that it hadn't been in use since the remodeling two years ago, it was still in working condition. He could thank Pete Larson for that; the guy had arranged the whole setup. Pete informed the other aide that Jack would be doing the cares for Nana that afternoon. Larson even told the staff not to expect her for supper and that he would arrange for her to eat in her room. Jack smiled to himself as he thought about how Pete even managed to sabotage the tub room on first floor. The phone call he had gotten from him earlier explained it in a way that only Pete could describe it.

"It was a piece of cake," Pete bragged, as he talked about how he had *fixed* the first floor tub room so it couldn't be used.

"How did you do it?"

"Hell, I just drilled a hole in one of the pipes and suddenly there was a slight leak. After enough water covered the floor, I turned off the main water valve, and then put up an *Out of Order* sign."

"That's slick," Jack said. "But how about others who may want to take a bath? Won't that be a problem?"

"Nah. Baths aren't normally given around here on Sundays, so no one is going to care. I'll fix the pipe the first thing tomorrow morning. Nobody will know the difference." Pete's chuckle had an ominous ring to it. "Besides, come tomorrow morning this place will be buzzing with other things. Nana will be the talk around the breakfast tables." He chuckled again. "It'll give the rest of the old broads something to yak about instead of complaining about the food."

Jack wanted to make sure he had everything straight. He wasn't feeling as sure about this one as he did about the last one. "What am I supposed to say if anybody asks why she's having her bath today?"

"Nobody's going to ask you."

"But what if they do?"

Irritation crept into Pete's voice. "Just tell them it's because her birthday party is tomorrow, and there's no time in the morning to do it."

When Pete paused, it sounded as though he was taking time to light up a cigarette. Jack heard the flicking of the cigarette lighter and the exhaling of his first drag. He imagined Larson leaning back in his chair, his feet up on his desk.

"The old bat also has a hair appointment scheduled for mid-morning tomorrow," Pete continued. "That worked in our favor since the afternoon wouldn't be a good time. No woman wants to take a bath after getting her hair done up."

"Man, you thought of everything, didn't you?"

"Damn right!" Pete laughed. "Old Pete has all the angles figured out." After he took another drag of his cigarette, his tone turned sober. "Are you ready for all of this now? Do you know what you're supposed to do?"

"Yeah, sure. No problem."

"What do you do first, then?"

"Hey, what's this? The third degree?"

"Don't get wise with me," Pete snapped. "I'm paying you a lot of money and I just want to make sure you've got it straight and don't screw it up." His tone softened. "So humor me and go over it again."

Jack took a deep breath. This was the last time he was doing a job for Larson. "I take her downstairs to the tub room and get her situated on the lift, belt her in, and once I lower her into the water, just excuse myself for a moment. Okay?"

"How about the belt?" Pete said with a hint of anger in his voice. "You forgot to mention what you do with the belt before you leave."

"I loosen the belt before I take off."

"Good, and don't forget." Pete paused. "Now, once you're out of there, I'll come in and give that old lady the bath of her life. After it's over, I'll come get you and then we'll go and tell the other staff how the *accident* occurred."

"You don't think anybody's going to get suspicious, do you?"

"Not if you keep to the story that you stepped out for a minute because she wanted to soak in the tub by herself for a while," Pete said. "And don't worry, if anybody even so much as raises an eyebrow, I'll be there to back you up."

As Jack was now on his way to pick up Nana for her bath he considered how he would present his story to other staff. He would, of course, be horrified and nearly in tears as he reported the accidental drowning. *Hey, shedding some tears would be a nice touch.* He rehearsed his story as he started up the stairs to get Nana. He stopped at the landing and tried to bring forth some tears to see if he could do it. Nothing. For a moment, he thought he would have to forego the tears. *Wait a minute. I'll just think about old Sammy.* Even now, the thought of Sammy brought a lump to his throat. Sammy was the Irish setter he had as a teenager. He had loved that dog and was heartbroken when Sammy had to be put to sleep. The memory of bringing Sammy into the vet's office was still painful. As he started up the stairs again, he brushed aside a tear. *Get your mind off Sammy. You've got a job to do.*

Nana was sitting outside her room in her wheelchair when Jack approached her. "Okay, it's time to go," he said cheerfully. Without waiting for any reply, he started to wheel her toward the elevator.

"What are you doing?" Nana cried, putting her feet down on the floor, causing the wheelchair to stop. "That's not the direction of the tub room." She looked back at him with a distrustful eye. "Where are you taking me?"

"To the tub room downstairs," Jack replied, keeping a smile on his face. "The one up here is out of order."

Nana looked at him in disbelief. For a second, he thought she was going to ask him to show her the first floor tub room.

"You'll have to wait until I go to the bathroom," she said.

"I'm sorry, that's not going to be possible, and we have a schedule to—"

"Young man, if you don't get me to the bathroom, I'm going to pee all over this wheelchair and then I'm going to scream for a nurse."

"Calm down, I'll take you to the bathroom," Jack said, flashing a professional smile. "And after that, it'll be my pleasure to take you downstairs."

# Chapter 5 7

"HE'S TRYING TO open his eyes," Rachel said as Adam finished untying the ropes binding LaMar's feet. "Are you okay?" she quietly asked while gently stroking the side of LaMar's head. He groaned, but didn't reply.

Adam was surprised that LaMar looked so well. Other than needing a shower and a shave and some clean clothes, the guy appeared to be in fairly good shape. He wondered how long LaMar had been locked up in this cell and what had been done to him while being held captive. With the light coming in from the open doorway, he didn't see any bruises on LaMar's face. Adam and Rachel propped him against the wall, and knelt on each side of him like bookends. "Talk to him some more," he whispered to Rachel.

"LaMar...LaMar...it's me, Rachel." When no response came, she looked to Adam. He nodded to try again and she repeated her words, but still nothing.

"Try once more," Adam urged, anxious to get out of there. If Jones didn't come around this time, he would have to be carried out.

After Rachel tried a third time, LaMar's eyes finally fluttered open as he focused on the face behind the voice. They waited while he swallowed a couple of times and tried to wet his lips. He spoke slowly in a raspy voice. "Is...is that...really you, Ra...Rachel?"

"Yes, it's me." She offered him a sympathetic smile, but spoke in urgent tones. "You have to get up. We have to get you out of here."

"Who's...who's that?" Lamar asked as his eyes shifted to Adam who had moved over and kneeled besides Rachel.

"I'm Adam Trexler. I work for the MAC Detective Agency."

"Your sister hired them," Rachel said.

"She...she did? What? I...ah..."

"It's a long story," Adam said. "We'll tell you all about it later." He was anxious to get back to Howie's. There would be plenty of time for questions later. The number one question was who drowned in that vat of chocolate. "Are you able to walk?"

"I...I think so. Just give...give me a minute," LaMar groaned. "My ribs...are...are so tender." LaMar gingerly moved his arms back and forth in front of him and then began slowly rubbing his thigh muscles.

"Do you know who did this to you?" Rachel asked.

LaMar nodded. "I...I don't know...his name, though..." He paused, wet his lips, and swallowed. "But...but the way...they talked, I—"

"They? Who are they?" Adam asked.

"Ja...Jack was one..."

"Jack who?"

"Jack Miller."

"You mean your roommate?"

"Yes." A scornful expression swept over LaMar's face. "The...the other guy..." LaMar paused as he took a deep breath. "I...I didn't recognize, but when he...he talked to Jack..." Stephanie's brother moved his tongue over his parched lips. It was difficult for him to talk, but Adam urged him on, needing to hear who else was involved. "The other guy... he...he works at a...a nursing home."

"What!" Adam cried. "Which one?"

"Some...somewhere in the area." LaMar mumbled so quietly that Adam cocked his head, moving within inches of the man's face. "Jack mentioned the name, but I...I don't remember it." LaMar coughed a dry, harsh, hacking cough that caused him to wince in pain as he held his sides. "There...there was some resident that...that Jack had to—" He coughed again. "She...she was getting in their way."

A foreboding feeling enveloped Adam as he thought about whether Nana could be that woman. Maybe there was no connection, but Howie needed to know. "I'm going to run up stairs for a moment," he said to Rachel as he touched her on the arm. "I need to make a quick phone call."

"What's the matter?"

"I hope nothing, but I've got a nagging feeling that a friend of Howie's may be in danger. He put his hand on her arm. "Will you be all right?" he asked, not liking the idea of leaving her alone.

"Yes, I'll be okay." She patted his hand. "Don't worry."

"I won't be gone but a few minutes. I'll leave the door open at the top of the stairs. Holler if you need me."

"I will." She leaned over and gently kissed Adam on the cheek.

"I'll be right back," Adam said as he stroked her hair. He turned to LaMar. "And I'll bring you some water, okay?"

The corners of LaMar's mouth turned ever so slightly upward. "I'd like that," he whispered. He tried to swallow again but couldn't.

Adam took the stairs two-at-a-time, rushed over to Rachel's desk, and picked up the phone. The first time he thought he had dialed Howie's number, but he had misdialed. A little girl had answered the phone. "Sorry," he said and hung up. His heart pounded. His lip was raw from his gnawing at it. This time, he was more deliberate in dialing, breathing a sigh of relief when Howie answered on the first ring.

"MAC Detective Agency."

"Howie. It's Adam."

"Anything wrong? Are you and Rachel okay?"

"We're fine." Adam spoke with a sense of urgency. "Now, listen up. The person locked in that room was LaMar Jones."

"What!"

Adam pictured his boss fumbling for his notepad, and opening his desk drawer for a pen to jot down the information.

"Did I hear you right?" Howie asked. "You did say Jones, didn't you?"

"That's right. And there's something else you should know." Adam quickly went over what LaMar had shared. "He named Jack Miller and talked about some other guy who worked at a nursing home."

"Did he mention which one?"

"No, but I think you better check on Nana and see if she's okay."

"I'll do that right now."

"Good. We'll bring LaMar up to the office. If you're not there, we'll wait for you."

After Adam hung up, he rejoined Rachel downstairs. He hoped that LaMar would be able to walk on his own after having some water, but the poor man still needed to rest. After ten minutes, LaMar said he was still too weak to move. They decided to wait for another couple of minutes, and if he wasn't able to walk then, the two of them would get him up the stairs and out to the car. They waited silently, occasionally glancing at each other as the time passed.

"We've got to go now," Adam said. "Do you think you can do it?" he asked LaMar.

"I...I think so...if I...I can lean on you."

With Rachel's help, they managed to get LaMar on his feet. The stairs proved to be more difficult. They took the stairs slowly and every so often stopped to rest.

"Come on," Adam urged. "We're more than halfway up. There are only a few more steps to go." No sooner had he uttered those words than he sensed the presence of someone at the top of the stairs.

# Chapter 58

AS SOON AS Howie hung up the phone after talking with Adam, he dialed the number to Nana's room. While he waited for her to answer, he wrote the name of LaMar Jones in his notepad and underlined it twice. "Come on, Nana, pick up your phone!" After the eighth ring, he slammed the receiver down. He drummed his fingers on the desk, looked at the clock, and quickly scribbled a note for Mick. It being Sunday afternoon and not having workweek traffic to contend with, he could make it to the nursing home within ten minutes.

From the time Howie flew out of his office to the moment he turned the corner and the Golden Years Retirement Home came into sight, nine minutes had elapsed. Not wanting to waste time, he pulled into a no parking zone, locked the car, and rushed up to the entrance. After giving a quick nod to the residents sitting in the lobby area, he hurried down the hallway to Nana's room. He rapped on her door and then without waiting for any reply, opened it only to find the room empty.

"Yoo-hoo! Young man!"

Howie whirled around. A lady with bluish-silver hair was stooped over her walker and pointing at him from the doorway across the hall. The woman, whose lipstick and rouge matched the color of her bright-pink bathrobe, eyed him with inquisitiveness. Nana had informed him that this particular neighbor, whom she had referred to as Zelda-the-Snoop, made it her business to know everybody else's. "Are you looking for Nana?" the Snoop asked in a tone that signaled she was eager to live up to her reputation.

"Yes. Have you seen her?"

"Just a minute. My hearing is lazy this morning." The woman shuffled further into the hallway, but kept a safe distance. Her fuzzy slippers were as bright pink as her nails, and her diamond ring looked too large to be real. "Now, what did you say?"

"Have you seen Nana?"

"I have indeed."

"Do you know where she is?"

"With some blond-haired young man." Zelda glanced up and down the hallway, and then lowered her voice. She spoke slowly, deliberately, and the stern look in her eyes told him that she was a person not to be rushed. "When I inquired at the nurses' station, I was told that he was a member of the staff." She shuffled out a few more steps. "But he must be new because I've never seen him before."

"Where did they go?"

"It's mighty peculiar if you ask me."

Howie thought about taking off, but the Snoop was his best hope in locating Nana. "Can you tell me where they went?"

The woman shuffled closer, glanced in both directions again, and then leaned toward him. "Do you want to know what I think?"

"Yeah, I do," Howie replied quickly, hoping that she would get the idea that he didn't have time to waste.

A smug smile appeared on Zelda's face, causing cracks to appear in her makeup. "Well!" she huffed. "It's my opinion that Nana and her young male friend wanted to find a quiet out-of-the-way spot so that they could do some smooching." She eyed Howie as if he might not know what she was talking about. "You know...making out...trading spit." She paused for a moment and then shuffled so close that Howie thought he would be overcome by her perfume. "Don't you think that's what they're up to?"

"I don't know, but I'll find out if you just tell me where they went."

"A lot of younger men go for us older women," the Snoop said in a tone that indicated she felt she had just revealed a well-kept secret of her generation. "Why else would he be taking her downstairs where nobody is around?"

"He took her downstairs?"

"Nana said she was going to have a bath down there." Her pencil thin eyebrows arched halfway up her forehead. "I don't know of any tub on the lower level. If you ask—"

Howie took off toward the elevator.

"Yoo-hoo! Young man! You come back and tell me what you found out, you hear?" the Snoop called out. "I just know they're making whoopee."

Howie pressed the *Down* button for the elevator. He pressed it again and then, spotting the stairway sign, made a dash toward it. His footsteps echoed in the cement stairwell as he sprinted down the stairs. When he opened the door to a deserted hallway, he wasn't sure which way to go. He started to his right, but then heard a scream coming from the other direction. "Nana!" he cried and ran in the direction of the scream. He came upon a door marked *Tub Room* and when he yanked it open he was both horror-struck and furious at what he saw.

# Chapter 59

HOWIE EXPLODED WITH rage at the sight of Pete Larson holding Nana's head under the water. "Why you..." Without giving Larson a chance to react, he lunged at the guy, knocking him against the wall. The would-be killer hit the wall and fell to the floor. When Nana came up gasping and sputtering for air, Howie went to her aid. "Are you—"

Larson charged the detective, throwing a body block that slammed Howie against the tub, knocking the wind out of him.

"Leave him alone!" Nana yelled and flung a bar of soap at Howie's attacker.

In the few moments it took Howie to recover, Larson was out the door. His running footsteps could be heard echoing down the corridor.

For a split second, Howie considered going after the guy but decided to stay with Nana. "Are you all right?" he asked, looking for bruises, and then quickly turning his head when it dawned on him that Jerome's grandmother was as naked as the day she was born. "Oh, I'm sorry. I...I didn't mean—"

"Don't be so hoity-toity," Nana sputtered as she pulled herself to a standing position, leaning against the side of the bathtub for support. "Get me out of this thing."

"Sure, right away."

"I feel like a water-soaked old prune." Nana squeezed the water from one of her pigtails with one hand while using the other to steady herself as she continued to lean against the tub for support. "Hurry up!" she cried. "I've got enough wrinkles as it is."

"Just a minute." Howie looked around for her bathrobe, spotting it lying in the corner by the door. He scooped it up, came back to the tub, and held it in front of him, keeping his eyes focused on a thin jagged crack in the wall just beyond Nana's head.

"You're going to have to use the lift," Nana said. "I can't get out of this tub by myself. And take that bathrobe away."

"But—"

"But, nothing. It's my favorite robe. My grandson, Jerome, gave it to me and I don't want it to get wet. I'll put it on when I'm out."

Howie had visions of Zelda-the-Snoop walking in on them any minute. He thought about going to get one of the nurses, but didn't want to leave Nana alone. Larson just might double back and he wasn't about to take that chance. "What do you me to do?" he asked as he hung her bathrobe on a hook on the wall.

"Help me back onto the lift-seat," Nana said as she held on to the tub's edge. "I can't stand much longer."

"Just hold on for one more second." Howie leaned over and placed his hands under her armpits. The phrase "light as a feather" came to mind as he lifted her onto the contoured plastic seat. "Now what?"

"Strap me in." Nana leaned against the backrest and waited until her embarrassed assistant secured the strap. "Now push down on the left pedal at the bottom of the lift." She turned and pointed toward the floor. "Do you see it?"

"Yeah, but there are two pedals. What's the other one for?"

"For lowering the lift."

"So all I have to do is to press the left pedal to raise you up and..."

"Then you swing me out from the tub."

"And once I do that, I press the right pedal to lower you?"

"That's right, and I'm ready whenever you are," Nana said impatiently. "Let's get moving, this water is getting cold and my buns are freezing."

It took Howie a couple of minutes to get Nana situated onto the lift-seat and to go over again what needed to be done. He wanted to make sure he understood each step so that she wasn't hurt in the process. Once he was sure of what he was doing, he tentatively pressed the left pedal with his foot. "It's moving," he announced with relief.

"It's about time!" Nana said, her tone reflecting a growing impatience. "Jerome would've had me out by now."

Howie was amazed at how easy the hydraulic device worked. Within a short time, Nana had been lifted out and over the tub, and then lowered to a point where her feet touched the floor. He gave her towels to dry with, managed to help her into the bathrobe, and then got her seated in her wheelchair.

After Nana had settled in, she glanced up at him and winked. "I haven't got such a bad body for an old lady, do I?"

# Chapter 60

HOWIE WHEELED NANA out of the tub room and down the corridor toward the elevator. All of the time he was pushing her, he kept looking behind him, making sure they were alone. He wasn't about to take a chance of Larson sneaking up on them. "Who brought you down here?" he asked as he pushed the *Up* button once they got to the elevator.

"One of the nursing aides." Nana shifted in the wheelchair. Water continued to drip from her pigtails. "He said his name was Jack."

"Was his last name Miller?"

"I don't know. He never told me."

The elevator door opened and Howie wheeled Nana in. He pressed the first floor button as she gave him a description of Miller.

"He had curly-blond hair, and blue eyes, but those peepers of his weren't warm like my grandfather's. And he was a few inches taller than you." Nana looked at him with a questioning eye. "Do you know him?"

"No, but I plan to get acquainted with him." Howie wondered how Miller was connected with LaMar's ordeal, and who was his connection at the candy factory? Hooknose? That didn't make sense, but the whole case wasn't making much sense at this point. "So this guy, Jack, was the one who brought you down?"

"That's what I told you, didn't I?" Nana reached back and, leaning to one side, squeezed one of her pigtails. Drops of water fell to the floor. "And to think that he had such nice straight choppers," she said as she repeated the movement on her other pigtail.

"Do you have any idea where he went after he left?"

"No, he—" The elevator door opened and Howie wheeled Nana off as a housekeeper got on with her cleaning cart. Once they headed down the hallway toward the nurse's station, Nana began again. "After this Jack left, Pete Larson showed up." She slapped the arm of her wheelchair. "And I thought he was just doing some kind of security check. Humph! I should've known better."

"How were you to know?" Howie said, trying to reassure her. He planned to stop at the nurses' station. Although Nana appeared okay and seemed to be almost energized by her ordeal, he still wanted someone to check her over more thoroughly. "Did Larson say anything to you when he came in?"

"Just that it was time for my bath, but he said it real sarcastically." Nana screwed up her eyes and pursed her lips. "Before I knew it, he came over to the tub, slipped me off that lift-seat, and started pushing my head under the water." She stuck her chin out. "I think I clawed him a good one on the face, though."

"Good for you."

"That'll teach him to mess with me." Nana raised her hand, doubled it into a fist, and shook it in the air. "He'd better not show up around here again if he knows what's good for him. If he does show his kisser, I'll bop him one on the nose!"

"I'm sure you will, but I'm glad I got there when I did."

"That makes two of us." Nana reached around and patted Howie's hand. Her tone softened. "I would've been a goner if you hadn't come."

"It had to have been frightening."

"Are you kidding?" Nana nearly shouted, straightening up in her wheelchair. "Why, I was more frightened on my honeymoon night." She chuckled. "Do you want to know what was going through my mind all the time he was holding me under water?"

Howie nodded, wondering if she would tell how her entire life flashed in front of her.

"That all those old hens would be cackling about me at breakfast tomorrow over their raisin toast and oatmeal, and how I'd be missing my birthday party."

"But I bet they would also have felt sad."

"Maybe some would, but most would still want the party so that all that cake wouldn't go to waste."

When they got to the nurses' station, a woman with graying hair looked up from the chart she was writing in. "Hi, Nana. How was your bath?"

"Bath!" Nana cried. "I nearly drowned! That's how it was."

"Oh, my God!" the nurse exclaimed, her eyes grew to saucer size.

Nana pointed to Howie. "He saved my life."

"Oh, my God!" she repeated twice more before coming over and squatted beside Nana. With trembling hands, she stroked Nana's hair. "You poor thing," she uttered and then looked up at Howie. "What happened?"

"She was left unattended in the tub downstairs and...ah, slipped off the lift-chair." Howie looked at Nana and winked, hoping she would go along with the tale he was spinning. He didn't want the police brought in just yet. If he and his partners could close the case on their own, it would be a great way to promote their agency. "When I came by she was yelling for help because she was...ah..."

"Bobbing and sucking water!" Nana exclaimed, giving Howie a knowing glance. "But he rescued me."

"And who are you?" the nurse asked Nana's rescuer.

"I'm, ah…" Howie cleared his throat. "I'm her grandson. I came by to wish her an early happy birthday."

"It was lucky that you did," she said, glancing at Nana.

"I know." Howie paused and then asked as casually as he could, "Have you by any chance seen Pete Larson, the security man? I need to talk to him about something."

The nurse gave Nana a gentle hug, and then stood up. "I saw Pete not more than ten minutes ago."

"Do you know where he was going?"

"No. He rushed by the desk here and said something about needing to leave for a while to run an errand."

Nana tugged at Howie's sleeve. "Ask her about the young man with the blue peepers."

"Who?" The nurse looked to Howie for an explanation.

"She's talking about the man who was working on this floor tonight. He's a blond-haired guy by the name of Jack."

"You mean Jack Miller?"

"Yes, that's his name. We'd like to talk to him about Nana's…ah, birthday party tomorrow. We have some last minute details to go over."

"I haven't seen him." The nurse turned to Nana. "Is he the one who left you unattended?"

"He did, but…" Nana glanced at Howie. "It was my fault. I demanded that he go to my room and get me my bottle of lilac bubble bath." She didn't give the nurse a chance to comment. "He didn't want to leave, but I put up such a fuss that he had no choice." She smirked. "You know how I can be."

The woman nodded. "Yes, I'm afraid I do." She looked at both of them with tired eyes. "Nana, he shouldn't have left you alone." She sighed. "You know, I'll have to write this in your chart."

"Go right ahead!" Nana snapped. "It should make some interesting reading for my doctor while he's prescribing all those medications I don't need."

"I think you should maybe let the nurse look at you," Howie suggested. "Just to see if you're okay."

Nana shook her head so hard that one of her pigtails slapped her in the nose. From the look she gave him, he knew that was simply not going to be an option. "Just take me to my room!" she demanded.

"I think your grandson is right," the nurse said. "Just let me check you over. It won't take but a minute."

"Oh, no you don't!" Nana backed up in her wheelchair. "I know my rights. I don't have to be probed and poked if I don't want to."

"But, Nana—"

"Don't Nana me! I told you no and I mean it!"

Howie smiled knowingly at the nurse who shrugged in return. He turned the wheelchair around and headed down the hallway. When they got to Nana's door, he noticed Zelda-the-Snoop peeking out at them from her room. When he waved at her, she quickly closed her door. "Do you want me to stay awhile?" he asked Nana once they were in her room.

"Now, don't you go and treat me like I can't take care of myself," Nana chided, wagging her finger at him. She gestured toward the wall opposite her. "Go in that closet and get something out for me."

"What am I looking for?" Howie asked as he opened the closet door.

"You'll see it." Nana wheeled along side of him. "It's that thing there leaning up against the wall on the right-hand side."

"You mean the cane?"

"Yep, that's what I'm talking about. It belonged to my father." Nana waited until Howie handed it to her before explaining further. "This old thing is made of cherry wood and it's good and hard. I can use it to wallop anyone who gets near me."

Howie frowned. "I don't know if that's such a good idea."

Nana whacked the floor a couple of times with it. "They get hit with this, they'll know it."

"Are you sure you'll be all right?" Howie asked, but backed off when Nana scrunched up her nose at him. "Okay, I'll see you tomorrow." He gave her a hug and left, closing the door behind him. He figured that Pete Larson wouldn't be back and that Jack Miller was probably long gone as well. Just the same, he decided to tell the nurse that he felt that Miller had treated Nana a little bit too rough and that he didn't want him coming near her. He wasn't surprised when the nurse told him that the supervisor had just called to inform her that Miller said he was sick and had to go home. Even though Miller and Larson were gone, he nevertheless left his phone number and told the nurse to call him if either of them showed up. He had to go back to the office now and sort the whole case out.

# Chapter 61

WHILE HOWIE WAS having his encounter with Pete Larson in the tub room, Adam was about to have his own encounter with Hooknose. Leo Rappaport stood at the top of the stairs, glowering down at him and Rachel. The only way out was through the doorway at the top of the stairs and right now the giant's massive hulk blocked it entirely. Adam doubted that Leo even recognized LaMar in the dimly lit stairway, unless, that is, he was responsible for him being put in that cell. And if that was the case, there was no way that he was going to let them leave.

"What are you doing here?" Leo shouted, glaring at Adam. "And who's that other guy?" he growled.

"That's LaMar Jones!" Rachel cried out.

Adam's eyes shifted between Rachel and Leo. When he first spotted Leo at the top of the stairs, he thought that he would have to leave LaMar with Rachel and take his chances to see if he could get the best of Leo in a fight. The odds of winning out over the big guy, however, were not in his favor.

"Will you help us?" Rachel pleaded.

"Of course, I'll help," Leo replied without hesitation and in a compassionate tone of voice that stunned Adam. Without another word, he hurried down to where the three stood on the staircase. "I'll take him from here," he said and then lifted LaMar in his arms and started back up the stairs, carrying him as a bridegroom would carry a bride over the threshold.

"Bring him over to my desk and set him down in the chair," Rachel said as they moved into the reception area. "He needs to rest for a minute."

Leo gently placed LaMar in the chair and then turned to Rachel. "I thought he was dead. What's going on, anyway?"

"You'll get the answer to that question and others later," Adam said, relieved that Leo appeared to be on their side, but still stunned by his gentle demeanor. "I need you to do something for me," he said to Rachel. "Will you and Leo get LaMar out of here and bring him to Howie's office?"

"What about you?"

"I want to check out a couple more areas while I've got the chance." Adam turned to Leo. "Is your car outside?"

Leo nodded.

"Would you drive them?"

"Sure, but who's Howie?"

"He's my partner. We're detectives."

"You! You're a detective?" It was Leo's turn now to be stunned.

"That's right," Adam said, taking pleasure in announcing that fact and seeing the bewildered look on the giant's face. "Rachel can explain everything to you on the way over. I don't have time right now."

"Where...where are...you taking me?" LaMar mumbled. He attempted to stand but fell back into the chair.

"They're going to bring you to a safe place," Adam said. He turned to Rachel. "Can I have the keys to your car?"

She handed her keys to him, holding on to his hand for a moment. "I don't want anything happening to you. Please be careful."

"I will. And when I'm done here, I'll come right over. One more thing, I also need your set of office keys." Once Adam got the keys, he urged them to go.

Leo walked over to LaMar, but was waved aside. "You...you don't have to...to carry me...I ...I can walk."

Adam went with Rachel and the two men to the entrance door. "Tell Howie that I'll be coming as soon as I can," he said to Rachel. He wanted to kiss her, but not with Leo present. Once this case was over with, he planned to further pursue their relationship.

After they were gone, Adam went downstairs and checked out both of the rooms thoroughly, but found nothing suspicious. He came back upstairs and headed directly to Gilbertson's office, hoping that one of the keys fit the lock. The third to the last key he tried was the one. He unlocked and opened the door, stepped in, and flipped on the lights. Everything seemed the same as before except he now noticed a black four-drawer file cabinet in the corner. Moving quickly to it, he discovered that it was locked. He tried every key on the ring of keys Rachel had given him, but none fit.

"I think I have what you're looking for," a man's voice said from behind him.

Adam swung around to face a person he had never seen before. His eyes, however, were quickly drawn to the revolver in the man's hand.

# Chapter 62

BY THE TIME Howie got back from the nursing home, Mick was waiting for him. His partner was lounging in his usual chair and paging through a *Police Gazette*.

"How are things over at the nursing home?" Mick asked as he closed the magazine and laid it on the desk.

Howie walked over and collapsed into his chair. He sat for a moment before opening the top drawer of his desk. He took out a bottle of aspirins, popped a couple in his mouth, and washed them down with coffee left in his cup from that morning.

A hint of a smile appeared on Mick's face. "What's the matter? Don't tell me that Nana has cooked up another scheme for finding the crooks?" His light-heartedness, however, dissipated as he studied his partner more intently. "Hey, buddy, you seem a little frazzled." He eyed Howie. "Is anything wrong? Is Nana okay?"

"She is now." Howie took a deep breath and let it out slowly. Although his back hurt from the altercation he'd had with Larson in the tub room, he was more emotionally exhausted than anything else. Under different circumstances, he would have loved to just crawl into bed and get some much-needed sleep. "I just saved Nana from being drowned in a bathtub."

"You what?" Mick cried as his body jerked forward and his mouth dropped open. "What are you talking about?"

"Pete Larson, the security guard at the home, tried to kill her."

"What!"

"He tried to murder her." Howie hoped the aspirins would soon take effect. One of these days he would have to check with a doctor about his headaches. "It was just fortunate that I got there when I did."

"I can't believe it."

"And Jack Miller was involved. He helped set the whole thing up."

"How did—"

"Wait, that's not all." Howie paused, finding the whole story hard to believe himself. "Get this. LaMar Jones isn't dead. Adam and Rachel found him locked up in one of those rooms in the sub-basement."

"You're kidding." Mick slumped back in his chair and stared at his boss while the wall clock ticked away the seconds. Somewhere on the street below, a driver honked an angry horn.

"I tell you we've got some bizarre things going on with these cases." Howie wasn't sure what their next step should be. As far as he was concerned, tracking down Pete Larson was their number one priority. After what Larson had attempted to do to Nana, he was anxious to get his hands on the guy. He thought about calling the administrator of the nursing home, but decided that might not be such a good idea. The administrator could be involved in the whole thing as well. There could be others also working with Larson and Miller. "Maybe even Zelda-the-Snoop," he mused out loud.

"What did you say?"

Howie cleared his throat. "I...ah, said that these cases have to be connected in some way, but I'm not sure how." He massaged his temples. A doctor would probably say that his headaches were work related. He could just hear the doc advising him to change jobs. Fat chance of that. If that was the advice, he would simply follow Nana's lead and change doctors before even considering another line of work. "It's hard to know who to trust at that nursing home," he said, hoping he wasn't getting as paranoid as Nana.

Mick stood up and walked over to the window. He looked out at the street below for several moments, and then turned around and sat on the windowsill. "It seems to me that we have to figure out just how this Miller and Larson are tied in with Jones." He scratched the side of his head, an indication that his initial shock had passed and he was now beginning to analyze the situation.

Howie watched Mick with pride. One of the characteristics that he liked about Mick was his ability to think through and sort things out. His partner's emotions could flare, but his actions were seldom based on emotions.

"Do you have any thoughts about why Jones would've been locked up in the first place?" Mick asked.

"No, and I've asked myself that same question." Howie drummed his fingers on the desk. "It could have something to do with him working with Pritchett. Maybe he found out something he wasn't supposed to know."

Mick nodded his agreement. "And let's not forget what Pritchett said about those chocolate angels not being so angelic." He scratched the side of his head again and then folded his arms across his chest. "Someone had to have gotten to him before he could tell us what he discovered. I don't know what those angels are made of, but they can't be made just of chocolate."

"I agree." Howie liked the idea that his partner was thinking more like a detective with each case they worked on. "But there's an even more perplexing question."

"What's that?"

"If it wasn't LaMar Jones who died in that vat of chocolate, who was it?"

"That's right!" Mick exclaimed, his eyebrows rising. "I hadn't thought about that."

"I just wish I…" The downstairs street entrance door banged shut and the stairs began to creak. "That must be Adam," Howie said. "Let's hope we'll get some answers from him."

Mick cocked his ear toward the door. "It doesn't sound like he's alone. Who's with him?"

"Rachel and LaMar."

"LaMar is coming here?"

"Yeah. Adam figured this is the safest place for him." Howie opened his notepad and took out a pen from the top drawer. "Besides, I have a number of questions I want to ask Jones." He and Mick waited, listening to the creaking of the stairs.

"What kind of shape is LaMar in?" Mick asked.

"According to Adam, the guy was doing okay considering what—" The door swung open and Rachel came in, holding it open for the two behind her. Howie's body stiffened when he saw Hooknose. *What's he doing here? And where's Adam?* Before he could speculate upon his own questions, his attention focused on the person leaning against Hooknose. The man, clothed in grubby jeans and a tee shirt that had been ripped at the neck, could have passed for one of the winos that wandered the back alleys of Broadway. Even though he was sure who the person was, he had to ask. There had already been too many surprises in this case. "That is LaMar, isn't it?" he asked Rachel, not sure if Jones could answer for himself.

Rachel nodded and then, as if sensing Howie's uneasiness concerning Leo's presence, offered an explanation. "Adam wants you to know that Leo has been a big help in all of this. He asked Leo to help me bring LaMar here."

Howie glanced at Hooknose, knowing that what Rachel had just related was Adam's way of letting his partners know that he thought Hooknose could be trusted. "Thanks," he said, not willing at this point, however, to trust him completely. One of Adam's faults was that he was too trusting of people and Howie considered that an occupational hazard of preachers. In this line of work, however, a person couldn't afford to be so trusting. It was a lesson that Adam had to learn and someday he was going to learn it the hard way.

Mick stood, stepped to the other chair, and turned it facing Leo. "Bring him over here so he can sit down."

LaMar, with Leo's assistance, moved slowly, his gait unsteady. Although he looked exhausted, he was conscious.

Howie came from around his desk to help. "We all thought you were dead," he said as he held the chair to steady it.

LaMar replied only with a thin smile.

"Everybody at work also thought that," Leo said as he helped LaMar ease into the chair. Howie noted how gentle and compassionate Hooknose seemed to be. There was none of the roughness in his tone of voice or manner that there had been when they first met him. Even his facial features seemed softer.

LaMar rested his head on the back of the leather chair and focused first upon Leo, eventually shifting his focus to Howie. When he spoke, it was in a hoarse whisper. "I...I only look dead, but I'm...I'm very much alive." He cocked his head, studying Howie. "But who are you?"

"Howie Cummins." He pointed at Mick. "And that's Mick Brunner, one of my partners. Adam Trexler, the guy who found you, is my other partner. We're detectives."

It took a second for Howie's information to sink in. "Did my...my sister hire you?"

Howie nodded. "Do you want to call her?"

"No...my voice..." LaMar cleared his throat a couple of times. With each word he attempted to speak, he became more hoarse. "Hard to talk...you call...let her know...I'm alive."

"I'll get in touch with her as soon as we get some things straightened out about my other partner." Howie looked to Rachel for an explanation. "Where's Adam?"

"He's still at the candy factory."

"What's he doing there?"

"He wanted to check out some other areas in the building." She glanced over at Leo. By the way she looked at him, it was obvious that she had complete faith in his goodness. "After Adam called you, Leo showed up and volunteered to help. And that's when Adam asked him to drive us over here."

When her eyes flickered, Howie couldn't tell if it was concern or fear or possibly guilt about leaving Adam behind. Or could it be she was afraid of what Adam would find out about her father? "How long did he say it would take?" he asked.

"Not long."

Howie's brain was spinning; things were happening too fast. It was almost beyond belief that Hooknose was standing in his office and being commended as if he was an overgrown boy scout. Something else was troubling him, however, and he couldn't put his finger on it until he recalled a statement Hooknose had made. He glanced at the others in the room, wondering if anybody had caught the obvious flaw in what had been stated; if they had, they gave no indication.

Mick offered Rachel the other chair. She sat down, brushing the hair away from her eyes. Harsh lines on her face revealed the stress and strain of the experience. Howie noticed that Hooknose kept glancing at her.

"I'll be okay," Rachel said, giving Leo a reassuring smile. "I'm just feeling a little drained from everything."

"Do you think this has any connection with what happened at the nursing home earlier?" Howie asked Mick. Although the question was directed at his partner, it was an intentional ploy to see how the others would react.

"What are you talking about?" Rachel asked.

Howie noted that Hooknose seemed to be just as puzzled as Rachel over the reference to the nursing home. He gave an abbreviated version of what happened, but left out the identities of the individuals involved.

LaMar stirred in his chair. "I...ah...need...the bathroom."

"Come on," Howie said. "I'll show you where it is, and while you're there, you can take a shower. And I'll get you some different clothes." He showed LaMar to the bathroom, giving him an old shirt and a pair of sweatpants to slip into after he cleaned up. The clothes would be short on LaMar since he was several inches taller than Howie, but at least they were clean. When Howie walked back into the office, Mick was standing by the window, leaning against the wall. Hooknose had moved the other chair next to Rachel's chair and the two of them were talking quietly. He checked the time. "Shouldn't Adam be here by now?"

"I would've thought so," Rachel said in a worried tone.

"You don't think something happened to him, do you?" Mick asked as he looked out the window again. The sound of him cracking his knuckles gave testimony to his growing concern.

Howie glanced at the clock for a second time. "I don't know what to think, but if he's not here within fifteen minutes, we're going over there. In the meantime, I'll call LaMar's sister and let her know that he's alive."

# Chapter 63

"OPEN UP THAT cabinet!" ordered the man with the gun, tossing Adam a set of keys. Although the curly, dark-haired intruder was several inches shorter than Adam, he appeared to be at least thirty pounds heavier.

The man's voice sounded familiar, but Adam couldn't place where he had heard it. "Which one is it?" he asked as he intentionally fumbled through the keys to give himself time to formulate a plan of action.

"Quit stalling!" the gunman snapped. "There's only one key that looks like it fits the cabinet, so hurry up and find it before I lose my patience." Once Adam unlocked the cabinet, the man ordered him to pull open the top drawer and then step aside. "Stand over there by the end of the table!" he said. "And don't even think about making any moves on me!" Satisfied that Adam was far enough away, he moved to the cabinet, reached into his coat pocket, and pulled out a small, black-velvet-covered box. He placed the box inside the cabinet drawer toward the back and then closed the drawer.

"Aren't you going to lock it?"

"Don't get smart with me." He locked the cabinet and then put the keys into his jacket pocket. "Come on."

"Where are we going?"

"For a little ride and then we'll see how much of a wiseass you are." He kept the revolver pointed at Adam.

"What if I don't go?" Adam's heart pounded so hard that he feared that his would be abductor could hear it.

The man sneered as he cocked the hammer of the revolver. "I'm only going to tell you one more time. Get the hell going!"

Adam moved toward the door. He would make his play once they got outside. "Where did you say we were going?"

The gun barrel jabbed into Adam's back. "When you have this, then you'll get to ask all the questions." He shoved the gun into his back again, only this time harder. "Now, put your hands behind you."

"Why should—"

The kidney punch nearly dropped Adam to the floor and for a split second he thought he would pass out. The vicious blow, however, caused a flashback and he now knew where he had heard that voice before.

"Well, Mr. Detective, you better start doing what you're told."

As soon as Adam put his hands behind his back, he felt the handcuffs go on. "You put me in that cell, didn't you? You're the guy with the flashlight."

"Just get going." The man shoved Adam forward. "When we get outside, don't try anything stupid." He thrust the gun into his back for a third time. "Just remember that I'm not afraid to use this."

Once outside, Adam glanced around. Other than a couple of kids riding their bikes at the end of the block, no one else was in sight. They walked down the steps and over to a dark-blue Oldsmobile parked in front of the building. The man opened the passenger's side and ordered him to get in.

"How am I supposed to do that with these handcuffs on?"

"Like this!" When the man shoved him into the car, Adam's head hit the top of the doorframe. "That's how it's done," he said. After he got his prisoner into a sitting position, he moved quickly to the driver's side and got in. He started the car and pulled away from the curb. Only after he had driven a couple of blocks did he speak. "Allow me to introduce myself since we have a mutual acquaintance."

"And who would that be?"

"Why, Howie Cummins, of course." He glanced over to see Adam's reaction. "The name is Pete Larson."

"Larson?" Adam disguised his surprise. "You're that security man who works at the nursing home."

"That's right."

"What's all this about?"

"Just sit tight and enjoy the scenery."

Adam watched the familiar landmarks go by. They drove by Kass' Drug Store. When he looked up at Howie's apartment, he wondered if his partners were there. They turned left on Lyndale going south. "Where are we going?" he asked after they skirted the downtown area.

"To a nice quiet spot outside the city limits."

"What's out there?"

"Some property belongs to my partner. He lets me use it whenever..." Pete paused, glanced over at Adam and gave him crooked smile. "Whenever it becomes necessary."

# Chapter 64

"STEPHANIE WILL BE here in less than a half hour, but I can't wait that long," Howie said as he hung up the phone after talking with LaMar's sister. As expected, she was stunned but overjoyed at the news of her brother being found alive. "Have you checked on LaMar?" he asked Mick.

"Yeah, he's taking it slow but he's doing okay." Mick stood in the open doorway leading to Howie's living area. "I told him that you were talking to his sister and that she would be coming over. He's looking forward to seeing her."

Howie glanced over at the clock and then motioned to his partner. "Come on. Let's go see what happened with Adam. He's been gone too long."

"I'm coming with you," Leo said.

"No, you stay with Rachel and LaMar. They'll need you here." That was true, but Howie wanted somebody with him he could trust completely. Although it now appeared as though Hooknose was no longer a suspect, Howie still wasn't about to take any chances. He thrust his hand out, palm up, toward Leo. "But I'll need your key to the building."

Leo hesitated, but when Rachel nodded, he gave his key to Howie.

"Thanks." Howie turned to Rachel. "You make sure that LaMar doesn't go anyplace. His sister should be here shortly."

"Good luck," Rachel said as Howie and Mick headed for the door.

"We'll take my car," Howie said as he and his partner flew down the stairs and out the entrance door.

When the two detectives arrived at the candy factory, Rachel's car was parked on the side street. "He must still be here," Mick said with a note of hopefulness.

"Let's go find out," Howie said. They hopped out of the car and ran up the steps to the entrance. He unlocked the door and the two of them quietly slipped in. "Where did Adam say Gilbertson's office was located?"

"On the main floor." Mick pointed to the double doors. "It's got to be through those doors."

As soon as they entered the main work area, they saw the office down at the other end. The door to the office was ajar.

"The light's on in there," Mick whispered.

"Let's take it careful," Howie said. "We can't be sure it's Adam." They moved slowly, quietly to the source of the light. He peeked through the door opening and saw a tall, distinguished older man standing at a table. The man's back was to the door. "Let's do it," he said to Mick as he yanked open the door and walked in.

The older man whirled around, a startled look on his face. "What in the world! Who are you?" he asked as he snapped the lid shut on a small, black-velvet box. "What are you doing here and how did you get in?"

"I'm Howie Cummins and this is Mick Brunner. We're from the MAC Detective Agency." Howie glanced around the office. "It doesn't matter how we got in. The question is who are you?"

"My name is Charles Gilbertson and I own this factory." Although his tone was indignant, his eyes hinted of fear.

"Where's Adam Trexler?" Mick demanded.

"How should I know?" Gilbertson stole a glance at the table. "Adam quit a couple of days ago. He doesn't work here any longer."

"I think you know where Adam is," Howie said. He, with Mick right along side of him, moved closer to the table. Not having a search warrant, he was on thin ice, but it was a risk he was willing to take. "Let's see what you're up to here."

"I insist that you leave this moment."

"We're not leaving without Adam," Mick said.

"I tell you, he's not here!" Gilbertson cried.

"What's in that?" Howie pointed to the box that Gilbertson had closed the moment they had come in.

"None of your business."

Both Gilbertson and Howie grabbed for the box at the same time, and in the process, the box was knocked to the floor. The lid flew open, scattering its contents.

"Holy cow!" Mick exclaimed.

Howie offered Gilbertson a smug smile. "Well, what do you know? So that's what makes your chocolate angels so special."

# Chapter 65

"SEE THAT OLD wooden bridge up ahead?" Pete asked, glancing over at Adam and pointing to the structure they soon would be crossing. The longer they had been in the car, the more relaxed and talkative Pete had become. "That's the Cedar Avenue Bridge." He chuckled. "Man, that thing has been there since the horse-and-buggy days. Have you ever been over it?" He continued as if his passenger had replied in the affirmative. "Going over it certainly is a test of whether you have balls or not."

Adam hoped he would spot a police car or the highway patrol and when he did, he had a plan. In the meantime, he had to keep Larson off guard. "So, you've driven across that bridge a number of times?"

"Are you kidding? I've been over that so many times I could do it blindfolded. Every time I cross that rickety old thing, I get a charge, especially when I meet oncoming cars. I like to stomp on the gas and go at them." Pete spoke in a causal tone, as though speaking to an old friend. "It's like playing chicken."

"Sounds like great fun." Adam kept his eyes straight ahead at the oncoming traffic. "The bridge is pretty narrow then?" he asked, hoping to keep Larson talking.

"You bet it is. Two dimes rolling in opposite directions would be in trouble if they met on the damn thing." Pete accelerated as they approached the bridge. They hit the bridge going at least seventy. "Listen to those wooden planks!" Pete cried. "Rat-tat-tat-tat. It sounds like a machine gun going off, doesn't it?" He slapped the steering wheel. "Man, I love that sound!" An oncoming car had stopped short of the bridge, waiting for them to cross. The driver shook his fist at them as they came off the bridge and flew past him. Within moments, Pete slowed the car as he glanced over at Adam. "Do you ever wonder what would happen if two trucks met on that bridge?" He looked in his rearview mirror. "I sure as hell would like to see that."

"It looks like we are out in the boonies," Adam noted, his hopes quickly fading about seeing any cops. "How far are we going?"

"My, aren't you the inquisitive one," Pete replied in a cocky tone. "I guess that's to be expected since you're a private eye. If you ask me, though, you're not much of a detective." They drove for a couple of miles before he spoke again. "I suppose it won't matter telling you what's going on. I bet you're wondering, aren't you?"

"Let's say that I have a professional curiosity."

Pete snickered. "I tell you what. Why don't you ask the questions and I'll answer them. I want to see how good you are at playing detective."

Adam decided that he would carry out his plan whether there was a cop car in sight or not. In the meantime, he would humor Larson by playing his little game. "What's your connection with the candy factory?"

Pete laughed as he slapped the steering wheel again. "Candy factory? It sure is some *candy* factory all right."

"I'm not sure what you're getting at," Adam said as Pete flipped on the turn signal and began to slow down.

"Don't you know what the pious Mr. Charles Gilbertson spices up his special boxes of chocolate angels with?" Pete's tone indicated that he didn't hold Gilbertson in high regard. "Can you guess?"

"No, why don't you tell me?"

"You're not very good at being a detective, are—"

Adam made his move, but Pete saw him coming and braced himself. Although Adam hit him with as much force as he could muster, Pete held his ground. Keeping one hand on the steering wheel, he grabbed Adam by the hair and threw him against the passenger's side window. Within a split second, he pulled out his gun and whacked him across the side of his face with the barrel. As the vehicle hit the gravel shoulder Pete slammed on the brakes and the car skidded to a stop leaving clouds of dust behind it. This time, the gun barrel struck Adam right above his eye.

"That was a stupid thing to try," Pete growled. "You were trying to make me lose control of the car, weren't you? I bet you were hoping that we'd go into a ditch and I'd get knocked out or something."

"Don't I get an 'e' for effort?" Adam managed to reply.

Pete jammed the end of the gun's barrel against Adam's temple. "You're just lucky, wise guy, that I don't want your brains all over the inside of my car. You try something like that again, though, and you'll wish you hadn't."

# Chapter 66

CHARLES GILBERTSON'S FACE turned ashen the moment the black-velvet box hit the floor and broke open, scattering its contents of diamond rings. Beads of perspiration broke out on his forehead as he stood speechless, facing Howie and Mick. The expression on his face was that of a little boy who had just been caught red-handed with stolen cookies from his mother's cookie jar, except these weren't cookies.

"You've got some explaining to do," Howie said as he glanced at the dozens of rings strewn about. Although he hadn't figured out yet what part the diamonds played in this case, he knew that Gilbertson had lied about LaMar. Back at the office Hooknose had made the comment to LaMar about how everybody at the candy factory had thought he was dead. On the ride over, Howie had explained to Mick that there was *one* person, however, who knew LaMar couldn't have been dead.

"Who was that?" Mick had asked.

"The person who identified LaMar's body by his high school class ring."

"Gilbertson?"

"That's right. He was the only one who knew that the ring found on the body had to have been taken from the real LaMar."

"Wow! No wonder Gilbertson made the arrangements so quickly and was willing to cover the funeral costs."

As Howie now faced Gilbertson, he was determined to get answers to his other questions. "Who died in that vat of chocolate?"

"I don't know what you're talking about."

"Come on. We know it wasn't LaMar Jones."

"It was, I tell you. I even identified the body."

"Is that right?" Howie shot Gilbertson a sarcastic smile. "Then we must have LaMar's twin brother sitting in my office right now."

"Wha...what?"

"You heard me. He's in my office as we speak. And he likes it a lot better than that dungeon you had him locked in downstairs."

Gilbertson wiped his brow as his eyes shifted nervously between the two detectives. Moisture formed on his upper lip. "I...I told him not to do it."

"Told who?" Howie demanded, casting a sideways glance at Mick. His partner, though, just raised his eyebrows and shrugged. "Told who?" he yelled when Gilbertson didn't answer.

"A man who—"

"What man? What's his name?" Howie's bitterly sharp tone warned Gilbertson that he wasn't going to allow any leeway.

"I...I can't tell you."

"And I think you will!"

"No, I—"

"Yes, you will!" Howie took a step toward Gilbertson. "Because if you don't, you're going to jail for murder."

Gilbertson's mouth dropped open and his eyes widened as he winced at the word *murder*. "I didn't kill him."

"Tell us who did, then," Mick said.

"Please...I..." Gilbertson swallowed hard. "I...I need to sit down." Howie motioned to Mick to get the chair from the desk. Once he brought the chair, Gilbertson collapsed into it. His face remained ashen. When he spoke, it was in the tones of a man who knew his world was falling apart. "It was a man by the name of Pete Larson."

Howie and Mick exchanged glances. Howie wondered if his own mouth had dropped as wide open as his partner's. "Are you talking about the Pete Larson who is the security guard over at the Golden Years Retirement Home?" he asked.

Gilbertson nodded.

Mick picked up one of the diamond rings and examined it for several moments. After examining two more rings, he showed them to Howie before turning his attention to the owner of the candy factory. "Are any of these rings from the residents at the nursing home where Larson works?"

Rachel's father didn't reply. He kept his eyes downcast, staring at the floor.

"Answer us!" Howie demanded. "And do it before I lose my patience. We'll only ask you one more time. Did these rings come from the nursing home?"

"Yes," Gilbertson whispered. He slumped further into the chair, not making eye contact, no doubt ashamed at what he had just confessed.

Howie hadn't initially made the connection, but now that Mick had, it was beginning to all make sense. His thoughts briefly turned to Nana. His client will be so thrilled to know that she was right about the crooks at her place stealing diamonds. He imagined her celebrating by doing wheelies down the hallways. "How did you and Larson ever get hooked up?" he asked, feeling repugnance at the thought of someone stealing from old people.

"Through a friend who suggested that Pete might be able to offer me some financial backing to start the business." Gilbertson swallowed a couple of times and wet his lips again.

"Keep talking." The man could use a drink of water, but Howie was in no mood to offer him any.

"When I went bankrupt years ago, I couldn't face anyone. It was a terrible time." Gilbertson paused, waiting as though expecting sympathy. When none came forth, he continued. "If it weren't for Rachel, I think I would've..." He looked away for a moment, his face distorted with anguish.

"Go on," Howie said.

"What kept me going was that I knew that I had to provide for my daughter to make up for all those hard times I put her through." Gilbertson looked at Howie and Mick with pleading eyes. "She suffered so much."

Adam had shared with Howie how difficult it had been for Rachel when her father had to sell the house and move into a cheap apartment. When Adam told him that, he had felt sorry for Rachel and her father. Now, as he looked at the man sitting before him, he felt sorry for Rachel for the kind of father she had. "Tell me about Larson. You said that you met him while you were starting this business."

"Yes, he had some money to invest and I took him up on it. I was desperate." Gilbertson shifted in his chair. He sat silently, staring at the diamonds scattered on the floor.

"You can forget about those," Howie said. "Just keep talking."

Gilbertson breathed deeply. "In those first couple of years it was a struggle to make any profits and I was afraid that I'd lose the factory." He ran his hand back through his hair. "I shared my concern with Pete. The next day he came to me and said he had an idea of how we both could benefit. All he had to do was make a contact in Chicago."

Mick asked, "Is that where you shipped the diamonds?"

"Yes."

"And you shipped them in with the boxes of chocolate angels?"

Before Gilbertson could answer, Howie spoke up. "You didn't ship them inside the boxes along side the angels, did you?"

"No."

Howie picked up one of the angel molds from the table. "When you made up your own batch of angels, you slipped the diamonds into the melted chocolate so that when it hardened, nobody could tell that it was really a chocolate-covered diamond." He tossed the mold back on the table with the others. "Those packages you made up to send to your so-called friends were really diamond deliveries to your contact in Chicago. Am I right?" When Gilbertson didn't reply, Howie took hold of the front of his shirt at the neckline. "Am I right?" he yelled.

Gilbertson nodded as beads of perspiration formed on his forehead again. He appeared to be a man who had reached a breaking point.

"So tell me," Howie said. "Who was it then that died in that vat of chocolate?"

"I don't know."

Howie pulled Gilbertson toward him, yanking and twisting his shirt into a tourniquet around his neck.

"I never knew his name." Gilbertson gasped. The veins in his temples bulged. His face turned crimson. He could barely get his next words out. "I...I swear."

"I think he's telling the truth," Mick said, giving Howie a look that told him that he was letting his anger get the best of him.

Howie stared at his partner for several long moments. When he released his grip, Gilbertson's collar button flew off and landed on the floor, rolling until it settled next to one of the diamond rings.

Gilbertson rubbed his neck and took a couple of deep breaths while pulling at his collar to make sure it stayed loose. "It was a fellow Pete knew from some place. He had come in every now and then to clean at the nursing home."

"And you didn't even know his name?" Mick asked, the look on his face revealing utter disbelief mixed with revulsion.

"He was just some bum off the street that Pete said nobody would miss. Pete had gotten him so drunk that night that he passed out." Gilbertson buried his face in his hands. When he looked up, his eyes revealed the horror he had seen. "Pete said he would take care of it. All I would have to do is identify the body as LaMar's."

"But why go to all that trouble?" Howie asked, feeling nothing but loathing for Gilbertson. "Why not just do away with LaMar?"

"Because he found out about the diamonds. When Pete learned about that, he went berserk. He wanted to know if LaMar had told anybody about it." Gilbertson paused as he wrung his hands, his eyes shifting back and forth between Mick and Howie. "He said that we'd keep him locked up downstairs until he came clean."

"And then what?" Mick asked.

"He promised that he would let LaMar go once he told us who else knew."

Howie nearly laughed out loud at Gilbertson's naïve belief that Larson would ever keep such a promise. "And you believed him?" Gilbertson started to reply but Howie cut him off. "Listen, and listen good. If LaMar would've talked, that would've been the end of him. That room would've become his tomb."

"No! No!" Gilbertson cried as he shook his head. "I wouldn't have allowed that. I wouldn't." He clasped his hands as if he was going to pray. "I'm not that kind of person. You have to believe me."

"Oh, sure." Howie had to control the urge of slapping Gilbertson around. If Mick hadn't been there, he would have roughed him up more. "You're not that kind of person, huh? Did you tell that to the poor guy who was invited to go for a swim in that vat of chocolate? Did you tell him how nice you were as he was being scalded to death?"

"I...I..." Gilbertson buried his face in his hands. When he finally looked up, his once smoothly lined face look like it had aged ten years. "I only wish..." He hung his head; his voice quivered. "I'll never forgive myself for that...never."

"We don't have time for your self-pity," Howie said, growing more disgusted by the moment. As far as he was concerned, Gilbertson and Larson were made from the same mold. "Where's Adam?"

Gilbertson eyes flickered as he stared off to one side. His lips moved as if in conversation with himself. "Pete has him," he finally mumbled.

"What!" Mick cried.

"Where are they?" Howie shouted, knowing what Larson was capable of. "Where did he take our partner?"

Gilbertson chewed on his lip. "I own some property south of the cities. He probably took him there." His eyes revealed a sense of dread as he glanced at Mick and then at Howie. "I think you better hurry, I'm..." He paused and then swallowed hard. "I'm afraid of what Pete might do. He's crazy, I tell you."

Howie cast a concerned glance toward his partner. "Where is this property?" he asked Gilbertson.

"South of the cities on Cedar Ave."

"Where on Cedar?"

"Do you know the Cedar Avenue Bridge?"

Howie nodded.

"Once you cross the bridge, it's about five more miles. It's on the right hand side. There is a cluster of pine trees near the main entrance."

"What do you mean the main entrance? Is there more than one?"

"Yes, there are two roads going into it but take the gravel one. It's the second one and it's easier to spot."

"Any signs marking this entrance?" Mick asked.

Gilbertson nodded. "There's a *No Trespassing* sign that has an angel painted on each of the four corners." He looked at Howie. "You have to believe me. I never thought it would lead to this."

Howie turned to Mick. "Let's take this creep downstairs and lock him up in one of those rooms. We'll deal with him later."

# Chapter 67

As Pete turned off the main highway onto a gravel road, Adam took note of the sign at the entrance. *Private property. No Trespassing. Violators will be prosecuted!* On each of the corners of the sign was an outline drawing of an angel. The gravel road disappeared into a clump of evergreens. Once they passed the trees, they continued on the gradually downward slope for another hundred yards or so. Up ahead, the road ended at a weathered wooden shed, about the size of a double car garage. The shed, in need of several coats of paint, appeared to be leaning to one side. Beyond the shed a path led toward another clump of evergreens.

"Once you go past those trees, there is nothing but marshland," Pete said. "I hope you'll like it because that's going to be your future home."

"All that's for me? You shouldn't have bothered."

"Oh, no, you'll have to share it." Pete smirked. "There's someone else out there already."

"And who's that?"

Pete chuckled, but said nothing. He parked to the right of the shed, got out, walked over, and opened the passenger door. "Okay, get out."

"Where are we going?"

"To the shed. I've got a little surprise for you in there."

# Chapter 68

MICK SHOVED GILBERTSON as they headed down the stairs to the sub-basement. "Come on. Move a little faster. We don't have all day."

"Wha...what are you going to do with me?"

"Don't play dumb," Howie said as he followed the two of them. "We're taking you to one of your private guest rooms so you can meditate on how you've been a naughty boy."

"You have to believe me, I—"

"Just shut up and move!" Howie yelled, tired of listening to the guy and anxious to get going to find Adam.

After locking Gilbertson in one of the cell-like rooms that had held Adam, they rushed back up the stairs. "What should we do about those diamond rings?" Mick asked as they came into the reception area.

"Just leave them."

"Really?"

"Yeah. We don't have time to fool with them now. We'll get them later." They flew out the entrance door and down the steps to their car. Within moments, Howie turned the ignition, put the car in gear, and squealed away. He had a score to settle with Larson. "How much time do you think it's going to take to get out there?" he asked.

"I don't know. Maybe forty to forty-five minutes." Mick braced himself as they turned the corner onto Broadway. The car picked up speed as Howie weaved in and out of traffic. He shot a look over at his boss. "On second thought, we might make it in thirty minutes."

Howie stepped on the gas just as the light at the corner turned red. He whizzed through the intersection as drivers who had the green light angrily honked. He glanced in his rearview mirror for any cop cars, and then gave a sideward glance toward Mick. "What do you say that we make it in less than thirty?"

# Chapter 69

"DAMN!" PETE CRIED as he had trouble turning the key in the rusted lock on the shed's door. "I told Gilbertson that he should've replaced this lock the last time." He slammed the lock against the door and swore again.

While Pete cursed the lock, Adam glanced back toward the main highway. The faint drone of passing cars could be heard, giving him hope that if he could get up there, he might have a chance of flagging down a car. He didn't think he could get very far, however, with his hands handcuffed behind his back. "Why don't you unlock these things and I'll open it for you," he said as he turned sideways, giving Pete a view of the handcuffs.

"What!"

"Take these cuffs off and I'll help you."

Pete looked at him as though he was crazy. "You've got to be kidding!" he cried and then offered Adam a smirk. "I have to give you credit for trying, though. You've got balls." He muttered something under his breath and went back to working on the lock. "Got it!" he finally announced as he yanked the lock off and swung open the door, its hinges creaking. He motioned to Adam. "Step in and be my guest."

Although the open door along with windows on both ends of the shed provided a measure of light, it took a while for Adam's eyes to adjust to the dimness of the space. He hadn't taken but a few steps inside when a decaying stench assaulted his senses.

"Do you know what that smell is?" Pete asked, a grin on his face.

Adam shook his head.

"I guess you've never smelled a dead mouse before, huh?" Pete looked around. "There are probably a couple of them in here. The little critters come in during the winter months thinking they'll be safe, but I set traps." He smirked. "Have you ever seen a trap shut on their heads?"

"No."

Pete chuckled. "Their eyes bug out just like in cartoons. Funny as hell."

Adam noticed a workbench off to his right with a window above it. A hammer, hacksaw, and some other tools he couldn't quite distinguish lay on the bench. On the wall directly ahead hung several heavy chains from hooks. A bicycle, missing its front wheel, leaned against the wall to the left of him.

"Well, what do you think about my little surprise?" Pete asked, gesturing toward the chains hanging from the hooks.

"I don't know what you're talking about."

Pete shoved Adam forward. He took one of the chains off its hook, held it up, and waved the end of it so close to Adam's face it caused him to flinch. "Now do you see?" he asked. "That's a leg iron attached to the end. It clamps around your ankle and is secured with a small padlock. I made it myself."

"Is that so?" Adam offered Pete a half smile. "I thought maybe it was a souvenir from when you served on the chain gang."

"Okay, wise guy. See what you think of this." Pete rammed his fist into Adam's stomach; the blow nearly sent him to the floor as he gasped for breath. "That's just a little reminder of who's in charge. You got that?" When Adam didn't reply, Pete hit him again. "I asked you, have you got that?"

Adam nodded as he slowly straightened up while trying to catch his breath. He couldn't take another blow and remain standing.

"That's more like it," Pete said in a patronizing tone, patting him on the back as if they were old friends. Without saying another word, he wrapped one end of the chain around Adam's neck several times until the leg clamp dangled in the middle of his chest. "Now let's get the hell out of here. It stinks in here." Once outside, he took a deep breath and then directed his prisoner to the back of the shed. Several cement building blocks lay in a pile near the far corner of the shed. "What do you think those blocks are for?" he asked.

"I wouldn't know," Adam said, still trying to catch his breath; his stomach muscles were sore and tender from the punches. The weight of the leg iron and heavy chain tugged at his neck, making it difficult to keep his head straight. But he was not about to appear in any way as if he was bowing in deference to Pete. "Are you planning on building something?" he asked, keeping his tone innocent, not wanting to risk another punch.

"Building something!" Pete cried. "Is that what you think?" He jabbed his finger into Adam's chest; his lip curled as he spoke. "Man, you just don't cut it as a detective, do you?"

"I try."

"Well, if you ask me, you and your partners are a bunch of amateurs, and I ought to know."

"How's that?" Adam needed to buy some time until he thought of what he could do if he ever caught Pete off guard. As far as those cement blocks, he knew exactly what the guy had in mind. "Were you in the business at one time?"

"I was never a detective, but I was a cop for nearly fifteen years before I got the job at that crummy nursing home."

Adam hoped his face didn't reveal his surprise at Pete's revelation. "How come you didn't stay a cop?"

"I got tired of trying to make it on a cop's salary and dealing with street scum." Pete sneered as he spit the words out. "There are easier ways of making money." He glanced at the pile of cement blocks and motioned to Adam. "Come on." He grabbed two of the blocks, lifting one in each hand. "Let's go sit out in front for a while. I need a cigarette before I take you on your boat ride." They moved to the front of the shed and he set the blocks down about ten feet apart from each other. "Go ahead and sit down," he said as he settled onto his.

"I think I'll stand if you don't mind," Adam replied, keeping his tone submissive while his mind raced for a plan of action.

"It's your choice. As for me, I'm going to relax and have myself a smoke." Pete reached in his pocket and pulled out his pack of cigarettes. "Just don't get any wise ideas, though." He plucked a cigarette out, lit it, took a puff, and then offered it to Adam. "Hey, would you like a drag? It may be your last chance."

Adam shook his head.

"What's the matter, don't you smoke?"

"Never took it up."

Pete took another drag, blew a smoke circle toward Adam, and then watched it dissipate in the light breeze. "That's right. I forgot. You're the one studying to be the preacher, aren't you?" He ran his tongue over the front of his teeth and made a smacking sound. After studying his intended victim for a couple of minutes, he leaned forward. "Do you want to say your prayers?" His tone was taunting, his eyes dancing with laughter. "I'll let you. It's okay with me. I won't tell anyone."

"Don't you ever pray?" Adam asked. His only chance was to continue to engage Larson in conversation.

"Me? Pray?" Pete seemed surprised by the question. "Nah, I don't go for that religious mumbo-jumbo stuff."

Adam strained to keep his head straight. The chain around his neck dug into his flesh. "Why not?"

Pete took another drag. "Because when I was a kid, my old man would get drunk and beat the hell out of me every week. And then come Sunday, he would sit me down and make me listen as he read his bible."

"That's too bad he beat you."

"That's not all of it." Pete flicked the ashes off his cigarette. "Get this: the jerk was a respected deacon at the church." His laughter was mixed with anger. "Man, if they only knew what he really was like."

"Doesn't sound like he was much of a father," Adam said, inching toward Pete.

"You got that right."

"What happened to him?"

"I don't know and I don't care." Pete pulled his gun out from inside his jacket and pointed it at Adam. "I see you moving up." He gestured with the gun. "Move back a couple of feet and let me enjoy my smoke in peace, will you?" When Adam stepped back, Pete nodded his approval. "Now, do you understand what I mean about you not being very smart? You and your partners have no business being detectives."

"We found out about you, didn't we? And we found LaMar."

"That was a fluke. If Gilbertson would've had a backbone and let me handle it the way I wanted to, you guys would never have found LaMar." Pete looked toward the marsh. "But I guarantee one thing...they'll never find you."

# Chapter 70

"THERE'S THE CEDAR Avenue Bridge up ahead!" Mick's voice revealed the anxiety of not knowing what was happening to their partner. For the past ten miles he had cracked his knuckles, only stopping after Howie pointed it out to him.

"How far did Gilbertson say we had to go once we cross that bridge?" Howie asked, his own nerves on edge.

"Four or five miles."

Howie pressed the gas pedal down even further. Even though they had been on the road for only twenty-five minutes, it had been a long, agonizing race against the clock. "Gilbertson said that the sign had angels on it, didn't he?"

"Yeah, in each of the four corners. They may be faded by the weather, but should be visible from the road."

"Watch for it, okay?"

"Don't worry, I'm looking."

"For his sake, he'd better not have sent us on a wild goose chase." Howie took the bridge at a fairly good clip.

"You'd better slow down," Mick urged, glancing over at his partner. "There's another car coming at a pretty good speed."

"I see it." Howie, however, didn't let up on the gas.

After the two cars narrowly passed each other on the bridge, Mick breathed a sigh of relief. "Why do you think Larson brought Adam all the way out here?" he asked once they had gotten beyond the bridge. "You don't think..."

Howie glanced over and saw the dread in Mick's eyes; his partner had already answered his own question.

# Chapter 71

PETE FLIPPED HIS cigarette away, stood up for a moment and stretched before he sat back down. "Hey, Mr. Detective. Have you figured out what I'm going to do with this cement block yet?" he asked in a tone matching his sarcastic grin.

"It's going to make a nice little anchor, isn't it?"

"You've got that right."

"And I'd guess that it's not going to be for the boat."

Pete chuckled. "Hey, you're not as dumb as you look." He laid his gun beside him, folded his arms, and then stretched out his legs. He spent a few moments watching puffy white clouds drift across the sky before turning his attention back to Adam. "Hey, do see that cloud up there?"

"Where?"

"Right above you. It looks like a puppy dog." Pete stared at it for several moments before turning to Adam. "You know, they say drowning isn't so bad."

"That's nice to know."

"No, really. I read someplace that the best thing to do is not to fight it, just breathe in the water and let it happen."

"You're not going to get away with this."

"You know, that's what Pritchett said before he died." Pete paused, eyeing Adam as though hoping for some kind of reaction like terror or horror, or perhaps expecting him to beg for his life.

Adam was shocked at hearing that Pritchett was dead. The poor guy was probably at the bottom of the marsh someplace anchored down with a cement block. Adam, however, wasn't about to give Larson the satisfaction of seeing how shaken he was by the news. "Why Pritchett?" he asked, keeping his voice calm.

"Because he got too nosey."

"THAT MIGHT BE it coming up!" Mick cried, the tension in his voice increasing. "There are the evergreens Gilbertson talked about."

Howie slowed the car as he pulled over to the shoulder, stopping short of the entrance road. "Are you sure that's the sign we're looking for?"

"Yeah, and I can make out the angels on the four corners." Mick checked the area. "Where are you going to park?"

"On this side of the trees." Howie turned onto the gravel road and let the car come to a rolling stop. "We'll walk from here. I don't want to advertise that we're coming."

PETE STOOD UP, stretched again, and grinned at Adam. "Well, I think it's about time for us to head out."

"Why don't you have another cigarette?"

"Funny boy." Pete picked up his gun and the cement block. "Get moving, but not too fast. This block is heavy."

"Unlock these cuffs and I'll carry it for you."

"Is that so?" Pete gave Adam a crooked smile.

"Just trying to be helpful."

"I've got to hand it to you. You may not be much of a detective, but you're one cool character. Too bad you're on the wrong side. I might have gotten to like you." He motioned with his gun. "Now, let's get going."

Adam turned and headed in the direction Pete had pointed with the gun. The worn pathway through ankle-high grass sloped downward toward the marsh. They had gone not more than a couple hundred feet when Adam saw a wooden rowboat up ahead. The weather-beaten boat rested peacefully in the watery marsh, anchored to the shore by a cement block at the end of a rope. Beyond the boat was nothing but marshland.

"SEE THAT?" HOWIE whispered. He pointed to a dark green car parked near a shed about a hundred yards or so up ahead.

"But I don't see any sign of anybody," Mick said. "Do you?"

"No, but let's get closer." Howie led the way as they moved to within twenty feet of the shed.

Mick nudged Howie. "The door's open."

"Yeah, but it doesn't look like anybody's in there." Howie and his partner moved quickly to the door and cautiously looked in.

"Look at those things." Mick pointed to the chains with the leg irons hanging on the back wall. He turned toward Howie. "I don't have a good feeling about this."

"That makes two of us," Howie said, knowing that Larson didn't bring Adam here to go on a picnic in the country.

"They've got to be around here someplace," Mick said.

Howie pointed to the path leading toward the marsh. "Let's follow that and see where it goes."

"WHAT IF I don't cooperate and get in the boat?" Adam asked in a tone as defiant as the look in his eyes.

"You know, that's interesting," Pete said. "Those are almost the exact words that Pritchett used. But I convinced him to do otherwise."

"How did you do that?"

Pete set the block down. "I told him that I'd shoot him in the hand, and if he didn't change his mind after that, I'd do the other hand." He studied Adam as though looking for signs of fear. "And then after I told him his arms and legs would be next, he quickly came around to seeing my way of looking at it."

"I'm not going to go so easy." Adam locked eyes with Larson. "You're going to have to shoot me because I'm not getting into that boat."

"You're calling my bluff, aren't you?" Pete seemed genuinely taken back by Adam's refusal to cooperate. When he stepped closer, Adam rushed him, but it was no contest. Pete whipped him across the face with the gun and then threw a kidney punch that dropped the defenseless Adam to his knees. "Well, hot shot, have you had enough?" he asked as he stood over his fallen victim. "Or do you want some more?"

Adam gasped for air. "I'm...not going."

Pete walked behind him and kicked him in the back. He kicked him again, and then again, until Adam finally fell sideways to the ground.

"I'm...I'm...still not going."

"We'll see how tough you are." He aimed the gun at his right leg. "On second thought, I'm not going to mess around with you." He pointed the gun at his forehead and cocked the hammer. "I'll tell once more. Get into that boat!"

Adam shut his eyes and swallowed hard, but refused to move.

WHEN THE GUNSHOT rang through the air, Howie and Mick froze in their tracks. They looked at each other with horror. "Come on!" Howie cried. Without waiting for Mick to reply, he started running down the path in the direction of the shot.

# Chapter 72

HOWIE'S HEART POUNDED as he and Mick ran down the path. The gunshot had echoed throughout the area, sending birds flying and a cold chill down his spine. All he could think of was Adam. *What if he's...* He tried to block the word from his thoughts, but couldn't. Sweat poured down his forehead. Images of his partner lying in a pool of blood assaulted his mind. Looking around for any signs of Adam, he tripped over a root and nearly tumbled headfirst.

"Are you okay?" Mick cried as he flew past.

"Just keep going!" Howie yelled as he picked up his pace again, his thoughts turning back to Adam. He blamed himself for persuading him to go undercover at that factory. *If Adam hadn't, he might still be— Stop thinking like that*, he chided himself.

"There he is!" Mick cried as he pointed ahead, having turned on the speed and was nearly twenty yards in front of Howie.

"What the—" Howie couldn't believe his eyes. Adam was standing, looking off into the distance to their right. He glanced in the direction Adam was looking and caught a glimpse of the tail end of a dark-colored car disappearing behind several evergreen trees. The car, spitting gravel behind it, was headed toward the main highway.

By now, Mick had reached Adam and had knelt down in the foot-high grass. It appeared as if he had discovered something. Adam stood next to him, staring at whatever Mick was examining.

As Howie came closer to his partners, he saw the body. By the time he reached them, he was nearly out of breath. Although his lungs gasped for air, his eyes quickly focused on the body of Pete Larson. A large, dark-red stain appeared near Larson's left-breast shirt pocket. The man's eyes, wide open, stared vacantly at the puffy white clouds passing above.

Mick placed his hand on the side of Larson's neck and felt for a pulse. The sounds of crickets and the shrieking of a bird in the distance filled the moments while his partners waited. He looked up at Howie and Adam, shook his head, and quietly announced, "He's dead."

# Chapter 73

ADAM'S BREATH CAME in short gulps. Still shaken by the events of the past few minutes, his legs barely steadied him. For one terrible split second when he heard the shot, he thought that it was Pete firing, but simultaneously he heard a dull thud and Pete moaned. The next thing he knew, he was struggling to get Pete's body off of him. By the time he managed to get to a standing position, a car's engine roared in the distance. He looked just as the dark-blue car disappeared beyond the trees. Feeling a sense of relief that he was still alive, he experienced overwhelming elation as Mick ran up to him. His partner quickly unwrapped the chain from around his neck and then knelt down to examine the body. Within moments, Howie joined them. Their joy, however, was tempered when Mick announced that Larson was dead.

"Whoever shot him took off in a car," Adam said to Howie, realizing the thud he had heard was the bullet striking its victim. He motioned with a nod of his head. "It vanished behind those evergreens over there."

"I know," Howie replied, still trying to catch his breath. "I caught a glimpse of it. Are you okay?" he asked Adam.

"I will be when I get these cuffs off."

"Do you know where he has the key?" Mick asked, still kneeling beside Larson's body, looking paler than the corpse.

"Check his right-hand jacket pocket," Adam said.

Mick found a set of keys and handed them to his partner.

Howie unlocked the cuffs and tossed the keys back to Mick. "Does that feel better?" he asked Adam.

"You bet it does." Adam winced as he crisscrossed his arms in front of him several times in an attempt to work out the stiffness in his shoulders. The skin on his neck had been rubbed raw from the chain and his back ached from where Larson had kicked him, but he felt a renewed strength from being freed.

"I'm sure glad you're okay," Mick said as he stood up.

"You and me both." Adam pointed to where the shot had come from. "See those trees over there?" he asked Mick. "How far away do you think they are?"

"I don't know. Maybe forty, fifty yards."

"Whoever fired the gun from there had to be an excellent shot," Howie said. "I can't even hit the broadside of a deer from ten yards."

"What did you say?" Adam asked, stunned by what his partners' words had triggered.

"That I couldn't hit a deer from that distance." Howie looked at Adam with inquiring eyes. "What's wrong?"

Adam gnawed on his lip as he stared at the grove of trees from where the deadly shot had been fired. He turned to Mick. "Give me the keys you took from Larson's jacket! I'm taking his car."

"Where are you going?" Howie asked.

"Back to the candy factory."

"Why?"

"Because the answer to who shot Larson is back there."

"What are you talking about?"

"I don't have time to explain now." He held out his hand to Mick. "Give me the damn keys!"

Mick looked to Howie who nodded his okay. "Do you want one of us to go with you?" Mick asked as he handed over the keys.

Adam shook his head. "You guys contact the police and explain what happened. You can tell them that I'll talk to them later."

IT TOOK ADAM thirty-five minutes to drive back to the North Side. When he arrived at the candy factory, he wasn't surprised to find the dark-blue car parked out in front. He pulled in behind it, sat for a moment while collecting his thoughts, and then got out and slowly walked up the cement steps to the front door. Once he was inside the building, he moved to the doors leading into the main work area, opened one, and peeked in. At the far end, the door to Gilbertson's office was open and the office lights were on. He slipped into the work area, closing the door quietly behind him. He moved past the tables toward Gilbertson's office. The stained glass windows silently witnessed his movements, their brilliance muted now that the sun had nearly set. He stepped unnoticed into Gilbertson's office. The person he had suspected was busy picking up diamond rings off the floor and putting them into a black cloth bag.

# Chapter 74

ADAM STOOD SILENTLY watching Rachel Gilbertson on her hands and knees picking up the diamond rings. He wanted to leave, to go someplace, anyplace, else but instead he took a breath and then quietly spoke her name. "Rachel."

She swung around. Startled at first, her face softened. "Adam, how long have you been standing there?" she asked in a casual, friendly tone as though what she was doing was nothing out of the ordinary.

"Why did you kill him?"

"Kill who?"

"Let's not play games." It hurt that she would even attempt to deceive him. "You know who I'm talking about…Pete Larson."

Rachel stood up and leaned against the desk, looking just as beautiful as the first time he saw her. "I didn't want him to kill you," she said and then asked calmly, "How did you know it was me?"

"I didn't, but when one of my partners made a comment that whoever it was must've been a crack shot, something your father said flashed through my mind." Adam felt sick to his stomach. He wished this was a horrible dream and that he would soon wake up. "Do you recall the first time you introduced me to your father?"

She nodded as her eyes flashed with curiosity.

"Do you remember what he said about you?"

"Not really."

Adam chewed on his lip. The pain he felt now was far worse than what he had received at the hands of Pete Larson. "Your father talked about the two of you going hunting. Do you remember now?"

She cocked her head, but remained silent.

"He said you were a crack shot."

A hint of a smile appeared on her face. "You should be proud of yourself. That's pretty good detective work." She reached down and picked up a diamond ring.

"All the time I was coming here, I was praying I was wrong." Adam watched as she opened the black bag and dropped the ring in. "I'd hoped I wouldn't find you here." He shook his head, trying to understand as he pointed to the black bag. "Why?"

The gentleness in Rachel's face that had been there just a moment ago faded. "Because my father has no business sense!" she answered, her tone tinged with anger. Any hint of a smile had disappeared.

"I still don't understand."

"Those years of living in that crummy little apartment after he had gone bankrupt were the worst years of my life." Her eyes narrowed as anger flashed in them. "I promised myself that would never happen again."

"How did Larson come into the picture?"

"When he came to my father and suggested the scheme, my father said no." Rachel's eyes hardened. "I convinced Daddy, though, to get involved."

"You did?"

"Yes, and he agreed to do it for my sake as a way of making up for those other years." She paused, her face and tone becoming gentler. "I stayed in the background and let him and Pete handle it."

"Did you know about LaMar?"

"Yes, but only after the fact." A note of sadness mingled with her words.

"And how about Pritchett"

Her lip curled. "He deserved what he got."

Adam closed his eyes for a moment, feeling light-headed and nauseous. "It's over now," he said, barely able to speak the words.

"It doesn't have to be."

"What do you mean?"

"We've got enough cash in a bank in Chicago. I can easily get my hands on it." Rachel held up the bag full of diamond rings. "And with these you and I could start a new life someplace else."

"I...I...can't," Adam said, choking out the words, daring not to even think about her suggestion.

"Don't you care for me?"

"Very much so. I thought we'd..." Adam took a deep breath with the hopes that it would relieve the heaviness he felt. "You're going to have to come with me."

"I don't think so." Rachel pulled out a small revolver from the black sack she was holding, and pointed it at him.

"That's not the answer."

"I'm not as good of a shot with this as I am with my rifle, but from this distance, I don't think I'd have a problem." The look in her eyes told Adam that she would pull the trigger if she had to. "Now you move over here." He and she exchanged places. "You have to promise you won't come after me."

"You know I can't do that."

"Then come with me," she pleaded, her eyes reaching out to him with tenderness.

"I can't do that either." Adam took a step forward. "Give me the gun."

"Stay where you are!" Rachel warned. "Don't make me—"

"It's over," Adam said, having seen Leo come up behind her. Hooknose probably had come to the candy factory with the intention of keeping a protective eye on Rachel. "Leo's here now. You can't shoot us both."

"You don't expect me to fall for that old trick, do—"

"Sorry," Leo cried as he wrapped his huge arms around her from the back, doing it so swiftly and with such force that she dropped both the gun and the black bag.

"Let me go!" she screamed.

"I'm sorry, I'm so very sorry," Leo kept repeating as tears streamed from his eyes.

# Chapter 75

"WHAT DO YOU think will happen to Rachel?" Adam asked from the back seat as he rode with Howie and Mick to the nursing home for Nana's birthday party.

"It's hard to say." Howie turned the corner and spotted a parking place near the entrance. He'd had to nearly twist Adam's arm to get him to come with them. "But I'm afraid that she's not going to be selling chocolate angels for a long time."

"Have you talked to JD about her?" Adam no doubt hoped that their police detective friend would have some definite answers.

"Not yet," Howie lied. JD had told him privately that Rachel would be tried for first-degree murder and probably get life. He would eventually share that information with Adam, but now was not the time. Although his partner was still hurting from the physical beating he took from Larson, it was nothing compared to the emotional beating inflicted upon him with Rachel's involvement in the case.

"How about her father?" Mick asked.

"He's going to be charged with accessory to murder." Howie pulled into the parking space, shut off the ignition, and turned to Mick. "And he's going to have to answer for the murder of whoever died in that vat of chocolate and for Pritchett's death as well." JD had also shared that the police would be conducting a full-scale investigation into any unexplained deaths of residents who had died at the two nursing homes in the past couple of years.

"It's just fortunate for Gilbertson that Rosie is still alive," Mick said.

Howie nodded. Charles Gilbertson had confessed that Rosie Carpenter was being held at the nursing home in St. Paul. When the police went there, they found her in a room on the third floor, drugged.

"Have they found Miller yet?"

"Not yet," Howie said. "But I don't think they'll have much trouble, since he's not all that smart. And when they do, it wouldn't surprise me if he agrees to testify to get a lighter sentence." He glanced at his watch. "We'd better go or else Nana will be sending out her grandson looking for us." He glanced back at Adam. "You okay?" he asked, glad that his partner had agreed to come along.

"I'll be all right."

"Don't forget your present for Nana." Mick handed Howie the box of chocolate angels he had been holding. "She's going to love you to pieces for this. How much did this set you back, anyway?"

"Enough, but she's worth it."

The three detectives moved through the lobby area, nodding and saying hello to those residents who greeted them. The party for Nana was held in the dining room on the first floor. Close to forty residents and staff members were in attendance. Elmer, the former truant officer, held court in one corner of the room as half dozen residents listened attentively to how he had single-handedly helped those young detectives crack their case. Jerome, Nana's grandson, took notes as Elmer spun his tale. As soon as Howie saw Nana, he walked over and presented her with his gift.

"What's this?" Nana asked, eyeing him and the gift suspiciously.

Howie offered her his winsome smile. "It's a gift from me to celebrate your birthday and for helping us solve the case."

"Why, isn't that sweet of you," Nana said. "Is it a bottle of booze?"

"I'm afraid not."

"My arthritis is acting up today." She handed the box back to Howie. "Unwrap it for me, will you?"

"I'll be glad to." Howie tore off the paper and presented the box of candy to Nana.

"I can't read this," she complained, squinting at the stylized writing on the cover. "What in tarnation is in such a fancy box, anyway?"

"It's a five pound box of chocolate angels. This is the finest—"

"Yuk!" she cried, wrinkling up her nose and pushing the box away. "Get that away from me right now!"

"What's the matter?"

"I hate chocolate! It makes my face break out."

"But—"

"No buts about it!" Nana snapped and then motioned for Howie to bend down closer. "You need to come to my room after the party," she whispered.

"Why?"

"I've got something important to talk to you about."

"And what would that be?"

"Haven't you learned anything yet?" Nana scolded, wagging her finger at him. "We can't talk here." Her eyes scanned the room. *"They* might be listening. I'll meet you later. Come alone and be sure you're not followed."

The party lasted for nearly two hours. Adam and Mick said they would wait for Howie in the reception area. "What are you going to do with the candy?" Mick asked.

Howie offered his partners a coy smile. "I'm going to use it to bribe a certain blond nurse to go out with me." On his way to Nana's room, he stopped at the nurses' station. An older woman in white was sitting at the desk and writing in a chart.

"May I help you?" the nurse asked.

"Ma'am, there is a certain nurse who works here." Howie cleared his throat. "Ah, I don't know her name, but she's blond and I would guess in her mid-twenties." He glanced around hoping that she might suddenly appear. "I'd like to talk to her."

"Oh, you must mean Cindy." She set her pen down. "I'm sorry but she quit yesterday and went back home up north."

"What! Do you know why?"

"From what I heard, I guess she was lonely." The nurse closed the chart she had been writing in. "She didn't have any boyfriends and wasn't dating, so she decided to go back home."

"Thank you," Howie mumbled. Before going to Nana's room, he stopped and laid the box of chocolate angels at the door of Zelda-the-Snoop. Allowing himself a half smile, he turned and went to Nana's door and knocked. Within moments, she answered and invited him to come in and sit down. "What's the problem now?" he asked after he found a corner of the bed to sit on.

"I've got another case for you." Nana went to the door and put her ear to it. When she came back she wheeled up to him until their faces were only inches apart. "Racketeering!" she announced as she tugged at one of her pigtails. "The Tuesday afternoon bingo games are rigged!" Her eyes narrowed. "My grandson thinks the Mafia's involved!"

Howie sighed and took out his notepad and pen. "Okay, Nana..." He took a deep breath. "Let's start at the beginning."

Charles Tindell's writing career began one hot July day in 1995 while sitting in a canoe in the Boundary Waters Canoe Area in northern Minnesota. His first book Seeing Beyond the Wrinkles is the recipient of the National Mature Media's coveted GOLD AWARD designating it among "The Best in Educational Material for Older Adults." His second book The Enduring Human Spirit is the recipient of the National Mature Media's Silver Award, symbolizing that the work is among the best of the best.

He and his wife, Carol, have three sons, four grandchildren, and two cats. Oil painting, ventriloquism, baking bread, canoeing, jigsaw puzzles, collecting hourglasses, and writing are among his interests. He serves as a volunteer police chaplain for his community. He also has had the privilege of speaking around the country on the subjects Spirituality and Aging as well as The Courage to Be.

This Angel Doesn't Like Chocolate is his second mystery in the MAC Detective Agency Mysteries featuring Howie Cummins and his partners, Adam Trexler and Mick Brunner. His first mystery is This Angel Has No Wings. He is currently working on his third mystery in the series, This Angel's Halo is Crooked.

Printed in the United States
40057LVS00006B/1-75

9 781591 331209